Lady **LURE** *Flora Speer*

Bestselling Author Of *For Love And Honor*

"Flora Speer opens up new vistas for the romance reader!"
—*Romantic Times*

A FINAL WISH

"Grant me another wish. It will be my last wish, Perri."

"What do you want of me?" Perri asked, adding regretfully, "We do not have much time."

"It won't take long." Halvo's hands slid up to her shoulders and then farther, to cup her face between his fingers. His voice deepened to a seductive whisper. "All I want is one kiss and for you to kiss me back as though you meant it. Can you do that much for me?"

"I should not," she said in protest. "It would be most improper."

"Improper to kiss a dying man?"

"No, don't say that!" She knew he was playing on her emotions. She was sure he sensed her disgraceful yearning to feel his mouth on hers once more. "You want me to pity you and to help you escape."

"Pity is the last thing on my mind. I want you to want me," he whispered. "Just one last time, I want to know a beautiful woman desires me."

Lady Lure

Flora Speer

LOVE SPELL **NEW YORK CITY**

LOVE SPELL®

January 1996

Published by

Dorchester Publishing Co., Inc.
276 Fifth Avenue
New York, NY 10001

The name "Love Spell" and its logo are trademarks of Dorchester
Publishing Co., Inc.

Printed in the United States of America.

Peri 1: A supernatural being in Persian folklore
descended from fallen angels and excluded from
paradise until penance is accomplished.
2: A beautiful and graceful girl or woman.
                        —*Webster's Seventh New
                        Collegiate Dictionary*

Lady Lure

Prologue

"Perri, daughter of the Amalini Kin, will you freely accept this commission?" the Chief Hierarch asked in formal tones.

Determined not to show him how troubled she was by what he had just revealed to her, Perri straightened her slender shoulders and met the pale green eyes of the most important member of the Regulan Hierarchy.

Until that day she had never met any of the seven Hierarchs face-to-face. On special occasions she, like other Regulans, watched on her telscan while the splendidly robed Hierarchs conducted the appropriate ceremonies in their sumptuous official chambers.

Yet even in the Chief Hierarch's private office,

where few would ever see it, there was ample evidence of the far-ranging influence of the Regulan government. On one wall hung a long Cetan sword. The sunlight coming through the window set the curved, highly polished blade aglow. Perri could remember the ceremony during which the sword had been presented to the Chief Hierarch on the occasion of the signing of the commercial treaty between Regula and Ceta.

On the wide desk sat a golden lizard, the heraldic symbol of the ancient Styxians, one of the first Races of the Jurisdiction—and a very peculiar Race, from all Perri had heard of that people. Since Styxia lay on the far side of the Jurisdiction and had only the most tenuous relations with Regula, Perri wondered how the Chief Hierarch had come by the artifact.

And, of course, inlaid into the desktop and into the wall immediately behind the Chief Hierarch's chair were representations of the Sign of Regula, a silver spiral that curved inward and in again upon itself until it doubled back to its own beginning, a never-ending, sinuous line as complicated and mysterious, it was said, as the minds of Regulan men.

Those multiple symbols of the dignity and authority of high office left Perri all but speechless with awe. She could scarcely believe that the Chief Hierarch himself had deigned to see her. She had expected to deal with his underlings.

"Well, Perri? You did say you would do anything to help Elyr. Do you intend to balk at this one request?"

Unusually tall, ascetically thin, with snow-white hair and beard, the Chief Hierarch always stood out from the six Lesser Hierarchs. Even while wearing a plain white robe in his simply decorated private apartments, the man inspired fearful reverence in Perri's youthful heart. It was all she could do to prevent herself from going to her knees before him.

Reverence or no, Perri did have a few questions. It seemed she always had a few questions, no matter what the subject under discussion. Silently she prayed for the Chief Hierarch to show greater patience with her than Elyr and his mother, Cynri, usually did.

"Sir, I do not doubt what you have told me," Perri said. "But I have known Elyr for thirteen years, since I went into his parents' household at the age of nine. I cannot believe Elyr could be guilty of a serious crime."

"You do not doubt, yet you cannot believe?" The Chief Hierarch raised thick white eyebrows in astonishment. "Are your thoughts truly in such disarray?"

"It is only that Elyr has never given any indication to me of having an unkind opinion of the Hierarchy." Elyr had never given Perri an indication of what his opinion was on any important subject, but that was not the point.

"Did I say he has done so?" the Chief Hierarch asked.

"You did not need to say it, sir. You implied it."

"You have allowed your irrational female thought processes to lead you to an unwarranted conclusion."

"Sir, please tell me what the crime is of which Elyr stands accused. When his servant, Vedyr, came to me with the terrible news, he said he could not discover what the charges are."

"There are certain matters too serious to put into words." The Chief Hierarch was frowning, and Perri trembled in response to this sign of displeasure. "I can tell you no more than I have already. Unless you carry out the task I have described to you, your betrothed will die in a manner best left unmentioned. Perhaps of more personal interest to you, since by virtue of your betrothal to him you are a member of Elyr's kindred, the entire Amalini Kin will be exiled from Regula."

That was a terrible sentence, one far worse than death. Most Regulans dreaded the thought of leaving their homeworld for more than a brief period. Perri could feel the blood leaving her face. Her head swam with terror and confusion and her trembling increased so much that she was afraid she would fall to the floor. But still, she asked questions.

"Sir, I am only a poor, ignorant woman with,

as you have so kindly pointed out to me, irrational thought processes. How, then, can I be expected to succeed in the difficult and dangerous task you have set for me?"

"It is in your interest to succeed," the Chief Hierarch said.

"But I do not know how to pilot a spaceship! I have never been away from Regula." Nor ever wished to leave, Perri added in a silent protest she dared not speak aloud.

"No matter." The Chief Hierarch was unmoved by Perri's emotional outburst. "Your personal robot is being programmed with the necessary information to enable it to act as your pilot. The technicians should be finished soon."

"What have you done to Rolli?" Perri cried, forgetting awe and respect for the Chief Hierarch in her fear for the one entity on Regula that understood her.

"You display more concern over a robot than you did for your betrothed." The Chief Hierarch did not appear to be either shocked or angered. He merely nodded his head as if to indicate that a deeply held belief had just been confirmed. "It is often so with women, foolish creatures that you are. Rest assured, your precious Rolli's basic memory bank is unchanged. Rolli will still be able to teach you the finer intricacies of needlework or recall the recipes for Elyr's favorite menus."

The Chief Hierarch spoke with the contempt

men reserved for the daily work of women. His manner annoyed Perri. Considering what he was asking of her, she expected him to show a bit more sympathy for both her and her robot. That thought produced another question.

"Sir, how can you imagine that I have even a minute chance of luring my prey onto the ship you will lend to me and Rolli?"

"Because you and your prey, as you so aptly call him, have one trait in common; curiosity. Both of you ask far too many questions." The Chief Hierarch paused, eyeing Perri with a tinge of malice in his pale green glance. "However, if it becomes necessary to lure him in other ways than by his curiosity, then do so."

"Even—" Perri could hardly breathe, but she kept asking questions. "Sir, you cannot want me to—Do you? I am sure Elyr would not agree."

"If it were to save his life," the Chief Hierarch murmured, "Elyr might well forgive your misconduct."

"I cannot think he would," Perri stated firmly. "Elyr's morals are of the very finest quality."

"Well, then, you must do what you think is best." Breaking off his talk with Perri, the Chief Hierarch looked beyond her, toward the entrance to his chambers. There a manservant appeared and paused just inside the door. "Yes, what is it?"

"Sir, the robot is ready." At a motion of the Chief Hierarch's hand, the man quickly bowed himself out of the room.

"Rolli!" Perri took a step toward the door.

"Perri of the Amalini, you forget your manners!"

"I am sorry, Chief Hierarch. It was not my intention to leave your presence in a rude way." Perri was relieved to see him incline his head in acceptance of the apology.

"I do assure you once again," the Chief Hierarch said, "that nothing about your robot has been changed save for the introduction of piloting and navigational knowledge. It would be highly inefficient to add skills or information not required for your upcoming tasks."

"Of course it would. I should not have doubted you, sir." Setting aside the moral issues involved in the assignment she had just been given, along with her own personal qualms and her lingering questions about what she was being asked to do, Perri reminded herself that she had no other way to save Elyr. Taking a long breath to steady herself, straightening her shoulders with a sense of firm resolution and commitment, she looked directly into the Chief Hierarch's eyes and said in the formal tones required by the occasion, "Very well, sir. Of my free will and volition, I hereby accept the commission you have given me. I will do everything in my power to carry it out as you wish."

"I was sure that all the Hierarchs—and Elyr—could depend upon you, Perri. I am pleased to

Flora Speer

hear that I was not mistaken in my assessment of your character." Pleased or not, there was no softening in the Chief Hierarch's expression, not even the trace of a smile. Nor did his cool eyes warm.

"When shall I leave?" Perri asked, envisioning days or weeks of preliminary training. In the meantime, perhaps she would be allowed to visit Elyr. Thanks to the Chief Hierarch's willingness to help, she could offer her betrothed some hope that the death sentence laid upon him would be revoked. But, she reminded herself, only if she succeeded.

"From these chambers," the Chief Hierarch answered her, "you are to proceed directly to the ship that is being prepared for you."

"Right now? Without going home to pack or to tell Elyr's mother? She must be so worried. This news would relieve her mind."

"Cynri does not know of Elyr's plight, and you are not to send her any messages."

"But, I thought—Why not?"

"Time is of the greatest importance in this matter, Perri, second only to secrecy."

"Secrecy?" Perri's dark green eyes grew wide. "Sir, what do you mean?"

"Understand," the Chief Hierarch said, "that I speak for the entire Hierarchy in this. Having confidence that you would accept this commission, we have agreed for the moment to withhold full disclosure of the charges against Elyr.

16

Those charges will not be made public unless you fail in the task set for you or unless you take too long to complete it. Remember, Perri, not only do Elyr's life and the future of all his relatives rest in your hands, but something far more important than life. The honor of the Amalini Kin—and their continued residence upon Regula—depends on you."

"She will never be able to do it." With Perri dismissed from the Chief Hierarch's chambers, the man who had been listening behind the heavy folds of a window curtain stepped forward. Of medium height and slim build, he had fair hair and green eyes set in a long face, which at the moment bore a solemn expression.

"It does not matter whether Perri achieves her mission or fails in it. Either way, she will not live long," the Chief Hierarch said. With a chuckle of genuine amusement the ordinarily humorless Hierarch added, "And with any luck at all, whether she succeeds or fails, the man she calls her prey will not outlive her. Then, my friend, you and I—and our futures and fortunes—will be safe."

Chapter One

"Stand and deliver!" The voice coming over the interspace comm system spoke with the emotionless rasp of an ALF—an Artificial Life Form. Hearing it, Capt. Jyrit and his communications officer looked at each other in astonishment for one split second before Jyrit spoke.

"You know the response to that order, lieutenant. Tell whatever metallic creature is hailing us to go oil itself—after it gets out of our way."

"Aye, captain." The lieutenant repressed a smile.

"Heave to and prepare to accept a boarding party!" the unemotional words continued.

"Perhaps we should offer to supply the oil," the lieutenant said.

"Heave to?" a quiet, human, and distinctly masculine voice from the direction of the hatchway said.

Capt. Jyrit and his lieutenant turned as one at the sound. They and the armaments officer all stiffened into formal attention as their only passenger came onto the bridge of the spaceship *Krontar*.

"Admiral. Sir." Behind his impassive exterior Jyrit found himself wondering if this tall, big-boned man had insisted on wearing his dark blue uniform jacket and trousers even when he lay near death on the finest hospital planet in the Jurisdiction. It seemed entirely possible. Jyrit had known the man for years and had never seen him out of uniform.

"At ease, gentlefolk." Admiral of the Fleet Halvo Gibal squinted at the viewscreen, being careful not to tilt his head while he sized up the situation. It only took an instant. At least his eyes were still functioning properly, even if the rest of his body resisted the demands he made of it each day. There on the viewscreen before him a ship hung motionless against the backdrop of inky black space and a few thousand scattered stars. Their opponent was boldly painted with the green-and-purple design of a space dragon belching orange flames, but in comparison to the *Krontar* the tiny ship looked

19

more like a gnat than a dragon.

"The captain must be mad," Halvo said. "No sane person could possibly believe a warship of the Jurisdiction Fleet would ever submit to a puny vessel like that one. It's no bigger than an ordinary shuttlecraft that's used to carry passengers and material from a planet's surface to a larger spaceship. And what coward would allow a machine to do his talking for him?"

"One who doesn't want his voice remembered later," Armaments Officer Dysia murmured. Raising her own voice and addressing Jyrit, she added, "Captain, the configuration of that ship is vaguely familiar to me. It may have been altered in an attempt to disguise its origin. I can check the viewscreen image against our old computer records and try to find a ship that roughly compares with this one."

"Do it." Jyrit snapped out the order. He was a Jugarian; thus his antennae were flaring bright red in indignation at what was happening. It was humiliating to be stopped by a shot fired across the bow of the *Krontar*. Jyrit's personal inclincation was to destroy the *Space Dragon* without discussion. He was under strict orders to conduct Adm. Halvo Gibal safely to Capital, and he could not afford to take chances with Halvo's life. Still, it was Halvo's right as the ranking officer of the fleet to issue any orders he wished. Knowing that Halvo had never run from a battle, Jyrit allowed a note of hope to creep into his inflections.

"We are nearing the outskirts of the Regulan Sector, Admiral. Pirates have recently become a serious problem in this area and all reports say they are growing ever bolder. In my opinion, they need to be taught a lesson similar to the one we taught their brothers last year, near Styxia. I will be happy to destroy that ship if you but concur in the decision, sir." Anticipating agreement, Jyrit nodded to Armanents Officer Dysia and half raised one hand, prepared to give the signal to fire upon the pirate at Halvo's assent.

"No." So easily did Halvo make the decision that was to change his life forever. Later, he would reflect on that one little word and wonder if he, rather than the commander of the pirate vessel, was the one who was mad. "They are too small to do us any serious harm. We could annihilate them with a single blast, and they must know it. Therefore, the question to ask ourselves is, why would so small a ship, traveling alone, accost us in this outlandish way?"

"Perhaps they have some new weapon we don't know about that could blast us out of the sky," Armaments Officer Dysia suggested.

"Perhaps. If so, why haven't they used it or threatened us with it?" Halvo stared at the image of the ship on the viewscreen for a moment longer before, without moving his head, he shifted his glance to Capt. Jyrit. "Aren't you curious?"

"Curiosity is not a Jugarian trait, admiral," Jyrit responded, barely controlling his anger and his desire to destroy the ship confronting him.

"No," Halvo said, "but courage and ferocity in battle are."

Capt. Jyrit inclined his head in mute acceptance of this compliment and waited to learn what Halvo wanted to do.

"During the past year," Halvo went on, "there has been precious little to arouse my curiosity. It is aroused now. Capt. Jyrit, I have a suggestion for dealing with this interruption in our journey. Since I am curious and you are not, I shall meet with the leader of the boarding party and attempt to discover what he wants. Meanwhile, you may keep your weapons trained on the *Space Dragon*. Do not hesitate to fire if they take any action that threatens the safety of the *Krontar*. Comm Officer, order a security team to Entrance Hatch Six. With your permission, Captain," Halvo added, to appease Jyrit's sensitive ego, though he knew the captain would not override his suggestions, however much he might disapprove of them.

"Sir." Jyrit was the picture of affronted Jugarian pride, but as Halvo had guessed, he would not openly disagree with someone of Halvo's rank. "You can interrogate them in the brig. I shall order Security to have the entire boarding party imprisoned at once."

"Not at once, Jyrit." Deliberately, Halvo used the personal name, speaking as though the captain were his friend. That, too, would ease Jyrit's pride, which must surely be outraged at having his expressed desires countermanded on his own bridge. "Let us discover first exactly what it is they want. I leave the bridge, and the weapons control, in your capable hands, Jyrit, while I personally greet our unwelcome guests."

"As you wish, Admiral. Sir." His tone was formal and polite, but Jyrit, his antennae glowing, looked after the departing Halvo in wondering disbelief at the admiral's irregular actions.

Halvo himself scarcely knew why he was taking the trouble to investigate the intrusion upon his homeward voyage. Perhaps it was because the journey had been so boringly uneventful or because, once he reached Capital—the planet where the Assembly and the Jurisdiction government offices were located—Halvo would be relegated to an administrative position behind a desk for the rest of his life.

Faced with the prospect of never commanding his own ship again, let alone the entire Jurisdiction Fleet, Halvo was bound to view any delay that kept him in outer space for a while longer as an undisguised blessing. He might even discover an opportunity to prove himself still capable of handling a challenging situation, just one last time, before the intrigues and the rules of Capital enmeshed him forever. It was all he could hope for at that stage of his life.

Balancing cautiously, moving slowly to avoid as much of the ever present pain as possible, Halvo made his way through the familiar corridors of the Jurisdiction warship, heading toward Entrance Hatch Six. Capt. Jyrit was certainly efficient. Half-a-dozen security personnel were waiting for him beside the hatch.

"The pirate ship has just docked, sir," said one of the security team as he caught sight of the slowly approaching Halvo. "The air lock is being pressurized now."

A moment later a blinking yellow light signaled equalization of pressure and the hatch slid open. Between the *Krontar* and the pirate ship stretched a flexible passageway that temporarily joined the two ships. Halvo saw that the entrance to the smaller ship was also open, though there was no sign of any member of the crew of the *Space Dragon*.

"Where is the boarding party we were promised?" Halvo demanded. He received an immediate response from the interior of the smaller ship.

"I wish the presence of Adm. Halvo Gibal," said the same metallic voice Halvo had heard while on the bridge.

"I am Halvo." He stepped toward the passageway.

"If you would care to join us aboard the *Space Dragon*," said the voice, "we would be pleased to welcome you."

"It was my understanding that you were planning to board us. Why the change in plans?" Intrigued, Halvo was about to take another step when he was prevented by the warning of the alert leader of the security team.

"Sir, let me go first. They haven't shown themselves yet. We don't know who is in there. You are too valuable to risk your life in an encounter with a pirate."

"You are mistaken, my friend," Halvo said. "My life has no value at all these days, not to the Jurisdiction Fleet, nor to myself. Not the way I am now. You, on the other hand, are young and healthy, with a long future ahead of you. I will go first."

"Sir, it is my duty—"

"Stay here. That is an order."

Halvo could almost see the protest forming on the young man's lips, and he noted the instant when the obedience trained into all security personnel took over. The man stepped back, leaving Halvo's way clear.

"Aye, sir. Please be careful, sir."

There was a metal ridge running all around the far edge of the passageway; it held the flexible material tightly in place against a docked ship, thus sealing the passage against the vacuum of outer space. As he stepped onto the

Space Dragon, Halvo nearly tripped over the ridge. He caught himself and straightened to an upright position again. A shaft of pain surged along his left leg and up his spine. As a result, he entered the cockpit of the little ship with his mouth compressed into a tight line and his mood altered from interested curiosity to distinct irritation. It did not help matters when he saw what awaited him in the cockpit.

"I did not come here to speak to an ALF," Halvo muttered. Preparing to turn around and leave, he unwisely shifted his weight to his left leg. Once more he was assaulted by pain, and the dizziness came upon him, making his surroundings appear to spin. Closing his eyes, he paused to grit his teeth and gather his strength before making the effort to lift his foot over that cursed ridge a second time as he got out of the pirate ship.

"I am but an emissary," the robot sitting at the controls said. "Nor am I, precisely speaking, an Artificial Life Form."

Halvo opened his eyes again to discover the robot looking at him, if looking were the right word, through two pale blue lights set into its spherical head of gray metal at the approximate place where eyes ought to be in a human head.

Mercifully, the cockpit and the passageway just outside it had stopped whirling. Reluctant to cause any further disturbance to his inner ear and his sense of balance, Halvo did not move.

The robot continued to stare at him, its blue lights blinking, until Halvo felt compelled to respond to the remarks it had made.

"It is my understanding that robots always speak precisely." Halvo growled the words out of his own malaise and frustration with his physical inadequacies. "Therefore, I expect you to explain to me at once precisely why this minuscule ship should attempt to bar the *Krontar's* way. Then you can tell me what you want with me."

There was another life form aboard the ship. Halvo was aware of a movement off to one side of the cockpit, but he did not dare turn his head to check on it lest the dizziness return and disable him completely. Instead, he continued to stare at the robot until a figure glided into full view.

"Greetings, Admiral." From its appearance, this life form was humanoid. Whether it was actually a human being was difficult to tell at the moment, because the form was encased in a silvery suit of the kind used when performing extravehicular repairs in outer space and the head was covered by an oval-shaped helmet equipped with a gleaming black faceplate. There was no way for Halvo to discern who— or what—was behind that black surface. The voice was muted and distorted beyond easy identification. There was no question, however, about the weapon now trained upon him. "How convenient to have you greet us in person since you are just the man we wanted to see."

"I am flattered." The drugs he had been using recently to ease his pain had dulled Halvo's physical reflexes. And apparently they had also slowed his wits. How could he have allowed his curiosity to override all security precautions? He should have told Jyrit to go ahead and blow the *Space Dragon* to bits as the sensible Jugarian had wanted to do. Now it was too late. For just an instant Halvo could hear the outraged exclamations of the security team. Then the hatch of the *Space Dragon* clanged shut behind him, cutting off both sound and his return path to the *Krontar*.

"Damnation," Halvo muttered, bitterly regretting that his own common sense was only now awakening. He knew what was coming before the creature in the silvery space suit motioned him to a bench at one side of the cockpit. Halvo snarled his response to the gesture. "Whoever you are, I regret that I cannot cooperate with you."

"Would you rather die?" the distorted voice asked.

"I think I would," Halvo said with perfect honesty. "However, I do not believe your intent is to kill me. If it were, I would be dead by now."

"You are partially correct, admiral. You will not die just yet, unless you misbehave."

"If you are thinking of ransom, forget it. I am of no use to anyone these days," Halvo said, adding in a low whisper, "least of all to myself."

"I have not taken you for ransom. Lie down on that bench and strap yourself in."

"I can't." Afraid he would disgrace himself if he tried to move, Halvo stayed where he was.

"I do not have time to argue." The silver-clad arm waved. "Rolli, put him down."

Halvo saw the robot approaching him and realized that it had not actually been sitting at the controls but, rather, standing before them. The robot's body was a metal box approximately two feet on each side and about four feet tall; it moved on small wheels. The spherical head sat atop this body, joined to it by a short neck that allowed the head to swivel like a human head. The robot had two jointed metal arms, which protruded from opposite sides of its body. At the ends of the arms were flexible appendages remarkably similar to human hands. These hands grasped Halvo by the shoulders before he could force his aching body to react; then the hands pushed him downward.

Halvo yelped at the sudden pain in his back. Instinct took over and he fought what was being done to him. The robot was stronger, and as always, sudden movement brought on the dizziness that left Halvo helpless.

He must have lost consciousness for a few minutes, because the next thing Halvo knew, he was flat on his back on the hard bench and there was a tight metal band wrapped across his upper arms and chest, with a second band over his thighs, holding him there on the bench, confining him beyond any hope of escape. Groaning, he cursed himself for getting into such a fix and for endangering the captain and crew of his transport.

"If you harm anyone on the *Krontar*," Halvo declared through teeth gritted against unrelenting pain, "I will see you hunted across the galaxy until you are caught and punished."

"I have no intention of hurting anyone else." The voice was muffled because his captor, having stripped off the silver gloves, was removing the helmet. "Rolli, send this message to the captain of the *Krontar*: 'Admiral Halvo Gibal is now a prisoner. He will not be seen again within the Jurisdiction. Therefore, it is useless to send out search parties.' Is that done, Rolli?"

"Done, Perri." Waiting for the next order, the robot paused, its metal fingers raised above the control panel.

"You know what to do," Perri said. "Activate Starthruster."

Halvo did not waste time speculating on how a space pirate had acquired the latest Jurisdiction technology, a device supposedly kept as a deep military secret. Starthruster was able to propel a space vessel so rapidly that the ship he was imprisoned on would be out of range of the sensors and the weapons of the *Krontar* within a few seconds.

There would be no way for Capt. Jyrit to trace the course the pirate ship was taking, no way for him to follow on a rescue mission. Halvo knew the chances he would ever be found had just diminished to near zero. Furthermore, what had happened to him was his own fault.

These thoughts flitted quickly through Halvo's mind, only to be eclipsed by amazement as he watched his captor doff the bulky, concealing helmet. The bared hands working at the clasps at the neck of the helmet were slender, with delicately shaped nails. Then the helmet was off and a flood of shining, dark red hair tumbled down around the shoulders of the silver space suit. Perri laid down the helmet and turned to regard Halvo out of dark green eyes.

Never had Halvo seen such a face, not on any of the various worlds he knew. Beneath the glorious cascade of shimmering, curling red hair, Perri's brow was wide, her cheekbones high, her nose straight and a little too short for perfect beauty. Her mouth was small and full, hinting at a tempting sensuality, but that particular message was contradicted by her pointed, determined chin. The green eyes—wide and serious and set at a slight tilt in her charming, heart-shaped face—gave her a curiously catlike look. But she was human and entirely bewitching.

And deadly. Perri was holding her weapon pointed directly at Halvo's heart.

Chapter Two

"He is not in the best of health," Rolli said. "He is too pale."

"I have noticed." With one hand on the weapon in the holster at her belt, Perri regarded her prisoner with cool eyes.

Halvo was feeling increasingly apprehensive. After her first threatening gesture toward him, Perri had put the weapon away. Then she and the robot had left him alone for hours. Strapped down on the cursed, hard bench, his back and legs ached while his captors piloted the *Space Dragon* across the galaxy. Hoping to discover where they were going, Halvo had strained to hear what his captors said to each other, but they kept their voices too low for him to distinguish any words. He knew it scarcely mattered. Wherever they were, they had left the *Krontar* far behind. They might even be out of Jurisdiction space by now.

It was too late to regret his own stupidity in walking into an obvious trap. What was done was done. The best Halvo could hope for was a quick death. Somehow he did not think that was likely to happen. A brave death then, or as brave as he could make it. Halvo tried not to think about some of the methods he had encountered for putting prisoners to death, nor about the many reasons space pirates were bound to have for wanting the Admiral of the Jurisdiction Fleet dead.

"He will require nourishment," the robot said.

"I know, Rolli." Perri took her weapon in hand and pointed it at the helpless Halvo. "I want your solemn word, Admiral. If I release you from those bands, you will not attack me."

"Believe me," Halvo responded, "I am in no condition to attack anyone." If they were going to feed him, it must mean they were planning to keep him alive for a while longer. Which, in turn, meant he just might have time to think of a way to escape. He could tell by the discomfort he was experiencing that the benefits of the long-acting painblockers he had last taken while aboard the *Krontar* had dissipated. His next dose was overdue. But there was an advantage to not having his medicine available. Without it, he could think more clearly.

"Your word, Admiral." Perri frowned at him. She was no longer wearing the bulky space suit that had served to disguise her identity from crew members of the *Krontar*. Both suit and helmet were packed away in a locker next to the entrance hatch. Perri was now clad in a form-fitting tunic and trousers in a deep shade somewhere between blue and purple. Over her shoulders and down her back the waves of dark red hair flowed, glowing against the somber fabric background.

"I promise," Halvo said, tearing his thoughts away from her enticing appearance. "I will behave." Didn't the wench know that a promise made under duress was not binding? Or was she playing some intricate, unexplained game with him?

Perri reached above his head to push a button on the bulkhead. Halvo tried not to look at the rounded breasts revealed as the blue-purple fabric stretched at her movement. The flexible metal bands holding him slipped soundlessly back into their slots.

"Get up," Perri said.

"I'm not sure I can."

"Get up!" Her green eyes flamed.

Halvo tried to roll to his side, hoping he could push himself to a sitting position that way. He discovered he could not move. Perri looked impatient and tightened her grip on her weapon.

"Sorry." Halvo grunted. "I am doing my best. You kept me in one position too long."

"Rolli, get him up. I want him on his feet."

"Not too fast," Halvo warned, "or I won't be able to stay up."

The robot took hold of him and this time Halvo did not resist the metal hands. He could not, however, prevent the cry of pain that tore from his lips as Rolli drew him upright.

"You are malingering!" Perri shouted.

"I am not!" Halvo could barely speak because of the searing agony in his left leg and his spine. Closing his eyes, he held on to Rolli as if his life depended on the robot's support, which, for all he knew, it did. If he crumpled to the deck, the beautiful tormentor watching his every movement might well decide to blast him out of existance. "Just let me stay like this for a minute or two. Then I'll be all right and I'll be able to walk."

"If you are pretending," Perri said, "you will regret it."

"I do not think this is pretense," the robot said, still supporting Halvo with hands that had become surprisingly gentle. "Perri, you will remember the report of the injuries he sustained last year in the pirate war near Styxia."

Was Halvo imagining it or did Perri look at him with a slightly more sympathetic gaze? He would have expected her to be infuriated by mention of the battle that had effectively wiped out all piratical activites in the Styxian Sector. It was reasonable to assume that she had lost friends and, perhaps, relatives in the successful war against the pirates.

"I haven't forgotten his injuries," Perri said to her robot. Then, to Halvo, she said, "Are you hungry, Admiral?"

"I haven't thought about it until now, but, yes, I believe I am," Halvo responded.

"Then come to the galley. We will eat together. Let me warn you. There are monitors all over this ship. Rolli will be watching every move you make and listening to each word you say. Make no foolish attempt to overpower me in hope of commandeering the *Space Dragon*."

"I wouldn't dream of it." Feeling steadier on his feet by that time, Halvo let go of the robot and waved one hand in an elegant gesture. "After you, Capt. Perri."

"Never." Perri tilted her pointed little chin as if to tell him without words that she was on to that particular trick. "You go first, Admiral."

"It was worth a try." She didn't have to know that he was in no condition to take her on in hand-to-hand combat. On second thought, she would be a fool not to know it. Keeping his head as level as he could, moving slowly, Halvo found the galley.

"Sit." Perri motioned to a contoured chair at the dining table.

"Thank you. I must warn you that it will probably take a while." Slowly, carefully, Halvo lowered himself into the chair, which immediately molded itself around his body. With his spine and his legs properly supported at last, Halvo let himself relax for a moment of pain-free comfort.

"Only Regulan food is programmed into the processor," Perri said.

"Regulan? Then order up some fruits and vegetables for me. I'll skip the main course." Halvo should have known she was a Regulan by her accent and by her incredible, deep green eyes. He might have made the connection if he hadn't been so concerned with his own physical discomforts and embarassed by the humbling realization that he had been so easily captured by a slim young woman.

"I did not expect a man of such wide experience to be squeamish about his food, Admiral." From her position by the mouth of the food processor, where she waited for their order to appear, Perri sent him a sly glance. "But then, I did not expect you to be weak as a toothless babe either."

"The doctors say with time and continued therapy the weakness will pass."

"If you live long enough. Here." She set a fork and a bowl of salad in front of him and added a loaf of coarse Regulan bread. "You will have to break the bread with your hands. I won't give you a knife."

"I am flattered to know you think me so dangerous," Halvo said wryly. He would have given anything he possessed for a plate of hot Demarian stew with big chunks of meat in it and a carafe of wine, but he wasn't going to tell Perri that. The salad of fruits and vegetables wasn't too unpalatable. He tried not to look at the mess Perri was devouring with every evidence of pleasure.

"I would like to know what you intend to do with me," Halvo said when he was finished eating.

"I will turn you over to the Regulan Hierarchy."

"The Hierarchy? If that is so, then this kidnapping makes no sense at all," Halvo said. "Regula holds Membership in the Jurisdiction. Why would you abduct me from a Jurisdiction ship only to hand me over to a Jurisdiction Member? The Hierarchy will be duty bound to hold you as a prisoner for what you have done." There were sure to be several twisted reasons for his abduction. Of that, Halvo was certain. A man in his high position could not avoid being aware of the Regulan love of political intrigue.

"I do not know what the Hierarchy intends," Perri said. But her eyes slid away from his, her delicately shadowed lids lowering until dark lashes lay softly upon her cheeks. She knew.

She just wasn't going to tell him.

Since first sighting the *Space Dragon*, Halvo's emotions had ranged from curiosity to anger to regret and disgust at his own failure to employ either the brain nature had given him or the training imparted by the Jurisdiction Service. Now, inexplicably, he was consumed by another emotion. He wanted to protect his captor.

The wide experience Perri had mentioned had not only taught him to eat strange foods. He had also learned during his years in the Service to gauge accurately the emotions of many different Races. Thus, he knew Perri was frightened. She concealed her fear well, but Halvo could sense it pervading her every word and action. Except for the robot, she was alone. As he was alone. He stared at her, sitting across the table from him and eating as if she were famished, and he wondered what in the name of all the stars had made a beautiful young woman embrace a career as a space pirate. His curiosity fully awakened by the mystery of her actions, Halvo knew he would not rest until he had plumbed Perri's deepest secrets. . . .

Chapter Three

Perri had not expected to like Halvo. Liking him made her task infinitely more difficult. Worse, she had never thought to find him so attractive. She had been told that Adm. Halvo Gibal was overweight, out of condition, and no physical threat to her. He had also been described as an aging parasite who was fattening himself on the Jurisdiction Service and indulging himself in an unnecessary rest cure after suffering minor wounds.

The man she had captured was bone thin. His handsome, chiseled face was marked by lines of pain. His every movement was controlled and cautious, as if he took great care to avoid further discomfort. Perri could see that, far from being minor, Halvo's wounds had been terrible. She could also tell that he was determined not to give in to the threat of permanent disability.

Nor was he as old as she had been led to believe. True, the dark hair at his temples was liberally streaked with silver, but that only made him look distinguished. The Demarians were a beautiful Race and Halvo was no exception, not even when he was angry—and he was angry most of the time.

The discrepancies between the information given to her by the Chief Hierarch and the reality of Halvo's presence puzzled Perri, generating a disquieting sense of unease.

She had tried to be kind to Halvo. Knowing Rolli would stop any attempt their prisoner might make to take over the *Space Dragon* and escape, Perri no longer kept her weapon pointed at Halvo whenever they were together in the galley or the cockpit. She allowed him to avoid the restraining bands of the bench, letting him sleep in a real bed in one of the three private cabins. Perri tried to keep all of their conversations pleasant.

Halvo was unmoved by her efforts to be agreeable. He constantly demanded facts she was unwilling or unable to reveal. Mealtimes were especially disturbing, perhaps because of the forced intimacy of a galley too small for

Flora Speer

more than one person to occupy with any degree of comfort.

At the moment, Halvo stood in the galley, glaring at her out of shadowy gray eyes. He hung onto the edge of the table as if he would fall without its support, and when he bared even white teeth in a fierce snarl he reminded her of a Demarian leopard-wolf, the fabled beast from his home planet that could swallow a human in two gulps. Perri decided she would in the future eat all of her meals alone in her own cabin if she must to avoid Halvo's simmering resentment and persistent questions.

"Tell me, Perri, how much are you being paid for this piratical venture?" Halvo growled.

"You do not understand. I had no choice." It was what she always said in response to his questions. As usual, he snorted at the platitudes she repeated so patiently.

"Then make me understand," he said in a tone that told her why he had become an admiral at such a young age.

Never had Perri met a man so single-minded. For the past three days, while they rushed through space toward Regula, he had been so relentless in his questioning of her that she wished it were possible to use Starthruster constantly instead of just in short, occasional bursts of power. Rolli had warned her that the stress of using Starthruster too often or too long could cause the aging *Space Dragon* to disinte-

42

grate. Thus, she would have to endure Halvo's persistent questions for another two or three days. Perri knew he was physically weak, and she controlled the only weapon on board, yet she was beginning to fear he would eventually defeat her by the strength of his will alone. Looking into Halvo's eyes, she almost called for Rolli to come and help her.

"I deserve an explanation," Halvo said.

"I cannot—"

"Tell me what to expect on Regula," he said. "At least let me be mentally prepared."

There was something about him—the habit of command, she supposed—that finally convinced her to respond with a few bits and pieces of a truth she would have preferred to keep entirely hidden from him until the last possible moment.

"The Regulan Hierarchy wants you," she said.

"You have already told me as much." He sounded thoroughly exasperated. "Why do they want me?"

"I am not sure exactly what they plan to do with you," Perri said, stalling while she tried to compose a simple explanation.

"Oh?" The single syllable demanded that she continue.

"It is an exchange, you see." Put that way, the whole situation did sound simple.

"An exchange," he said, "of myself for someone else? I know I have a fair-size ego,

43

Perri, but who could be valuable enough to be exchanged for the Admiral of the Fleet? Is some Race outside the Jurisdiction holding an important Regulan official and demanding me in return for that person's life?"

"It has nothing to do with Races outside the Jurisdiction," Perri said, offering another crumb of information. She watched him consider her response before he began asking questions again. She could not avoid a flare of sympathy for the man. So often in her own life she had questioned—and questioned again—and received unsatisfactory answers or no answers at all. It troubled Perri to discover that basic similarity of character between herself and a person whom she ought to think of as a dangerous enemy. She did not doubt that, if he could find a way to escape from her, Halvo would be ruthless about doing so. But if Halvo escaped, Elyr would die. Perri reminded herself never to forget that frightening fact.

"I can understand why the Regulans wouldn't want to commit a ship with their own markings to an illegal enterprise like this one," Halvo said, "but why send a lone woman and a robot to abduct me, especially when Regulans don't think much of the mental abilities of females?"

"I was sent because I am the one who cares most."

"You?" His shrewd eyes threatened to expose all of her secrets. "For whom am I to be exchanged then? Your parents perhaps? A dear friend? Or is it a lover?"

"It would be better if we did not talk about this anymore."

"That is what you always say when my questions get too close to the truth. What you mean when you say, 'Don't talk,' is that you are ashamed to admit what you are involved in." Halvo ran a hand through his hair in a gesture of pure frustration. "I am rapidly reaching the end of my patience with this situation."

Again he glared at her, making Perri wish she could shrink to atom size, then disappear altogether. He was right. She was ashamed of what she was doing, but she could see no other way. She was forced to depend upon the Chief Hierarch to keep the promises he had made to her.

With a sound of utter disgust, Halvo spun on his heel and took a step toward the hatch leading out of the galley. The movement was cut short. Halvo swayed, gasping, and put his hands up to his head.

"Cursed dizziness," he rasped, swallowing hard.

"What causes it?" Perri asked, glad of a chance to change the subject. "I know you were injured in combat."

"Injured?" Halvo groped for the chair in which he usually sat, found it, and dropped into it with a sigh. He fixed Perri with the cold glance she was becoming accustomed to seeing from him. "I was torn to pieces, as good as dead. There have been times during the last year when I have wished the medics had never found me."

"How can you say such a thing?" she cried, shocked by his intensity.

"Because it's true," Halvo said between gritted teeth. "A quick, clean death would have been infinitely preferable to what I went through."

"What, exactly, happened?" Perri met his eyes, determined not to flinch before the rage and the pain she could see there. Perhaps if she could make him talk about himself, he would stop questioning her. And perhaps talking about his injuries would ease his anger. Because she was not used to people answering her constant questions, she was a little surprised at how readily Halvo began to speak.

"We were fighting pirates who had massed on the Styxian border to attack one of our space stations," Halvo said. "Purely by chance a quarter of the Jurisdiction Fleet was nearby. Why the pirates didn't know about our presence I can't say. Perhaps their intelligence reports were faulty. We held a quick conference and decided to take advantage of the opportunity to dispose of a worsening menace to space travelers."

"The pirates were defeated," Perri said. "I do know that much. The news was the talk of Re-

gula for days." She saw no reason to add that
not everyone she knew had rejoiced over the defeat of the pirates. She had not understood
Elyr's attitude about the battle, but he had told
her that her questions on the matter were so
silly they were not worthy of answers.

"I was informed later that it was a great victory," Halvo said. "I do not remember the end
of the battle."

"Because you were so badly wounded," she
said, still meeting his eyes. There was a flash of
something between them, an odd connection
forming. She did not have time to think about
it before Halvo was talking again, and she was
listening with growing horror.

"When the bridge of the Jurisdiction flagship
was blown up, my left leg was torn off at the
hip, I was thrown onto my face, and my back
was broken by falling debris. My inner ear was
all but destroyed by the blast. It took months,
and three operations, before I could hear again.

"But the ship's medics saved me," Halvo said.
"They got me to a hospital planet where my leg
was reattached and my spine rearticulated.
Then the therapy began. Have you ever been severely injured, Perri?"

"Not like that, but I can imagine—"

"No, you can't. Shall I tell you what it's like?
They wrap you in elastic bands and make you
stay flat on your back for days on end," Halvo
said as if he were talking to himself, reliving the

pain and the despair. "Then they take the bands off and stand you up and tell you to walk. But your injured leg is completely numb and you stand there trying to wiggle your toes or flex your ankle so you can take a step, but nothing happens. For the first time in your life your own body refuses to obey you and you slowly begin to understand that the connections between your leg and your brain have been severed and will have to be restored—and only the most intense therapy can accomplish that restoration.

"They dump you into a pool of warm water and a nurse who is a sadist in disguise moves your leg for hours at a time, day after day, until your skin is permanently red and wrinkled, like the carapace of a Jugarian crab, and you understand at last why Jugarian crabs are so testy. You lie in bed at night crying from the pain, so they give you drugs to help you sleep. But when morning comes and they want you up and working again, you are too groggy from those drugs to put two thoughts together.

"But you keep on trying to force your body to move as it should, because the nurses won't let you stop trying. A year later, when your back still aches every day and your balance is never dependable, the doctors discharge you. Then comes the real injury, worse than anything that has gone before." Halvo paused for a moment, and when he went on, his voice was drenched in bitterness. "When you are finally able to report to Fleet Headquarters, the officials there tell you that you will never again be fit to command a ship, so they are retiring you from active duty. Do you know where I was going when you kidnapped me, Perri?"

"You were heading for Capital," she whispered, too shaken by this passionate account of his sufferings to speak more loudly.

"Yes, to Capital, to my formal retirement ceremony. In the grand old Jurisdiction tradition, I was asked to name my own successor as Admiral of the Fleet, while I was to be permanently consigned to a desk job," Halvo said, and Perri had never heard such grief in anyone's voice. "After all I've done for the Jurisdiction, after all I've been through, they were finished with me. And now, as the gravestone of my career, you have kidnapped me in order to exchange me for someone whose name you refuse to tell me!"

She sat there, close to tears of sympathy for him, gazing into his tormented eyes. Suddenly remembering a method her dear old nurse, Melri, had used with her when she was a child, Perri knew what Halvo needed to snap him out of his mood.

"Admiral," she said as coldly as she could, "I have never met a man who felt so sorry for himself!"

"I am not absorbed by self-pity," he said. "I got over that a long time ago. Now I am angry.

49

I am furious at the way I have been treated by my own people and even more outraged by what you have done to me."

"It was necessary." She faced his glare, aware once again of the bond that was slowly, irresistibly, forming between them.

"I have told you what you want to know," Halvo said. "I have answered your questions. Now I insist that you do the same for me. Tell me why you abducted me."

"Oh, please," she whispered, "can't you wait until we reach Regula?"

She could not look at him any longer. She lowered her gaze to the tabletop instead. She had become remarkably tough and determined during the past 20 days or so, while she and Rolli searched through space for the *Krontar* and then, having located it, tracked it to a spot where they could waylay it without concern of interference from another ship. Perri did not like what she was doing, but her mission had to be completed. Still, she could not help the sympathy she felt for Halvo. What was going to happen when they reached Regula was not fair to him. Not for the first time since beginning this venture, Perri wished she could think of some other way to secure Elyr's release.

"No, I cannot wait." Startling her out of her unhappy ruminations with his sudden movement, Halvo grabbed both of Perri's hands in his and held on tightly. She thought the dizziness must have assailed him once more because when she looked up at him, he immediately went pale, but he did not let her go.

Perri was aware of the latent power his hands possessed even after a year of illness and rehabilitation. It was more than physical strength. There was a quality in Halvo that touched Perri's spirit, awakening in her needs and possibilities she had never considered before meeting him. She wanted to curl her fingers around his, to sit with their hands clasped on the cold, bare metal surface of the galley table and their eyes locked, while they sought in each other unexpected truths.

Did Halvo experience the same reaction to the touch of her hands? She did not think so. Halvo was interested in only one subject: gaining his freedom. She could not blame him for that. Elyr was probably thinking similar thoughts.

"I have a right to know what I will face on Regula," Halvo said, adding with a faint smile, "It is my life, after all, such as it is."

"It is Elyr's life, too," Perri whispered, unable to stop the words because her thoughts were at that moment upon Elyr. At once, Halvo seized on what she had said.

"Who is Elyr?"

"Please." Telling herself the emotions swirling through her heart and mind were most unseemly, she tried to tug her hands away from his. Still he held on to her. Afraid to look into his eyes again, Perri concentrated on his hands. They were large and strong. A man weakened as Halvo was should not have hands so strong. Her own looked remarkably fragile in his grasp. Halvo's hands were warm. For an instant, before she caught herself in shame and dismay, Perri wondered what it would be like to lie unclothed with Halvo, to be stroked with tenderness by those hands.

"Who is Elyr?" he said again, more insistently.

"Let me go, Halvo."

"Not until I have some answers that make sense of what has been done to me."

"You have been planning this moment for days, haven't you?" she cried, alarmed by her wayward emotions. "You tricked me! You have been pretending to be weaker than you really are and you told me about your wounds to soften my resolve, didn't you? You were counting on my sympathy."

"Prisoners are expected to use whatever weapons they have available, including their wits. You saw only my apparent weakness and thus you misjudged me." He paused before adding in a wry tone, "It was a tactical error not common to successful pirates."

Perri opened her mouth to call for Rolli, who was as usual monitoring the ship's controls in the cockpit. Again she misjudged her opponent.

Before she could make a sound Halvo pulled on her hands, dragging her across the table until her face was close enough for him to silence her by covering her mouth with his. Like his hands, Halvo's lips were warm and far stronger than she expected. He grasped a fistful of her hair, holding her head so she could not twist away from him.

Aware that one of her own hands was free, Perri lifted it to scratch at his face or pull his hair, to make him stop what he was doing. She did neither. Instead, her fingers settled limply on his shoulder. Unable to control her instinctive response, she opened her mouth and gave herself up to the kiss blistering her lips. With the last wisps of thought available to her fevered mind, she wondered how anything so hot and demanding as Halvo's kiss could also be so sweet.

Afterward, when he finally allowed her to sink back into her own chair, she gaped at him, seeking for words to express her outrage. For it was—it must be—outrage making her heart pound and her stomach quiver. The guilt would come later. It always did, after she had time enough to consider any act of disloyalty to Elyr, however minor. But what had just happened was not a minor event. Perri felt as though she had been jolted by an earthquake.

"You are neither as sick, nor as weak, as you pretend to be," she said at last, her voice husky from continuing breathlessness.

"I fervently hope you will never experience injuries or weakness like mine," Halvo said, "though, I must admit, I would be pleased if you were to be as emotionally stressed as I am at the moment."

"I am not stressed, not in the least." Denying all she had just felt, Perri took a deep breath, willing her pulse and her stomach to return to normal. "Halvo, if you touch me again, I will call Rolli and have him put you back on the bench. There you will stay, under restraint, until we reach Regula."

"Fair enough."

Was he laughing at her? she wondered. Did he perceive how confused she suddenly was? Perri could not tell for certain, but the possibility further unnerved her.

"All I want from you," Halvo said, "is a straightforward explanation. Am I accused of some crime? If so, I am unaware of the nature of my offense."

"This situation has nothing to do with you personally."

"Forgive me if I dispute that contention," he said. "It is personal. I am the one who was kidnapped. By the way, in case you did not know, under Jurisdiction law you could be sent to a penal planet for the rest of your life for what you have done to me."

He leaned forward as if he would take her

hands again. At a sharp warning glance from her he stopped with his fingertips almost touching hers where they lay on the table. Perri imagined she could feel a current emanating from his fingers and arcing toward hers. Hastily she moved her hands to her lap. Halvo did not appear to notice.

"Perri, you are no more a pirate than I am," he said to her. "I believe the appearance of piracy was a ruse to mislead Capt. Jyrit and the rest of the crew of the *Krontar* so they will provide inaccurate information when they are questioned by Jurisdiction authorities. Perri, from the few hints you have let slip about your background, I have a dreadful impression that someone is using you. Perhaps I can help you. Tell me who Elyr is."

"He is my betrothed." Perri did not know why she should be embarrassed to admit the truth to him. After all, she had not instigated that passionate kiss. It was Halvo's misdeed, not hers, and she would take care that it was not repeated. Fiercely she told herself she had no reason for shame or embarrassment.

"A few minutes ago, you said that Elyr's life was involved in this, as well as my life," Halvo said.

The decision came to her with perfect clarity as Halvo spoke. Perri acted on it instantly, before she could think of the many reasons there must be for her to proceed with greater caution, and before she could consider how Halvo's kiss might have something to do with her decision.

"The full details of what the Hierarchy will do once you are delivered to them have not been revealed to me," Perri said. "However, I must confess to a belief that you ought to be made aware of your true circumstances. I will tell you as much as I know."

"It's about time." Halvo sat back in his chair, waiting for her to continue.

"Elyr has fallen afoul of the Regulan Hierarchy," Perri revealed. "For men like Elyr, who are highly placed in our society, this is not a difficult thing to do. The seven Hierarchs are all jealous of their power. They sometimes quarrel among themselves, and their disagreements can spread to involve those who are not Hierarchs."

"The Regulan Hierarchs are famous throughout the Jurisdiction for their complicated political intrigues," Halvo remarked. "Perhaps I ought to say they are infamous, since people have been known to die as a result of their machinations. It isn't difficult for me to believe that your Elyr could be drawn into one of those schemes. Go on, Perri. Tell me the rest. I need to know how I got involved in this."

"I was unaware of what was happening until the day when Vedyr, one of Elyr's most trusted servants, came to me in great distress to warn me that Elyr's life was forfeit," Perri said. "Be-

lieving that Elyr must have been innocently im-
plicated in the latest plot, I did the only thing I
could think of to help him. I went to see the
Chief Hierarch to plead for Elyr."

"I am beginning to understand," Halvo said.
"You were told to capture me and turn me over
to the Hierarchy. In return, Elyr's life would be
spared. Am I right?"

Perri's nod confirmed his speculation. "I was
also warned not to give you any information. So
I have broken faith with the Chief Hierarch for
what I have just said. But I could not let you go
before the Hierarchy without knowing as much
as I do. I am sorry, Halvo. I saw no way to save
Elyr except to do what the Chief Hierarch commanded."

"Wasn't there someone on Regula who could
have helped you? If Elyr is so highly placed, his
family might have enough influence to do
something for him. Or perhaps your family
could have. Do you have any family, Perri?"

"A few distant relatives," she said, dismissing
his idea with a shrug. "I do not know any of
them well. Perhaps you are not familiar with
our marital customs. I was betrothed to Elyr
when I was nine years old. Immediately after
the ceremony I was sent to live in his parents'
household so I could be trained in their ways
and thus grow up to be a pleasing wife to Elyr.
I have not seen my own family since the day of
my betrothal."

"You must love Elyr very much to be willing to risk your life in order to save him," Halvo said.

"Love?" Perri frowned. "I do not know. We are on friendly terms. Elyr is an honorable man. His mother, Cynri, has often told me so. I know that I have improved in the last few years in my attempts to please him. He says I am almost an acceptable cook and my needlework is very fine. I make all of Elyr's clothing with my own hands," Perri said proudly.

"What more could a man ask of a wife?" Halvo said in a dry tone. "What does he do for you in return?"

"In another year or two, when I have perfected my skills, he will marry me," she said. To her chagrin, Halvo chuckled. "Do you find me so amusing?"

"Not at all. I was only wondering what my mother would think of your attitudes. She would turn Regula upside down if she were to visit it."

"I have heard that the Lady Kalina is formidable. On Regula, she is considered most unwomanly." To indicate that she meant no insult to his mother by these remarks, Perri allowed the corners of her mouth to tilt upward, but she could not resist one final comment. "Perhaps it is just as well that the Leader of the Jurisdiction has not sent his wife to us on one of her state visits."

"I assure you, my mother's needlework is impeccable and she is an excellent cook," Halvo said. Then, more soberly, he said, "Perri, for all your cleverness and your bravery, you seem to me to be remarkably naive. Don't you see the terrible possibilities behind your mission to capture and deliver a hostage? For example, the Hierarchy surely has its own secret service. All planetary governments have. Why did the Chief Hierarch recruit you for such a dangerous job instead of using professional operatives?"

"Because I am the one most concerned with saving Elyr," Perri said. "For me, it is a matter of honor to succeed quietly before Elyr's name can be publicly besmirched."

"Are you saying he has not been officially charged with any crime?"

"The Chief Hierarch promised me the affair would be kept confidential until I have a chance to carry out my mission."

"Perri." Halvo shook his head as if he could not believe what he was hearing. "How old are you?"

"Twenty-two Jurisdiction years," she said. "What has my age to do with any of this?"

"I am almost forty-three," he said. "I'm old enough to be your father."

While middle age did not begin for humans until at least age 60 and, depending on one's planetary environment, the onset of old age might be delayed for many years or even for decades, the difference between Halvo's age and Perri's included an education and a career in space that set him far beyond her in experience.

"I do not think of you as a parental figure," Perri said, blushing a little.

"I am glad to hear it," Halvo said with a smile. "We will discuss that later. For the moment, let someone who has more practical knowledge of government intrigue make a few suggestions as to what may be going on here."

"I know what is going on," she said, not wanting to hear what Halvo might say. But she was forced to ask herself with brutal honesty why she didn't want to hear his ideas. Was it because she had begun to wonder if she had been told everything by the Chief Hierarch? Of course she had not been told every detail of Elyr's situation; some matters of state were far too important for her ears.

"The first possibility," Halvo said, "is that for some reason the Hierarchy wants to be rid of both Elyr and you, and they plan to achieve their goal by blaming the two of you for my kidnapping. Thus, after I am delivered to the Hierarchy they will free me, thereby gaining a great deal of credit for honesty with the Jurisdiction government, with the Service, and not incidentally, with my parents. Of course, you and Elyr will have to be killed before you can say anything to suggest that the Hierarchy's version of my abduction and release is false. Please note that, for all I know, my kidnapping was concocted between you and your betrothed, and your tale of the Chief Hierarch's involvement in the scheme is a vicious lie."

"No!" Perri cried. "No one who knows Elyr or me would believe such a wild, unfounded story. Nor would the Chief Hierarch be so dishonest with me. He was willing to help Elyr."

"The Hierarchs are always involved in some plot or other, though this one does seem unnecessarily complicated," Halvo said. "If the Hierarchy wants you and Elyr dead, some local, trumped-up charge would have done the job. I suggest to you that the Chief Hierarch has not told you the truth—or at least, not all of it."

"You are wrong about him!" Perri said, recalling the dignified man whose bearing had seemed to her the very essence of impressive—and fearful—government power. But that same man had given her inaccurate information about Halvo.

"Alternately," Halvo said, ignoring her protest, "suppose that for some reason the Regulan Hierarchy just wants to get rid of me. Why, I can't imagine. I have never to my knowledge done anything to harm the Regulans, and since I am about to be retired from active duty with the Service, my status as admiral cannot be important to them. In fact, I have been out of the Service decision-making process for more than a year. But just suppose the Regulans, or some other planetary government with whom the Regulans want to curry favor, have an old grudge against me. How could they get their revenge by doing away with the Admiral of the Fleet without bringing the entire Jurisdiction down on their heads?"

Halvo proceeded to answer his own question. "What better way than to send out an intelligent but innocent young woman, in a ship that blatantly mimics a pirate vessel, to abduct me by force or to lure me to Regula by some other means? Capt. Jyrit and the crew of the *Krontar* can testify to your act of piracy. Jyrit will have made an immediate report to Capital. Most of the Jurisdiction will know by now everything that Jyrit knows about what has happened to me. However, no blame will attach to the Regulan Hierarchy for what they do, because the fault will appear to be entirely yours. Think about it, Perri."

"No, that's not—" She stopped, considering all he had said. Her conclusions chilled her. "They would have to kill me after killing you. Otherwise, I could tell that it was the Chief Hierarch himself who sent me to capture you. There is always the chance that someone will believe my story, so they could not let me live."

"Good girl. You are learning fast," Halvo said.

"But the Chief Hierarch will keep his word to me. I know he will. Whatever happens to me,

62

Elyr's life will still be spared."

"If you are willing to give up your life for his, then you must love him," Halvo said with a trace of regret in his voice that even Perri, innocent as she still was, could not help but notice.

"It is not a matter of love. It is a matter of family honor."

"As for Elyr," Halvo said, "I can extend this nasty scenario a bit further. Suppose it is Elyr who wants to be rid of you, perhaps so he can marry someone else. Possibly a member of the Hierarchy has a daughter of marriageable age. From what you have told me, this entire affair is a secretive thing. Elyr may have committed no crime at all. He—and the Hierarchy—may simply be killing two birds with one stone. A neat analogy, if I do say so, though I still have no idea why the Regulan Hierarchy would want me dead."

"Your mind is warped, Halvo." Perri leapt to her feet. "This wild story cannot be true. Elyr would never do such a thing to me! You have no evidence. Your suggestions are concocted out of space debris.

"I was beginning to like you," Perri said, tears prickling her eyes. "I felt sorry for you because you have been so sorely injured and because I believe the Hierarchy does have a harsh punishment planned for you. You have made me regret talking so freely to you. In fact, I regret speaking to you at all!"

"I was only trying to make you understand that you have been entirely too credulous. You ought to give some serious thought to the mess in which you are involved. I don't believe you considered at all about the ramifications of what you were doing. You just acted on impulse." Halvo stood, too. "Admittedly, it was a kindhearted impulse, to save Elyr's life. But can it ever be right to save one man by destroying another?"

He was so tall, so overwhelmingly masculine. Elyr had never made Perri feel so helplessly feminine or so eager to seek comfort in his arms. Sternly, Perri reminded herself that it was Elyr to whom she owed her loyalty. The man standing before her was an enemy who would not hesitate to use her to gain his own freedom. Every word he had just spoken to her was false.

"Perri, I believe you are being manipulated in some underhanded scheme," Halvo said.

"Indeed I am," she sneered at him. "By you! This conversation is ended, Admiral. Do not attempt to open it again. In fact, I would be grateful if you would refrain from speaking to me at all during the remainder of our journey."

"If you are so upset by what I have said, it must be because you know there is a grain of truth in my suppositions. But suit yourself. It's all the same to me. If I am dead, it won't matter to me what happens to you."

If I am dead. . . . If I am dead. . . . The ominous words echoed over and over in Perri's brain all the way to her cabin. There she flung herself onto her bunk. She pounded her pillow in fury a few times. Too upset to stay in one place for long, she got up again and began prowling around the tiny room. Halvo's insinuations of wicked plots that threatened her life had thrown all her assumptions into disarray. She did not want to think about what he had said, but she could not stop thinking about his words.

Elyr did not want to be rid of her! He was pleased with her. She owed it to him to try to save his life. She belonged to Elyr. Yet she knew in her heart that there was little real warmth in his attentions to her.

What had Elyr done to make the Hierarchy sentence him to death? And why had Perri not known about the trouble he was in until Elyr's servant, Vedyr, told her of it? Why, if Elyr had done something terrible enough to warrant the death sentence, was the Hierarchy willing to commute that sentence if Perri delivered Halvo to them? Wouldn't Elyr still be guilty of a capital crime? She had been so eager to save him that she, who had been told all of her life that she asked too many questions, had neglected to ask those important questions. Halvo's lecture made her consider them now.

If I am dead. . . . She did not want Halvo to
die.

There was nothing she could do to prevent
Halvo's death. It was the price the Hierarchy
would exact for sparing Elyr's life. The words
had not been spoken aloud during her interview
with the Chief Hierarch, but Perri knew it was
so. A life for a life.

*Can it ever be right to save one man by destroy-
ing another?*

"I cannot believe a word Halvo says," Perri
muttered to herself. "I mustn't believe him. He
is only attempting to save his own life. He
doesn't know Elyr; he doesn't understand Regulan customs. The Hierarchy will dispense justice to Halvo in its own way, but Elyr will not
be involved. Halvo is lying when he says otherwise. Lying!"

Yet still, over all the unwelcome thoughts and
rationalizations, above her determination to do
what was right for Elyr whatever the cost to herself, Perri remembered Halvo's kiss and the
emotions it had stirred in her. Elyr had never
aroused such warmth in her, never slid his
tongue into her mouth in the sensuous way that
Halvo did.

Elyr's kisses were quick and dry and the once-
a-month couplings he had insisted upon since
the night of her sixteenth birthday were brief
and almost casual. Once she had recovered

from her initial shock at the mechanics of the couplings and her distaste for their messy endings, Perri had accepted them with indifference. She knew it was always that way between men and women because Elyr told her it was so. She belonged to Elyr; therefore, there was no reason for him to mislead her. Elyr would tell her when the time was right; then she would be allowed to give him the single child permitted by Jurisdiction and Regulan law. Afterward, the couplings would cease, but Perri would still be an important part of Elyr's household because she would be in charge of his comforts.

She wondered what Halvo liked to eat when he had a choice of food. Did he prefer his bathwater hot or warm? Did he like a cold rinse after the bath and the finest, cleanest fabrics for his personal clothing? His kiss had been so heated. Would his couplings be heated, too?

"I must stop thinking like this or I will go mad. The Hierarchy will do as it wants with Halvo. Once he is turned over to them, the matter is out of my hands. Elyr will live. It is Elyr who is important."

Halvo. Oh, Halvo, why did you kiss me?

Chapter Four

In the cockpit of the *Space Dragon,* Halvo was attempting to learn how much Rolli knew about the Hierarchy's plans for him—and for Perri.

"Are you specially programmed to pilot a space ship?" Halvo asked the robot.

"Among other things." The metal head swivelled in Halvo's direction, the eyelike blue lights blinking in a steady rhythm. "Why do you ask?"

"I was wondering if we really are going to Regula."

"We are going to Regula." The robot turned back to the ship's controls.

Why do you ask? Never before had Halvo known a robot to display curiosity. Since it was one of his own strong personal traits, Halvo made a mental note to pay attention to any other evidence of curiosity on Rolli's part.

"Have you and Perri been together long?"

"Since she was nine years old."

"Were you a gift on her betrothal to Elyr?" Halvo asked.

"It is the custom on Regula for children to have such guardians," Rolli said. "I have served as Perri's nurse, teacher, and servant."

"How heartwarming." When the blue lights turned in his direction again, Halvo said, "Personally, I prefer a living nurse who has a soft lap a child can curl up in after a nightmare. Someone who understands from her own experience the desire for sugar cakes at odd hours."

"I do not believe I have ever been deficient in supplying Perri with good emotional or nutritional advice," Rolli said.

"Perri told me about Elyr and how she is trying to save his life," Halvo said, trying another tack. When the robot did not respond to that remark, Halvo asked, "Does she love him? More importantly, does he love her?"

"Perri will do what is necessary. She has a strong sense of honor."

"Come on, Rolli. You aren't helping. I am trying to save my own life and, incidentally, Perri's life, too."

"Why do you care about Perri's life?" There it was again, curiosity from a robot.

"I care because I'm a romantic fool." Halvo grinned, suddenly feeling like a knight-errant in an old story. "Here I am, weaker than I have ever been since I was a baby and too often dizzy and light-headed, yet I am ready to do battle to save a woman who is determined to sacrifice herself—and me—in a lost cause!"

"You truly believe Perri's life is in danger?"

"Don't you? Use your circuitry, Rolli! It's simple logic. By abducting me, Perri has put herself outside the law. You have deduced your own fate, haven't you?" Halvo went on, watching the robot closely for any unusual reaction to his next words. "You do understand that shortly before or immediately after the Hierarchy kills Perri, you will almost certainly be dismantled? At the very least, your memory banks will have to be altered. Or perhaps they will be erased completely. Whether Elyr lives or dies, the three of us won't survive very long once we reach Regula."

"You believe Elyr would permit this?"

"I have no idea what Elyr would permit. He may not have anything to say about what happens. According to Perri, the Hierarchy will decide our fates. I know enough about the mighty seven who rule Regula to realize how poor our chances really are. Perri has high hopes, but she is wrong. You might say dead wrong."

Rolli was silent for a while, the blue lights blinking rather faster than usual.

"Do you dare trust Perri's life to the Regulan Hierarchy?" Halvo asked. "Or your own continued existence?" Again Rolli did not respond. The seconds passed in silence.

"I cannot allow Perri to be harmed," Rolli said at last. "Guardians are charged with the protection of those placed in their care."

"Then, my friend," Halvo said with a sense of satisfaction he did his best to hide, "you and I are going to have to devise a way to save Perri when the Chief Hierarch reneges on his promises to her."

"Give me a few more days aboard the *Space Dragon*," Halvo said, "and I could reprogram the computer to produce some decent food."

"There is nothing wrong with Regulan food." Perri clamped her lips shut. She had not intended to speak to Halvo at all, but he had a peculiar ability to evoke unwanted responses from her.

"I suppose for someone who doesn't care whether she lives or dies food doesn't matter, either." Halvo sounded as if he were carrying on an ordinary conversation. Perri was forced to grit her teeth to keep from answering him.

"Out there in the rest of the Jurisdiction, far beyond Regula," Halvo said, "people who are sentenced to death are given their choice of a last meal. It's an old tradition, one I gather the Regulan Hierarchy is not inclined to follow."

"We have our own traditions," Perri snapped, infuriated by his drawling tone.

"You amaze me, Perri. It is one thing to face death bravely. It's quite another thing to face the unknown—and you do face a distinctly uncertain future—without flinching. Your composure is remarkable."

"I am not facing an unknown. You are."

"In that case, let's stop this carefree banter and proceed to serious conversation, shall we?"

"I do not wish to talk with you, Halvo."

"You keep saying that, but you always answer any remark I make. And every time I walk into this galley, you follow me. I do believe you want to be alone with me."

"Of all the egomaniacal—" Determined not to rise to his continuous baiting, Perri made herself lower her voice. "I am concerned that, if you are left unsupervised, you will attempt to sabotage the *Space Dragon*."

"Sabotage? From the galley?" His eyes lit up with sardonic amusement. Perri was absolutely certain he did know a way to sabotage the ship from the galley. She was not going to give him the chance to try. They were too close to Regula, too near the successful completion of her mission for her to allow any such lapses of judgment on her part.

She had spent the two days since their quarrel reviewing every action she had taken after learning of the sentence upon Elyr. She honestly did not think she could have chosen any other path. Looking the other way and refusing to help Elyr would have left her with a conscience so burdened by guilt that she could not have continued to live after his death. By all she had ever been taught, she was doing the right thing.

Why, then, did she have so many unanswerable questions, so many doubts? Oddly, she did know the answer to that. It was Halvo's fault. She also knew that, even if she were to return to her old life in Elyr's household, her questions would not cease and, inevitably, they would cause trouble for her. Elyr did not like her to ask questions. He never had. So whether she asked or kept the questions to herself, the peaceful security she had once known had been permanently destroyed.

"Perri." Halvo spoke in the firm tone of command. Stepping closer, he took her by the elbows. "Tell Rolli to change course and take us away from Regula. Do it now, before their instruments can indicate our approach. This is our last chance."

"I cannot." Gazing deep into his eyes, she drew a long, shuddering breath. "I wish I could help you, Halvo, but I have promised to deliver you to the Chief Hierarch. I cannot break my word to him." She wondered why the tense expression on Halvo's face did not change at what must have been the final blow to any hope he held of regaining his freedom.

"All right," he said. "If you won't give me a last meal of my choice, and you won't order Rolli to change course, then grant me another wish. It will be my last wish, Perri."

"What do you want of me?" Perri asked, adding regretfully, "We do not have much time."

"It won't take long." His hands slid up to her shoulders and then farther, to cup her face between his fingers. His voice deepened to a seductive whisper. "All I want is one kiss and for you to kiss me back as though you meant it. Can you do that much for me?"

"I should not," she said in protest. "It would be most improper."

"Improper to kiss a dying man?"

"No, don't say that!" She knew he was playing on her emotions. She was sure he sensed her disgraceful yearning to feel his mouth on hers once more. "You want me to pity you and to help you escape."

"Pity is the last thing on my mind. I want you to want me," he whispered. "Just one last time, I want to know a beautiful woman desires me."

"I am not beautiful," she said, aching to tell him she did desire him and fully aware of how wrong it would be to admit such a thing to him.

"If you are not beautiful," he murmured, "then all other Regulan women must be incredible." Unbidden, without waiting for her permission, he lightly brushed his mouth across hers.

"Halvo." The sound of his name was a soft whimper of undeniable longing for an unknown possibility that, within a few hours, would be forever lost to her. She knew if she gave him what he wanted then she, too, would be lost.

He took the choice away from her. His mouth covered hers with a firm sureness that stopped her breath. His arms gathered her close.

If she had been able to think clearly, Perri might have marveled at the way in which Halvo could combine such hot, primitive demands on her with a tenderness that enriched their physical contact, enlarging it to a depth and intensity she had not dreamed possible. Deep inside Perri something stirred and spread like a sprouting seed in spring, a force still new and fragile, yet demanding life, insisting upon space and warmth in which to grow. And moisture. There was moisture aplenty in the heated blood coursing through her veins, in the burning between her thighs. Never, never before. . . .

Halvo moved, drawing her hips against his, letting her feel his hardness. He lifted her off her feet, still holding her against the length of his body. Her arms were around his neck and she clung to him, moaning, whimpering, wishing they had hours and days . . . wishing they had forever.

Dimly, she realized that they were out of the galley. She imagined he was heading toward her cabin, or perhaps toward his, to the nearest bed. She did not want to resist him, but she knew she must. She could not forget her imperative duty, not when she was so close to success. Halvo's arms were still around her. She could barely move. He was holding her much too closely.

"What?" She opened her eyes to look at him. It was not desire she saw on his face. And she knew what he was trying to do. While he kissed her, he was easing her toward the bench with its restraining bands. "Don't, please. No, Halvo. No!"

"I'm sorry, Perri. If you won't save yourself, then I'll have to save both of us." He should have covered her mouth with his hand, or kissed her again so she could not cry out, or held her so tightly that she could not fight what he was doing.

"Rolli!" she screamed. "Help me! Help!"

The controls were already on automatic, so it took only a split second for Rolli to wheel to her side. Perri was struggling as hard as she could, kicking and scratching and yelling at Halvo to let her go. His strength surprised her. She had believed in the weakness of which he constantly complained. It took Perri and Rolli together to subdue Halvo, and Perri suspected it was only a bout of dizziness that forced him to give up at the last. Whatever the cause, a few minutes later Halvo lay flat on the bench, straining against the flexible metal bands that held him fast.

"You are going to regret this," he said in a cold, deadly voice. "You little fool, I could have helped you. Now whatever happens will be on your own shoulders."

He would not stop talking. He swore at her, demanded that she let him off the bench, warned her of a dreadful fate to be visited on her, and finally, in a voice so poisonously sweet it made her teeth hurt to hear him, he informed her that she would never be able to forget that she was responsible for his inevitable death and for her own demise and the end of Rolli's existence.

"Be quiet!" Perri covered her ears with her hands. "Oh, merciful stars, Halvo, leave me alone! When will I ever be at peace again?'

"Not on Regula," Halvo said with unconcealed relish. "Not anymore. This adventure has changed you, hasn't it, Perri?"

"Yes, it has!" Taking her hands away from her ears, where they were having no effect quelling the sound of his voice, she balled them into tight fists. "I have learned never to trust males who are not Regulans. You tricked me once too often, Halvo. You pretended to make love to me, but you only wanted to put me on that bench where you are now."

"That," Rolli said, blue eyelights blinking in Halvo's direction, "was exceptionally devious of you, Admiral."

"Rolli, remember our conversations on this subject and release me," Halvo said. "You must understand that I am trying to help Perri as well as myself."

"You said nothing about attempting to seduce her into compliance," the robot replied. "You should have tried logical arguments first."

"I did!" Halvo said. "Logic doesn't work with her."

"Perhaps it was not the right kind of logic," Rolli said.

"Then you try to talk some sense into her! She is stubborn, willful, and deliberately blind to the danger she is in."

"The only danger I have been in has been from you," Perri told Halvo. To emphasize her resolution in regard to him, she pulled a small, oblong box from the shelf beneath the bench and held it up for him to see. "In this medical kit there is a strong sedative. If you say one word more I will inject you with it and you will not awaken until you are dragged before the Chief Hierarch. I believe you would prefer to walk, would you not?"

Halvo's only reaction to her threat was a groan as he strained his shoulder muscles against the metal bands.

"Do you understand me?" Perri leaned over

him, searching his face. If she had seen there any trace of the tenderness she had thought she detected in him earlier, she might have listened to his arguments against continuing to Regula. His passionate embrace, false though it undoubtedly was, had done more in his favor than all his sensible talk. The thought of turning Halvo over to the Chief Hierarch produced an ache in her heart that she knew would never heal.

But Halvo's eyes were cold and hard as they bored into hers, and his mouth was pulled into a narrow, grim line. Telling herself she had argued enough, with herself and with him, Perri straightened.

"What do you wish me to do?" Rolli asked, the blue eyelights fixed on her face as if to read all the emotions registered there.

"We continue to Regula as planned." Perri spun away from Halvo and the robot. "You may not release Halvo until we reach our destination."

"Understood." The robot wheeled quietly back to the ship's controls. Unable to bear the bitterness of Halvo's gaze any longer, Perri fled to her own cabin.

Halvo craned his neck, watching Perri leave the cockpit. "The woman is suicidal."

"Merely inexperienced in treachery," Rolli said. "Regulan females are deliberately kept innocent of the intrigues that so happily—and so

79

dangerously—occupy their menfolk. The males prefer their women uninformed about the truth of Regulan life, believing feminine ignorance will result in compliance with every masculine wish."

"Does the theory work?" Halvo asked.

"It has kept one half of Regula's population in subjugation," the robot said. "Sometimes to their great detriment, and occasionally to their deaths."

"I thought you were supposed to protect Perri." Halvo's eyes sharpened, watching the robot, but there was no way to tell what the effect of his words were on Rolli. The robot appeared to be doing nothing more than monitoring the ship's controls.

As silence fell and lengthened in the cockpit of the *Space Dragon*, Halvo knew the time had come for any sensible man to accept his fate, to steel himself to meet the immediate future with dignity. He had always been a sensible man. And yet . . . and yet. . . .

Chapter Five

"Perri, daughter of the Amalini Kin, make your report." The sonorous voice of the Chief Hierarch filled the cockpit of the *Space Dragon*. "Have you successfully completed the mission I delegated to you?"

"Yes, sir, I have." With a growing sense of foreboding, Perri faced the large main viewscreen. In the background she could see evidence that the Chief Hierarch was in his private chambers, in the same room where he had granted Perri her initial interview with him. She recognized the spiral on the wall behind the desk and she could just see one end of the Cetan sword on the adjoining wall. The Chief Hierarch was standing in front of the desk. Instead of his hierarchal robes he was wearing a white tunic and trousers, an outfit that made him appear even thinner and more ethereal than he ordinarily did.

Perri had assumed that for this occasion, when he accepted delivery of her prisoner, the Hierarch would require all the ornaments of his high status and would want to be formally attired and to sit behind the desk in his public office. The lack of official accoutrements suggested that the matter of Elyr's conviction was still being handled on a confidential basis. Perri should have been reassured by these signs, but she was not. Even the Chief Hierarch's benevolent expression could not soothe her uneasiness. Telling herself she had allowed Halvo's insinuations to influence her thinking, Perri smiled at the face on the viewscreen.

"Sir, where shall I deliver the prisoner?"

"First, bring him forward," the Chief Hierarch said. "I wish to confirm with my own eyes that you have found the right man."

"I have confined him, sir. As we approached Regula he became a bit unruly." She had decided not to tell the Chief Hierarch how Halvo had attempted to deflect her from her proper course of action. If he knew, he would surely hold it against Halvo and order a more grievous punishment. Perri did not think the Chief Hierarch was going to have an easy time with Halvo, but she would let him discover that fact for himself. Thus, Perri would not be responsible for what happened after Halvo was out of her hands. She told herself she would feel less guilty that way.

"Have your robot release the prisoner and hold him in front of the viewscreen," the Chief Hierarch commanded.

"This really is Adm. Halvo Gibal," Perri said, stung by the implication that she had not done her job correctly. "I confirmed the fact with the identification material you ordered loaded into the *Space Dragon's* computer before we left Regula."

"Do as I tell you, Perri!" The Chief Hierarch's benign expression changed slightly. The new, cold gleam in the pale green eyes, the stiffer posture, the strange harshness in his voice—all registered in Perri's mind. These subtle alterations, however, did not have their previous effect on her. She no longer trembled in fear and respect. Instead, she merely noted his effort to manipulate her. Nonetheless, she obeyed him.

"Rolli." Perri motioned to the robot. At once Rolli moved toward Halvo, who was ending his involuntary journey strapped down on the bench upon which he had begun it.

"Rolli," Halvo said in a low voice, "consider once again the arguments I have made in these last few days."

"I know my duty," Rolli said. "For your own good, Admiral, I urge you not to cause any further trouble. Come with me to the viewscreen."

With Rolli's help Halvo got to his feet and took up a position where the Chief Hierarch could see him. Rolli then quietly moved away toward the ship's controls, stopping just out of the Chief Hierarch's line of sight.

"So." A triumphant smile curled the Chief Hierarch's thin lips as he regarded the famous admiral. "It is you."

"I told you it was," Perri said, annoyed by the sign of the Chief Hierarch's lack of confidence in her ability to accomplish the task he had given her. "Now, sir, if you will just tell me what you want me to do with him."

"He is to be off-loaded onto a personnel shuttle that is on its way to intercept you even as we speak," the Chief Hierarch said.

"Then we will see you in person in a short time." Perri signaled to Rolli to close the transmission.

"Just a moment." The Chief Hierarch forestalled the action. "You and the robot are to remain aboard the *Space Dragon*."

"I told you so," Halvo whispered to Rolli, turning slightly so that his face was not visible on the viewscreen.

"I don't understand," Perri said to the Chief Hierarch. "Sir, is there some problem? Oh, please, it's not Elyr, is it? You haven't—you did promise you would take no action against him until I returned."

"See for yourself." The Chief Hierarch moved aside, allowing a second person to step into view. A young man with fair hair, green eyes, and a long, solemn face looked out of the view-screen.

"Elyr!" Perri said. "You are alive and well. How happy I am to see you."

"In fact," the Chief Hierarch said, "I have just appointed Elyr to be my principal assistant."

"I knew you would understand that he could commit no crime," Perri said. All the doubts and fears generated by Halvo's insistence that the Chief Hierarch had not been straightforward with her fled at the good news, leaving Perri's honest heart overflowing with happiness. "Thank you, Chief Hierarch. I know you will not regret your decision. And congratulations to you, Elyr. I look forward to greeting you in person in just a short time. Dear Elyr, I can scarcely wait." She could not resist adding that last, warm note. Surely, after what she had done for him, Elyr would be as eager to greet her as she was to embrace him.

"Alas, Perri, your hope cannot be fulfilled." Elyr spoke in a doleful voice. "You must comprehend that what the Chief Hierarch and I have decided is for the best."

"What are you saying?" Perri asked. "Rolli and I will land on Regula soon. Chief Hierarch, if you have an assignment for Elyr, I beg you to allow him to delay its start until we can have just a few minutes together. It will mean so much to me."

Perri was too intent on her conversation with the Chief Hierarch and Elyr to pay any attention to what was happening off to one side of the cockpit, out of range of the viewscreen.

"Admiral." Rolli spoke at a lower volume than usual, keeping to a level that could not be heard over the video link with the Chief Hierarch's chambers. Halvo caught the odd note of warning and did not so much as turn his head or shift his eyes. He responded by barely moving his lips and he used the same low tone.

"Yes, Rolli."

"There are three Regulan warships approaching the *Space Dragon*. Their weapons are set on firing mode."

"You know what this means." Still Halvo gave no indication of a conversation going on between himself and the robot. To the two men on the other end of the video link, he was merely waiting for Perri to finish speaking with Elyr. Halvo had heard enough of that particular conversation to be entirely enlightened as to the true relationship between Elyr and his betrothed.

"Now you have proof that my predictions were correct," Halvo whispered to Rolli. "Those vessels are being sent to blow up this ship, and you and Perri with it. Soon neither of you will be available to deny the Chief Hierarch's version of the events that brought me to Regula."

"Death would be a blessing to me," Rolli said.

"But not to Perri." Halvo did not pause to question such a peculiar statement from an emotionless robot. He was too busy trying to think of a way out of a seemingly impossible situation. Rolli appeared to be the only hope left, and Halvo was determined to convince the robot to act. "Perri is young and deserves to live. As far as I can tell, her biggest crime is trying to save her ungrateful fiance. What Perri did to me, she did at the Chief Hierarch's behest."

"Elyr is not worthy of her," Rolli said. "Not worthy at all."

"Then do something to help her," Halvo said, "because it is clear to me that Elyr won't."

Meanwhile, Perri was still dealing with Elyr and the Chief Hierarch.

"You are to stay on the *Space Dragon* until you receive official permission to land," the Chief Hierarch repeated in response to Perri's continued insistence that she wanted to meet with Elyr in person.

From the bewildered look in Perri's eyes, Halvo could tell that she suspected what was going on, though he thought she was not ready yet to admit out loud that she was the victim of a treacherous plot. Halvo decided it was time for him to take control of the conversation.

"Why don't you tell us exactly what you have planned for me once I reach the surface of Regula?" Halvo asked, turning back to face the two men on the viewscreen. "Don't you think Perri has the right to know the full extent of your machinations? After all, it won't make any difference how much information she has. She can't stop you now, can she? Speaking for myself, I would like to know which of the possible scenarios I set out for her is the correct one."

"Admiral, the personnel shuttle should be in position for docking with the *Space Dragon* within ten seconds," the Chief Hierarch said, his disregard for Halvo's questions providing the final proof Halvo needed about his conclusions on the Hierarch's plans. "I advise you to disembark promptly."

"What if I don't want to leave?" In the Chief Hierarch's last remark, Halvo had discovered the opportunity he sought. It had been a long time since he had participated in such a dangerous game. A part of him that he had believed permanently put to rest was beginning to awaken again. Danger or no, Halvo was enjoying himself. He just hoped he could avoid a sudden bout of dizziness until the confrontation with the Chief Hierarch was finished. And he sent a fervent prayer to each of the ancient gods of Demaria that Rolli's programmed instructions to protect Perri at all costs would not fail.

"Regulan personnel shuttle to starboard, requesting permission to dock," Rolli reported from a position near the ship's control panel.

"Permission granted," Elyr said, apparently speaking at the same time to both the *Space Dragon* and the shuttle.

"Belay that order!" Risking vertigo, Halvo turned to look into Rolli's constantly blinking twin blue lights that took the place of eyes. "Rolli, you have about ten seconds to unscramble your circuitry and do the right thing. After that, it will be too late for all of us."

"Elyr, please," Perri cried to the uncaring face on the viewscreen. "I have done my best to help you. Now tell me the truth. Elyr, what is happening?"

The viewscreen went blank.

"Rolli," Perri cried, "get the picture back."

"No," Rolli said. "I need the power for Starthruster."

"You mustn't! We can't run away. Not now, not when Elyr is free." Perri's green eyes were swimming with tears, and she sounded more and more desperate with every word. It was clear to Halvo that she was trying to convince herself of the truth of what she was saying. "Our mission is a success, Rolli. You and I together have saved Elyr from the death sentence. It is a time of rejoicing for us and for all the Amalini Kin."

"Elyr was never charged with any crime," Halvo said. "If he were a criminal, he would not be allowed in the same room with the Chief Hierarch unless he was chained or under heavy

89

guard. Elyr's so-called imprisonment was a ruse, a deliberate lie invented to lure you into an act of piracy. In your heart you know it, Perri. Admit it."

"No! Elyr would not betray me, not when I risked my life and my honor for him."

"Admiral." Rolli's calm, metallic words broke into Perri's frantic reply. "You have exactly thirty seconds to strap yourself and Perri into your seats before I activate Starthruster. I calculate that it will require forty-five seconds for the commanders of the Regulan ships now approaching us to order their weapons to be fired and for the ensuing blasts to reach the *Space Dragon*. This will leave us fifteen seconds in which to quit the immediate area."

"No!" Perri screamed again. "I won't leave. I won't!"

Halvo could tell she was on the verge of hysteria. Under the circumstances, he couldn't blame her. There was no time to reason with her that she was better off without the treacherous Elyr. He would do that later, if they lived long enough. Catching Perri by her upper arms, Halvo slammed her down on the bench. Though she was apparently too stunned by his unexpected action to fight him, he held her with one arm and knee while he fumbled for and found the button that controlled the straps. By the time Perri fully realized what he was doing, she could not move. The flexible metal bands that once had held Halvo kept Perri immobilized. But Halvo could not move either.

"My back!" he yelled, stiffening with pain.

Rolli either did not understand what was wrong with Halvo or did not choose to respond. At the appointed moment, exactly 30 seconds after promising to do so, Rolli hit the button to activate Starthruster. The *Space Dragon* shuddered, then rocked as if it had been struck by a giant's fist.

The motion threw Halvo to the deck. Fortunately, he landed on one side. He rolled over onto his back and lay there, groaning. Perri, equally unable to move, gazed down at him in a decidedly unfriendly way.

"You deserve a backache," she said to him. "Let me off this bench at once."

"I will just as soon as it's safe," Halvo said. Raising his voice, he called, "Rolli, when you can leave the controls, come and help me. I'm having trouble getting up."

There was no response from the robot.

"Rolli?" Grunting with the effort, Halvo attempted to raise his head so he could see better. "Rolli!"

"Something is wrong," Perri said, straining to lift her own head. She appeared to have recovered from her bout of near hysteria, her thoughts apparently no longer on Elyr, but upon her robot. "From where I am, I can see the control panel better than you. Rolli is sitting absolutely still at the controls. Halvo, do you smell something burning?"

"Insulation." Halvo sniffed the air again, just to be sure. "Can you see any smoke?"

"No, I don't think so." Perri squirmed around on the bench as much as she could, trying to get a better view of the controls and the robot. "Rolli's eyelights are out. Halvo, I think the *Space Dragon's* controls are on overload. I'm sure Rolli told me that is what the big red light means."

"The blast from one of those Regulan ships must have hit us just as Rolli activated Starthruster," Halvo said. "If the robot's metal fingers were on the control panel at exactly the right moment, they would be perfect conductors for the charge from the Regulan ships."

"Is that why our ship is vibrating so much?" Perri asked.

"This ship is vibrating because Starthruster is still working. We are hurtling through space at uncontrolled speed," Halvo said. "If Rolli is out of commission, then I have to get to the controls fast."

"Well, I am certainly not in a position to stop you," Perri said in a resentful tone. She watched him struggle to move off the deck.

"Damnation," Halvo growled. "I can't get to my feet on my own."

"Do something!" Perri shouted at him. "I don't think the *Space Dragon* can take much more vibration without tearing apart at every seam. Rolli warned me against using Star-thruster for too long a time."

Perri could not move very much, but she managed to wriggle downward along the bench until the restraining band across her chest and arms was rubbed up just above her left elbow. This was on the side toward Halvo. Perri lifted her lower arm, rotating it outward as far as she could. "Here. If you can raise your arm and take my hand, perhaps you can use me to pull your-self up."

"It will hurt you," Halvo said.

"Do we have any other choice?" she snapped. "If you injure my wrist or my elbow, we will fix it later. Just get up from that deck, Halvo, and find a way to slow the *Space Dragon* before it tears apart from the stress!"

Reaching up, Halvo caught Perri's hand. Then, grunting with pain, he bent one knee and pushed as hard as he could, levering himself off the deck as Perri had ordered. He heard her catch her breath as he pulled on her arm, and he saw her set her teeth.

Of course, inevitably, as soon as he began to move the cursed dizziness returned. Closing his eyes to shut out the spinning cockpit, Halvo clung to Perri's forearm and to the ad-ditional body parts he discovered with his other hand as he blindly raised himself a lit-tle higher.

"I wish I could be of more help to you." Her voice was tight with the discomfort he was inflicting on her.

"I can do it," Halvo said. "Just a moment or two more."

The *Space Dragon* shivered as if it would come apart at any second and Halvo, already unbalanced by the effects of the old injury to his inner ear, went sprawling. He landed on something soft and heard the air go out of it in a quick little cry. He opened his eyes to find himself lying facedown atop Perri.

She was soft and sweet beneath him. Her lips were parted as she gasped for air. With that first deep breath her breasts moved against Halvo's chest. Her green eyes met his with concern and fear.

Halvo felt his body stir into hard, masculine life. It had been so long since that had happened, the entire year of his hospitalization and for some months before that. He had worried, in the black loneliness of many a night since his injuries, that he would never feel like a virile man again. That it should happen here, in a spaceship about to disintegrate into tiny pieces, while he lay immobilized on the body of a girl half his age who was responsible for his present situation, seemed to Halvo just one more piece of a bad joke the cosmos was playing on him. And yet gazing into Perri's eyes, he was aware of a jolt of irrational happiness.

He wanted to kiss Perri and feel those soft red lips opening beneath his own hard mouth. He wanted to take her in his arms and hear her moan while he—

"Halvo, are you in terrible pain? Speak to me. Are you paralyzed?"

"Just give me a minute." He could not take his eyes off her lovely face.

"Get off me, Halvo, and go fix the controls." Perri pushed at him with her left hand. The urgency in her voice increased. "Please hurry."

He wanted to hurry. He wanted to thrust rapidly into her soft, feminine body and rush to a joyous, all-consuming climax. . . .

"Halvo!"

"I know. I know, Perri. I have to get to my feet." Halvo had spent more than 20 years in the Jurisdiction Service. He was trained to duty, and duty called to him. In a monumental act of willpower he consigned the storm of desire afflicting him to a far corner of his mind and kept it there.

"If you can reach the release button just above my head," Perri said, "the bands will retract and I will be free to help you stand up."

"Yes. Good idea." With some difficulty Halvo got his right arm over his head. His searching fingers found the button and pushed. He tried to make his mind a blank so he would not react out of passionate desire when Perri touched him. She seemed to be unaware of his response to physical contact with her, but Halvo knew he would not soon forget the sensation of her lithe body sliding out from under his or the gentle strength of her small hands. Then he was on his feet, and the pain in his spine was minimal. After carefully straightening his back, Halvo made his way to the controls.

"Perri, come and help me move Rolli."

"I'm here." She was right behind him, and she gave him an encouraging glance before turning her attention to the robot. "Oh, poor Rolli," she said, regarding the blackened fingers still resting on the control for Starthruster.

"Don't touch anything that's metal until I have shut down the panel," Halvo said.

It only took a moment, then he let Perri roll the robot out of the way.

"We'll fix it later, when we have more time," Halvo said, seating himself.

"Do you know how to pilot the ship?" Perri crouched down beside him, eager to help. Halvo wasn't sure why she was so calm when she had previously been so upset, but he blessed her self-control.

"I was flying ships like this before you were born," he said. "I haven't forgotten how. Your knees and back are younger than mine, so you are going to have to do the repair work. I want you to crawl under this control panel and follow my instructions."

"Don't say that."

"Don't say what?"

"You are not so much older than I."

"Tell that to my doctors."

"Your injuries will heal in time, Halvo." Did she know what the soft touch of her hand on his thigh was doing to him? "It seems to me that you are not as pale as you were when you first came aboard the *Space Dragon*."

"I am sure that's true." Halvo looked down upon her dark red hair and barely restrained himself from twisting his hands into it and lifting her face to his. "Here is what I want you to do. It's fairly simple. You won't even need tools." Swiftly, he gave her the repair instructions.

"Are you certain I won't destroy the ship?" she asked. "I have no mechanical ability at all."

"It's a perfectly simple adjustment," Halvo said. "If you aren't sure about something, just ask a few questions."

"That I can do." After giving him a wry smile, she lowered her head and went to work.

Halvo tried not to react when she brushed against his legs as she moved around down there beneath the control panel. However, he did find it impossible to keep his eyes off the beautifully rounded buttocks that shifted and moved back and forth just beside his seat. His gratitude knew no bounds when Perri finally completed the repairs and crawled out again to stand behind his chair.

"Will it work now?" As she bent forward to look at the control panel, her breast pressed on his shoulder and her warm fragrance filled his senses.

"Stand back," he ordered brusquely. "You are in the way."

She said nothing more, but she did move. Halvo breathed a sigh of relief and refused to think about his growing frustration. Then he brought the control panels back on-line and de-activated Starthruster. At last he was able to fire the braking rockets. The *Space Dragon* slowed, and as it did, the dangerous vibrations gradually stopped.

"Oh, thank you." Looking as if she might cry, Perri collapsed into the navigator's chair. "You saved us. The ship will hold together, won't it?"

"I think so. For the time being, at least. You did the actual repairs, Perri. I should be thanking you." And he knew just how he would have liked to thank her, too. Gods of Demaria, what was wrong with him? Why did he think about making passionate love to her every time he looked at her? "Because it has been too cursed long a time," he muttered, answering his own questions.

"I beg your pardon, Halvo?"

"It has been too long since I last piloted a ship like this," Halvo said hastily. "In my younger days, I used to be a hotshot pilot."

"I think you still are." The brilliant smile Perri gave him nearly took Halvo's breath away.

Chapter Six

There had not been much reason for Perri to smile in recent days. Nor was there cause for rejoicing at that moment. Her relief at the knowledge that death by disintegration was no longer imminent quickly gave way to pangs of guilt.

"Halvo, I do not know how to express my regret for what I have done to you." She was still seated in the navigator's chair, with Halvo in the copilot's chair. The pilot's place was empty because it was Rolli's place and the robot did not require a seat.

At her words, Halvo turned to look at her with a burning intensity that Perri interpreted as anger.

"I am truly sorry," she whispered, hoping she might avert his rage by enlarging her apology. "I will do anything I can to make it up to you."

"We will discuss it later. I'm sure I will be able to think of something you can do for me." A silver light smoldered in Halvo's gray eyes.

"I ought also to thank you for being clever enough to save our lives." Perri was disconcerted by Halvo's steady gaze. Remembering Elyr's cold anger whenever she did something wrong, she was a bit fearful of Halvo's present mood. "You were right about everything, Halvo. I was a fool to trust the story I was told without asking questions. Elyr, his servant who first brought the tale of his arrest to me, the Chief Hierarch himself—all of them lied to me. None of them cared a bit for my life. Nor was my concern for Elyr an adequate excuse for committing a criminal act. I am deeply ashamed."

"Abject penitence does not become you, Perri. I much prefer to hear you snapping and snarling at me. Besides, this adventure isn't all bad. I haven't had this much fun in years. Being an admiral can be awfully stuffy business." His cheerful grin shocked Perri.

"Your attitude is most gracious," she murmured. "But I still owe you some recompense for your recent trials."

"Don't worry. As I said, I'll think of something you can do in return."

"You have only to name it, Halvo."

He laughed and suddenly he looked like a much younger man. Perri noted how sure his hands were on the controls. When a light blinked or a buzzer sounded, Halvo did not hesitate for a moment. He knew just what to do. His competence gave her a feeling of complete security. Unfortunately, she knew her contentment could not last. In her experience of life, good things never did.

"Halvo," she said, "where are we going?"

"I have a more important question," he said. "Where are we now?"

"Don't the navigational instruments provide that information?"

"I'm not sure we can depend on them. All the evidence indicates that we were hit by a blast from one of the Regulan ships just as we shifted to Starthruster. Add the effects of using Starthruster for too long a time to any structural damage the Regulan shots did and you get some very peculiar readings on the instruments. We can make some repairs here in space, but we really ought to find a planet where we can set the *Space Dragon* down and go over her completely inside and out, checking all the systems."

"Would it be safe to land?" Perri asked. "Won't the Regulans pursue us?"

"They have to," Halvo said grimly. "The Chief Hierarch cannot take the chance that we will reach a Jurisdiction outpost and report everything we know about his scheming."

"What shall we do, then?"

"Our best chance of eluding capture lies in staying as far away from Regula as possible, which may not be too difficult, given the length of time Starthruster was controlling this ship. The Regulans have no way of knowing how long we used Starthruster. That lack of information ought to slow their search somewhat and provide us with a little time. At the moment, it's the only advantage we have. Let's hope it will be enough."

"You are saying that I cannot return to my homeworld." Perri had not meant to sound so despairing.

"Do you really want to go back?" Halvo sent her an understanding look.

"I don't know. I have never thought of living anywhere except on Regula. For Regulans, exile is a punishment worse than death. But there is nothing left for me on Regula now. Elyr has made it clear that he does not want me." Perri took a moment to purge her voice of any hint of sorrow before she continued. "I have been separated from my blood kin for so long that they are all strangers to me, and my parents have been dead for several years. If I were to return, I would have to stand trial for what I have done, and with the Chief Hierarch and Elyr testifying against me, as they surely would in order to protect themselves, I would be convicted and given a long prison sentence—or a worse punishment."

"Permanent exile," Halvo said. "Which is what you have now without the nuisance of a trial."

"Oh, dear," Perri said. "Just a little while ago, I was feeling so content."

"Perhaps we can discover a way to restore your contentment." Halvo's voice sank to a low, caressing tone that resonated in the depths of Perri's being. His smile warmed her heart. It told her he held no grudge against her. She smiled back at him, feeling for a brief and lovely moment as if she was not a stranger in a cold, empty universe with all the forces of her native world aligned against her.

"Now," Halvo said, speaking more briskly, "I am going to switch to the slowest possible speed and set the controls on automatic. Let us hope we don't have any trouble with that setting, because while it is on, you and I are going to try to repair Rolli. We are going to need that robot to help us get the *Space Dragon* back into top condition and to correct any defects in the navigational system, not to mention in the sensors, so we can detect the Regulan ships that are surely going to follow us."

Half an hour later, with the ship running on its own and with the available tools laid out on the bench in neat order as if they were a surgeon's instruments, Halvo went to work.

"I know it is only a metal construction, but I have begun to think of Rolli as a person," Halvo said. "Removing its head feels to me like a decapitation."

"It is." Perri watched Halvo's nimble fingers with growing amazement. As a female, she had never been permitted to use masculine tools. Her first attempt to work with them had been the repair to the controls that she had done under Halvo's guidance. Now, her fingers itched with her desire to take up one of the instruments and help Halvo. Knowing she would very likely prove to be more of a hindrance than an assistant, she resisted the impulse. To distance herself emotionally from the actual work, she decided to tell Halvo some of Rolli's history. She was just about to begin when Halvo finished removing the last screw and lifted Rolli's head off the slender metal neck.

"Oh," Perri murmured, looking into the opening thus revealed. "I did not know how complicated Rolli is." She was pleased when Halvo did not order her to move away. Instead, he began to explain what it was she was seeing.

"There is the damage, right in front of us. No wonder Rolli's hands froze on the controls." Using a tool that looked to Perri like a large pair of tweezers, Halvo extracted several long strands of blackened fiber from Rolli's neck. "This is why we smelled burning insulation. The mechanism for Rolli's physical movement is located in what, on a human, we would call the chest. Information is routed from Rolli's memory circuits in the head we just removed, down through the neck along these fibers to the secondary circuits in the chest, where a message to use the hands is implemented, or a message to move around on those little wheels. The system is roughly analogous to the human body: Your brain tells your hands or your feet what to do by sending commands through your nerves."

"How fascinating. Can we fix it?" Gently, Perri touched the scorched fingers of her daily companion. "The *Space Dragon* does carry a few repair supplies."

"It shouldn't be too difficult." After another survey of the robot's neck and chest cavities, Halvo continued his explanation. "When Rolli's hands were burned, a safety device automatically disconnected the robot's main circuitry in its head from the circuits in the lower body. This prevented a burnout in the main circuits, which would have destroyed the robot's memory banks. To put it simply, Rolli won't require brain surgery. I can replace the destroyed fibers and reset the safety device. Then, after we put the head back on and fasten the screws to make the necessary connections, Rolli should function normally again."

"I am glad to hear we won't have to open Rolli's head. Halvo, I ought to tell you about the memory—"

"Would you locate the repair supplies and see if we carry the right-size fibers?" Halvo asked, his attention on the robot. "We ought to have some. It is a standard size."

Deciding there would be time enough later to tell him what she knew about Rolli's main circuitry, Perri obediently headed for the small cargo bay.

"Your manual dexterity is remarkable," Halvo said. "It is probably why you are a good seamstress."

"I have never been permitted to use men's tools before. I expected to be clumsy."

"You weren't, not for a moment. You have been a real help to me, Perri."

His praise warmed her. She had been feeling guilty and worthless. But after her successes on the control panel and on Rolli, she thought she might be good for something after all.

"As a matter of fact," Halvo said, "I think you ought to learn to pilot the *Space Dragon*."

"I?" She stared at him, not sure she had heard him correctly. "Only men can pilot spacecraft."

"Regula is one of the last male-dominated planets," Halvo said. "On other worlds, and in the Jurisdiction Service, females are required to develop all possible skills. The first officer, armaments officer, and the navigator of the *Krontar* are all females."

"They are?"

Halvo paused in his inspection of Rolli's apparently undamaged head to look hard at Perri. He was so clever that she believed he must be fully aware of the new currents arising in the stream of her thoughts.

"You have been deliberately kept in ignorance," Halvo said.

"Ignorance is not the same as stupidity," Perri said at once, stung by what she perceived as an insult.

"You are not stupid, Perri. Quite the opposite."

"If I cannot return to Regula, then I must make a new life for myself elsewhere. To do so, I will have to educate myself as quickly as possible."

"I will be happy to help you, Perri."

His words were said in all seriousness, but something told her that Halvo was not talking only about the various ways of life encompassed by the Jurisdiction or the study of mathematics and the sciences. When he smiled at her, standing there with Rolli's metal head in his hands, Perri knew Halvo had a more intimate education in mind. A warm fluttering began deep inside her, a sensation that brought a blush to her cheeks.

"We can discuss your curriculum later,"

Halvo said, returning his attention to the robot. "For the moment, let's put Rolli back together. If I hold the head in the right position on the neck, will you replace the screws?"

"Do you trust me for so important a task?"

"Why not? You haven't made a mistake yet."

"I have made many, Halvo." The residue of sadness and guilt sounded in her voice.

"Not on Rolli." Halvo regarded her soberly. "You can learn from the other mistakes you have made. It will be part of your education."

"Thank you," Perri whispered, lowering her head so Halvo would not see the sudden moisture in her eyes. In effect, he had just said that he forgave her for what she had done to him.

Halvo put Rolli's head down on the bench and took Perri's hands in his. "Look at me."

Reluctantly, Perri lifted her eyes to meet his.

"You have been thinking of me as a victim, but I am not," Halvo said. "It was my deliberate choice to leave the *Krontar* and board the *Space Dragon*. Capt. Jyrit disapproved of my decision. The leader of the security team warned me that I was making a dangerous move. I refused to listen to either of them. But just suppose for a moment that I had listened. Suppose I had decided to be sensible. What would you have done then?"

"Done?" she repeated blankly. "I don't know. I was depending upon your curiosity to impel you to do as I wished you to do."

"Exactly. Don't you see, Perri? You could not have captured me without my cooperation. Never think of me again as a victim. I am having far too much fun."

"I turned your life upside down," she said.

"We did it together—the same way we escaped from Regula and got this ship under control together. The same way we are working together now to repair Rolli. I won't betray you, Perri." Halvo's hand rested against her cheek for a moment.

Perri thought he was going to kiss her. She would have welcomed his embrace. But Halvo dropped his hand and returned his attention to Rolli.

"We have a lot of work ahead of us," he said, somewhat abruptly. "And we are not out of danger yet. We can never forget those Regulan ships that are following us."

"That should do it." Relaxing in the knowledge of a job well done, Halvo sat back in the copilot's chair and sent a glance toward Rolli. The robot was just finishing the last test on the ship's controls.

"Most systems on the *Space Dragon* are now functioning within tolerable limits," Rolli said. "Which is not to say they are in perfect working order or will continue to function. Still, the last two hours have been most productive. Admiral, I have so far neglected to express my appreciation for the prompt and technically accurate repairs you made to my own systems."

"I acted out of self-interest, Rolli. Perri and I need your skills if we are to survive. No thanks are necessary, but if you are offering them, you ought to include Perri, too. She helped me."

"I do not doubt her ability to rise to such an occasion." Rolli's head swiveled in Perri's direction. She sat in the navigator's chair looking remarkably dejected considering the success she and Halvo had achieved in getting Rolli working again.

"I want Perri to learn to pilot the *Space Dragon*," Halvo said, sounding as if he expected to hear an objection from Rolli.

"An excellent idea," Rolli said. "It would be an added safety factor if all three of us were able to pilot the ship. Shall we begin at once? Perri, if you will stand directly behind me, I will explain the control panel to you. I believe you have already memorized most of it since I answered the questions you put to me during our voyage to intercept the *Krontar*."

"No." Perri rose from her seat, but she did not move toward the main control panel. "Later, perhaps. Please, Halvo, I can't do this right now."

"You ought to rest for a while," Halvo said, hearing the strained note in her voice.

"I am a bit tired." A lone tear trickled down

Perri's soft cheek. She fled the cockpit, heading toward her own cabin.

"I do not believe she is ill," Rolli said.

"Not in the way you mean. Not physically ill," Halvo said. "I have seen similar reactions in young Service personnel under my command. Excitement and a determination to prove themselves can carry them through the worst pre-battle tension. They set aside their very natural fears and any doubts they have about the rightness of what they are doing. Then, once the action is over, they often lapse into depression or guilt, as Perri is doing now. The reaction is always strongest when the battle has ended badly and there is no triumph to buoy their spirits."

"I comprehend the problem," Rolli said. "Abducting you was an act entirely foreign to Perri's nature. She undertook the mission only to save Elyr. To foreswear her beliefs about right behavior, to give up such a vital part of her own value system in order to help another, then to meet betrayal from that other, could only result in emotional devastation."

"You do understand." Halvo gave the robot a close look, but there was nothing to see except the smooth metal head and the steadily blinking eyelights. Certainly, there had been no emotion in Rolli's voice. There could not be. Robots did not feel emotions.

"I was originally programmed to conform my circuitry to Perri's needs and to her thought patterns," Rolli said. "It takes no great leap of logic to discern that she is suffering a severe reaction to unbearable stress."

"I would call that an accurate diagnosis," Halvo said.

"Perhaps it would help if you talked to her, if you explained to her the psychological implications of what has occurred in the same way in which you have just explained them to me."

"I'm not sure that would be a good idea," Halvo said.

"You must offer counseling to junior officers under your command when they are distressed as Perri is now. Why not do the same for her?"

"The truth is, Rolli, I am having a bit of trouble with my own feelings toward Perri."

"If you express your resentment directly to her, will it not become easier for the two of you to work out your differences? Should we encounter further dangers, it will be necessary for you to work together in harmony to alleviate any resulting crisis."

Halvo could not tell the robot that, far from feeling resentment toward Perri for abducting him, he was suffering from a nearly uncontrollable desire for her. It was more than sheer lust; it was a vibrant longing for the most intimate kind of communion. Halvo had known many women on many worlds. Never before had he been so passionately drawn to a female that he had difficulty in thinking about anything else but her. As honest in his own way as Perri was in hers, Halvo knew what a joining with her would mean. He could not take Perri, then walk away from her. If he made love to her, it would be love in truth, and they would be bound together forever after.

While he could see a great many benefits to himself from such an arrangement, he did not think it would be fair to Perri. He was much older than she, and his life experiences were entirely different. Perri, released from the Regulan subjugation of females, ought to be free to pursue her own life in any way she wished.

All of his reasoning assumed that Perri wanted Halvo as much as he wanted her. He could not be sure that she did.

"Damnation," Halvo muttered to himself. "I don't know how to handle this."

"While your reluctance to intrude upon Perri's privacy is commendable," Rolli said, "she does need a friend."

"I thought you were her best friend," Halvo said.

"The differences between a metal robot and a human being are obvious, Admiral. You yourself have previously pointed out some of them to me. I do not have a soft lap, nor would I offer sugar cakes indiscriminately."

"If I didn't know better," Halvo said, "I would accuse you of having a sense of humor."

"I am merely stating the obvious, which may,

of course, appear to be humorous to the human mind." Rolli paused as if to let that statement sink in, then said, "Perri has a liking for heskay tea. She finds it comforting."

"Is that the vile-smelling stuff she drinks with every meal?"

"It is programmed into the food processor," Rolli said, "which has been fully functional for the last thirteen-and-one-half minutes. You should have no difficulty in obtaining a hot beverage from it."

With a chuckle, Halvo rose, pleased to note that his physical condition appeared to be improving. He was able to get out of the copilot's seat with neither pain nor vertigo.

"Heskay tea and straightforward logic. Now I know how you keep Perri under your thumb," he said to the robot. "I must remember your methods."

"Thumbs?" Rolli asked. "Precisely speaking, I do not have thumbs in the human sense. I am merely equiped with five jointed digits at the ends of metal arms."

"Right. And you don't have a fondness for Perri integrated into your main circuitry either." With one of his own hands about to descend on Rolli's square metal shoulder in a gesture of comradely affection, Halvo stopped himself just in time. Rolli did not appear to notice either the motion of Halvo's hand or the muttered oath with which he turned away from the control panels and left the cockpit.

Hot heskay tea was a thick orange brew with a fetid odor that threatened to turn Halvo's stomach. Holding a mug of it he left the galley and headed toward Perri's cabin.

The interior sliding doors were not functioning. All of them were wide open. This was one of the ship's systems that would require further repair work once they located a safe landing place. Thus, Halvo was able to walk right into Perri's cabin. She was curled up on the bunk, her knees drawn almost to her chin and her eyes closed. Setting the tea mug down on the shelf beside the bunk, Halvo sat next to Perri. He stroked her glowing hair gently, letting his fingers tangle into the thick waves while he reflected that it was a good thing he could not close and seal the door and be alone with her.

Perri's eyes opened, but she lay unmoving while Halvo's hand slipped through her hair over and over again. Finally, she stretched, turning onto her back. Catching Halvo's hand, she held it against her cheek.

"I do not want you to think I am feeling sorry for myself," she said. "I have only been thinking about what has happened and trying to make my peace with it."

"I know how difficult that is. It can break your heart to learn that the people to whom you have devoted your life set your value so low."

"You brought me tea." Dropping his hand,

she pushed herself up to a sitting position. Halvo put the mug into her hands and she sipped appreciatively.

"I don't know how you can drink it," he said, grimacing at the smell of it.

"It is an indulgence left from my childhood. My mother used to prepare it for me. I shall probably never outgrow my taste for it. However, a fondness for heskay tea is all I ought to retain from my youth. It is clear to me that I must discover a new way to live."

She looked so downcast that Halvo took the chance of spilling the disgusting tea on himself. He put his arms around her. Perri nestled against him so easily that Halvo knew he was risking far more than a dousing with hot, smelly tea. He was about to lose his self-control.

Perri was small, warm, and beautifully rounded. Her hair flowed over his arms, strands of it catching in his hands. Halvo rested his cheek on the silky red curls and, for just a few moments, gave himself up to sweet desire. His hands molded her shoulders, then wandered downward to the small of her back and farther, to trace the feminine curves of her hips.

"Halvo." She leaned away from him. Her eyes were wide, her rosy lips softly parted. The hand holding her mug of tea trembled slightly. "I am not sure you ought to touch me like that. It makes me feel most peculiar."

"Touching you has the same effect on me." He

took the mug from her unresisting fingers, stowing it safely on the shelf. Then he put both arms around her and kissed her hard.

She did not protest. Her hands slid up his chest and around his neck, and her lips opened at once to Halvo's thrusting tongue. The interior of her mouth was as smooth and every bit as hot as the richest Demarian cream. Halvo did not even mind the faint, lingering taste of heskay tea on her tongue. Perri moaned softly, pressing closer to him, and Halvo's senses spiraled into a mad clamor, demanding instant gratification.

He could feel her breasts crushed against his chest and he longed to caress them. He wanted to see her nipples standing up hard when he touched them. He stroked her thighs and ached to feel them opening beneath him.

Halvo realized that he was standing. He had drawn Perri upward from her bunk because he instinctively knew what would happen if he lay down beside her. He would not be able to stop himself from taking what he so desperately wanted.

Frantically, he told himself that Perri was too young for him, too innocent. She was emotionally wounded at the moment and therefore incapable of making a rational decision as to whether she really did want him or not—as if desire as intense as theirs could ever be rational! Lastly, and far from an unimportant matter to Halvo, was the fact that they could enjoy no privacy.

The mental image of Perri and himself naked on her bunk, with Rolli appearing in the open cabin doorway to observe them from those calm, blinking blue eyelights, was what gave Halvo the strength to set his hands upon Perri's shoulders and hold her away from him.

"Don't you want me?" she whispered, her face flushed, her lips bruised by his passionate kisses.

"We have more important things to do than roll around together on your bunk," he said. He saw her face close into the tight, expressionless mask she had shown to him on their first meeting, and he almost cried out with grief and longing for the softer, sweeter Perri he had just deliberately banished with his own harsh words. But Halvo had not become an admiral by giving way to unseemly emotions at the wrong times.

"I did not come to your cabin to make love to you," he said through set teeth.

"Didn't you?" Her emerald eyes were altogether too brilliant. Halvo was certain she was trying not to cry.

"I just wanted to reassure you that you may begin your piloting lessons whenever you feel ready."

"How kind of you. If you don't mind, Admiral, I would prefer to be alone for a while. It is why

I retired to my cabin in the first place."

She sounded as if she would like to kill him, which was just as well. If she had wept or tried to touch him, Halvo wasn't sure he could have resisted her in spite of all the sensible reasons for self-restraint that he rehearsed in his mind over and over again on his way back to the cockpit.

"Did Perri drink her tea?" Rolli asked when Halvo slid into the copilot's seat.

"Yes." To Halvo's surprise, the robot did not turn its eyelights upon him after that terse response.

"She is not ill then?"

"Perri is going to be just fine." Halvo resisted the impulse to smash his fist down on the control panel—or into the robot's smooth, metal face. "Perri is a survivor. I am the one who may not live through the next few days."

Chapter Seven

"What we are searching for," Rolli said, reiterating the conclusions reached during a long discussion of their situation, "is a planet or a large asteroid with an atmosphere acceptable to human physiology. As you have previously noted, Admiral, a place with a friendly, technologically advanced civilization would be the ideal, but if necessary, we can make the required repairs ourselves so long as conditions permit us to work outside the ship and take our time about it."

"Unfortunately, I can't locate any suitable planets in this sector." Halvo was acting as navigator and he was making one of the periodic tests he and Rolli had instituted as soon as the ship's instruments were operating again. "I can't swear to the accuracy of the findings on these sensors, but there does appear to be a definite lack of inhabited—or habitable—territory in this area of space."

"We still don't know exactly where we are," Perri said. She was ensconced in the copilot's chair while Rolli provided her with continuing instructions on how to handle the *Space Dragon*.

"Which is one more reason why we need to set down as soon as possible," Rolli said. "If we stray toward the edge of the galaxy or into the Empty Sector, we could find ourselves in serious trouble. In its present condition, the *Space Dragon* will not be capable of withstanding renewed physical stress."

"All of which means," Halvo said, "that we are going to have to settle for something less than our ideal. I have just found a planet orbiting a small yellow star." Halvo worked the buttons on the navigator's panel, bringing the image of a rocky, barren-looking world onto the small screen in front of him.

"Turn your circuitry loose on this image, Rolli, and tell us what your conclusions are. I have seen places like that one before, and I have even walked on a few of them. That little world will be blazing hot during the daylight hours and unbearably cold at night. I mean that literally. Such planets are intolerable to humans except for a short time after sunrise and again after sunset."

"Then, this planet you have just discovered cannot be of any use to us." Perri pointed at the navigator's screen. "What do those symbols mean?"

Rolli answered her, responding as her finger moved from symbol to symbol, explaining patiently as always. "A thin atmosphere. On the uppermost hillsides a human could not breathe. At lower levels, where the air pressure increases, the atmosphere is marginally acceptable, but a space suit will be necessary for outside work. In deep ravines or caves, it should be possible to remove a space suit and still survive."

"This symbol indicates the presence of water molecules," Halvo said, taking up the explanation. "The ship's computer doesn't tell us whether it is in frozen or liquid state, but from the other data I would say that on the planet's surface it would have to be frozen and confined to places where the sun never shines. Otherwise, it would melt and boil away during the hot daytimes."

"I concur," Rolli said, and went on to explain the other symbols displayed on the navigator's screen.

Perri stared at the small screen, attempting to combine the image and the symbols in her mind so she could make sense of what she be-

Flora Speer

held. In the last 18 hours she had learned a lot about the *Space Dragon* and the way its various systems functioned. Rolli and Halvo had answered every one of her questions. Neither the man nor the robot had so much as hinted that a mere woman had no right to know how a spaceship operated.

As a result of their tutoring Perri understood why the food processor had once again stopped functioning, though understanding did not make her less hungry. She also knew she was cold because the air in the ship—which, fortunately, was still safe to breathe—was no longer being heated adequately. Halvo and Rolli had explained a series of system breakdowns to her. Taken individually, the problems were minor. Added together, they were making the *Space Dragon* an increasingly unpleasant place to be. Ultimately, Halvo had warned her, the ship would become a dangerous environment. Still, to one who was not experienced in space travel, the familiar ship represented security, while everything in the vast blackness outside it was threatening.

"That planet doesn't look like a very hospitable place," Perri said. "Can't we explore a little farther? Is our situation really so desperate?"

"At the moment, we are not in dire straits," Halvo answered, "but in another day or two we will be, and we have no guarantee of finding a better spot. If Rolli agrees, I vote for a landing

124

on that planet." He paused, looking toward Rolli, but the robot was taking longer than usual to process the data on the screen.

"Rolli?" Halvo said. "Do you have any reservations about that planet?"

"No, Admiral," Rolli said slowly. "The planet shown on the screen would appear to offer the best opportunity for survival that we have yet encountered."

"Then, this planet it is." Halvo began to call up landing information from the navigator's panel.

Alerted by a strange clicking sound from Rolli, Perri spun around in her seat to look at her robot. The clicking sound continued, and Rolli's eyelights were blinking much more slowly than usual.

"What's wrong?" Perri asked.

"I am dealing with . . . an insignificant . . . malfunction," Rolli said.

"I thought you were processing information too slowly," Halvo said. Having finished with the ship's computer for the moment, he also turned his full attention to the robot. "Has something happened to the repairs we made? Shall I take you apart again and recheck the connections on those fibers?"

"The repairs . . . are suitable." Rolli continued to speak in an oddly hesitant way. "The anomaly lies in . . . a recently inserted program."

"Do you mean the information implanted by the Chief Hierarch's technicians?" Perri cried, horrified by the possibility Rolli had just suggested. "If that program isn't working properly, you may not be able to pilot the *Space Dragon* any longer. Without the new program, you will revert to a nurse companion."

"Admiral Halvo is . . . an excellent pilot. If required, he can take over for me. Ah," Rolli said, the spherical head moving back and forth on its metal neck, "the malfunction has repaired itself. Apparently, it was only a minor glitch."

"When you are in space, there is no such thing as a minor glitch." Halvo regarded the robot with questioning eyes. "Tell me about the new programming you were given back on Regula."

"The Chief Hierarch assured me it was only knowledge that would enable Rolli to pilot the *Space Dragon*," Perri said.

"Don't you know by now that you cannot trust anything that man told you? I want to hear everything he said to you on the subject, Perri, and all you know, too, Rolli, about what was done to you."

It did not take long, only a few sentences, because, in truth, they had not been given much information.

"I intend no insult to either of you," Halvo said when they were finished, "but I think I ought to take over as sole pilot until we have landed safely. Perri, change seats with me."

Perri would have protested, preferring to leave the ship under control of a robot that was bound to have a reaction time quicker than that of a man who was not in the best of health. But when she turned to Rolli she saw that the eye-lights were no longer blinking. If they had been real eyes, Perri would have said they were staring at the navigator's screen without seeing it. Furthermore, the robot was slowly wheeling backward, away from the control panel. When Rolli spoke again, the robot's metallic voice took on a strained quality and an urgency that Perri had never heard in it before. She began to rise from her seat as Halvo had ordered, but her attention was on her robot.

"Admiral." Rolli continued to move away from the controls. "Immediate action . . . is required."

"Explain." Halvo shoved Perri out of the way, putting himself between her and Rolli.

"Search . . . circuitry," Rolli said in that strange, new voice. "I regret . . . have only now become aware . . . Use great caution . . . Perri's life . . . primary programming . . . Protect Perri at all costs."

"Rolli!" Perri cried, trying to get past Halvo's firmly planted form. "Rolli, what's wrong with you?"

"Stay away from it." Halvo pushed Perri down into her seat again before he advanced to the robot, which was standing next to the exit hatch. Rolli fumbled at the exit button with one metal hand.

Perri knew perfectly well that Rolli never fumbled. The robot's fingers were deft at every task. If she had seen or heard no other evidence of malfunction, Rolli's awkwardness would have alerted her.

"Disconnect," Rolli said. "Disconnect! Cannot . . . must not—"

"It's all right, Rolli." Halvo caught at the metal shoulders. "Hold still. I can do it in just a second."

"Perri! Danger! Dang—" The robot stopped in midword as Halvo hit the disconnect switch.

"Halvo?" Warned by Halvo's tense stance and by Rolli's last words, Perri stayed where she was. Halvo pulled open the metal grate on Rolli's chest and began to work on the circuitry there. "Halvo, did we do something wrong when we fixed Rolli before?"

"No, we aren't the ones who interfered with Rolli's programming. There, that should do it."

"Will you please tell me what just happened?"

"You don't want to know." Halvo spoke somewhat absently, because he was unfastening the screws that held Rolli's head in place.

"Don't you dare tell me what I want to know!" Perri shouted at him. "I have been denied information all my life and constantly warned to stop asking questions. Just look where my obedience has brought me!"

Then, she said in a quieter voice, "Rolli has been my closest companion, my only true friend. I have a right to know what you just did to my robot."

Halvo did not respond at once. Instead, he lifted Rolli's head from the neck with what seemed to Perri to be exaggerated care. With equal caution he placed the head into the air lock of the entrance hatch. Then, still moving slowly, he wheeled the body right up to the hatch.

"Perri, I need your help to lift Rolli's body over the ridge and into the air lock so we can store it there. I will explain why later. For now, please just trust me. And be careful. Don't drop it."

"Of course, I won't drop Rolli." Perri came forward to give Halvo an accusing look and ask more questions. She closed her mouth on further discussion when she saw how serious he was. Without another word she took hold of Rolli and helped Halvo to get the robot into the air lock. Halvo sealed the hatch, then stood with one hand on it while he released a long breath.

"I want to know why that was necessary," Perri said in what she hoped was a reasonable tone.

"The Chief Hierarch lied to you about what was done to Rolli, as well as about everything else to do with your mission to kidnap me,"

Halvo said. "And his technicians lied to Rolli." He swung away from the hatch to confront Perri as he continued.

"You heard what Rolli said. There was something dangerous to you in that robot's programming. Fortunately, Rolli's primary program contains a directive to protect you at all costs and it was able to override the new instructions. That is why Rolli insisted on being disconnected. If I hadn't said at once that I could do it, I believe Rolli would have tried to get into the air lock and then eject from the air lock into space in the hope of saving you."

"Rolli would have died to protect me." Perri took a moment to digest what Halvo had said. She did not think it any more peculiar that she should think of death in connection with her dear friend, than that Halvo should speak of Rolli hoping to save her. "What do you think the danger was?"

"Is," Halvo said, correcting her. "The new instructions are still in there, planted in Rolli's memory banks. To find out what those instructions are, we will have to take Rolli apart for a complete examination and discover where in the main circuitry the tampering was done. Only then will we know exactly what Rolli was trying to warn us against."

"On Regula, it is a crime to change the primary programming that protects all owners of robots," Perri said. "What the Chief Hierarch's technicians did was illegal."

"That shouldn't surprise you. After everything else he has done, ordering a change in Rolli's programming can have been no more than a trivial detail to the Chief Hierarch," Halvo said, but Perri had already moved on to a more immediate concern.

"You will try to repair Rolli, won't you?" she asked. "You won't just find out what the problem is and then eject Rolli from the air lock—or leave my dear old friend in pieces?"

"You don't have to worry about that," Halvo said. "We need Rolli to help us fix the ship. After we land, we will start repair work, and I promise you we will get Rolli into functioning condition again."

"Thank you." Perri blinked away the moisture that had risen to her eyes at the thought of Rolli's unwavering loyalty.

"It's a funny thing," Halvo said, moving toward the ship's controls. "I usually don't care one way or the other about Artificial Life Forms, but Rolli is the most likable robot I have ever met. I would be very unhappy if we had to jettison that collection of metal parts."

"There is good reason for your feelings," Perri said.

But Halvo was no longer thinking about the robot. He ordered Perri to the navigator's position and began giving her instructions on what to do as they approached and then moved into orbit around the planet they had chosen as their temporary base. Once more Perri postponed telling him what she knew about Rolli.

Chapter Eight

"It wasn't the smoothest landing I have ever made," Halvo said, shutting down the *Space Dragon's* engines, "but not too shameful for a pilot who is badly out of practice."

"Who has only a completely inexperienced navigator to help him." Perri was feeling remarkably pleased with herself. She had followed Halvo's directions to the letter and he had made no complaints about the navigational information she had provided.

"First, we repair Rolli," Perri said, leaning back in her chair.

"No, first we find shelter," Halvo said.

"Why can't we just stay on the *Space Dragon*?" Perri asked.

"Because thanks to our damaged heating system, it is already too cold for comfort in here. Where we have landed it is late afternoon. In a few hours it will be night and the temperature will drop so low that we will freeze to death well before morning."

"Are you sure?" She knew he would not make such a claim if he were not sure but, as usual, Perri was compelled to ask questions. "Couldn't we put all the remaining power into the heating system and survive the night?"

"We might, but if we did, we would literally stew in our own juices after the sun rises tomorrow morning. That is what happens on a world where the atmosphere is too thin to moderate the temperature by more than a few degrees. We discussed this with Rolli before we chose this planet, but there is one positive factor we did not mention. If the Regulans are close on our trail, they may overlook this little world for the very reasons that made you regard it as unwelcoming. If our pursuers think the way you do, this unfriendly chunk of rock may prove to be the safe haven we need."

"How clever you are. Very well." Perri straightened her shoulders, standing as tall as she could. "Give me your orders, Halvo, and I will carry them out."

"The only space suit on this ship fits you," he said. "I am too big to squeeze into it. You are going to have to locate the shelter we must have before nightfall."

"You want me to go out there alone?"

"We will be in constant contact. There is a comm system built into the suit."

"Yes, there is." She could not add that she was afraid. She knew if the suit had fit him, Halvo would not have hesitated to step onto the alien soil outside their ship. And she understood how urgent their need was. The *Space Dragon's* sensors could not provide information about areas below ground or in deep clefts within rocks. Using a portable, hand-held sensor, someone would have to search out a place where they could shelter—and do it quickly before the heating system in the space suit became as ineffective against the terrible cold as the ship's system was.

When Halvo opened the locker next to the exit hatch and pulled out the familiar silver suit, Perri took it from him without comment and began to put it on. He knew how to help her and soon the closures were fastened, the gloves and boots sealed tightly, and Halvo stood with the helmet in his hands.

"Which way shall I go?" Perri asked. "We don't have a map of the cliffs."

"We have something better. Look here." Tucking the helmet under his arm, Halvo reached over to call up on the large, main viewscreen an image of the terrain just outside the

Space Dragon. As he manipulated a dial to change the view, Perri could even see the swept-back glider wing that kept the ship steady during landings and takeoffs. Halvo pointed toward a row of cliffs in the background. "This area isn't as far away as it looks on the screen and our sensors indicate some deep folds in the rock. All you have to do is shine your light into those folds. You ought to be able to tell pretty quickly where there are caves."

"If there are caves." Perri hoped he could not discern from her voice how apprehensive she was.

"There will be. Rolli agreed with me on that." He handed her the light she was to carry and she slipped the strap over her left forearm, fastening it securely. "Just point in the direction in which you want to see. There is one other thing, Perri. The sensors have shown no evidence of any life-forms on the surface of this planet. You don't have to worry about wild beasts."

"You will be tracking me?" Perri took up the hand-held sensor.

"Every step of the way. Ready?" Halvo lifted the helmet to set it over her head.

"Halvo?"

"Yes?" He paused, holding the helmet in the air, ready to lower it to her shoulders.

"If I find a suitable place, how will you reach it?"

"I will run fast," he said and secured the helmet with a gesture that suggested to Perri a reluctance to answer any more questions.

Perri went out the air lock, stepping over Rolli's disjointed form on the way. Then the outer hatch closed and she was alone. Panic assailed her. Taking a deep breath, pulling her shoulders straight, she made herself look around. Immediately, she became so fascinated by the view that she forgot to be afraid.

The sky above her was the darkest blue she had ever seen and in spite of the daylight she noticed a few stars. The soil beneath her feet was a dull reddish brown and appeared to be loose and dusty. The land sloped upward to the tall cliffs Halvo had pointed out to her as her destination. The distant, pale yellow sun was setting behind these cliffs, and the lengthening shadows the cliffs cast were an ominous pitch-black.

"Head straight for the cliffs," Halvo's voice said in her ear. "Walking shouldn't be too difficult for you. The gravity is a little less here than on Regula."

Perri stepped away from the *Space Dragon*, then turned around to look at the ship.

"I can see some damage to the hull," she said.

"Never mind that now," Halvo said. "We can worry about the ship tomorrow."

"Did you realize we have landed in a huge crater? I was too busy to notice while we were still in the air." Perri's gaze traveled over the line of jagged, red-brown cliffs that bounded the horizon. All she could see of the planet was contained within the bowl of the crater. "I wonder what lies beyond the rim?"

"More of the same kind of terrain. I was not too busy to notice. Head for those cliffs," Halvo said. "Stop wasting time."

"I have never before set foot on a world outside Regula," she said. "You must allow me a few moments of explorer's license." She thought she heard a smothered chuckle before Halvo told her once more to get moving.

"You were right," she said as she went along. "The walking is easy. I am at the beginning of the shadows." Refusing to divulge to Halvo just how uninviting she found that opaque darkness, Perri switched on the lamp attached to her arm. The bright, sharp-edged beam shone out, lighting the way directly ahead of her. By it she discovered that the ground within the shadows was the same red-brown shade as out on the plain. However, a different substance, packed tightly against the cliffs in several places, reflected her light.

"Halvo! There is ice! I can't tell how thick it is."

"Good," Halvo's voice said. "Keep looking for caves."

Within a few minutes she had found five promising folds in the face of the cliff. Two of them proved to be little more than indentations.

Two others were deeper, but on further investigation, she found that they were not deep enough to offer adequate protection from bitter cold or scorching heat. Perri headed toward the fifth opening.

"Keep looking." Halvo did not sound at all discouraged by the unhelpful discoveries she had made so far. "You will find something."

"You are a good officer, Admiral. You know how to keep the spirits of your troops high." Perri halted for a moment beside the last opening, shining her light into it. "Just in front of me there is a very narrow crack in the ice at the base of the cliff. It looks as if it leads back into the cliff itself. I am going to try to slip inside it."

"Be careful. We can't have you injuring yourself. And keep talking so I know you are safe."

Halvo's own voice faded as Perri moved along a twisting fissure, through a layer of ice and into the solid rock. There, inside the cliff, a rock corridor opened, sloping gently downward. Crystals imbedded in the rock glittered when she shone the beam of her lamp on the walls. A trickle of water coursed downward to a half-frozen puddle. The sensor in her hand told her the water was pure and the air was acceptable for humans to breathe. Perri could not tell how deep the cave was, but she knew she had found the shelter she sought.

She also knew how valuable time was. Well aware that there was still a lot of work to be done before she and Halvo could rest in this rocky haven, she at once began her return journey to the outside world.

"Perri!" Halvo's shout nearly broke her eardrums as she emerged into the open. "If you do not respond in ten seconds, I am coming after you!"

"You needn't bother. I am safe. I'm sorry you were worried about me," she said, though privately she was touched by his concern. "I think the thickness of the rock cut off the transmissions between us. Halvo, I have found a place for us."

"Describe it." There was a definite note of relief in his voice. Perri smiled to herself as she complied with his order.

"It sounds fine. We don't have much time left before the temperature drops well below zero," Halvo said. "I want you to stand outside the cave entrance and point your lamp toward the ship. Don't ask questions. Just do it."

Perri obeyed. Since she was facing away from the cliffs and toward the flat plain at the center of the crater, she could see how far outward the shadows had advanced while she had been exploring. The sun was sinking rapidly and the *Space Dragon*, which on landing had stopped just outside the edge of the shadows, was so completely enveloped in darkness that Perri could barely make out its location. She lifted her left arm, directing the beam, and the light shone on a swirl of orange flames being belched out by the dragon painted on the side of the ship.

Through her feet she could feel the vibration of the *Space Dragon's* thrusters starting. Slowly the ship began to move toward her, skimming just above the surface of the ground. It stopped with the exit hatch facing Perri, just a short distance away from her, in a spot where it would be well concealed both day and night within the shadows cast by the cliffs.

"Come back inside the ship," Halvo said when the thrusters were silent once more. "But keep your helmet on. You aren't going to stay long."

Perri made two trips between the *Space Dragon* and the cave she had found. Each time, she carried to the cave the supplies Halvo collected while she was gone. On her third visit to the ship Halvo announced that he was ready to leave.

"I am going to run to the cave," he said, as if there were nothing at all unusual in a man with a bad back and bouts of vertigo attempting to race uphill across crumbly soil.

"You're mad!" Perri cried. "Halvo, it is already bitterly cold outside and my sensor tells me the air pressure at this altitude is just barely within acceptable limits for a human."

"Without a space suit that fits me, what else can I do?" he asked. "I will take a couple of deep breaths inside the ship and then run as fast as

I can. It shouldn't be much worse than a high dive into cold water. All you have to do is see me out the hatch, after which you are to close and seal it as you go through."

"I can't leave Rolli behind," Perri said.

"We cannot take the robot!" he said. "From what you have said, Rolli's body is too big to squeeze it through the slot in the ice."

"If the temperature inside the ship tonight is going to be low enough to freeze us to death," Perri said, "then it may also be low enough to damage Rolli's main circuitry. We are going to need the information stored in there, Halvo."

"You do have a point," he said, "and I have sent some other temperature-sensitive equipment to the cave in those bundles you carried out of here. But only Rolli's head goes, along with a kit of tools, so I can work on the circuitry before we come back to the ship." Disappearing into the aft portion of the *Space Dragon*, Halvo reappeared a minute or two later with a sheet from one of the beds. Into it he placed Rolli's head and the special tools he would need. Slinging the bundle over his shoulder, Halvo stepped to the exit hatch. There he paused to look around.

"All you need to do after I leave is make certain the hatch is properly sealed so the air in here won't seep out," he said.

"I know what to do. Halvo," Perri said, "take care. Get into that cave as quickly as you can.

142

And do not, under any circumstances, stop to wait for me or come back to help me. I promise you I will be all right."

"You are no mean officer yourself," he said with a grin that warmed her heart. Then he was gone from the ship and Perri quickly finished her last tasks aboard so she could follow him.

Halvo had moved the *Space Dragon* so close to the cliffs that he did not have to run any great distance, and as Perri hurried forward she could see his light ahead of her in the all-encompassing darkness.

She caught up with him in the narrow fissure, just before the ice ended and the rock began. He was gasping for breath, struggling to move on, and Perri could see he was dizzy and possibly disoriented by lack of air. She pushed him into the rock corridor, shoving at his back with all her strength. Halvo burst into the wider opening, stumbling and dropping to his knees.

The sheet containing Rolli's head and the tools fell to the ground. The corners of the sheet pulled apart, releasing the contents. The tools stayed where they landed, but Rolli's head went bouncing and rolling downward along the slope of the corridor. Perri ran after the head, awkward in her space suit, trying not to damage the suit since it was all the protection they had against the extremes of temperature and the inadequate air pressure outside the cave.

Rolli's head came to rest against a curve in

the corridor wall. Perri bent to retrieve it. When she straightened up, the light still attached to her arm shone into the distance.

In the blackness beyond the edge of the wall something moved and gleamed softly. Swallowing her fear, Perri advanced a step and directed the light ahead of her.

It was a liquid that had reflected her light. Setting Rolli's head down again, Perri used her hand sensor to check the composition of the liquid. It was a large pool of water, filtered through the rock and as pure as water could be, though it was so cold it was almost ice. In contrast to the damp outer corridor, a smooth little niche in the high-roofed inner chamber was dry and had a reddish-brown, sandy floor that made a tiny beach where it met the pool.

Perri returned to the outer corridor in triumph, carrying Rolli's head and eager to tell Halvo of her findings. He was sitting propped against the wall, breathing deeply. His face was moist from the trickling water he had just gathered in one hand and splashed onto himself.

"Did you catch Rolli?" he asked.

"Yes, and I discovered something wonderful." Placing the robot's head on the sheet, Perri eased off her gloves. Then, with her fingers working at the fastenings of her helmet, she sank down beside Halvo.

"You looked so funny," he said, "running downhill, chasing poor Rolli as if that metal head were a ball about to bounce out of your reach." Leaning his own head back against the rock, he began to laugh.

"I don't think it was funny at all," Perri said sternly. Pulling off her helmet she added it to the sheet next to Rolli's head. "Rolli could have been damaged beyond repair. Worse, if I had fallen, the space suit could have been torn."

"If it had been, we would have discovered a way to repair it—or to do without it. I am beginning to think you and I together can overcome most problems."

"Are you sure you are all right?" Perri was startled by his humor and by his too casual response to her remarks about the space suit. "I was afraid you were going to die there, just at the entrance, before you reached the good air."

"Thanks to your timely shove, I am rapidly recovering from oxygen depletion and from the euphoria that goes with it. The feeling is rather like the altitude sickness a mountain climber suffers when he ventures too high. A few more deep breaths and I will be fine. Since you don't need it in here, you ought to take that entire suit off. We can fold it and store it there in the sheet. Shall I help you with the seals? Those boots can be awkward to remove."

"Please." Perri held out first one foot, then the other. With an upwelling of emotion, she regarded Halvo's head bent to his task. It was all she could do to keep herself from stroking his thick dark hair. When he looked up at her, his gray eyes shining, she almost believed that he felt a similar urge to touch her. To distract her thoughts she told him about her discovery of a pool of water.

"It appeared to be a dry chamber," she said, finishing her description a few minutes later. "Perhaps we could make our camp there."

"All right." With a steadying hand on the rock wall Halvo pushed himself to his feet. To her confusion, Perri could detect no emotion in his voice and his face was closed to her, his eyes suddenly cool. "Hand me a couple of bundles to carry and lead the way."

They had four blankets with which to make their beds, Perri's hand weapon, the tools Halvo would use to work on Rolli's head, and several pieces of ship's equipment he had disconnected and brought along.

"Heat won't be a problem for the ship itself since we are parked in permanent shadow," Halvo said, piling the equipment on the spread-out sheet to keep it away from the sand, "but these are extrasensitive items."

"Where did you find these packets?" While unrolling one of the blankets, Perri had just uncovered packages of compressed food. "I didn't know these were aboard. We could have eaten them."

"Then it's a good thing we didn't know about them until I started rummaging through the stores a couple of hours ago. We will have to ration ourselves until the food processor is repaired once more, but at least we won't starve for a while."

"But Rolli told me all of our food must come from the processor." Perri began stacking the packets into a neat pile.

"Perhaps these stores were left aboard after the last time the *Space Dragon* was used," Halvo said. "I, for one, do not intend to question our good luck. There is nothing on this planet that we could eat, so I am glad to have our own supply of food."

"I believe you when you say it is as safe a place as we will find," Perri said, "but I do not like this world. It is entirely lifeless. During my explorations my sensors never registered so much as a microbe." She moved a little closer to Halvo as she spoke, seeking the only other source of life on that barren planet. To her dismay, Halvo immediately stepped to the other side of the sheet upon which they were arranging their supplies.

"All the more reason to make our repairs and get away as quickly as possible," Halvo said, studying their meager belongings. "I also found a small heater. With it we can warm the air and feast on hot food. Then you ought to rest while I work on Rolli. As soon as the temperature begins to rise just before dawn, we have to go back to the ship and start the repairs."

"Halvo, are you angry with me?" Perri asked. "Have I done something wrong?"

"Not at all. You have performed remarkably well. Now, if you would just fill this container with water, I will set up the heater and we can eat." He was careful not to touch her fingers when she took the container from him, and he did not look directly at her.

"Be sure to fill it only half full," he said.

"Stop giving me orders!" Baffled by Halvo's behavior, Perri could only snap at him.

"Sorry. The habit is hard to break." Standing with the portable heater in one hand and a packet of compressed food in the other, Halvo appeared to be searching for something in the collection of gear laid out on the sheet.

To Perri, it seemed that he was avoiding her eyes. When she approached him with the container of water, he moved away again, motioning to her to put it on the ground.

"Why don't you want me to touch you?" she asked.

"This is a subject you would do well not to pursue." He spoke as if he expected her to understand his meaning, but Perri did not understand.

"Why, Halvo?" Not to be denied, Perri went to him with determined strides and took his arm. The eyes he finally turned upon her blazed with an emotion she did not recognize. Perri took a step backward, but she did not let go of his arm.

"Don't pretend you don't know," he said. "It has been perfectly obvious. On the ship, with Rolli in working order and all the doors jammed open, it was difficult enough to keep some control. Here, alone with you, it is going to be far harder than I imagined. But if I do what I want, it would not be fair to you, Perri. You are so much younger than I, and I don't think you have had much experience along these lines. Nor do I want to bind you to me when you have just been freed to live your own life.

"So, my dear," Halvo said pointing across the chamber, "you will sleep over there, against the rock wall, while I sit here to work on Rolli, as far away from you as I can possibly get inside this cave."

"Now I understand." Comprehension flooded over Perri. She had loathed what she had to do for Elyr each time he appeared in her bedchamber, but for Halvo, she would not mind. For Halvo, it would be a pleasure. Perri did not pause to think what that difference in her attitude meant. Her only concern was to put Halvo at ease. "Forgive my denseness. I should have recognized the symptoms. It is time for your manly need to make you uncomfortable."

"What?" Halvo stared at her as if he could not believe his ears.

"You do not have to feel embarrassed, Halvo, I can relieve your discomfort. On the night of my sixteenth birthday, Elyr showed me how to pleasure a man."

"Did he?" There was a note of steel in Halvo's voice. Very deliberately, he bent and put down the food packet and the heater. He kept his face turned away from Perri's sight for a few moments.

"Yes," she said eagerly. "I know exactly what to do. I have become more expert since that first time. Halvo, it would be an honor to serve you in that way."

"Serve me?" he said. There was no mistaking the meaning of the fierce glare that lit his eyes. "Why? Because of my rank? I have known many women who were willing to service the Admiral of the Fleet."

"No," she whispered, intimidated by the anger he had not troubled himself to hide. "It is because I like you. Because you have been kind to me and have handled me gently. Because when you kiss me I feel a wonderful warmth. If you want to kiss me again before I begin, I will be happy to respond. But if you do not wish to kiss me, I will not be insulted."

"Really?" Halvo's eyes had narrowed to mere slits and his face was guarded and tight. Perri decided a few intimate revelations might help him to relax.

"Elyr only kissed me on greeting," she said,

"and then again on leaving me, which he always said was right and proper. But never while I ministered to his discomfort. However, I will not object if you wish to do so. Your customs are surely different from Elyr's."

"I don't doubt that for a moment," Halvo said. "No kissing? How interesting. How unexciting for you. Was there no touching either?"

"What do you mean?" Her genuine confusion at his peculiar comments must have communicated itself to him. Some of his anger appeared to dissipate.

"Perri, I am not sure that you and I are talking about the same thing."

"Of course we are." She smiled to show him she did not mind what he would require of her. With Elyr, her smiles had always been forced. Glancing downward along Halvo's stiffly held figure, she could see that they were, indeed, speaking of the same phenomenon because she could tell he was uncomfortable. In fact, her eyes told her that Halvo was extremely uncomfortable.

For the first time in her life, the image of what lay beneath a man's clothing fascinated Perri, and the thought of what she could do to relieve the distress Halvo was obviously suffering was a desire blossoming in secret places where she had not known it was possible for a woman to feel such warm urges.

"Let me help you," she said, offering all she

had to give. "I am yours to use as you wish."

"Thank you, but it would not be fair to you," he said.

"What does fairness to me have to do with it?" she asked.

"I have tried to live my life as an honorable man," Halvo said. "I am not going to take advantage of a young woman who clearly has no idea of the full implications of what she is suggesting."

"But Elyr did not object."

"I don't care what Elyr did or did not do! Perri, in the name of all the stars, I am trying to do what is right for you!" Halvo lifted one hand, pointing again to the far rock face. When he continued, his voice was the coldest Perri had ever heard. "Dinner has just been canceled. I cannot talk to you anymore or even look at you. Do not ask why. You know why. Take a blanket and go over there and lie down. Stay there and do not speak to me again. Do you understand me?"

Perri's lower lip was trembling so hard that she had to bite down on it to keep herself from bursting into sobs of humiliation and anger. She did not know what Elyr would have done if she had voluntarily offered to ease his discomfort when he had not indicated that he wanted such a service from her. Feeling as she did about the way in which Elyr demanded and then directed her aid, she had never offered.

But Perri did not think she would have felt so forsaken and hurt if Elyr had rejected her as Halvo had done.

Nor did Perri understand her own physical reactions to the scene just ended by Halvo's cold commands. She desperately wanted Halvo to kiss her and she ached to feel his arms around her. She recalled in vivid detail the incident in her cabin aboard ship when he had kissed her and put his tongue in her mouth and had drawn her upward so she stood pressed along his body—and the disturbing heat and hardness of him when he had held her that way.

She also remembered the time when, trying to get to his feet so he could disconnect Starthruster and slow the *Space Dragon*, he had fallen on top of her while she was confined on the bench. She had not given the physical sensations much thought at that moment, because Halvo and she had been in grave danger. But the feeling of Halvo's full weight on her and his thrusting, masculine hardness against her thigh had impressed themselves on her senses, allowing her to recall every detail. He had been uncomfortable then, too, though it had definitely not been an appropriate time.

Her skin prickling and sensitive, her body restless with a yearning she could not understand, unable to stop thinking about Halvo and the discomfort he denied, Perri stirred on her makeshift bed . . . and tried not to weep . . . and wondered if she would ever again feel like her usual self.

Beside the silent pool Halvo sat with both lights propped in the sand so they would shine on Rolli's head while he worked on it. Hearing Perri move behind him and make an unmistakable feminine sound of unfulfilled need, he grimaced.

Uncomfortable? He was ready to explode! And from the way she was thrashing around and moaning, Perri was equally uncomfortable.

Damnation! Why did he have to be so cursedly moral about sex? She had offered herself. She was willing. And he was bursting with more than a year's pent-up energy and frustration.

She was so lovely, with her flawless ivory skin and her hair the color of dark red wine. He could easily imagine her naked, with that hair curling around her shoulders, her breasts caught in his hands, moving as she was at that moment. He could hear her moving. He remembered the feel of her wriggling beneath him when she was strapped onto the bench. His mouth dry, Halvo laid down his tools.

He looked toward Perri. If she sent the least glance his way, the slightest hint of invitation. . . .

She was asleep. She must be, since her eyes were closed and her breasts moved gently with each slow breath. Those beautifully rounded breasts! The skin of Halvo's hands burned to touch them, to feel the nipples harden against his palms. A man could die of wanting Perri.

With a disgusting spaceman's oath that he was aware would be all the satisfaction he was going to get for that night, Halvo turned back to Rolli's head, knowing full well that if he tried to work on it in his present mood he would only damage it further. Propping his elbows on his knees, he rested his chin in his hands and stared into the robot's unlit, sightless eyes . . . and wished he were anywhere but where he was.

Chapter Nine

Halvo and Perri worked on the *Space Dragon* for several hours shortly after sunrise, with Halvo inside the ship and Perri, again wearing the space suit, performing some simple repairs to the outer hull. The sun was not very high before they were forced by lung-searing heat to race back to the cave. There they sheltered until nightfall brought cooler temperatures that would allow them to go out and work again.

The emotional distance Halvo maintained from Perri, coupled with his crisp orders and unembroidered instructions about the work she was to do, provided a constant irritation to her. She could not imagine why any man would be annoyed with a woman who had offered, with the best of intentions, to ease his urgent discomfort.

Her own discomfort was another matter. Perri had never heard of a woman feeling the way she did. Thus, she did not know how to help herself. She arrived back at the inner chamber of the cave tired, overheated, and thoroughly out of sorts.

"Do you know how to prepare the food in those packets?" Halvo asked with cold detachment in his voice. "I want to eat at once, before I start the repairs on Rolli. I didn't get much accomplished the last time I tried, so I don't want any interruptions this time."

"Of course I know how to prepare food!" Perri snapped, adding with great irritation, "What other purpose is there to a woman's life but preparation of meals and supervision of the servants who clean a man's house?"

She did not mention the third thing a woman was expected to do for a man. Having stripped off her space suit and folded it, Perri was clad in her purple-blue tunic, trousers, and boots. She snatched up the water container and headed for the pool to fill it.

"You are capable of far more than traditional tasks," Halvo said as she stalked past him. "Your assistance on the *Space Dragon* has been exemplary."

"Thank you, Admiral," she said. "I trust you will note that fact on my personnel report."

"Perri, you are making this situation more difficult than it has to be." He sounded weary.

"I," she said with great dignity, "was only trying to make you more comfortable. You are the one who is making your situation difficult." She pretended not to hear the unrepeatable oath he swore beneath his breath.

Certain she was in the right and still deeply offended by Halvo's rejection, Perri barely deigned to speak to him while they ate. Once the meal was over, Halvo spread out his sleeping blanket on the sand and arranged his tools on it. He positioned their two lights exactly as he wanted, then he picked up Rolli's head. At that point Perri forgot her injured feelings in favor of open curiosity. Being careful not to disturb anything on the blanket, she went to her knees beside Halvo to watch what he was doing. He acknowledged her presence with a quick glance and a nod before he began to investigate the opening at the base of Rolli's head, where the neck fitted to connect the robot's head to its metallic body.

"If I tell you to run for the corridor," Halvo said a few minutes later, "don't stop to ask me why. Just follow my orders."

"I must ask questions," she said. "If I do not, no one tells me what I need to know."

"Very well, then. What you need to know here is that I am certain there is still a danger lurking in Rolli's head. I have some mechanical ability and I understand how computers and robots function, but I am not a surgeon. I cannot repair damaged human bodies."

"Nor can I," she said, meeting his eyes. For the first time since their quarrel they regarded each other without anger or reservation. Perri could see that he was worried. "Be careful, Halvo. In this environment, our lives depend upon each other."

"That is what I have been most afraid of." The look in his eyes was unreadable, but a faint smile curved his lips. "I have been lying to myself about my motives," he added quietly.

"I cannot imagine you afraid of anything," Perri said, and she got in response another long, searching look.

"Not even of a young woman's scorn if I do not measure up to her expectations?"

"Halvo, you have always exceeded my expectations."

"You really don't know what I am talking about, do you? Perhaps it's just as well," he said and returned his attention to the metal head in his hands. "We can discuss it later, if you like. Shall I explain what I am doing to Rolli?"

"Yes, please." She settled herself more comfortably in the sand. "Halvo, several times I have attempted to tell you about Rolli's memory banks. There is something you ought to know that might help you in your repairs."

"Oh? And what is that?" As he spoke, Halvo

lifted away the faceplate to expose the inner workings of Rolli's head. To Perri, it was a confusing tangle of wires in many different colors that connected together square or oblong pieces of metal or plastic. What she saw made little sense to her, and the sight made her queasy, as if she were watching actual surgery and the doctor had just opened the skull of a dear friend. Her stomach churning, she looked elsewhere, preferring to watch the icy water of the pool. But she did answer Halvo's question.

"When I was a little girl still living in my parents' house, I had a nurse named Melri to care for me."

"I am glad to hear it," Halvo said. "From what Rolli told me of your past, I thought you were raised by a robot."

"In a way, I was. Shortly before my ninth birthday, which was the date designated for me to go into Elyr's household, Melri fell ill and the doctors told her she would die soon.

"No companions are permitted to go with a girl into the home of her betrothed. Such lingering ties to her old life can only impede adjustment to her new circumstances. But a robot, presented to the girl as a gift, to be a personal servant and guardian of her safety, would be allowed, and in fact, such robots are common on Regula.

"My father was a brilliant man, a famous inventor. He built Rolli for me. And on the last evening before my betrothal, knowing she had at most only a day or two more to live, Melri asked my father to drain her mind of memories and then transfer those memories to Rolli." At this point in her story Perri stopped talking because Halvo had just made a strangled sound.

"By all the gods of Demaria," Halvo said angrily, "what was done to Melri was neither morally right nor legal. Mind draining is forbidden on every world of the Jurisdiction!"

"It was Melri's last wish," Perri said, "her own idea, done willingly, because she loved me. She knew we would be parted forever within a day, by my betrothal and her inevitable death—and she died of natural causes, Halvo! She and my father assured me it was so, and I have no reason to doubt either of them. Rolli's memory banks are their dearest gift to me.

"What neither Melri nor my father foresaw," Perri went on, "was the change that being a robot would impose upon Melri's memories. Melri is truly dead. Her physical body died, still holding my hand, early on the morning of my betrothal. Rolli is a new and different entity, with all the deficiencies and the superiorities of a robot. But Rolli can recall my birth and all of my childhood. And like Melri, Rolli loves me."

"No wonder you have been so worried about her," Halvo murmured. "Does anyone else know about this?"

"Only my father and Melri, both of whom are

dead, and Rolli and myself. We agreed not to tell my mother. She would have been appalled," Perri said with a little laugh.

"I am appalled," Halvo said.

"No harm was done to Melri," Perri said, "nor anything against her will. She died at peace. And for her devotion, I have blessed her every day of my life since then. Halvo, you will not tell anyone about this, will you? You are the only other person who knows."

"You were only nine years old, too young to be responsible for what was done, and far too young to bear the burden of an illegal secret. The adults who were responsible and who laid that burden upon you are dead, and thus beyond punishment. No, I cannot see any reason to reveal the truth to anyone else. You are the one who would suffer if I did." Halvo paused, squinting a little, looking hard at the exposed circuitry. "I cannot see anything in Rolli's head that is different from any other robot. I doubt if the Chief Hierarch's technicians, who were only interested in putting a new program into Rolli's main circuitry, could have discovered anything unusual. So Rolli's secret is probably safe."

"If Rolli appears to be a normal robot, then where does the danger she warned us about lie?" Perri asked.

"That is what I intend to find out right now." Taking up the long tweezers he had used for previous repairs, Halvo began to move some of the brightly colored wires aside, disconnecting a few of them so he could lift out a metal piece and gain access to the next layer of wires. So precise and delicate were the movements of his fingers that Perri did not dare to move or ask questions about what he was doing. She held her breath, watching. As Halvo moved deeper into Rolli's head, Perri thought he had stopped breathing, too, and his tension communicated itself to her. After a while, he let out a long, low whistle.

"Very clever." With great caution, Halvo lifted the tweezers away from Rolli. Caught between the pointed tips was a red triangle so small that Perri could barely see it. "This is what was troubling Rolli."

"What is that thing?" Perri asked. "And how were you able to find it?"

"I found it because it is the only mechanical anomaly inside Rolli's head. If I am right, this innocent-looking object was planted as a well-hidden backup weapon that would instruct Rolli to blow up the *Space Dragon* and anyone on it. It was to be used in case you should by some slim chance slip past the Regulan warships that were sent to intercept the *Space Dragon*. The Chief Hierarch never intended for you to return to Regula alive, Perri.

"Melri may have done more for you than make your life in Elyr's household more pleasant," Halvo said, holding up the tiny red triangle so the horrified Perri could see it more closely. "I suspect it took the combined power of Melri's loving memories of you and Rolli's primary programming to protect you, to overcome the commands issued by this lethal weapon. The safeguards your father planned for your protection are why Rolli was trying so frantically to get out of the *Space Dragon* and as far away from you as possible."

"Is it still dangerous?" Perri cried, wishing she could close her eyes and shut out the hideous proof of the treachery of those whom she had trusted.

"Not at the moment." Halvo turned the tweezers this way and that, holding the triangle up to the light. "Not unless it is reimplanted into some poor robot's main circuitry."

"Throw it away!" Perri was on her feet, putting space between herself and the hateful object. "Get rid of it! I don't want to see it, Halvo."

"I can't get rid of it." From the first-aid supplies he had brought from the ship, Halvo took up a clean medical specimen capsule about an inch long and sealed the red triangle into it. "This is evidence. When we reach an inhabited planet—and we will, I promise you—this will be our protection against Elyr and the Chief Hierarch. In fact, this little piece of technology could bring down the entire present Regulan Hierarchy.

"I believe," Halvo said, "that there is a lot more to my kidnapping and to the Chief Hierarch's desire to see you dead than we have yet realized. This entire affair is a mystery—and I do not like unsolved mysteries."

Perri was scarcely listening to him. She was trying to absorb everything she had just learned. She was disgusted by the immorality involved in the subversion of Rolli's primary programming, and she was terrified by the thought of what might have happened to Halvo and herself if the weapon implanted in Rolli's main circuitry had succeeded in its deadly purpose.

Over and above those terrible emotions was the realization of a perfidy so complete that she could barely comprehend it. An anger beyond ordinary rage filled her to the depths of her being, demanding an outlet and transforming her from a hurt and bewildered young woman into a vengeful fury.

"They wanted us dead." She repeated that unquestionable fact in a voice cracking with emotion. "The Chief Hierarch and Elyr, too, connived at my death and yours—and Rolli's. Liars! Wicked, wicked—If these are the leaders of Regula, then I will no longer be counted a Regulan or a member of the Amalini Kin, for I belong to the Amalini only by my betrothal to Elyr.

"I renounce them all!" Flinging her arms in

the air with clenched fists, she screamed the words at the top of her voice. "I will be a homeless wanderer all of my days rather than belong anymore to the despicable Regulan Race!"

Her words echoed and reechoed, the sound bouncing off the rock cavern walls. To Halvo, watching and listening to the outburst from where he still sat on the blanket, Perri appeared to change in a moment. Her pale cheeks were reddened with the flush of the blood heating them, her deep green eyes sparkled with a dangerous fire, her lips were drawn back over her teeth. And her hair curled and writhed about her face and her shoulders like seething tongues of flame, swinging and swirling with each step she took as she paced across the sand.

Never before had Halvo heard her use her voice in such a manner. It ranged from a low, throbbing pitch to the high screech of an enraged harridan. If Perri could have cast a spell from where she stood to entrap and torment Elyr and the Chief Hierarch for all eternity, Halvo had no doubt that she would have done so without present compunction or later regret. She was magnificent, the very image of avenging, wronged womanhood.

Halvo understood the loss and pain that accompanied Perri's outrage. Her pain touched his heart, for he, too, had known pain both physical and spiritual. He, too, had lost that which was most important to him in life. Like

Perri, he was forced to rebuild his broken existence, to try to find new meaning in a life that had left him with nothing that mattered to him save his own self. Hearing Perri scream curses against the men who had betrayed her, Halvo knew that only with her would he ever again be able to make sense of his own life.

In that moment, all of Halvo's qualms and qualifications about the matching of a young woman with a much older and more experienced man, all his needs for masculine freedom and for a position approximating the one he had once held—all these misgivings, whether scrupulous or not, vanished, and in their place came absolute certainty. He had been right about one thing: Joining with Perri would bind them together forever. The difference was that he no longer feared their joining or the responsibilities it would entail. He wanted to be bound to Perri.

And she did not know it. She thought of him as someone whose manly discomfort required periodic easing, and she believed that service was all he wanted of her. What a lot she had to learn. How joyful would the learning be for both of them. Laying Rolli's open head down on the blanket, Halvo rose to face Perri.

"Fix the *Space Dragon*!" she commanded him, her eyes still blazing with all the righteous wrath she felt. "We will return to Regula. No, we will go instead to Capital, where you can tell

167

your father what crimes have been committed. Surely, Leader Almaric will want to see justice done! He will destroy those villains!"

"Indeed, he will." Approaching Perri, Halvo took her by the upper arms. She grasped him, too, holding on as if she thought her companion in vengeance might decide to soften his attitude. She did not seem to understand that revenge was not on Halvo's mind at the moment. "Perri, please try to calm yourself. You cannot stay this angry for long without becoming sick."

"I cannot be calm," she cried. "Don't you understand what has been done to me and to Rolli—or to you, Halvo? Those wicked men meant to take your life, too!"

"I do understand." Halvo could feel through her hands and arms the tremors that shook her body. He heard her sobbing breath and knew she was near to collapse. The emotions she was experiencing were out of her control. There was only one way to subdue them and that was to direct them toward a new object.

"Halvo." She sounded as if she could not catch her breath. Her eyes rolled up, her lids closed, and she fell against him. Halvo caught her in his arms, then carried her to her sleeping blanket, which was still spread neatly at the far side of the rock chamber. There he laid her down. Her eyelids flickered, tears rolling from beneath them. "What are you doing?"

"Hush, my love. It's time for me to ease your discomfort."

"I am not uncomfortable, but if you are, I will—No, I will not!" With a strength Halvo did not expect from her, she pushed him away. "Why should I?" she demanded, her fury renewing itself. "I always did what Elyr wanted, but no more. No more!"

"Good. I am happy to hear you say so." Ignoring the fluttering hands that still pushed at his shoulders and his chest, Halvo caught her face between his palms. "I will do what you want, Perri, and only what you want."

"I don't know what I want!" she yelled. "Oh, Halvo!"

Then she was clinging to him, but she was not crying and she was no longer hysterical with rage. She was just holding on to him as tightly as she could, and Halvo was content to hold her with equal tightness. Some time later she began to pull away. True to his word, Halvo loosened his embrace.

"What I want," Perri whispered, "is for you to kiss me."

"Gladly." Halvo moved to do so, but she stopped him.

"Would you put your tongue into my mouth?" she asked. "I think it is not a very proper thing to do, but I like it."

"I like it, too." He did not mention what he understood from her innocent statement. Elyr had never kissed her in such a passionate way. Halvo was beginning to think Elyr had never done anything to Perri's benefit, least of all in matters sexual. Swearing to himself that he would make certain she found complete fulfillment with him, he lowered his mouth to hers.

Immediately, her lips opened and moved against his. The sweet invitation was too much for Halvo's tenuous hold on self-restraint. Fiercely, he thrust his tongue into her. He felt her startled withdrawal, then a moment later, her shuddering relaxation. She sank into his kiss. The interior of her mouth was hot and moist and slippery, and her little tongue was like velvet. When she began to suck on his tongue, Halvo quickly withdrew, fearing he would lose all control.

"Oh, how lovely," Perri whispered. Her face was buried in his shoulder, his arms were around her, and they were lying together on her blanket. Halvo fought the urge to roll over on top of her. He knew what would happen if he did. It must be enough for him, for the time being, just to hold Perri and reassure her. His own desires would have to wait until she was as eager as he was.

"Halvo?" Her fingers touched his face, moving slowly as if to memorize each bone and line through her hands. When her fingertips trailed along his lips, Halvo opened his mouth and drew them inside, sucking them, curling his

170

tongue around each finger in turn, while Perri gasped and stared at him as if he had lost his wits.

"Why are you doing that?" she whispered.

"Because you taste so good." To prove it, he nibbled on a finger; then, with great daring, he moved closer to chew softly on her earlobe.

"Halvo!" A silence followed, during which she did not protest his further excursions behind her ear or along her throat to the collar of her tunic. She caught her breath, her breasts lifting against his chest before she spoke again. "Your tongue in my mouth tasted . . . salty."

"Did it?" He tilted up her chin and advanced across the slenderness of her throat toward her other ear, kissing and nibbling along the way. "Your tongue and your skin taste sweet. Perhaps it is the difference between male and female."

"Halvo, why are you doing this?"

"I thought you liked it." He wove a hand through her thick, silky hair. "Shall I kiss you again, Perri? Would you like to discover if my tongue is still salty after licking across your skin?"

In response, she wriggled against him in an inflammatory way. Yet Halvo had the impression that she did not realize the effect she was having on him. There was something oddly innocent about Perri's lovemaking. He could tell she welcomed his advances, but she did not act as if she knew what they meant. As an experiment, Halvo let one hand drift downward in a casual way until it rested on her breast. She went perfectly still, then with a whimper, she pushed herself into his hand. Her eyes were wide with surprise, but Halvo could tell she found the sensation pleasant. Slowly, he began to stroke and knead. Perri sighed, allowing the caresses.

"How kind you are to me," she whispered.

It was then, with Perri swooning in his hands and his own senses rapidly approaching a state of flagrant disarray, that Halvo had a brilliant idea.

"Perri, would you like me to show you the Demarian way of giving comfort?"

"Oh." She went rigid in his arms, making Halvo regret his suggestion. "What would I have to do?"

"You don't have to do anything," he said. "The purpose of the activity is for a man and woman to comfort each other, to their mutual pleasure."

"You do need comfort, Halvo. I can see you do." Perri considered the matter for a moment, her eyes contemplating first Halvo's glaringly obvious need and then his serious face. "Perhaps it would be best for you if it were done in your own way."

"I agree completely." Halvo could feel her trembling, though whether it was from fear or eager anticipation he could not be certain. He did know that Perri had locked inside her a wealth of vibrant emotion. It only wanted release. Perhaps a judiciously administered shock or two would help. "The first thing we must do is remove our clothes."

"You wish to see me naked? No one ever has, not since the day I was born, except for Melri—and Rolli, of course."

"I thought you wanted to do this in the Demarian way," Halvo said.

"Well, yes. I am sure the Demarian method would be more pleasing to you."

"Exactly. Shall I help you with your tunic?"

"Thank you." Her fingers were already at the shoulder fastenings. With Halvo's assistance she pulled the tunic over her head. The sleeveless shirt she wore beneath was as white as her skin and made of a sheer, clinging fabric that revealed the luscious curves of her breasts and their small, firm nipples.

Halvo could not resist. He placed his hand over one breast. The sound Perri made was not a gasp or a moan or even a sigh, but rather a combination of all three and yet her own inarticulate expression of astonishment and delight. She went perfectly still when Halvo pulled the undershirt out of her waistband and lifted it high so he could replace his covering hand with his mouth.

She was unbelievably sweet and soft. Her

skin was like rich cream, her nipple a tightly budded flower beneath his lips. Halvo was close to losing himself in her, frighteningly near to forgetting that the lovely creature in his arms had some peculiar gaps in her experience.

"Why are you making me feel this way?" Perri cried. "I cannot think clearly."

"What I am doing is an old Demarian custom," Halvo said with all the gravity of an ancient wise man.

"But if I lose my wits, how can I serve you properly?" she asked. "I do not wish to hurt you, Halvo, but I may if I am not fully aware of what I am doing."

He did not tell her he intended for her to lose her wits completely. He did not say the only way she could hurt him was by refusing to go on with what they were doing.

"You must remove your trousers and boots," he said. "Then it would be very nice if you would help me to take off my clothing."

"You want to be undressed, too?" Plainly, she was puzzled by his Demarian ideas. "It is not necessary for a man to undress."

Blast you, Elyr! What have you done to this girl? What did you make her do for you? Halvo was beginning to have a pretty good idea as to the answers to those questions, but he decided not to dwell on thoughts of Elyr. It was Perri who was important to him.

"It is the Demarian custom for both participants to be unclothed," Halvo said.

"Oh, I see. Well, I would not want to infringe on the traditions of your homeworld." Without any further protest, Perri removed every garment she wore.

For his part, Halvo was too entranced by the beauty she revealed to do anything but lounge on one elbow, watching each graceful movement she made. Her waist was slim, her hips curved perfectly, and her legs were long and shapely. And there, where her thighs joined, was the place . . .

"Now." She knelt before him, blushing down to her lovely breasts, but not acknowledging any embarrassment. "You wanted me to assist you."

"Yes." He sat up and let her remove his tunic. He stayed very still while she looked at him and touched a few of the battle scars, both old and recent.

"Truly, you were badly wounded," she murmured.

"There are worse scars beneath my trousers," he said. "You should be prepared, Perri. My body is not a pleasant sight."

"I think you are a marvelous sight." Her fingers played lightly with the hair on his chest, then wandered down toward his belt. "Halvo, we ought to hurry. You appear to be dreadfully uncomfortable."

"I can wait a while longer," he said with a

throaty chuckle, "because I know at the end I will find complete comfort in you, Perri."

"I hope you will." She was having trouble with the fastening of his belt. Halvo undid it for her and then, brushing aside her hands, he peeled off his trousers and boots and stood so she could see him as he was, scarred and discolored and ugly. He had to know if she would show any sign of revulsion, if she would flinch away from what he had become after space pirates and Jurisdiction surgeons had had their way with him.

"Oh, poor Halvo." Her concern was not for the wounds he had once suffered, nor for the scars they left on healing. There was not the least flicker of disgust in her eyes, and she looked at him from head to heel. What she put out her hands and touched, what she took into her hands and caressed, was the swollen manhood he could not control. "How painful it must be. Let me ease you now."

"Not yet." He seized her hands in his, lest she instantly accomplish what he was trying his best to delay. He dropped to the blanket and pulled her down to lie beside him. "There are still some Demarian preliminary customs to be observed."

"I apologize. I assumed you would want immediate relief. Tell me what I should do, Halvo."

"What I want," he said, "is for you to instruct

me. I want to know what will please you, Perri. On Demaria, the man always pleases the woman first."

"Really?"

"Absolutely." Could any experienced woman actually be this naive? She claimed that since the night of her sixteenth birthday she had repeatedly been taught how to pleasure a man. She was certainly eager to get her hands on Halvo, and from the gestures she had made toward him, she knew what she was doing—was remarkably skilled, in fact—yet she appeared to be unaccustomed to feeling desire herself. The answer to that puzzle was obvious to Halvo. Elyr had taken his pleasure and left Perri unmoved. Halvo was determined that before he took his pleasure Perri would believe the stars had moved.

Knowing she enjoyed kissing, he resumed his lovemaking there, tasting her mouth so thoroughly that soon she was whimpering and moving against him in innocent provocation. Halvo had to force himself to remember his overall purpose so he could banish the urge to release his mounting desire in her before she was completely aroused.

He covered her face and throat with kisses, and while he did, he let his hands wander across her soft, smooth skin along breast and hip and thigh. She touched him, too, and he allowed it, knowing the tactile sensations would further

Flora Speer

awaken her desire. But there was one place where he could not allow her to go. Repeatedly he had to snatch her hands away and tell her to wait. He could see her confusion growing, even as she steadily warmed to him.

And finally, gently but firmly, he drew his hand upward along her inner thigh and began to explore her most sensitive spot, hidden beneath dark red curls. Perri bit off a scream.

"Why are you doing this to me?" she cried. "What does it mean?"

"Hasn't anyone ever touched you here?" he asked. He could not say that cursed man Elyr's name. Not there, not at such a moment.

"Is this the way a man feels when a woman touches him?" Perri gasped.

"Just this once," he said, "stop asking questions and allow yourself to feel, Perri." She fell silent. Slowly, Halvo let one finger slide inward, gently so as not to frighten her, steadily so she would know he was not going to stop.

She did not ask him to stop. She made a soft sound of acceptance, her body closed around him, and Halvo knew his time of waiting would soon be over. He nearly spent himself just thinking about it, but by concentrating on what Perri would require of him first, he managed to gather the last shreds of control and hold on. She would be worth the waiting.

Perri was lying beside him with her eyes closed, her body moving in a slow, sensuous reaction to the constant stroking of his finger. Halvo withdrew his hand. Her eyes flew open.

"Oh, please don't stop."

"I won't," he said. "I have only begun."

Drawing her thighs wider apart, Halvo positioned himself at the entrance to the one place in all the universe where he wanted to be.

"Halvo, what are you—" Perri moved as if she would fight what he was doing. Unable to stop himself, Halvo pushed against her. Sudden comprehension brightened her lovely features. "This is what Demarians do? Oh, Halvo, yes, please! Please!"

He required no more encouragement. Halvo moved boldly forward until he met an obstruction. Perri winced, then pushed against his presence to help him. Her small hands were flat on his buttocks, pressing hard, giving him a message she was too caught up in amazement and passion to speak aloud. Halvo was filled with joy at the discovery he had just made. Not wanting to hurt her, he tried not to be too precipitous, though his body was clamoring for its long-denied release. After a second or two, during which he fully expected to die from the strain he was exerting upon himself, Perri's body stretched to accommodate him. Halvo buried himself in his love. When Perri smiled up at him there was nothing he could do but kiss her, long and deeply and passionately.

Before he dragged his mouth away from hers

she was wriggling beneath him, getting the feel of him so far inside her. When he saw a question come into her eyes, he answered her before she could speak. He began to move, slowly at first, then, realizing that he was not causing her any pain, he stroked faster and more fiercely. To his delight, Perri moved with him.

Halvo told himself to hold on just a little longer. Perri was sighing and moaning and pushing herself against him. Her fingernails dug into his back, urging him to continue. It would not be long. She began to struggle, as if the pleasure were becoming more difficult for her, and Halvo reached down a hand between their bodies to help her.

She screamed and convulsed around him. Never had Halvo seen anything as beautiful as Perri experiencing her first fulfillment as a woman. Then his own reward was upon him. He could wait no longer. There was no more need for him to wait. Halvo poured all his passion and all his love into the woman still shivering in delight in his arms.

Halvo slept. Perri lay beneath his arm, secure and content. And while Halvo was asleep Perri thought about all the things that had been required of her on Regula and all the things that had been denied to her. She thought of what Halvo had taught her and how, in a burst of comprehension, so many previously misunderstood bits and pieces had come together in her mind, coalescing into knowledge. She could remember the women of Elyr's household murmuring together and the way they fell silent when she approached, how they refused to tell her what they had been saying. She recalled the sudden appearance of a tiny baby, the child of two of Elyr's married servants. No one would answer her questions about how the child had come into existence. With a dismissive gesture Elyr's mother, Cynri, had said that when the time was right, Elyr would explain to her what should be done so Perri could have her own child.

Now Perri knew how it was done. But she did not think she would have enjoyed the act so much with Elyr. The thought of Elyr invading her body made her ill. With Elyr, it would have been an invasion. And now Perri knew why. So many questions answered by one miraculous deed. And so many new questions raised.

"Halvo?"

"Hmmm." He stirred, awakening, and his arm tightened around her.

"Halvo, I have a question to ask you."

"Of course you have." He postponed what she would ask with a long, tender kiss, but eventually he had to remove his mouth from hers.

"Halvo, will we have a child?"

"Would you like one?"

"I think so. I would love it and care for it as

Melri cared for me. And of course, I would have Rolli to help."

"You do understand that it would be necessary to get official permission first," he said.

"But, Halvo, what if I am already—what if . . . . I fear I do not fully understand the complete process."

"I can see that you will need further instruction in this subject," he teased, "not to mention an explanation of the inevitable consequences."

"Halvo, what are you doing now?" she gasped, her mouth against his.

"It's an old Demarian custom," he said.

Chapter Ten

"Halvo, abducted?" Leader Almaric, ruler of the Jurisdiction, looked stricken. His sharp features had gone pale and his tall figure, still lithe and slim despite his advancing age, was held stiffly upright as if to ward off the terrible blow just dealt to him.

"Explain yourself, Capt. Jyrit," Lady Kalina said. In contrast to her husband, the First Lady of the Jurisdiction was a rather stout woman. Her bronze hair was liberally sprinkled with gray and her sparkling blue eyes—her sole claim to beauty—were filled with a shrewd intelligence. It was widely rumored that many of Almaric's best decisions as Leader were in fact his wife's decisions, and the entire Jurisdiction knew how fiercely protective she was of her husband and of the two sons she had been permitted to bear in contradiction of the Jurisdiction law limiting a couple to a single offspring. She fixed her clear blue gaze upon Jyrit and asked the most pertinent questions first. "How could Halvo be removed from a ship of the size and strength of the *Krontar*? Why did you not prevent this kidnapping?"

"Lady Kalina, it was Adm. Halvo's personal decision to interview the boarding party sent from the *Space Dragon*. Unfortunately, the claim of a boarding party proved to be a trick." Jyrit wished fervently that he were anywhere but at Capital, in the Leader's own house, facing the two most powerful people in the Jurisdiction. He saw his career in the Service evaporating and he feared the only honorable future open to him would prove to be a ceremonial Jugarian suicide.

"Leader Almaric, Lady Kalina, may I speak?" Armaments Officer Dysia had insisted on accompanying Jyrit to the meeting. Jyrit had permitted her presence because, like Almaric and his wife, Dysia was a Demarian and therefore might be better able than Jyrit to explain Halvo's mysterious motivation to his parents.

"Of course, you may speak. Tell us what you know." Almaric sank into a chair, his head in his hands. He looked as if he had not the strength to stand any longer. Going to him, Kalina put one hand on his shoulder.

"Sir," Dysia said, "Capt. Jyrit, and later the leader of the best security team on the *Krontar*, both advised Adm. Halvo not to see those pirates."

"Pirates?" Kalina cried. "Halvo was wounded fighting pirates on the Styxian border. Could his abductors be survivors of that war who are seeking revenge?"

"It is always a possibility, Lady Kalina," Jyrit said. "However, my armaments officer has some interesting information to relay to you that suggests that perhaps we ought to look elsewhere for the villains in this unfortunate affair." He nodded to Dysia to continue.

"The ship that accosted the *Krontar* appeared familiar to me," Dysia said. "Its configuration had been somewhat altered, but I was able to determine that the *Space Dragon* is one of an older class of Regulan vessels."

"Regulan, you say?" Almaric lifted his head to regard Dysia with new interest. "We all know how the Regulans love intrigue. Could they have some reason for kidnapping my son?"

"Sir, I am almost certain the Regulans are involved," Dysia said. "The *Space Dragon* disappeared suddenly. After it was gone, the *Krontar's* sensors picked up faint traces of some unusual molecules. Recent scientific studies have shown that these same molecules are left by the activation of Starthruster. Those traces indicated a heading directly toward Regula."

"How could pirates have gained possession of a Starthruster device?" Kalina asked, once again noticing the most important fact. "Did they remove it from one of our disabled ships after Styxia?"

"Every pirate ship near the Styxian border was destroyed or disabled and captured," said Jyrit, who had been there for the great battle. "The few ships that did escape fled from our pursuing forces as quickly as possible. No, Lady Kalina, no pirate had the opportunity to steal a Starthruster device from a Jurisdiction ship."

"Then, if a pirate has Starthruster now, it was deliberately placed aboard that ship by a government holding Membership in the Jurisdiction." Kalina looked grim.

"As you say, madam," Jyrit said.

"The first place you should have looked for Halvo is on Regula." Kalina spoke with the complete assurance for which she was justly famous.

"So I thought, too, Lady Kalina," Jyrit said. "However, since discretion appeared to me to be vitally important in this matter, I judged it best to return to Capital at once, to inform you of the situation privately and await Leader Almaric's further orders."

"Discretion?" Kalina cried. "My son's life is in danger!"

"Jyrit is perfectly correct, my dear, and if you

pause to consider for a moment I am sure you will agree with him." Almaric broke into whatever vehement remarks Kalina was preparing to make next. "Until we have more solid evidence of Regulan involvement than a few molecular traces leading in the direction of that planet, we cannot make accusations against the Hierarchy. Doing so might cause a war within the Jurisdiction."

"Just so, Leader Almaric." Jyrit bowed in respect to Almaric's sagacity. "We may suspect the Regulans. In our hearts we may feel certain that they are to blame for your son's disappearance, but without proof, we can do nothing against them."

"All the same, we must find Halvo as soon as possible," Kalina said. "Our son is not yet fully recovered from his wounds. He requires further therapy. His physicians have told us so."

"While he was aboard the *Krontar* he suffered frequent bouts of vertigo," Dysia said. "Nor do I believe his broken back is completely healed. I took note of how cautiously he always moved."

"There, you see?" Kalina said to her husband. "We have to find him, Almaric, and soon."

"With your permission, Leader Almaric." With respectful Jugarian politeness, Jyrit bowed again, waiting until Almaric's nod gave him leave to speak. Jyrit was feeling much more optimistic than when he had first arrived to make his report about Adm. Halvo. With luck and a bit of diplomacy, he might be able to avoid ceremonial suicide after all.

"Speak, Jyrit," Almaric said. "I value your sensible opinion."

"Sir, in the interests of discretion, I suggest that the *Krontar* be assigned to the search for Adm. Halvo. I have refused shore leave to my crew while we are at Capital, and I have ordered them not to discuss with anyone who is not a fellow crew member the way in which your son was lured aboard the *Space Dragon*. Reprovisioning will be completed within the hour. The *Krontar* is ready to depart from Capital the moment you give the word.

"Leader Almaric, Lady Kalina," Jyrit went on, "since it was from my ship that your son vanished, honor requires that I should be the one to rescue him. I assure both of you that I will not stop searching until he is found."

"Jyrit, I do not hold you accountable," Almaric said. "I know my son's character well enough to be certain that what happened was not your fault."

"Nor do I blame you," Kalina said. "However—" She paused, and Almaric turned in his chair to look up at her out of troubled eyes.

"I believe I know what you are going to ask of me, Kalina," Almaric said.

"And as always, you will give me what I desire, will you not, my dear?"

"I hesitate only because what you want will separate us for a time."

"Halvo is lost," Kalina said. "We must find him, and you are forbidden to leave Capital so long as you are Leader."

"Capt. Jyrit"—Almaric faced the Jugarian—"Lady Kalina will accompany you on your search."

"You need not worry that I will upset the routine of your ship," Kalina said, apparently perceiving the concern Jyrit was doing his best to conceal. "I was not always First Lady of the Jurisdiction. Indeed, it will be a relief to me to put off formal robes and lay aside protocol for a time. I will not take your cabin, Jyrit. I will be content with passenger's quarters, and I will take with me only two trusted aides and minimal baggage. A single outfit of state robes should be sufficient for this journey. I believe the dark red set will be most appropriate for my meeting with the Chief Hierarch."

"The Chief Hierarch, Lady Kalina?" Jyrit regarded her with astonishment and steadily growing respect.

"Since you tell us you have already scoured the area of space where you were when Halvo was taken," Kalina said, "I see no point in wasting valuable time with a further search there. Your armaments officer has determined that the *Space Dragon* was originally a Regulan ship and the small amount of evidence you have suggests it headed toward Regula after parting from the *Krontar*. Under these circumstances, it would be only right and proper for us to ask our dear friends the Regulans to help us trace it. We will, therefore, begin our search for Halvo on Regula."

"My thoughts exactly, Lady Kalina," Jyrit said. He hoped the remarkable woman would notice a fact of which he was fully aware. His antennae were presently a soft shade of orange red, the coloring of friendship.

Chapter Eleven

"Admiral," said Rolli, "you were correct about the matter that concerned you."

"What matter?" Perri asked. She was so conscious of Halvo's every reaction that she was immediately aware of his repressed anger at Rolli's words.

"There is no point in keeping it from you, Perri." Halvo spoke when Rolli did not answer Perri immediately. "In addition to the device implanted in Rolli's circuitry, the main instrument panel here on the ship has been fitted with a homing signal."

"Which is no longer functioning," Rolli said. "I have destroyed it."

"First the Regulans tried to blast us into

smithereens," Perri said, chilled to the heart by this latest revelation. "Then, in case they failed to kill us that way, they reprogrammed Rolli to destroy us. Now you tell me they arranged a signal so they could follow us and finish the job if their first two plans didn't work out. They aren't leaving anything to chance, are they?"

"Apparently not," Halvo said.

"Why are they so determined to see us dead? Do we know something they don't want us to tell? What could it be? I don't have any information that is vital to Regulan interests. Do you, Halvo?"

"I think it is more a matter of who we are," Halvo said. "I am beginning to formulate a theory about Regulan motives. Rolli, how are the repairs coming along?"

"Most of the systems are just barely operational," Rolli said. "Without a complete overhaul, the *Space Dragon* will not be fit to lift into space."

"Are you saying we must stay here until the Regulans find us?" Perri cried. While it was wonderful to have her old companion in one piece and working again, Rolli had been giving them nothing but bad news over the past hour. Every sentence the robot spoke indicated new problems worse than the previous ones. "We can't stay here, Rolli. If we do and our pursuers find and kill us, then Elyr and the Chief Hierarch will win—and I won't let them win! I want to see justice done to those two and anyone else who was involved in their immoral schemes."

"So you have repeatedly declared," Rolli said, adding with a robot's typical logic, "However, what you want does not matter if the *Space Dragon* will not fly."

"You should have heard her before we put you back together." Halvo addressed Rolli with dry humor. "She has calmed down considerably. Now, she will be content with justice; then, she was screaming for bloody vengeance.

"But Perri is right," Halvo said, still speaking to the robot. "Our first order of business must be to get off this star-blasted world."

"Star-blasted world is not an entirely accurate term, Admiral, since we are presently sitting on the floor of a crater formed by the collision of a meteor with this planet. No stars have blasted this world. Only meteors have crashed here."

"Rolli, be quiet," Perri said, interrupting her literal-minded friend. She tried to speak with calm assurance, though what she felt was cold fear. "I have been studying the specifications for this ship. The *Space Dragon* has a double hull. At strategic locations throughout the ship it also has hatches that can be sealed in case the hull is breached."

"Go on." Halvo was watching her with interest.

Knowing he would listen to whatever she had

to say and give her suggestions serious consideration eased Perri's fear a little. "The worst damage we sustained was in the aft section. Could we seal the interior hatches to that section, cut off the life-support systems to the sealed areas, and live just in the cockpit and the galley? We ought to save a fair amount of energy that way, and air leaks through the cracks in the hull that we are not able to repair won't matter because we won't be using those parts of the ship."

"The cracks could widen during the stress of takeoff," Halvo said, "and the ship might break apart completely when we try to land again. Rolli, give us your opinion on Perri's idea."

"I must defer to your experience in this matter, Admiral," Rolli said. "I am not programmed to repair battle damage. I am confined to piloting the ship, to navigational functions, and to making simple repairs on the computer."

"Perri, what you have suggested is so dangerous that I deliberately have not mentioned the possibility of using the ship under those conditions," Halvo said.

"Then we must not risk it," Rolli said. "Not if the attempt would endanger Perri's life."

"Perri's life," Perri said in a sharp voice, "is in danger every moment right here on this planet. To begin the list of our problems, we do not have sufficient food."

"The processor is working again," Rolli said.

"It will not continue to work for long," Perri snapped. "We cannot repeatedly run the ship's engines so the food processor will function—or run the engines to moderate the temperature inside the *Space Dragon*. If the Regulans do not find and kill us first, we will exhaust our fuel supply sooner or later. Then we will be forced to take shelter in the cave, where we will die of starvation or cold. Halvo, will you please explain this to Rolli?"

"Why should I when you are doing an excellent job of laying out our options?" Halvo asked. "I am impressed, Perri. You have been studying constantly and learning your lessons well."

"What I have learned from the ship's computer and from you," Perri said, "leads me to believe we have only two options. We can remain where we are, in which case we will surely die. It will be a long, slow, and painful process. Or we can accept the risk involved in helping ourselves. If we die trying to leave this planet or trying to land somewhere else, at least it will be a quick death.

"As Rolli says, you are far more experienced in this area than we are, Halvo. But if you were to ask my opinion, I would vote in favor of attempting to get into space again and, once there, to find a more pleasant place in which to make full repairs. We will also increase our chances of survival if we can lose the Regulans who are following us." She stopped because

Halvo was grinning at her, and she could not help smiling back at him.

"We still do not know where we are," Rolli said. "Nor will we until we are in space and our navigational instruments have been fully activated, assuming they can be fully activated."

"We'll manage," Halvo said, his eyes still locked on Perri's. "We'll find a way. Let's give the *Space Dragon* one more work period. And we will take two more long rest periods before we leave because once we are on our way we won't have time for sleep." The tone in which he spoke that last sentence told Perri that rest was not all he had on his mind.

"Yes," she said.

Much later, it was Halvo who had a question to ask Perri. They were back inside the cave, sheltering from the cold. Once again Halvo had raced from ship to cave entrance, where he had arrived gasping for breath, though it seemed to Perri that he was neither as weak nor as dizzy as the first time he had made that brief trip. To protect Rolli's main circuitry from the extreme temperatures they had again brought the robot's head with them. Securely wrapped in a sheet, it rested with their supplies. Perri knew the main circuitry was not working at the moment, but even so she was glad to have Rolli's eyelights covered.

Perri knew she and Halvo would make love

soon. She had been aware of his building desire all day. What astonished her was the realization of her own eager need. It had never been so with her before, but Halvo had changed the way she felt about many things.

"Eat all of it, Perri." Halvo had seen her picking at her food. "You are going to need every calorie before we reach safety."

"Safety?" she said, smiling. "You cannot promise that we will ever again be safe. And if you could, I am not sure I would be happy to arrive at such a place. Since this adventure with you began, my life has been far more exciting than I ever dreamed was possible. I am beginning to suspect that I am of a temperament to be bored with a safe existence."

"I have been bored on occasion," Halvo said. "When I was on active duty I endured occasional regimented dullness without complaint because propriety is expected of the Admiral of the Fleet and because I knew such times would not last long. The dullness was interspersed with periods of great excitement, thus I never had reason to be seriously bored. Planning new space ventures, fighting the Cetans and negotiating the treaty with them after they were defeated, visiting planets that were considering Membership in the Jurisdiction—those were good times. Then I was wounded and the boredom began, relieved only by my need for therapy. The boredom continued until I met you.

First you reawakened my curiosity, next you jolted me out of my despondency. Whatever happens to us, I am glad we met."

"Perhaps we were fated to meet," Perri said.

"I don't know much about Regulan philosophy. Do you believe in predestination?"

"I think I do now, though it is strange to think of those wicked men, the Chief Hierarch and Elyr, as the agents of some great cosmic plan." Perri lapsed into a pensive silence, and Halvo asked a serious question. "Perri, when he visited your bedroom, exactly what did Elyr make you do for him?"

"We never did what you and I have done," she cried, suddenly defensive.

"I know. Technically speaking, the first time we made love you were a virgin. However, you definitely were not inexperienced." They were sitting side by side while they ate. Reaching toward her, Halvo smoothed her hair away from her face, telling her without words that he did not despise her, no matter what she had done with her betrothed. "I have my suspicions about Elyr's demands upon you, but I think you and I ought to discuss the matter so there is no misunderstanding between us."

Perri sighed and relaxed. It was only fair to explain to him what her compliance with Elyr's wishes had meant—and how much she had always disliked what she was commanded to do.

"If you wish, I will show you," she said. "I do not mind, Halvo."

"I will only consent if this is something you truly want to do," he said.

"How could I not want to help you in any way I can?" she cried. "I have been kissed more in the last few days than in all the years since Melri died, and as for the way you made me feel when you demonstrated your Demarian customs—Halvo, I never dreamed such joy was possible."

"You still believe you have an obligation to please me," he said. "You are not obligated, Perri. You have a right to your own pleasure."

"In that case, after I have shown you what you want to know, I will ask you to pleasure me again."

"You do learn fast, don't you?" he said.

Perri loved the way his face lit up when he smiled. He always made her want to smile back at him.

"Do you wish to remain sitting?" she asked. "Or would you prefer to stand or perhaps to lie upon your back?"

"Why don't we adjourn this party to your blanket?" he asked.

"Whatever you wish, Halvo. You will not have to remove your clothing this time."

"What a pity. I like the sensation of my skin next to yours. But just this once, we will do things the Regulan way."

Perri followed him across the sand, then

stood waiting while Halvo stretched out on her blanket. He clasped his hands behind his head, crossed his legs at the ankles, and smiled up at her.

"I trust you, Perri. I put myself completely in your hands."

"Have you any special requests?" she asked.

"How can I make a request when I don't know what you are planning to do?"

"Of course." She did not tell him that at that point in the proceedings, Elyr had always made a sarcastic comment about her previous performances, followed by a warning to her to do better this time. But unconstrained by any demands, she would do what seemed to please Halvo. That thought pleased Perri.

"I can see," she said, "that our discussion has fueled your need."

She knelt beside Halvo. Reaching out one hand she laid it over his half-erect masculinity. Halvo drew in a short breath but lay quite still. Beneath her fingers she detected a swift surge of increasing hardness. Gently she manipulated him through his clothing until he shifted restlessly, uncrossing his ankles.

"Perri." His breath was becoming ragged.

"Yes, Halvo. Just lie still. I will tend to your need." She saw his face go hard and reminded herself that he did not like her to be subservient. She decided she would take the opportunity to show Halvo just how active she could be.

She lifted his tunic and unfastened his trousers. At once his engorged flesh sprang forth. Keeping her touch light, Perri began to stroke him. Halvo grew harder and larger, his eager need throbbing in her hands. Perri bent her head to lap the tip of him with her tongue.

Halvo's hands clamped around her wrists, pulling her away, holding her so they were face-to-face.

"This is what you did for Elyr?" he said. "Every time you were together and without removing your clothes?"

"Yes, of course," she said.

"He never did anything else with you?"

"Sometimes he wished me to take him in my mouth. He taught me how to do it so I would not hurt him. Halvo, if you found my fingers too rough, I can be more gentle. You must be desperately uncomfortable." She glanced at the source of his discomfort, then looked into his eyes.

"You cannot possibly imagine how uncomfortable I am," Halvo said. "But before we go any farther, I want to be certain that we understand each other. Did Elyr do anything to relieve your discomfort?"

"With him, I never experienced discomfort. I felt nothing but indifference toward him. I did dislike having to provide the aid he required, because it was something he demanded of me, regardless of my feelings."

"Did Elyr have other wives or mistresses whom he may have preferred to you? Or was what he made you do simply the Regulan method of birth control?"

"I do not know of any other women with whom Elyr found comfort," Perri said. "But then, as you know, much was deliberately concealed from me. Halvo, I see now how wrong it was for me to touch you the way I just did."

"It was not wrong!" he said. "Blast Elyr! If I ever have the chance, I may well strangle him for the way he treated you. Perri, what you just did is part of a perfectly normal repertoire of lovemaking skills. As you now realize, it is not everything. And it is only wrong if there is coercion involved, which apparently was the case with you."

"Elyr insisted. I could not refuse him. He was my betrothed."

"I understand. You were not to blame, Perri. By the way," Halvo said, "what you did was so delightful that I remain extremely uncomfortable, though my only serious complaint about the process is that I am still fully clothed. And so, unfortunately, are you. Do you think we could remedy this situation in the near future?"

"I have a proposal to make to you," Perri said.

"Yes?" Halvo brought her hands to his lips and began kissing them. "I am listening."

"I suggest that we attempt to discover a

means of blending the Demarian way and the Regulan."

"What a good idea." Halvo put on a serious face, but his eyes were dancing. "In my capacity as an admiral, I have occasionally been called upon to mediate disputes and assist in drawing up treaties, so I am aware of several interesting methods of carrying on negotiations between diverse cultures. Of course, considerable patience is usually required when translating the messages given and received, in order to be sure no misunderstandings occur. And then, one must always take care not to insult either involved party."

"Halvo, you are teasing me."

"Am I? How can you be sure?"

"I have never insulted you!"

"Oho! I could mention an occasion or two. However, in the interests of interplanetary peace, I will note only your peculiar insistence that I should remain fully dressed during the most intimate moments."

"It is the Regulan way!" Perri's pointed chin tilted upward.

"It is not the Demarian way!" Halvo's eyes showed a dangerous sparkle.

"If you wish to be unclothed, I will unclothe you, Admiral!" With that, Perri flung herself at him, tugging hard at his tunic. Halvo burst into laughter and rolled over, pulling Perri along with him. She ended with her back jammed against the smooth rock wall and Halvo tight against her.

"Do you see how easily negotiations can break down if one is not careful?" he whispered. "It appears that we will be obliged to look farther afield in order to find an acceptable compromise to end our disagreement, some activity that is neither Regulan nor Demarian."

Perri was not sure how she ought to react. Never having associated sex with laughter, she was bewildered by Halvo's actions and by his joking words. But she did like the sensation of his strong body lying along hers, and she held tightly to him.

"For example," Halvo murmured, his mouth against her throat, "we might attempt the Jugarian method, though since we lack antennae, we will probably not succeed in attaining the exquisite and prolonged ecstasy that well-mated Jugarians supposedly reach."

"Have you made love to a Jugarian woman that you know about this supposed ecstasy?" Perri asked, still clinging to him and achingly aware of his hardness pushing against her abdomen.

"Not I, though I was once told how it is done, in case I should ever need to know."

"So that's how admirals spend their time! You huddle together, gossiping about the reproductive customs of the various Races!" If he was not going to allow her to touch that rigid segment of his body with her hands again, then she wished he would revert to Demarian custom and do what he had done the last time they had lain together. The memory made her warm, and that warmth growing inside her made her long for a recurrence of the intimate closeness and the stimulating friction. If only. . . .

"Perri, would you mind telling me exactly what you are trying to do?" Halvo said. "You are driving me mad."

"I beg your pardon. I will stop at once." She had been moving around in his arms, attempting to find a position in which that wonderful, hard part of him could fit into the right place in her body. She was growing hotter and more frantic by the moment and she did not know how to tell him what she wanted so he could do it in time. She wanted him to do it soon—immediately if possible. She did not think she could live much longer without Halvo inside her.

"Then there is the Styxian way." His tongue touched the corner of her mouth. "Though we do not have scales to become iridescent as our passion rises, we might find the Styxian version of lovemaking an interesting variation. Have you an opinion on this matter?"

"No." Perri gasped.

"Well, then, since you are not particularly interested, perhaps we should imitate the Styxians another time. While you have a beautiful back and alluring buttocks, I do think I would prefer to look at your face while we make love."

"The Styxians do what?" Perri became aware of Halvo's hands at the waist of her trousers, pulling them downward. She welcomed what he was doing, but before she completely lost her wits to passion, she had a question or two to ask. "From behind? How?"

"You know, don't you, that Styxians are descended from reptiles? I am told their reproductive processes are fascinating to anthropologists." Halvo's hands caressed the bare skin of Perri's flanks, which he had just exposed to the cool cavern air. "Then there are the Famorat, a mysterious Race living on the tangential border of the Jurisdiction. They cannot mate unless there are three Famorati present."

"Halvo, stop talking! Oh, please, I want you— yes, I want you there!" Their legs were tangled together and Halvo's skillful fingers were arranging their bodies just as Perri desired. They were lying face-to-face, with Perri braced against the cavern wall. Halvo's hands were on her hips so he could pull her closer to meet his vigorous thrusts.

Behind Perri's closed lids strange images swam, the result of the shocking things Halvo had just told her. And as he must have expected, numerous questions tumbled through her mind.

While still living on Regula she had seen on her telscan a visiting delegation of Jugarian diplomats. They were humanoid in shape, with pale gray skin and twin antennae on their hairless heads. The antennae had changed color with their moods. What color would their antennae be while a Jugarian was in the transports of sexual passion?

What did a Styxian female feel when, her scales glowing, she was mounted from behind? Did it hurt? Or did she find as much joy in her peculiar mating as Perri was finding with Halvo? And how could the Famorati combine three at once? How did they all fit together?

Did the females of other Races love, as she loved Halvo? And she did love him. She had known love in her earlier life—for her parents and for Melri. What she felt for Halvo was similar, yet with the added dimensions of an intense physical attraction and a sense of equality with him that she had never experienced with anyone else.

These wisps of thought, floating through her mind, did not distract her in the least from what Halvo was doing or from her own body's response to him. In fact, the new information enhanced her reactions, which she suspected was just as Halvo had intended. Nor did her thoughts or questions last for very long. Soon Perri was completely caught up in Halvo's lovemaking and thinking of nothing else. Then she was incapable of thinking of anything at all.

Once more Halvo pulled her hips forward while he thrust hard into her. He stayed there, buried deep, until Perri had found complete release for all discomfort and Halvo had followed her into a similar, male state of contentment.

"It is always so satisfying to be able to bring negotiations to a happy conclusion," he murmured a short time later.

"Is it a Demarian custom to tease your women into compliance?" she asked in mock irritation. "Or to torment them with stories of how the other Races mate?"

"I thought you would find the knowledge interesting and, perhaps, useful." There was an undertone of amusement in his response.

"Thank you for your efforts to advance my education. I am aware that I was sadly deficient in certain areas until you undertook to enlighten me."

"If you have any further questions, do not hesitate to ask."

"About the Famorat," she said.

"I knew you would be intrigued by that particular piece of information. Oh, Perri, the quirks of your mind will never cease to delight me." Halvo began to laugh. Lying back on the blanket he pulled Perri into his arms again. She rested her head against his heaving chest while his laughter rang through the cavern, echoing off the walls. Halvo laughed until his cheeks were wet with tears.

When he was calmer, he told her what she wanted to know. By the time he was finished with his explanations they were both fully ready to undertake their own two-person variation on Famorat custom. As Halvo demonstrated for her, Perri wondered why any couple would want to add a third, possibly disruptive, personality to the equation when two was so obviously the perfect number required for complete happiness.

Chapter Twelve

"Lady Kalina, you are magnificent." Jyrit gazed in admiration at the wine-red robes the First Lady of the Jurisdiction was wearing. The high-necked, long-sleeved gown fell to Kalina's feet in dignified folds. The enveloping cloak was the same color as the dress, but it was transparent. Both garments were perfectly plain.

However, Kalina was not without adornment. The thin gold diadem of a Demarian noblewoman circled her brow. Gold spirals curled about her ears, and her heavy gold necklace was studded with red-gold Styxian sunstones, the rarest and most valuable jewels in the galaxy. The wide bracelets on either wrist were also set with sunstones.

Behind Kalina stood her two aides, both dark-haired, middle-aged Demarian women robed alike in gowns of deepest green.

"Whenever I don state robes, I feel as if I have been prepared for my own funeral," Kalina said, responding to Jyrit's compliment with self-mocking humor.

"In this particular case, perhaps you ought to think of those garments as a costume suiting the role you must play on this day," Jyrit said.

"So I shall." Kalina smiled warmly at the captain of the *Krontar*. A firm comradeship had grown between them during the voyage from Capital to Regula, a relationship based upon a mutual determination to discover what had happened to Halvo. Kalina understood that, for Jyrit, the search was a matter of deep personal honor.

"Sorry to be late, sir. I was instructing the security team." Armaments Officer Dysia appeared in the captain's reception room. Like Jyrit, she was clad in the silver-trimmed, dark blue dress uniform of the Jurisdiction Service. Both officers wore short, red-lined formal capes over their jackets and trousers and carried the anachronistic silver dress helmets that were seldom actually worn. Behind Dysia six members of the ship's security guard, also in full dress uniform, filed in and stood waiting patiently.

"Jyrit, you have arranged a splendid retinue," Kalina said, giving those in the room a quick inspection. "We ought to impress the Regulan Hierarchy. Don't you think so?"

"Madam, were you to descend to Regula alone and in everyday clothing, you would still impress the Hierarchy by your honesty and by the force of your character," Jyrit said. Turning to his armaments officer he added, "Dysia, you have made an intensive study of Regulan society during our journey here. Have you any last-minute advice for us before we disembark?"

"Only to remind each member of our party not to say anything we would not want over-heard," Dysia said. "We all know the Regulans are masters of intrigue and they are certain to have listening devices planted in anticipation of any unguarded remarks we might make. Unless there is a clear and urgent need to do otherwise while we are on the planet's surface, I suggest that we confine our conversation to polite triv-ialities and to questions phrased to elicit infor-mation while not giving away anything. After we return to the *Krontar* and can talk freely again, we can put together what each of us has been able to learn. Our watchword on Regula should be caution."

"Agreed." Kalina nodded her approval of Dy-sia's warnings.

"Lady Kalina," one of her aides said somewhat nervously, "won't this be a danger-ous visit? Shouldn't we wear sheer body armor?

We will be in full range of the entire Regulan Hierarchy."

"Amalla, I am surprised at you." Kalina frowned.

"It is not for myself I am concerned, but for you," Amalla cried. "I am sure Leader Almaric is worried about your safety, too."

" 'If you fear treachery, walk in the most public places,' " Kalina said, quoting an old Demarian proverb.

"No one would dare to harm Lady Kalina, nor any member of her retinue, lest the full force of the Jurisdiction be turned against Regula," Jyrit said. "No, our greatest caution should not be for our physical safety, but for the misspoken word. As of this moment, guard everything you say."

Kalina had insisted that her visit to Regula must be a brief and informal one. Nevertheless, the ceremonies arranged to greet the First Lady of the Jurisdiction proved to be long and tedious. The day was well into its second half before the honored guests were led away from the Great Plaza, out of the too bright, coppery sunshine and into the shade of the reception hall of the main government building, where a banquet was to take place. The hall was open on three sides, allowing a fine view of the governmental gardens, which included an artificial lake and beds of multicolored flowers. To Kalina's relief a pleasant breeze, scented by the flowers, blew through the hall. However, she was not pleased when she beheld the long table set with silver dishes and utensils. The number of chairs lined up at the table was enough to alarm her.

"My dear friend," Kalina said to the Chief Hierarch, who was her escort for the occasion, "it was my hope that we might enjoy a private conversation."

"Dear lady, I must protest your wish for privacy." The Chief Hierarch smiled upon Kalina with great benevolence. His silvery robes glinted as he walked, his white hair and beard and even his thick, white eyebrows were perfectly trimmed and combed. He was the very image of a pure-minded, openhearted ruler welcoming a long-awaited guest. "We could not deny our beloved people a glimpse of the first government representative sent to us from Capital. Perhaps you do not fully comprehend how deeply honored we Regulans are by your presence among us."

"As I explained to you before we arrived, my dear Chief Hierarch, this is not an official visit. I come to you in great urgency, hoping that you will be able to provide some clue to help me solve the mystery of my son's disappearance."

"Since our first conversation while you were still days away from us, dearest Lady Kalina, the entire resources of the Regulan Hierarchy have been devoted to discovering just such a clue." The Chief Hierarch spoke with such sympathy and sweet sincerity that Kalina, experienced as she was in diplomacy, was certain he was lying.

Guarding her tongue and hiding her reluctance, Kalina allowed the Chief Hierarch to lead her to the head of the elaborately set banquet table. As her first sight of the complicated place settings had led her to fear would be the case, the feast consisted of many courses and much wine. The service was almost painfully slow. Kalina knew why. The Regulan Hierarchy was going to keep its guests in the banquet hall for as long as possible. There, Kalina and the others would be unable to talk with anyone but carefully selected people who were no doubt as firmly cautioned to be discreet as were the members of Kalina's own party. Nothing was to be left to chance, not a single hint of uncontrolled information was to be leaked to the folk from the *Krontar*. And it was all done with such generosity, such hospitality, and so many promises of help that any protest would seem to be the height of rudeness.

Kalina could only hope that, despite the precautions the Hierarchy had taken, Jyrit, Dysia, and the rest of her group would be able to gather a crumb of information here, or a vague hint there, so that, when the little they had learned was put together, it would provide a bit of hope that Halvo still survived and some idea as to where he was.

Kalina was seated between the Chief Hierarch and his fair-haired, solemn-faced son-in-law. The rest of her people were scattered along the table in descending order of rank, each of them surrounded by the Regulan Hierarchs and their families. When the Chief Hierarch turned to speak to the woman on his left side and to Jyrit, who sat next to the woman, Kalina gave her full attention to her youthful companion.

"I have met so many people today," Kalina said with a self-deprecating laugh, "that I regret I cannot recall your name, sir."

"I am not surprised." Though the actual eating and drinking had barely begun, the young man swallowed the entire contents of his large wine goblet and held it out to a servant to be refilled. "I am Elyr. This lady beside me is my wife, Thori. Since we are but newly wed, we were seated together."

"Congratulations to you both," Kalina said.

"I have never been to a state banquet before." Thori leaned forward toward Kalina, but her eyes were on Elyr's face. There was adoration in her gaze and—was that a hint of fear?

"How long have you been married?" Kalina asked, her interest in the pair sharpened by what she thought she perceived in Thori's face.

"Only six days." Thori blushed. She was a pretty girl with reddish brown hair worn in braids and a bright blue gown.

"Now, as I understand Regulan custom," Kalina said in a friendly way, "you have been betrothed since your ninth birthday and living in Elyr's household since that day. I consider that a very sensible arrangement. Boys and girls should know each other well before they marry."

"Oh, no," Thori cried. "I hardly know Elyr at all. We were only betrothed for ten days before the marriage ceremony."

"I beg your pardon for my mistake." Kalina extended her smile from Thori to Elyr. She did not miss the fact that he looked decidedly pale and was on his third goblet of wine. "Obviously, I am not as conversant with Regulan customs as I imagined."

"No, Lady Kalina, you did not make a mistake. Elyr was betrothed to someone else first," Thori said, as if she were eager to tell someone about her unusual marital arrangements. "The silly girl stole a spaceship and ran away. Can you believe anyone would do something like that? It caused such a scandal!"

Plainly, Thori meant that she could not understand how anyone could run away from Elyr, but Kalina, who knew how women were treated on Regula, found herself wondering instead how a girl kept in virtual ignorance of the world outside the home of her betrothed could have learned to pilot a spaceship. Kalina decided it might be enlightening to learn more about Elyr's former wife-to-be.

"I am sorry," Kalina said to Elyr. "I owe you another apology. When I meet young people, I am so interested in learning about their lives that my questions sometimes overstep the boundaries of good manners. I did not mean to intrude into your personal unhappiness."

"I am not unhappy." Elyr's words were just a bit slurred. "Perri was an irritating, stupid girl. I am well rid of her. Thori is much more to my liking."

"You may be sure, dearest Elyr," Thori said blushing again at her husband's compliment, "that I will never run away as Perri did."

"I am sure you will not." Kalina smiled at her. "You appear to be a sensible girl, so I am certain that, when differences arise between you and your husband, you will find a way to settle those little arguments to your mutual advantage. As a wife of many years who loves her husband dearly, I can tell you that husbands and wives do quarrel on occasion."

"They do?" Thori's eyes went wide with surprise as she contemplated the novel idea.

"It is the sign of a healthy relationship. I never hesitate to speak my mind to my husband."

"Oh." Thori appeared to be thinking about that.

"My wife will never disagree with me." Elyr spoke with all the assurance of a Regulan male.

Thori looked from her husband to Kalina and back to Elyr again. Kalina was fully aware that she had just planted the seed of future dissent. She hoped Thori would be strong enough to nourish its growth.

"Ah, Lady Kalina," the Chief Hierarch murmured, returning his attention from his other dinner partner to her, "I fear you have been subjected to my daughter's overexcited version of the story of her marriage."

"Who is the dreadful girl who stole a spaceship?" Kalina asked.

"Oh, dear," the Chief Hierarch murmured, looking sorrowful. "I had originally planned to tell you about the incident after the pleasantries of the banquet were over. I have no wish to spoil this delightful repast for the sake of so slight an indicator."

"What indicator? Has this thief, Perri, anything to do with my son's disappearance?" Kalina raised her voice by half a notch and allowed a threatening note to creep into it. "Tell me now, Chief Hierarch."

"You have explained to us that your son was abducted aboard a small ship which you believe was crewed by pirates," the Chief Hierarch said.

"Yes." Kalina waited, barely daring to hope that the Chief Hierarch had some news of Halvo and that he would tell her honestly what that news was instead of engaging in a typical Regulan intrigue.

Flora Speer

"Perri did indeed steal a small ship," the Chief Hierarch said, "and several days after the date on which Capt. Jyrit reports your son was taken, she reappeared in Regulan space. We do not know what she intended to do next. Perhaps she planned to return home. What we do know is that several Regulan patrol ships approached the *Space Dragon*, promising Perri she would not be harmed. She seemed agreeable to their escort back to the surface of Regula. But then, suddenly, her ship exploded. Perri was certainly killed, and dear Lady Kalina, if your son was aboard, he must have been killed also."

Kalina did not cry out or faint or burst into tears. She was a well-trained diplomat in her own right, so she was able to keep her emotions in check while under close scrutiny by possible enemies, even when she had been dealt a blow that would break any mother's heart. Furthermore, though she recognized the name of the spaceship upon which Halvo had been abducted, she did not entirely believe what the Chief Hierarch had just told her. Nor could she determine what his motives might be for making such a terrible revelation at a public banquet.

Regulan intrigue, she said to herself. It is not true. My son is not dead. If Halvo were dead, I would know it in my heart.

"Do you have a place where women may retire for a few minutes to refresh themselves?"

220

she said aloud to the Chief Hierarch in a voice that was almost normal.

"Of course." He was all sorrowful sympathy. "Lady Kalina, shall I end the banquet in deference to your grief?"

"Certainly not. I will return shortly." Kalina rose.

"Cynri will show you the way," the Chief Hierarch said, motioning to a gray-haired woman who sat several places down the table.

The ladies' retiring room was small and windowless. It might have provided the few minutes of privacy that Kalina needed, but Cynri persisted in hovering around her on the excuse of helping until Kalina was sorely tempted to be rude to the woman. But then Cynri's fluttering, inane remarks took an interesting turn.

"Lady Kalina, we all know why you have come to Regula," Cynri said. "I, more than most people, hope you will find your son."

"Thank you for your kind wishes, Cynri."

"I hope you also find that appalling girl, Perri, and see to it that she is severely punished for what she has done to my son."

Kalina had been smoothing down her wiry bronze hair so she could settle her gold circlet more securely upon her brow. At the other woman's words she paused, her fingers still on her hair and circlet, and stared at Cynri in the mirror. The woman's eyes did not meet hers, but shifted here and there. A warning sounded in Kalina's mind.

"Would your son be Elyr?" Kalina asked, feeling very much as if she were wading through a bog filled with quicksand.

"Isn't he handsome? And such a good son, always so thoughtful of me." It was the kind of thing a loving mother would say, but to Kalina it sounded overdone.

"I am happy to hear it. Cynri, the Chief Hierarch has told me that this Perri creature died when her ship exploded. Why do you think I will find her alive?"

"She's not dead. Not that one!" Cynri drew nearer. "We can understand each other, can't we, Lady Kalina? Both the mothers of sons, both devoted to our boys, both willing to do anything to protect our darlings. As you fear for your son's life, so do I fear for Elyr's. Lady Kalina, may I speak freely?"

"Of course," Kalina said. "Whatever you say will remain strictly between us."

"I never liked that girl."

"You mean Perri?" Kalina was beginning to wonder if Cynri's wits were scrambled. Cynri's slightly disheveled appearance and her furtive manner suggested that might be the case. Or was this conversation a clever ploy of some kind? One could never be sure with the Regulans.

"Of course I mean Perri!" Cynri said. "For

thirteen years, day and night, the impertinent creature never stopped asking questions. It was exhausting."

"I am sure it was," Kalina said.

"Then, on that last day, she went to see the Chief Hierarch."

"Did she? Do you know why?" Kalina asked.

"Why else but to tell him what she had learned from asking all those questions? And then she ran off to be a pirate. The thing is"—Cynri drew closer still to Kalina—"the men are always plotting together."

"So I have heard," Kalina said.

"And they never tell the women what they are planning, which makes it difficult to arrange mealtimes or household chores. If I were in charge, things would be different."

"I am sure that is true." Kalina tried to sound sympathetic. "Cynri, to return to the subject of Perri—" She paused, hoping Cynri would say something useful.

"I'm afraid the Chief Hierarch and Perri together have drawn my poor, innocent boy into some terrible scheme," Cynri whispered. "I know Elyr has been frightened in recent days."

"Really?" By now, Kalina did not know what to believe about the woman. She could not decide whether Cynri was mad or extremely clever and devious.

"And then there are the pirates."

"Pirates," Kalina said.

"Of course. There are always pirates," Cynri said.

"I wasn't aware that there were any in this particular sector of the galaxy," Kalina said.

"We can't get rid of them." Her pale watery-green eyes darting here and there but never resting on Kalina's face, Cynri added, "Pirates are dangerous."

"They certainly are," Kalina agreed. She began to edge toward the door. Their conversation was going nowhere and Cynri was not making much sense. Kalina was sure she could learn more by talking with the Chief Hierarch.

"I don't want my boy to come to harm," Cynri said, sounding desperate. "And you want your boy safe, too. So if you do find Perri, you know what to do."

"If I find her, I will know exactly what to do." Kalina paused at the door.

"And don't believe a word she says. She's a liar, too." With that, Cynri pushed past Kalina and disappeared in the direction of the banquet hall.

"At least we now know the official Regulan line on the matter," Jyrit said. He, Kalina, and Armaments Officer Dysia were once again in the captain's reception room aboard the *Krontar*. The other members of their party who had gone to the planet's surface had made their reports before being dismissed for the night. "As we have just heard, all of our people were told basically the same story. This Perri girl stole the *Space Dragon*. How she did it on this planet where females are kept away from all but the simplest machinery, we do not know. Then, for a reason we are not clear about yet, Perri used the ship to kidnap Halvo. As she returned to Regula the *Space Dragon* suddenly exploded, killing both of them. End of story, according to the Regulans, and all of Regula regrets the incident. I need not point out the obvious inconsistencies in this tale. Have either of you anything to add?" Jyrit looked from Kalina to Dysia.

"I met the Chief Hierarch's new son-in-law. And the young man's mother." Quickly, Kalina reported both conversations. "Cynri appears to believe that Perri and the Chief Hierarch were working together, that Perri was spying on Elyr's household, and that the girl has somehow drawn Elyr into a major intrigue that puts his life in danger."

"Do you believe this?" Jyrit asked.

"I am not sure how much of what she said was true," Kalina said. "I do believe that Cynri was deliberately letting bits of information slip out—or perhaps it was misinformation. Whether she was told to do so or did it on her own in hope of protecting her son, I could not discern.

"I can understand Cynri's desire to protect

Elyr. I would do the same for either of my sons. Jyrit, after today I am more certain than ever that Halvo is not dead. But how do we get to the truth of this particular Regulan intrigue? More importantly, how do we find Halvo?"

"I may have information that will help." Dysia leaned forward in her chair, her face alight with interest and excitement. "As that party on Regula was breaking up this evening, I overheard a conversation. Now, I do not discount the possibility that I was meant to hear what I did, but still, what I learned may be useful.

"The Chief Hierarch was talking to Elyr," Dysia said. "Elyr appeared to be openly upset and acted as if he had been drinking heavily. There was a lot of repetition in their conversation but this was the gist of it. The Chief Hierarch told Elyr that he shouldn't worry, that there was no trace of the *Space Dragon* left for anyone to find, and that if the Regulans, knowing the *Space Dragon's* last position exactly, could not locate evidence, then the Jugarian captain will never discover a clue to its apparent destruction."

"Apparent destruction?" Jyrit said.

"Those were his exact words, sir." Dysia grinned with a touch of mischief in her manner. "Also, it just so happens that during that interminable banquet I was seated next to a knowledgeable fellow who is a high-ranking officer in the Regulan police. I will admit I fluttered my eyelashes at him a few times and perhaps gave him the wrong impression about my degree of interest in him. But I did learn the approximate location of the *Space Dragon* at the time when it supposedly blew up.

"As soon as we returned to the *Krontar*," Dysia said, "I ordered a thorough scan of that area. Even at this late date there ought to be lingering traces of the explosion that destroyed the *Space Dragon*. Our scan discovered nothing except a few molecules that indicate the use of Starthruster."

"Good work, Dysia." Jyrit made a hand motion that, on his native Jugaria, signified hearty approval.

"You are suggesting that the *Space Dragon* escaped from Regulan space," Kalina said.

"Only that they may have escaped," Dysia said. "I am compelled to point out that the Starthruster traces we found could have come from a Regulan ship using the device while on legitimate business. All we know for certain is that the *Space Dragon* did not explode where and as the Regulans claim."

"It is possible," Kalina said, "that everything we think we have learned today is false, that the Chief Hierarch meant for us to uncover these clues. I am particularly disturbed by Cynri's mention of pirates."

"Piracy is a scourge difficult to put down," Jyrit said. "Destroy one pirate base and before

Flora Speer

long another appears somewhere else. We knew that even as Halvo led us to victory against those pirates gathered near Styxia."

"I have worried since I first heard of his abduction that a pirate, or a group of pirates, wanted revenge against Halvo." Kalina looked at Jyrit. "What shall we do now?"

"We let the Regulans think we believe them." Jyrit rose from his chair and the two women stood, too. "We leave orbit within the hour. We will continue the search, Lady Kalina, and we will be even more thorough than we have been so far. If the *Space Dragon* was damaged instead of destroyed, Halvo would want to head for a good shipyard for repairs. We know that Perri is not an experienced pilot, so she just might decide to take Halvo's advice. We will start with planets or space stations known for making the best repairs to spaceships. If nothing else, the maneuver will confuse the Regulans and perhaps make them think we have a problem with the *Krontar*. And we will ask a lot of questions on worlds where the inhabitants are more honest than the Regulans."

"I have every confidence in you, Jyrit. And in you, Lt. Dysia." For the first time in that long and trying day Kalina broke into an honest smile. "I know you will find my son for me. Find that despicable girl, Perri, too. *I want to talk to her.*"

When Kalina had left them, Dysia looked at

228

Jyrit and said, "I could almost feel sorry for this Perri creature."

"Save your sympathy," Jyrit said with more than a touch of Jugarian harshness. "Perri is a criminal and Lady Kalina will see to it that she feels the full weight of Jurisdiction justice."

"The *Krontar* has gone," Elyr said, reporting to the Chief Hierarch early the next morning.

"I knew they would," the Chief Hierarch said, frowning. "There was no reason for you to worry. You must learn better self-control, my son. I tell you once again, my schemes always work. Now, I am going to visit my dear Thori. Will you join me, Elyr?"

"Just as soon as I finish my day's work, sir. My duty to Regula supersedes my personal desires, though I must confess I miss Thori every moment that I am apart from her."

"It's good to have a son-in-law on whom I can depend and who is so devoted to my little girl." The Chief Hierarch laid a paternal hand on Elyr's shoulder. "I am glad our mutual love for Thori has bound us so closely together, my boy."

Left alone in the Chief Hierarch's office, Elyr scowled at the desk full of work he was expected to complete for the older man. Still, work was more pleasant than listening to Thori's female chatter or the Chief Hierarch's constant fond remarks about his beloved daughter's beauty and goodness. Both of them could wait. Elyr was more concerned about the delegation that had just left Regula.

If the Chief Hierarch had his schemes, Elyr had his own. He had a mind attuned to notice details that others often missed, and that time the Chief Hierarch had missed an important detail. Elyr called in his former servant, Vedyr, who was acting as his aide.

"Vedyr, I want a spaceship to follow the *Krontar*," Elyr said. "It is to remain undetected by the *Krontar* and its captain is to report to me alone."

"Do you think the *Krontar's* crew might discover there is already a Regulan ship searching for the *Space Dragon*?" Vedyr asked.

"It is inevitable. Capt. Jyrit is no fool," Elyr said. "Do that right away."

"Yes, sir."

Alone again, Elyr smiled to himself at the thought of the *Space Dragon* lost in the far reaches of the galaxy and most likely badly disabled, tracked by a Regulan warship . . . both of which would surely be discovered by the *Krontar* . . . which was, in turn, secretly being followed by a second Regulan ship. Elyr almost wished that he could be there when the four ships converged and met in battle. But he could not be present. Elyr knew his destiny lay on Regula itself. Although the Chief Hierarch did not suspect it yet, Elyr intended to take his place. Thanks to his mother's help with Lady Kalina, the plot had already been set in motion.

Chapter Thirteen

"Halvo?" Perri stroked his thick hair, her fingertips lightly touching the silver strands at his temples. His head was resting between her breasts. She loved the feeling of his weight upon her and the warmth of his breath on her skin.

"I'm sleeping." He stretched against her like a large, well-satisfied cat—or a Demarian leopard-wolf content after a recent meal. For all his kindness to her and the gentleness he so often displayed, there was a strength and fierceness in Halvo that boded ill for anyone who might attack him—or her. She knew he would protect her with his life. There, in a chilly cave on a barren little world, with a disabled spaceship as their only means of escape, she still felt safe with Halvo.

"If you were asleep, you could not talk to me," she said.

"You would be amazed at what I can do in my sleep." When Perri giggled, Halvo lifted his head to look at her. "Are you ready to leave so soon?"

"I do not want to leave your embrace. Not ever." Perri sighed. Suddenly, no longer kept at bay by her romantic fantasies, all of the concerns and insecurities of the universe outside the cave flooded in upon her. "We are both agreed that we cannot stay here. Still, the moment we are skyborne everything will change." She stopped when Halvo's mouth covered hers. It was some time before she could speak again.

"Will you return to active duty in the Service?" she finally asked.

"I can't. I am presently assigned to administrative duties. What made you ask such a question when you know about my injuries?"

"I was wondering what the future would bring." She could not steel herself to inquire whether he intended to include her in his plans, so she tried an oblique approach to what was troubling her. "Your physical condition is greatly improved."

"I feel healthier now than I have since the day I woke up in a hospital and learned how badly I was wounded," Halvo said. "I attribute much of the improvement to the fact that I have recently had something else to think about, instead of constantly worrying over how slowly I was recovering. You have helped by providing many interesting diversions." He ended with one of those teasing smiles that usually made her respond with her own smile. But not that time.

"I see," she said, pushing him away so she could sit up. "I am a diversion. I am glad to hear it, since you are nothing more than a diversion to me, too."

When she scrambled to her feet to put distance between them, Halvo came after her. She had reached the edge of the icy pool before he caught her by her upper arms. Looking away from him and into the still water of the pool, she saw their reflections as if in a mirror. She thought their relationship was like that reflection. With the least touch, the slightest stirring of the water, the reflection would break into ripples and vanish. If she pushed Halvo too hard in an attempt to stay with him permanently the closeness between them would dissolve, and unlike the reflection in the water, a ruined relationship would not reassemble itself automatically.

"Never run away from me again," Halvo said, shaking her a little. "If you have a problem, tell me what it is and stay with me until we resolve it."

"By your clever interplanetary negotiating methods?" she asked scornfully.

"By any means necessary. Perri, tell me what is wrong. Are you apprehensive about leaving this planet, afraid the *Space Dragon* will explode with us inside it? If it does, at least we will be together and the end will be quick and painless. You said so yourself. Or do you think the Chief Hierarch and Elyr will come after us and try to force you to return to Regula?"

"None of those possibilities frightens me," she said.

"Then what is wrong? Tell me and we will deal with it together."

She could not tell him how terrified she was of losing him to his family and friends or to his career in the Service. She was an ignorant, provincial girl and he was a famous man, the son of the Leader of the entire Jurisdiction. Once he returned to his old life, Halvo would soon forget her. In the next few days they would face several different dangers and the distinct possibility of death. And at the end of all their travails—if they survived to the end—there would be no reward for her. She would almost prefer that both of them should die than that Halvo should leave her.

No. She could not bear the thought of his death, not after all he had suffered and the injuries he had overcome. Because she loved him, she would do everything she could to assist him until they reached safety, and when the time came, she would let him go without a quarrel. She would end their association with dignity. When Halvo was gone, memories and her dignity would be all she had left. Foreseeing that future, a bleak emptiness washed over her.

"Nothing is unbearable if you face it willingly," Halvo said. He was still holding her arms, still expecting a response from her.

"Some things are." Perri blinked back tears, refusing to shed them. She met his questioning eyes squarely. "I am being foolish. This cave has given me a false sense of security and now I regret the necessity of leaving it. But we have made our decision and for my part I will do my best to carry it out."

His approving smile was worth much to her. She made herself smile back at him.

"I knew I could depend on you," Halvo said.

"It is time." Halvo strapped himself into the copilot's seat. On his other side Rolli stood secured in the pilot's position, working the control panel.

Perri wanted to tell Halvo she loved him, just in case their lift-off ended in disaster, but she could see that his thoughts were on the ship and the tasks immediately ahead of him.

"Good luck to us," she said, instead of what she wished she could say.

The *Space Dragon's* engines roared to life and

the thrusters came on line. The damaged ship shuddered and creaked. Slowly it began to move away from the cliffs and toward the center of the crater. Halvo and Rolli worked together without need for words, while Perri reported what navigational information she could drag out of instruments not yet fully operational. With a lethargic effort that made Perri want to scream to release the building tension in the cockpit, the *Space Dragon* lifted off the surface of the planet and headed for the sky.

A few minutes later they were in orbit, holding there while Rolli and Halvo retested all the systems. Whether the systems worked or not, the *Space Dragon* could not return to the surface. It would be too dangerous to try. From that moment on, they must move cautiously through weightless space and hope they could find a space station with adequate repair facilities. If they did not, then a landing on some planet would be necessary and that would present their greatest danger since the *Space Dragon* might not hold together during the descent through an atmosphere. The disintegrating pieces of the ship—and the crew—would burn up like meteors.

Two hours after leaving orbit Perri discovered they were facing a worse danger than incineration.

"There is a Regulan warship following us." Perri looked up from her navigational instruments to see Halvo's face go hard and cold.

"Damnation," he muttered. "I hoped they would lose us after Rolli destroyed the homing signal we found."

"We can't fight them," Perri said, stating the obvious. "The few weapons we carry are not operational."

"We'll have to run from them," Halvo said. "At least now we know where we are."

"Near the Empty Sector," Perri said, checking the instruments again. "I read a book once about space exploration. There was a chapter in it about the Empty Sector. It is a fearsome place, where the common laws of physics do not always apply, where humans experience vivid dreams that drive them mad. We cannot go there, first because ships are not allowed to cross the border, and second, because no one ever returns from the Empty Sector."

"If no one returns to make a report on conditions there, how do authors obtain enough information to write whole chapters about it?" Halvo asked. "In fact, I know three people who did return safely."

"Admiral, are you suggesting that we should seek refuge from the Regulans in the Empty Sector?" Rolli asked.

"I think it is our only practical choice," Halvo said. "The warship following us is undoubtedly faster than the *Space Dragon* and far better armed. We can try to fight them, in which case they will destroy us. We can surrender at once and then they will destroy us because they dare not let us live. We can dodge and hide and try to throw them off our trail, but that tactic won't work for long because this ship is in no condition to carry on a sustained chase. Or we can head straight into the Empty Sector and hope they choose to obey Jurisdiction law and not follow us."

"Then it looks as if it is the Empty Sector for us." Perri considered the idea with trepidation, yet she was curious about the fabled area, where Jurisdiction ships were forbidden to go.

"I cannot permit any action that might endanger Perri's life," Rolli said.

"Rolli," Perri said with barely restrained impatience, "I know this constant insistence on my immediate safety is your programming talking, but I do wish you would begin to make a few logical connections and think long-term. The odds are better for us in the Empty Sector. I believe we should go there at once."

"I do like a gambling woman." Halvo winked at Perri. "Set the new coordinates. If Rolli decides to become fractious, I will just have to push her disconnect button."

"Admiral, I must protest your decision," Rolli said.

Halvo was still turned toward Perri, so she saw the anger at Rolli's response that Halvo quickly repressed. In the tightening of his mouth she recognized the same worry and strain she was experiencing. Halvo might conceal his feelings behind a calm exterior or a joke, but Perri knew he took their predicament as seriously as she did. The chief difference between them was that, while Perri conjured up fears out of her imagination, Halvo had enough real-life experience to know where the greatest dangers lay.

"Now hear this!" Without warning Halvo swung around to face the robot, gray eyes clashing with blinking blue eyelights. He spoke slowly and distinctly. "Far from wanting to put her into further danger, I am attempting to assure Perri's permanent safety. Can you understand that much, you metallic obstructionist?"

"Of course, I understand." Rolli sounded so affronted that Perri began to wonder if the robot might begin to malfunction again.

"In order to keep Perri safe," Halvo said, still speaking to Rolli in the same distinct manner, "some minor, immediate danger must be accepted. Perri's safety is of paramount importance to me. I will say it again. A lesser danger in the present will prevent serious harm to Perri in the future." Silence followed his slowly enunciated words until Rolli finally responded.

"Understood, Admiral." Rolli's eyelights were still fixed on Halvo's face.

"Then follow the orders I give you," Halvo said.

"Aye, sir." Rolli turned back to the control panel.

"That was amazing," Perri whispered to Halvo.

"Let's hope it worked," he said. "We may be able to trick the Regulans. Outwitting a robot is another matter altogether."

As the *Space Dragon* neared the frontier between the Jurisdiction and the Empty Sector, it reached a space buoy that emitted a constant warning signal that could not be missed or misunderstood by any spaceship with a functioning communications system. The *Space Dragon* passed the buoy and continued onward toward a second buoy, which was halfway between the first buoy and the edge of the Empty Sector.

"Our navigational instruments are beginning to display fluctuating readings," Perri said. "I can't tell exactly where we are anymore."

"However, the main controls are still operational," Rolli said. "Admiral, our sensors show the Regulan ship is reducing speed."

"It worked!" Perri cried. "They aren't going to follow us."

"They may only be hesitating while they decide what to do next," Halvo said.

"The second space buoy is dead ahead," Perri said. She clapped both hands over her ears. "What a terrible signal!"

"The Jurisdiction doesn't want anyone inad-

vertently straying across the border." Halvo cut
the comm system to half power and the shriek-
ing, rhythmic signal became tolerable. "Perri,
can you detect any indication of the border?"

"Not yet, but the readings don't make much
sense at the moment," Perri said, her eyes fixed
on the instruments before her. "What should I
be looking for?"

"I'm not sure, but you will probably know it
when it shows on your screen."

"Admiral," Rolli said, "the Regulan ship is increasing its speed and following us."

"They may think we will lose our nerve at the
second buoy," Halvo said.

Somehow, despite the undependable navigational instruments, Halvo and Rolli kept the
Space Dragon on a straight course. They
reached and passed the second buoy with the
Regulan ship still pursuing them.

"They are going to chase us right up to the
edge of the Empty Sector," Perri said. "Halvo,
what is this pink line in the middle of my
screen?"

"You can't appreciate it on that little navigational screen," Halvo said. "Turn around and
look at the main viewscreen."

Obeying him, Perri gasped, not in fear but in
amazement. A wide band of pale pink light
stretched horizontally across the viewscreen.
Below it a few distant stars glowed in the gen-
eral blackness. Above the band of light lay a

long swath of stars that curved backward in the direction from which the *Space Dragon* had come.

"That," Halvo said, pointing to the gathering of stars, "is the end of the outermost spiral arm of the galaxy. We are looking at it edge on. The Empty Sector is at the very tip of the arm and beyond it there is nothing for thousands of light-years."

"I didn't know it would be beautiful," Perri said.

"The Regulan ship is gaining on us," Rolli said. "It is now at maximum speed. It appears they intend to prevent us from crossing the border."

"Now that you've seen it, Perri, are you still willing to gamble on the Empty Sector?" Halvo glanced at her, then returned his full attention to the controls.

"Yes," Perri said. "If we die, let it not be at Regulan hands."

"I feel the same way." Halvo spared another warm look for her, then said, "All right, Rolli, let's take this dragon to top speed."

"Admiral," Rolli said, "this is dangerous. Our outer hull is cracked and most systems are close to shutdown. Any additional physical stress on the ship—"

"Are you with us? Or do we shut you off?" Halvo asked.

"I will endeavor to assist you. I merely wished

243

to lodge an opinion." Rolli's voice was almost plaintive, but in the minutes that followed, the robot promptly did everything that Halvo ordered.

Having directed all the ship's energy except for a minimal life-support system to the engines, Halvo opened the thrusters all the way. Under his guidance the *Space Dragon* raced toward the band of pink light, which, as they drew nearer, steadily increased in size until it filled almost all of the viewscreen. With the navigational instruments basically useless, Perri had little to do but watch the screen.

"Halvo, I can see stars inside the light," she cried.

"There are lots of stars in there," he said, "and planets. Entire solar systems. The Empty Sector is huge."

"Admiral," Rolli said, "the Regulans are closing on us."

"Why aren't we using Starthruster?" Perri's question brought a quick grin from Halvo.

"I am waiting for just the right moment," he said.

"When will that be?" Perri cried. "We are almost on top of that pink light. And Rolli is right. The Regulan ship is so close that I am afraid they will try to ram us."

"If they do, they will overshoot their mark. We won't be where they think we are. Hold on," Halvo said just before he activated Starthruster.

244

The jolt almost knocked Perri out of her chair. She heard every creak and groan the *Space Dragon* made. All of the instruments went wild. On her small navigator's screen, as well as on the main viewscreen, there was nothing but a blinding, bright-pink glow. The cockpit lights dimmed. Then both of the viewscreens went dark.

Perri held her breath, expecting to feel at any second the awful sensation of the ship breaking apart around her. Instead, she felt as if she were bouncing and sliding down a steep hill with no way to stop herself from plunging into an endless void. She put out one hand, reaching toward Halvo, but did not actually touch him. She merely wanted to be ready. If they were to die, she wanted her hand to be clasped in Halvo's.

And then the *Space Dragon* was drifting quietly in space. The lights returned to full strength and the viewscreens cleared. The pink light was gone, though Perri could discern a faint flush of the color around the edges of the screens. The picture she saw was of ordinary black space with a few stars and, here and there, streaks of blue or green, which she thought might be interstellar gas or cosmic dust illuminated by some unseen energy source.

Inside the cockpit there was complete silence for a while, as if the two human occupants and Rolli all needed time to assure themselves that they still existed. Feeling limp and weak, Perri stared at her companions before turning back to the large viewscreen.

"The Empty Sector doesn't look very frightening," she murmured.

"The engines are dead," Rolli said.

"If we have lights and the viewscreen, then we still have power." Halvo hit the start button. The engines immediately began to throb again. "Any sign of the Regulan ship?"

"Not on our sensors," Rolli said, "but I must caution you, Admiral, that all instrument readings are decidedly peculiar. The Regulan ship may, or may not, be lurking in our vicinity."

"Perri?" Halvo looked at her.

After a moment to collect her thoughts, she checked the navigator's panel and said, "I can't give you any definite information either. These instruments are useless."

"Then we'll do it the old-fashioned way," Halvo said, "by sight alone."

"A method that will only be successful," Rolli said, "if the image on our viewscreen is an accurate one."

Halvo said nothing to that. He just grinned and pushed a few buttons on the controls. Then the *Space Dragon* began to move again.

"Without dependable instrument readings," Rolli said some time later, "it will be impossible to discover a planet on which we could land the *Space Dragon* with any hope of survival."

"I suppose there are no space stations in the Empty Sector, are there?" Perri asked. Without waiting for Halvo's response to her question she said, "I have learned enough about navigation to understand that only a narrow portion of the Empty Sector directly borders on the Jurisdiction. If we leave in any other direction we will be outside the galaxy proper, with no hope of ever finding a place for repairs."

"That's right," Halvo said.

"Then why do you keep smiling as if you know a great secret?" Perri asked.

"I know where we can find the space station we need," he said. "Actually, it is a ship that has been placed in permanent orbit, but it has a docking deck large enough to accommodate the *Space Dragon* with no trouble, and if I know my brother, all the supplies we may require will be readily available."

Perri gaped at him, too astonished to speak. However, a robot could not be astonished, and Rolli at once said what Perri was thinking: "Admiral, your statement requires explanation."

"I know it does." Halvo was not only smiling, his eyes were twinkling. "My friends, I am about to reveal a state secret."

"Is that wise?" Rolli asked. "The value of any secret lies in keeping it from the knowledge of all but a chosen few."

"This secret can be kept easily enough," Halvo said. "I can fix your memory banks so you will never reveal what you learn about Dulan's Planet. As for you, Perri, I will accept your word that you will keep the secret."

"You have it," Perri said. "Halvo, how can you have a brother when Jurisdiction law only allows one child to a couple?"

"If you knew my mother, you would not have to ask," Halvo said, chuckling. "How she did it is irrelevant here, but Kalina did obtain official permission to reproduce a second time. My younger brother, Tarik, was the result."

"How can you expect him to help us when we are now outside Jurisdiction space?" Rolli asked.

"Tarik is outside Jurisdiction space, too. He lives here in the Empty Sector." While Halvo's listeners sought for words in response to this unbelievable statement, he went on with his explanation. "Four years ago, the Jurisdiction won a major battle against the Cetans, then made a treaty with them. Tarik, who played an important part in the defeat of that warlike Race, suggested to our father that it would be a good idea to keep a watchful eye on the Cetans so we could be sure they were adhering to the terms of the treaty.

"From a voyage he made just before the Cetan War—a journey that had ranged well beyond the boundaries of the Jurisdiction—Tarik knew of a suitable planet located not far from Cetan space. That planet is here in the Empty Sector."

"Then your brother is one of those you mentioned who returned from this sector," Perri said.

"He is," Halvo said. "Tarik is now the leader of a colony of ten scientists and communications experts who live on a world they named Dulan's Planet. They traveled to it on a captured, refitted Cetan ship that they renamed the *Kalina*, and it is that ship that is now in orbit around Dulan's Planet."

"You knew about this colony, and yet you did not tell us?" Perri cried. "This is why you came directly to the Empty Sector!"

"As I said, the existence of the colony is a state secret. I could not tell you. But now we are in desperate need of assistance, and Dulan's Planet offers the only possible hope for us."

"Do you know the coordinates?" Rolli asked.

"I know where the planet used to be," Halvo said, "though in this sector nothing ever remains stable for long. Still, I think I could find it . . . if we had instruments that were working properly."

"Have you ever been there?" Perri asked.

"No."

"Then what do you suggest we do?"

"The only thing we can do. We begin exploring and hope luck is with us."

Perri wondered if the peculiar effects of the Empty Sector had already begun to attack Halvo's brain. He looked remarkably cheerful. He even whistled a funny little tune as he checked the controls.

"Admiral," Rolli said, but fell silent when Halvo put up one hand for silence.

"Is the food processor working?" Halvo asked a short time later.

"I don't know." Perri looked to Rolli for advice, but the robot's eyelights were fixed on Halvo.

"See if you can get one of those large salads out of it, will you?" Halvo asked. "And some bread, too. I'm hungry, but not close enough to starving to eat a Regulan main course. I may never be hungry enough for that."

Perri did as he bid her. She was glad to get out of the cockpit for a while. With only cockpit and galley usable and the air recirculation system set at minimal level, the *Space Dragon* was beginning to feel like a prison. Perri longed to stand in an open place with no confining walls around her and take a deep breath. Fresh air might help the headache that was bothering her.

To her delight, the food processor was functioning well. It delivered not only the salad Halvo wanted, but a mug of steaming heskay tea for herself and two loaves of dark bread. After piling everything onto a tray, she returned to the cockpit. There she discovered that Halvo and Rolli had effected a partial repair of the navigational instruments.

While the two humans ate Rolli piloted the ship, but Halvo never moved out of the copilot's chair and he constantly monitored what Rolli was doing. Just as Halvo finished his salad and handed the bowl to Perri, Rolli spoke.

"Admiral, there appears to be a star of the type you have described to me—"

"Where?" Halvo's full attention was on the controls, then on the large viewscreen. "Good job, Rolli. A solar system with three planets, one of them with two moons. Yes, this may be what we are searching for. This may be Dulan's Planet."

Chapter Fourteen

Aboard the Jurisdiction ship *Krontar*, a grim-faced Capt. Jyrit paced the bridge, knowing he was about to lose the argument in which he was engaged.

"Jyrit, my friend," Kalina said, "I beg you to try to understand a mother's aching heart. I cannot concede to your insistence that Halvo will never be found."

"Lady Kalina, I do understand your feelings. My own emotions mirror your anguish. Though sadly maimed, your son still had much to live for, much to look forward to in his future life." More than I have, Jyrit added silently to himself. I have little life left at all.

"Jyrit, I do know about the Jugarian rules of

honor," Kalina said. "If the shame of losing Halvo to a kidnapper cannot be expunged by his rescue, then you must die as restitution for his loss. I have grown to know you well, my friend. I suspect you of scheduling your own death for the near future."

"It will be necessary," Jyrit responded, uncomfortably aware of Armaments Officer Dysia's troubled gaze on him as well as Kalina's clear blue eyes. Jyrit knew what Kalina would say next, because Dysia had already said the same thing to him several times. Much as he liked and respected them, they were both women, and Demarians at that. Therefore they could not be expected to comprehend the requirements of the strict code of honor that bound all Jugarian males. Jyrit was the son of a long line of warriors, and he knew what he would have to do.

"It would be sheer ineptitude on your part to take your own life prematurely," Kalina said. "We may still find Halvo. Jyrit, we are so close to the Empty Sector. I think we should search there, too."

"You know as well as I what the law says about the Empty Sector." Jyrit and Dysia exchanged sympathetic glances, both of them realizing that Kalina's suggestion was the last, desperate hope of a parent unable to admit her child was gone, never to be seen again. Out of his affection for Kalina, Jyrit made a decision he knew was hasty and probably ill-advised. But he could not do otherwise. He owed the grieving woman every consideration since her grief was his responsibility.

"What I can do without breaking any law," Jyrit said, "is take the *Krontar* as far as the buoy at the edge of Jurisdiction space. We can get information from the buoy about any ships that have approached that boundary. If there is no data available to show the passage of a ship answering the description of the *Space Dragon*, will you agree to turn back to the Jurisdiction without objection?"

"There are two buoys marking the Empty Sector," Kalina said.

"Very well. We will check both of them," Jyrit said.

"Agreed." Kalina looked almost cheerful.

Several hours after that conversation, the information extracted from each of the buoys by the *Krontar's* communications officer was identical.

"One small ship, similar in description to the *Space Dragon*, has entered the Empty Sector," the officer said. "It was followed by a Regulan war vessel." She continued with technical information about the time of entry and the course taken by each ship.

"Halvo." Kalina spoke the name in a whisper. "He is alive."

"All we know for certain," Jyrit said as kindly as he could, "is that the ship has survived."

"Halvo is in danger, Jyrit." Kalina's voice betrayed her tightly wound nerves. "That Regulan ship can mean no good to him. We must pursue them into the Empty Sector without further delay."

"This is a grave decision, Lady Kalina." But not as grave as ritual suicide, Jyrit thought. If we can locate Halvo and by some unexpected miracle save his life, then I may live to see my wife and child again.

"I have another son, who has established a colony in the Empty Sector," Kalina said. She gave Jyrit a brief expanation about Tarik's settlement on Dulan's Planet.

"I have heard rumors of such an outpost," Jyrit said, "but never anything definite enough to make me believe in it."

"I know the coordinates for Dulan's Planet," Kalina said. "Tarik gave them to me before he left Capital. They are engraved in my heart and in my memory. Let us follow those two ships, Jyrit, and when we can follow them no longer, we will find Dulan's Planet and stop there to visit Tarik. I will tell him myself what has happened to his brother."

Chapter Fifteen

"I did not expect to locate it so soon." Halvo stared intently at the viewscreen. The *Space Dragon* was close enough for those in the cockpit to be able to make out the three planets that Halvo had insisted would be orbiting the star. "You see that the middle planet of this system does have two moons."

"That doesn't mean this is the planet you want to find. Many stars have associated planets, and planets often have moons." Perri was afraid to hope they would reach safety so easily. She was even more afraid of what would happen when Halvo was reunited with his brother, who, she was certain, would not approve of her. "Halvo, Rolli has pointed out that we cannot even be sure the image we see on our viewscreen is a true one."

"We have to believe that it is," Halvo said. "After using Starthruster, the *Space Dragon* is in worse condition than before. The two largest cracks in the hull have increased in size. The life-support system is on the verge of collapse. We need help, and we need it soon. We are going into orbit around that third planet."

"Our sensors indicate a ship dead ahead," Rolli said.

"It's the *Kalina*!" Halvo said. "I would know her anywhere. My brother, Tarik, and I had her refitted to our own specifications before he left Capital with his people. This proves we have found Dulan's Planet. Rolli, try to contact the *Kalina*."

Perri sat back, waiting, a knot tightening in the pit of her stomach. She ought to be as happy as Halvo was that their dangerous journey was almost over. But all she could feel was fear and a sense of impending loss. With a sigh, she turned to her own instruments at the navigator's console.

"We cannot raise the *Kalina*," Rolli said. "The problem appears to be with our own communications system."

"I am sorry to add to our problems," Perri said, "but the Regulan ship is still following us."

"They have crossed into the Empty Sector? They do want us dead, don't they?" Halvo's voice was light, but Perri saw the cold look in his eyes. "Check your instruments again, Perri."

"My readings on the Regulan ship are consistent," she said after obeying his command. She frowned, seeing new information displayed. "I should say my readings on the *first* Regulan ship. There appears to be a second ship following the first—and now I am receiving a third image! Are there three Regulan vessels chasing us? Or could these readings be the result of some distortional effect of the Empty Sector?"

"If it is," Rolli added to Perri's excited remarks, "then my instruments are showing the same distortion. I also note three ships, but I do not believe the third one is Regulan."

"Could it be a Cetan vessel?" The knot in Perri's stomach twisted tighter as she spoke to Halvo. "You did say the Cetan sector is near."

"That is no Cetan." Halvo had the image on the larger viewscreen.

Having seen models and telscan images of similar vessels all of her life, Perri was able to identify the Regulan ships at once. As Halvo sharpened the picture she could see that the mysterious third ship was definitely not Regulan though it, too, was oddly familiar to her. She recognized it just as Halvo spoke again.

"That's the *Krontar*! Now how in the name of all the stars did Jyrit find us?"

Before either Perri or Rolli had time to speculate on the answer to that question, the *Space*

Dragon was rocked by an explosion.

"The Regulans are firing on us," Rolli said, her emotionless voice making the dire statement seem even more terrifying than it otherwise would have been.

"They want us blown into atoms before the *Krontar* can rescue us," Halvo said.

"Now the *Krontar* is attacking the first Regulan vessel," Rolli said.

"With a ship the size of the *Krontar* and the armaments it carries, Jyrit can probably take those two Regulans," Halvo said, "but the *Space Dragon* cannot fight. Nor can we survive even a single direct hit."

"What shall we do?" Perri asked.

"We have to get away from the field of battle," Halvo said. "We don't dare to use Starthruster again. If we try, the *Space Dragon* will break apart."

"Then what?" Perri's despairing cry was punctuated by another explosion.

"That was entirely too close," Rolli said.

"I can't argue with that assessment." Halvo's face was grim. "I think we ought to seek shelter behind the larger moon. I'll take full control, Rolli. This will call for some fancy flying."

The words were not out of his mouth before the *Space Dragon* began to change course. Halvo handled the ship entirely by himself, using only occasional navigational assistance from Perri.

She did not know how he managed to avoid the frequent blasts coming from the Regulan ships. There were a few near misses that rocked their little vessel, and Halvo performed so many twists and turns in direction and so many sudden, breathtaking swoops that Perri's stomach began to protest.

"Admiral," Rolli said, "you are taking an exceedingly dangerous course, which is placing intolerable stress upon an already disabled ship."

"Just a few seconds more," Halvo said. "I want to confuse the Regulans and make them wonder if perhaps they have succeeded in destroying us."

The larger of the two moons loomed on the viewscreen, an airless, meteor-pitted surface that reminded Perri of the small world on which she and Halvo had taken refuge earlier in their adventurous voyage. But on that particular world they could not land with any hope of survival because it had no atmosphere at all. As Perri watched in admiration of his ability, Halvo piloted the *Space Dragon* around the limb of the moon toward the dark side. Just as Perri thought they were safely out of range an ear-splitting blast shook the ship. The *Space Dragon* shuddered. Perri was almost thrown to the deck.

"They got us," Halvo said. "Nicked our tail at the very last second. We almost made it."

"Almost?" Perri cried. "No, we've won. We're still alive, aren't we?"

"Right." Halvo's smile held no humor. "Now all we have to do is reach Home with a ship that is slowly losing both its air pressure and its artificial-gravity system, not to mention the small detail of engines that aren't functioning at full power."

"Home?" Perri echoed, not ready yet to deal with the implications of Halvo's other remarks.

"It's what the colonists on Dulan's Planet call their headquarters," Halvo said.

"If we go there, assuming we are able to reach this Home," Perri said, "we will draw the Regulans right to your brother's doorstep. I cannot think he will be happy about the loss of concealment when secrecy is vital to his project."

"While we are on this side of the moon, communication and sensor scanning from any ship on the other side is blocked out, making us as good as invisible to all three of those ships," Rolli said. "I am certain you plan to use this situation to our advantage, Admiral."

"I do," Halvo said. "Right now, the *Krontar* is probably keeping both of the Regulan ships too busy for them to have time to pay much attention to us, which gives us a slim chance to reach the planet's surface without being closely tracked—and that is our best hope of staying alive and free."

"My knowledge of space flight is still sadly

limited," Perri said. "But from that one book I read, I learned that a vessel entering the atmosphere of a planet must do so at a precise angle in order to avoid being bounced out into space again or, alternately, being burned to a cinder."

"That is exactly right." Halvo cocked an eyebrow at her. "It is your life I am planning to risk, as well as my own, so you deserve a say in this decision. How do you vote?"

"Do it," she said at once. "I trust you, if not the ship."

His eyes held hers for a moment before he turned back to the controls.

It was a bumpy ride, and a hot one. The *Space Dragon's* heat shield, which had been damaged along with other parts of the ship, began to burn away as they entered the planet's atmosphere. They could all see on the viewscreens the resultant smoke, the debris tearing off the ship, and even a tongue or two of flame. The temperature inside the *Space Dragon* rose until Perri and Halvo were drenched in perspiration.

Perri was more terrified than at any other time since her adventures in space had first begun, but she would not let Halvo know it. Teeth clenched against a scream, shoulders rigid, she stayed at her post and obeyed Halvo's terse orders though her clammy hands slipped on the buttons and her damp hair flopped into her eyes and had to be brushed away so she could see.

But the greater part of the heat shield did hold and Halvo's piloting skills took them into the lower atmosphere. The last few loose pieces fell from the shield and the smoke disappeared.

Perri attempted to take a long breath, only to realize how thin and contaminated by foul odors the air in the cockpit was. Halvo, who was intent upon the controls and oblivious to all else, did not appear to notice the air was tainted, and of course, Rolli did not require clean air in order to function.

Considering everything that was wrong with the *Space Dragon*, Perri thought it remarkable that Halvo guided the ship to a safe landing. He used the nearly powerless ship as a glider, skimming over mile after mile of a wide ocean, keeping the *Space Dragon* in the air until Perri had located an island with a flat surface that was large enough to allow the ship to roll to a gradual stop in case the braking thrusters should fail. Which they did, after a short burst that slowed the *Space Dragon's* velocity by only a little.

"You are the most amazing pilot!" Perri was almost in tears from relief when their forward motion finally halted.

"Unfortunately, we overshot our preferred landing spot by far too much," Halvo said. "We are on the opposite side of the planet from where we want to be."

"Perhaps that is not a bad thing."

"Perri, you make me think you don't want to meet my brother," Halvo said.

"I think your brother will not want to meet our Regulan pursuers," she said, deliberately neglecting to add that Halvo's brother would not be happy to meet the woman who had abducted so important a family member.

"We are not likely to meet anyone unless we can make some major repairs," Rolli said, breaking into the conversation. "If you will recall, Admiral, our communications system is not working."

"The air is getting worse, too," Perri said. "I have a headache."

"Bad air is one problem I can easily fix." Halvo went to the entrance hatch and pressed the release button. A moment later a fresh, warm breeze blew into the cockpit bringing with it the fragrance of exotic flowers mixed with a salty tang.

Unable to wait any longer to be free of the confines of the *Space Dragon*, Perri stepped outside. She looked around and then turned to Halvo, who was lifting Rolli out of the ship.

"This is a much nicer place than our last stop." She spread her arms wide as if to embrace the entire planet. "Is that surf I hear?"

She knew—or thought she knew, for the navigational instruments had been increasingly undependable during the last hour—that the *Space Dragon* had landed on the upper left arm of an island shaped like the letter V. Perri stood in a narrow, sloping meadow that ended in an abrupt drop. The meadow was dotted with flowers in brilliant shades of clear yellow or blue or striped red and orange. A few dainty white blossoms were scattered here and there among the brighter colors. The wild grasses were intensely green. Off to the south was a dense forest, and beyond the trees on the southern horizon a line of high mountains reared upward, their tallest peaks capped with snow. On the other three sides of the meadow lay a purple-green sea. The sky was a blue so dark it was almost purple and the sun—the same star that had shone pure white when seen from space—was a glorious, warm orange and much larger than the Regulan sun.

"I want to see what is over the edge," Perri said. She started forward, only to have Halvo catch her arm to stop her.

"Go slowly," he said, "and carefully. We don't know what—or who—is beyond that drop in the ground."

"Then come with me." Pulling away from him she continued across the meadow, following the downward slope of the land.

"Perri, come back," Rolli said. "I must warn you that you are set upon a possibly hazardous course."

"What harm can there be in walking across a meadow?" Perri said. "We have just escaped a fiery death. I want to relax for a few minutes."

"She's right," Halvo said to the robot. "Happily for you, you are not capable of experiencing the fears that Perri and I have known over the last few hours. Humans need a while to recuperate after coming so close to death."

"Admiral, my programming compels me to protest. This is not the time for frivolity. The *Space Dragon* requires immediate repair."

"The ship may not be reparable."

Rolli had more to say to both Halvo and Perri on the subject of taking responsible action, but Perri was no longer paying attention. She was still alive when she had fully expected to be dead. Possessed by a sudden sense of complete freedom, she broke into a run and did not stop until she reached the edge of the meadow.

The gently sloping land ended in a cliff that was steep but only about six feet high. Below the cliff was a sandy white beach that curved around the northern end of the island. A short distance away a stream splashed over the cliff and across the beach. On the ocean side of the island, where the cliffs were much higher, waves roared onto the sand, great, foam-flecked curves of greenish water that slid back again into the sea, only to return with renewed force. The tip of land where Perri stood curved slightly inward, and beyond a wide bay of calmer water sheltered by the land she could see the mist-shrouded eastern arm of the island.

"I wouldn't advise you to swim here," Halvo said, coming up behind her and catching sight of the roiling sea. "There will be an undertow and rip currents in a place like this. Swimming will be safer down there." He waved an arm toward the more southerly reaches of the bay, where the beach gradually widened and the water was quieter.

"Dangerous or not, it is beautiful!" Perri said. "I can smell salt in the air. Halvo, do you think there are sea animals that we could eat? I don't think the food processor is going to work much longer, if it is still working at all. We are going to be hungry if we stay here for more than a few hours."

"We might find edible shellfish along the water's edge." Halvo squinted against the sunlight reflecting off the water. "The cliff dips just to our left. It will be easier to get to the beach from there. Shall we try a bit of exploration?"

"Right now?"

"Why not? There isn't much we can do to protect ourselves if we should be attacked, but we might discover something useful down there on the beach."

"Like a cave where we could hide?"

Halvo smiled at the memory, then shook his head. Taking Perri's hand in his, he began to walk toward the spot where the cliff was not so high.

"Unless we put a moon or a planet between

us and them, there is no place where we can hide and be truly safe from Regulan sensors," he said. "All we can do is wait and hope that Jyrit dispatches those two ships quickly, before they can find and capture us. Then Jyrit will send out a search party to look for us. Our task is to survive until he does and to stay with the *Space Dragon* so the job of locating us will be easier."

"Could the Regulans win against the *Krontar*?" Perri looked toward the sky. It was difficult to imagine the battle taking place beyond the atmosphere. From where she stood, Dulan's Planet was an entirely peaceful place, its serene sky holding nothing so threatening as a single cloud. The first of the twin moons was just visible, rising over the eastern arm of the island. Perri stared at that silver moon, recalling how close to it they had been only a few hours ago and how uninviting its surface was. From her present perspective the moon was a lovely, soft counterpoint to the bright sun.

"Jyrit is a born fighter, and his is the larger and better-armed ship. He will defeat those Regulans."

Having reached his goal, Halvo sat on the lip of the cliff to look downward. Perri copied him. Behind them, they could hear Rolli's metallic voice still calling out warnings to Perri.

"Why didn't your father build Rolli with legs instead of wheels?" Halvo asked. "With legs, a robot is much more mobile."

"Rolli was intended for use inside a house or on city streets while shopping," Perri said. "That is how Regulan women are expected to spend their time. My father never envisioned either Rolli or me traveling off-planet. Personally, I am very glad we have done so." She paused while Halvo lowered himself to the sand. He put up his arms and Perri jumped into them.

"I shouldn't have done that," she said at once. "Your back—"

"Is not troubling me at all," Halvo said, finishing the sentence for her. Still with his arms around her, he lifted his head, breathing deeply. "This air is wonderful. You are wonderful. What a shame that this cannot be a vacation for us."

"Perhaps until we are found it can be." She knew they ought to be on the alert for attacking Regulans or for a search party from the *Krontar*, but with the clear air of Dulan's Planet filling her lungs and Halvo's strong limbs pressed against her, Perri could not make herself worry about practical matters. Her arms went around Halvo's neck almost of their own accord. Her fingers slid through his dark hair. Halvo lowered his mouth to hers. In his kiss was all the sheer joy of being still alive after so many dangers faced, so many desperate risks overcome. Perri gave herself up to him, refusing to let herself think about what would very likely happen when they were found. Halvo might not blame her for abducting him, but whoever rescued them surely would.

"Are you hungry?" Halvo broke away, holding her only by her hands. "Shall we look for food as you suggested?"

He had told her more than once that it was a Demarian custom to joke and tease at the beginning of lovemaking, in order to prolong the anticipation and thus increase the ultimate delight. Perri was not sure whether that was truly a custom of his homeworld or whether it was Halvo's personal preference, but it was a most effective method of luring her into a sensual encounter. Looking into his eyes she saw his desire and his humor, and she knew that, delay though he might, before much longer he would be deep inside her, carrying her with him to a rich fulfillment they would share together. When she gazed into Halvo's eyes all other concerns fled from her mind. Only Halvo mattered, only his passion. And her passion for him.

"What do you think we will find?" She gave him a teasing smile to match his own before breaking away to hasten toward the water's edge. "Could there be shellfish or crabs on this planet? Dare we hope for seaworms? Are they indigenous to most worlds with salty seas?"

"Ah, I had forgotten for a moment the deplorable Regulan taste in main courses," he said. "No doubt you will expect me to eat several varieties of seaplants along with sliced, raw worms."

"Certainly not," she said, laughing at him. "We will cook the seaplants before we eat them."

But the only seaplant they discovered was a single, long strand of brown material that had been washed onto the sand and dried by the blazing sun. There were no seaworms to be found in the damp mud below the tide line and no shellfish of any kind. They did notice a few large fish leaping out of the distant, deeper water from time to time.

"Not having fishing gear or a boat to take us out onto the bay or the open sea, we cannot catch them," Halvo said with a sigh of hunger and longing.

"I fear we are going to be reduced to eating the bread that was left over from our last meal out of the food processor," Perri said.

Her stomach was empty, but she was not really thinking about food. All during their search along the seashore Halvo had made a point of touching her often, of taking her hand or tucking a strand of windblown hair behind her ear or letting his fingers trail down her spine whenever he stopped her to point out some new aspect of the landscape.

"Perhaps we should return to the ship," Halvo said at last. "Rolli will be burning out her circuits in worry and frustration because we have been out of sight for so long."

Perri's heart plummeted in disappointment. She had assumed that at some point they would lie down upon the soft, warm sand to make love. She wanted Halvo so badly. There was a familiar heat building inside her, the result of their prolonged, private stroll along the shore and his continual gestures toward her.

Was she mistaken? Did he not want her? Had she misinterpreted casual touches as preliminary caresses? She was not experienced enough to be absolutely certain what his intentions might be.

Having returned to the spot at which they had first descended to the beach, Halvo boosted Perri up, then hauled himself to the edge of the cliff to sit beside her with their legs dangling downward.

"I haven't been this relaxed in years," he said.

"I am glad to know you are happy," she snapped. "I, on the other hand, am still hungry."

"I want you to be starving," he whispered, leaning closer. "Aching with emptiness. Absolutely ravenous. As I am."

She could only stare at him, her emotions seething, her cheeks uncomfortably warm. She would have leapt to her feet to run away from him, but Halvo prevented her from moving. He did not take her hand or her arm. He simply placed one of his hands on her knee, then let it slide slowly up her inner thigh.

"You are playing a game with me," she said.

"It is no game, I assure you. Perri, you have been trained to gratify a man's need instantly, with no regard for what you might want. I would like you to begin to appreciate the full range of possibilities between a man and a woman."

"Another Demarian custom?" She sounded spiteful, but she did not care. Looking down at him she could see that he did want her. She lifted her own hand to lay it on him.

"The custom of a man who cares about his woman," he said mildly. Catching her hand before it could make contact with his eagerness, he lifted her fingers to his lips. "Self-restraint can be exciting. Don't you agree?"

How could cool gray eyes hold so much heat? How could a quiet voice throb with tightly leashed passion? Halvo got to his feet, pulling Perri up with him.

"I do think it is about time to put Rolli to bed for the night," he said, "since I prefer privacy." Still holding Perri's hand he began to walk across the meadow to the *Space Dragon*, where Rolli stood beside the ship, watching them.

Perri held back, dragging on Halvo's hand until he paused. The day was drawing to a close, the sun sinking lower in the western sky, while both moons had risen. Over the sea a soft purple haze was forming and on land the shadows were growing longer and deeper.

"Do you think they will come for us tonight?" Perri asked.

"I hope not." His teeth flashed white. "I intend to feast on stale bread and stream water. And on you. I have been dreaming all day of your shining hair strewn across those pale blue sheets in my cabin."

"What?" Perri cried, thinking his words were yet another piece of teasing. "Even when you were saving us from the Regulans?"

"Especially then," he said. "I thought about your soft body and your hot kisses—and your impatient eagerness—and I knew it was not time for us to die just yet."

"Oh, Halvo." She could see how serious he was and her heart melted, every bit of irritation with his delaying tactics vanishing in a wave of tenderness.

"My sweet, precipitous enchantress, can you wait just a little longer?" he asked.

"I will try," she whispered, "though my knees may give way at any moment."

"My own problems lie in other areas," he murmured, his face alight with laughter and another, warmer emotion that sent a thrill through her and made her tremble.

Halvo's method of putting Rolli to bed consisted of pushing the disconnect button, after which he and Perri lifted the robot back into the *Space Dragon*, settling it in the cockpit for the night. That done, Perri expected Halvo to take her in his arms at last and lead her to his cabin or hers.

"A bath is next on the schedule," he said, peeling off his jacket as he spoke.

"A bath," Perri said blankly. Her own hands were at her belt buckle in expectation of immediate disrobing. She tried to remind herself that Halvo had his own ways of doing things, but she wanted him. She was quivering with longing. And he knew it.

"There is plenty of water in the stream." His eyes were glittering when they met hers.

"That water is icy cold," she said.

"Stimulating."

"Admiral, you are a sadist." She saw the smile he quickly repressed as he stepped toward her.

"Actually, I have recently become something of a sensualist." He wound his hands through her hair, pulling her closer. She put up both hands to fend him off and they landed on his bare chest. Beneath her fingertips she could feel his strong heartbeat.

"If you grow cold in the water, I will discover a way to warm you quickly," he promised.

"Couldn't we just stay warm, as we are right now?"

"We were both overheated during the landing," he said. "A bath will be refreshing."

"Will it stiffen your resolve?" Pushing away from him, Perri headed for the private cabins. Behind her she heard his full-throated laughter, but he did not follow her as she hoped he would.

"My resolve is firm enough already." Halvo moved to the exit hatch. "Don't be long, Perri. Daylight is waning fast."

To her own surprise she thought of a clever response to his words, but she did not make it. She was not used to jokes and teasing, and she was not yet certain just how far she could go with Halvo. More than that, she was startled by the workings of her own mind. Halvo was bringing out a sense of humor in her that she had not known she possessed.

In her own cabin she undressed, and then, recalling Halvo's remarks about the blue sheets, she pulled the top sheet off her bunk and wrapped it around herself in lieu of a robe. She had no personal belongings with her except the clothes she wore by day. All of her intimate needs—cleansers, comb, tooth cleaners, and such—came from the regulation supplies kept in all spaceships. For the first time, Perri wished those supplies included perfume and face paint.

On leaving the ship a short time later she discovered that both moons were high in the sky, though the sun was still shining above the horizon, sending long rays of orange-gold light across the sea, turning the foaming whitecaps to gold and touching the land with mellow late day warmth.

The air was still soft and warm, but the

stream was cold and shallow. Halvo stood in rushing water up to his knees with his back to Perri. She dipped a tentative toe into the water and shivered. The stream wended its way across the meadow from the higher land in the south and after feeling it Perri was convinced the water had only recently melted from the ice and snow on the tallest mountains. Undeterred by the chill, Halvo was splashing water about, washing himself with his hands.

Perri dropped the blue sheet and got into the stream. At once her teeth began to chatter, but she went to her knees and stuck her head under the surface, then began to scrub at her hair. She had to admit it was an invigorating experience, especially when Halvo noticed her presence and came to help her. His hands were gentle on her back, sliding along her spine, downward to cup her hips. He pulled her against him and though the rest of him was as cool as Perri's own skin, the rigid part that prodded at her buttocks was deliciously warm.

With Perri leaning against his chest, Halvo's hands slipped around to caress her abdomen before moving upward to her breasts. There he played until Perri was gasping and it seemed to her the stream must be boiling. Halvo's lips were on her shoulder and her throat, her head was thrown back against his shoulder, her hips were writhing. When he let his hands slide downward again, across the water-slicked skin of her abdomen and into the heated place between her thighs, Perri cried out her raging need.

"So soon?" he murmured, tasting the edge of her ear with his tongue. "Well, then, if you insist."

"I must insist? If I did not want you so much, I would hate you," she said, pulling away from him.

"It is your uncontrolled passion I find so irresistible." With an unexpected swoop of his arms he lifted her off her feet and lightly set her upon the grass before climbing out of the stream himself.

Perri stared at him, surprised by his easy movements, waiting for the inevitable complaint about his back, but all he did was bend to spread out the sheet she had dropped. Halvo lay down on the sheet, waiting for her. Perversely, she decided to make him wait. Realizing that her long hair was dripping, Perri began to twist it, squeezing the water out onto the grass.

"When you are ready, come to me," Halvo said, his patience apparently still intact, though his readiness was indisputable. "Come freely because you want what I can give you and because you want to give me what I so desire."

How could she hesitate when her every sense urged her to throw herself upon him, when she was half mad with the need to feel his hardness inside her?

"You are under no obligation to me," he said.

She tightened the coil of her hair in an absentminded way, wringing from it the last few drops of water while she regarded his naked length stretched out in the blue twilight. Awaiting her. Wanting her. Refusing to take her unless she wanted him, too. And she understood that while he could find physical release in her, for him there would be no soaring joy unless she was with him in heart and mind when they came together.

"There is no greater gift than the gift of freedom," Perri said, falling to her knees beside him. "Halvo, my longing for you is a constant ache, not just in my body, but in my heart, too." Perhaps she should not have said so much. She thought she saw a shadow pass over his face at her words. Or perhaps it was only the deepening evening light.

Putting out one hand she let her fingertips trace the contour of his mouth. His eyes reflected the silver glow of the moons above them.

"I want to be one with you," she whispered. "It is my wish, my own true desire. There is no coercion in what I do here. I only ask that you wait no longer, for if you delay, I think I will faint and then I will be of no use to either of us."

With a broken laugh he seized her in his arms and rolled with her across the sheet. Her hair came undone from its tight coil and lay in dark, damp strands over the pale fabric. As the sun sank lower there was a growing chill to the early evening air, but Halvo's mouth was warm and his hands seemed dipped in fire when he caressed her. And then at last the empty, aching place in her was filled with Halvo's hot, masculine strength. Perri's hands clutched his shoulders, her lips opened to his thrusting tongue. Her hips moved in rhythm with his, slowly, gently at first, but after a while with a hard need, a wild, ecstatic passion. Her cry rent the still night, followed immediately by Halvo's shout of triumph. And for a little while they were truly one, joined in freely chosen joy.

Perri lay beside Halvo, looking up at the heavenly dome above them. The moons hung side by side at the very zenith of the dark sky, their combined light washing the meadow with silver, making the water in the stream glitter as it flowed.

The scene was so peaceful and Perri was so relaxed and content that at first she paid no attention to the fluttering movement just at the corner of her vision. When it happened again, she turned her head with a lazy sigh, expecting to watch a cloud drifting across the sky to partially obscure one of the moons. But the undefined shadow was too low to be a cloud, and it was moving too rapidly. There was more than one shadow. Squinting against the direct moon-light, Perri watched the strange objects for only a moment more before she nudged Halvo.

"Wake up," she whispered urgently. "Something is coming. I can't see it—them—clearly. Halvo, do you hear the noise?"

"Where?" He was wide awake and on his feet in an instant.

Perri could see that there were three objects flying across the sky. They appeared to be heading directly toward the meadow. The noise they made told her what they were, but recognition did not lessen her fear. Her eyes still on the sky, she scrambled to her feet.

"Birds?" she cried, moving into the protection of Halvo's arm. "I have never seen birds so huge. They must be dangerous."

"I do not think so." Halvo was amazingly calm. "My brother told me once about the birds that live on this planet. They are intelligent and telepathic."

"That's impossible!"

"Not on this world. In the Empty Sector few things are impossible." Dropping his arm from her shoulder Halvo said, "Stand a little apart from me and hold out your hands as I am doing."

"Why?" Perri was still afraid the giant birds would prove to be enemies. Now that they were closer she estimated that, if one of the three were to alight before them, it would prove to be

281

as tall as Halvo. She could not guess how wide the wings were.

"So they can see what we are," Halvo said. "Think of an island in the middle of a lake, Perri. Think of a settlement called Home."

"I don't know what the colony looks like," she cried.

"It doesn't matter. Just concentrate your thoughts. The birds ought to receive some sort of message from us, and they may pass the message on to Tarik."

She tried to do as he wanted. She tried to think of the birds as friendly creatures, though their size frightened her. She fought to overcome her distaste for the very idea of telepathy, which was forbidden within the Jurisdiction. Nor could Perri deny her reluctance to be discovered by Halvo's brother. Still, this was what Halvo wanted. For his sake, she would do as he asked.

Slowly the birds circled the meadow, turned, and came back, flying closer to the ground on this second pass. Perri imagined the lead bird was aiming itself directly at her to attack her. Near panic, she forced herself to think of a peaceful lake with an island in the middle of it. There would be trees on the island and a beach, perhaps a shuttle to ferry the colonists from the island to the spaceship *Kalina* in orbit above.

She could see it! As the lead bird flew over her head, coming so close to her that if she had the courage to do so she could have reached up and touched its green feathers, there came into Perri's mind a vivid picture of a lake, an island, even a gray Jurisdiction shuttlecraft sitting on the white sandy beach. There was a round white building in the very center of the island, with a row of white columns along its circumference and a domed roof above. Then the birds and the picture were gone. Perri saw the three winged shapes soaring off toward the east. She stared at them, transfixed, until they had disappeared into the night.

"Perri?" Halvo touched her arm. "Are you all right?"

"It was green," she said in a slow, low-pitched voice.

"Two of them were. The third was blue. You don't have to be afraid of them. According to Tarik, they are friendly unless you display violent behavior."

"I am not afraid." It was true. She was filled with wonder, with awe and amazement, but she was no longer afraid. She spoke with complete assurance. "They will tell your brother you are here."

"I believe they will," Halvo said. "We should return to the *Space Dragon* now."

"Yes." Still in a strangely peaceful daze, Perri caught up the sheet and wrapped it around herself, while Halvo collected his trousers.

Once inside the ship he closed and sealed the

entrance hatch, which for ventilation purposes had been left open since just after their landing. By now the air inside the ship was clean, though it remained several degrees warmer than the breezy temperature outside.

They retired to the cabin Halvo had been using during their travels. There, as she drifted toward slumber, Perri was aware of Halvo's fingers combing through her hair, spreading it out across the sheet, and then of his mouth warm and tender on hers, before he laid his head into the curve of her shoulder and closed his eyes.

Chapter Sixteen

Standing beside the shuttlecraft from the *Krontar*, Armaments Officer Dysia stole a quick look at her surroundings. The sun was a remarkably bright shade of orange, the air was cool enough to make her shiver in her uniform jacket, but the trees covering the island, though mostly bare, appeared to be normal. Nor, so far as she could see, was there anything unusual about the blue water in the lake or the white beach and the striated brown rocks scattered about the shore.

Never had Dysia dreamed of entering the Empty Sector, much less of actually landing on one of the mysterious planets within the forbidden area of space, yet there she was, with both of her booted feet firmly planted on a world where, if the legends about the Empty Sector were to be believed, anything might happen. However, at the moment it appeared as if the first thing that was going to happen would be a family quarrel.

"And so there are two Regulan warships in orbit above us, waiting for you to discover what this female pirate has done with Halvo?" There could be no doubt that Tarik was angry. His handsome features were marred by a frown and his fine, dark blue eyes were colder than the autumn wind off the lake. With a single companion at his side Tarik had come to the shore of his island headquarters to greet the shuttlecraft in person. His delighted surprise at finding his mother aboard had quickly changed to outrage when he heard the story that Kalina, Capt. Jyrit, and Dysia had to tell him. But his anger seemed to be directed more toward his mother than toward the villains in the shocking tale. "You knowingly led those Regulans here? How could you do this?"

"Do not take that superior tone with me." Kalina shook a finger at her son. "You look and sound just like your father when he is annoyed."

"I am far more than annoyed, Mother. You, of all people, know how important complete secrecy about the existence of this outpost is to the success of our treaty with the Cetans. Let them hear one word of our presence so near their space, one single hint that we do not completely trust them to live up to the terms of that treaty, and they could take offense and start another bloody war and claim it is the fault of the Jurisdiction. Yet you have brought not only a Jurisdiction vessel to Dulan's Planet, but two Regulan warships as well!"

"I will not be lectured by you, Tarik. We have just explained why we are here. Halvo is still recuperating from his injuries and beyond any doubt he is in danger. I intend to rescue him and take him back to Capital, where he will receive the best possible medical care to correct whatever further damage has been done to his already fragile health by that malicious creature who kidnapped him."

"Fragile? Halvo?" Tarik gave a harsh laugh, to which Kalina responded with a stern look.

"I would do the same for you if you were lost and injured, Tarik."

"I know you would, Mother. I am not jealous, only amused by the way in which you persist in regarding your grown sons as children in need of your help." Tarik's troubled expression cleared enough to allow a smile, and he put his arm around his mother. "Which reminds me that you have not yet seen your grandson. Come inside while we prepare for the search. Capt. Jyrit, Lt. Dysia, you are both welcome, too."

As Tarik drew his mother toward the round white building at the center of the island, Kalina came face-to-face with the man who had accompanied her son to the shore, whom Tarik had introduced simply as Osiyar. Kalina looked him over with great interest and Dysia, whose previous attention had been on the conflict between mother and son, spared her first full glance for that person.

Osiyar was blond, with sea-blue eyes and a perfectly chisled, remarkably handsome face. Between his burnished eyebrows was a small blue tattoo in the design of twin crescents facing each other, the crescents topped by a round blue dot. Dysia thought he was the most intriguing-looking man she had seen in years.

"We have not met before," Kalina said to Osiyar, "but I do know who you are. Your name was in one of Tarik's reports. You are the native telepath."

"That is true, Lady Kalina." The man responded to Kalina's curiosity with a charming smile. "Tarik has admitted me to his colony— and to his friendship."

"Yes, I know." Kalina looked into Osiyar's eyes with no trace of fear. "I have never met a telepath before."

"Tarik has told me of your efforts to have the Jurisdiction Act of Banishment against telepaths rescinded," Osiyar said. "For that kindness I thank you in the name of all telepaths."

"It is not kindness. It is a matter of common sense." Kalina put out her hand and Osiyar took

Lady Lure

it. "Perhaps you can be of use to us in our search for Halvo."

"I hope so, Lady Kalina."

The appearance of the First Lady of the Jurisdiction in their headquarters building was greeted with surprise by the colonists and with open joy by her daughter-in-law, Narisa.

"How I have missed you," Narisa cried, hugging Kalina. "You know most of the grownups, of course. Now come and meet the children." Kalina went readily, laughing and talking with Narisa as they caught up on family news.

"I never thought to see such a sight," Jyrit murmured to Dysia a short time later. His eyes were upon Kalina, and Dysia had been watching her, too. The usually dignified First Lady of the Jurisdiction, clad in a bright red tunic and trousers, was down on the floor playing with her grandson, a toddler with his father's black hair and intense blue eyes. A second boy with orange-red hair and golden eyes, whom Narisa had introduced as the child of colonists Suria and Gaidar, was with them and it was obvious that the two children were close companions. Taking off her gold necklaces, Kalina draped one around the neck of each child. The boys pulled and twisted the shining links, clearly delighted with these new toys.

"At the moment, both Suria and Gaidar are on duty aboard the *Kalina*," Narisa said to her mother-in-law.

"What a pity. I would like to see them again. I think of Gaidar as my third son," Kalina said. "Were it not for Gaidar taking us far away from Capital at a crucial time, Almaric and I might not have survived the Cetan War and the revolution that finally brought us to power. And now look at this handsome boy he has fathered. Gaidar must be very proud, and Suria must be as happy as she has always deserved to be."

However much she might enjoy playing with her grandson and her friend Suria's child, or reminiscing about dramatic events of the past, Kalina could not afford to forget her primary mission for long. An hour after landing at Home, she and Tarik, Jyrit and Dysia, along with a few of the colonists, held a conference on the course they should take.

"Our battle with the Regulan ships did not last long before they agreed to a cease-fire and negotiations," Jyrit said to the group. "I have tried to convince the Regulan captains that we believe the *Space Dragon*, which was badly disabled by Regulan fire, burned up during entry into the atmosphere. I am not certain they believe me, but they made no strong protest when I announced my intention to accompany Lady Kalina to the surface to meet with her remaining son and tell him of the death of his brother. In hope that we could complete our search for the missing ship before the Regulans begin their own, I emphasized that mother and son would want to comfort each other and thus we would be here for some time."

"But you do not believe Halvo is dead." Osiyar's eyes bored into Jyrit's, making the Jugarian openly uncomfortable until the telepath moved his gaze to Kalina.

"We do not," Kalina said very firmly. "Halvo is an experienced space pilot. If he is physically capable of handling a ship, then there is a good chance that he survived. We will find him, Tarik. We must. I cannot leave him to the mercy of that despicable pirate."

"It is only fair to tell you before you agree to join our search, Cmdr. Tarik," Dysia said, "that while we were on Regula we learned that this woman, Perri, does not know how to pilot a ship. It was being done entirely by her robot."

"Which means," Tarik said in a carefully controlled tone that did not completely hide his distress at the possibilities he was forced to consider, "that if Halvo was not well enough, or if he was not allowed near the controls, then the *Space Dragon* may have burned in the upper atmosphere or, if it did not burn, it may have crashed with loss of life."

"Exactly." Jyrit spoke over Kalina's renewed protest that her son must be alive. "Furthermore, we do not know where on Dulan's Planet we might find the *Space Dragon*—or if we will discover any evidence of the ship at all."

"Nevertheless," Kalina said, using her most

authoritative voice to break into the discussion of practical realities, "we will search the entire planet if need be."

"Why in the name of all the stars did this Perri woman head for the Empty Sector?" Tarik asked.

"We do not know," Jyrit said. "The Regulan captains appear to be as honestly baffled by the course taken by the *Space Dragon* as we are. Nor do I think they have been given much information by their Hierarchy."

"That would not be surprising." Tarik looked even more worried than before. "The Regulan Hierarchs are always up to something secretive. We may never learn the entire truth about their motives."

"I do not care what their reasons are," Kalina said. "I just want to find Halvo."

After some further discussion it was agreed that in addition to a direct search of the planet by shuttlecraft, planet-wide surveillance would also be conducted by Gaidar and Suria from the ship *Kalina*. Tarik would pilot one of the colony shuttlecraft, taking with him Kalina, Osiyar, and Herne, the colony physician.

"Capt. Jyrit," Tarik said, "you and Lt. Dysia ought to return to the *Krontar* to keep an eye on those Regulan ships."

"My first officer knows what to do," Jyrit said. "I will add my shuttlecraft to the search. If you wish to send more of your people along, they may come with me."

"It really isn't necessary," Tarik said.

"This is a matter of personal honor," Jyrit said, his pale gray face hard, his antennae beginning to turn red with emotion.

"He will not change his mind," Dysia said. "Nor will I. I will follow my captain until he orders me to return to the *Krontar*. You cannot get rid of us, Cmdr. Tarik, so do not try." She knew her own face was almost as set and hard as Jyrit's.

"I will not try. I appreciate loyalty. And I admit I will be glad of the extra ship. With it, the search should only take half as long." Tarik paused, then spoke again. "Do you know from which direction the *Space Dragon* entered the atmosphere? The information might give us some clue as to where to begin looking."

"As soon as we were near enough to establish instrument contact, our communications officer put a continuous trace on the *Space Dragon*, but she lost contact when the *Space Dragon* entered the lower atmosphere. Here." From her belt pouch Dysia pulled a small disk. "I made a duplicate of the trace record and brought it with me in case there was something on it that would be useful to you."

While Tarik ran the data disk through the colony computer, with Kalina hovering over his shoulder and offering a steady monologue of advice, Osiyar broke away from the group in the main room. Dysia had been watching the telepath, and when he walked across the room to the entrance, she hastened to follow him. Osiyar had such a strange look on his face that as she went through the door after him Dysia pulled her hand weapon from her belt. At once Osiyar halted, but he did not turn around. Dysia stopped, too, just a pace or two behind him.

"Do you imagine I will attack you?" Osiyar asked with some humor. "Or perhaps call up an enchantment upon you and your captain? Or worse, enter your mind and learn all of your thoughts?"

"Would you?" Dysia's hand trembled a little, but she kept the weapon trained on Osiyar.

"By a law the telepaths themselves made centuries ago, I am forbidden to enter anyone's mind without express permission," Osiyar said. "The only allowable exception occurs when use of my power is necessary to save a life."

"I did not know that."

"You of the Jurisdiction know little of my kind. It is not your fault. Most telepaths left the Jurisdiction or were killed because they would not leave long before you were born." Osiyar did turn then to smile at Dysia and shake his head at her weapon. "Did you sense that I was receiving a message? Is that why you followed me?"

"You had a peculiar look on your face. What

message? Are the Regulans up to something we should know about?"

"Not the Regulans. If you will put away your weapon, you may come with me. The Chon do not like weapons of any kind. Centuries ago, too many Chon were killed by Cetans using similar weapons."

"The Chon?" Mystified by the unfamiliar name, Dysia lowered her weapon.

"They are large birds." Quickly Osiyar explained about the intelligent, telepathic creatures. When he headed for the opposite side of the island, a fascinated Dysia went with him.

They came out of the trees onto a rough beach, with the lake spread before them. In this northern hemisphere it was autumn, and so the few leaves still clinging to the trees that in places grew right down to the water's edge were brown or gold, with an occasional flash of scarlet. In the far distance a single, snowcapped mountain rose. Not far from the island and to the left of where they stood reared a sheer stone cliff.

"That is where the Chon live, in those caves," Osiyar said, pointing to the cliff.

Some of the birds were fishing in the lake. A few were in the air, circling the island. As Dysia watched, one of them detached itself from the others to land on the beach just a few feet away from Osiyar. With a faint rustling sound the bird folded its wings and stood quietly regarding the two humans.

Dysia caught her breath. Never had she seen a bird so large or so beautiful. Its feathers were green as the finest jewel, its bright, dark eyes were undeniably intelligent, and its manner was perfectly calm when Osiyar approached it. The telepath put out a hand to lay it upon the bird's smooth breast, and the bird allowed it. Osiyar's eyes closed. There was silence on the beach, yet Dysia was aware of a humming vibration in the air.

That was telepathy in action. With her Jurisdiction training, Dysia should have been disgusted or frightened. Instead, she was thrilled by the simple, apparently quite natural demonstration of an awesome power. She stood perfectly still, listening to the hum, feeling the vibration, until Osiyar broke his physical contact with the bird. Man and bird separated, each standing quietly, Osiyar with his head bowed as if in deep thought. After a few moments the bird spread its wings and, with a graceful flutter, soared away across the lake. With its departure, Osiyar appeared to go limp. Dysia hurried to him.

"May I touch you?" she asked, reaching toward him in case he needed to lean on her. "Are you ill? Is there anything I can do to help you?"

"Thank you for your concern. I would not

have expected it from a member of the Jurisdiction Service."

"We are not all oafs and bigots," she said rather sharply.

"No, you are not." His sea-colored eyes seemed to pierce to her very soul. She was not even offended when he did not use her official title. "I am not ill, Dysia. It is only that when I break my communion with one of the birds, it takes me a moment or two to adjust my thoughts, to recall that I am only a man, who cannot fly as they do, who cannot remember each detail of a complicated scene after but an instant's glance at it."

"I suppose there are benefits to being a bird."

"Indeed." Osiyar chuckled. "There are times when I wish I were one of the Chon."

"You can't mean that!"

"Of course not." But Osiyar's smile was mysterious. "We ought to return to the others. I have learned a few facts that will be of use to Tarik and your Capt. Jyrit."

As they turned back toward the headquarters building and began walking along the path they were met by a dark-haired, intense-looking woman.

"Here is Alla, my mate," Osiyar said, introducing the woman, who immediately slipped her hand into the crook of his arm in a possessive way.

"I have just witnessed an amazing demonstration," Dysia said to Alla, forcing herself to squelch the irrational sense of disappointment she felt at the unexpected introduction. She did not know Osiyar. There could be no connection between them. A friendship with a telepath could only be detrimental to the career that meant everything to her.

"How lovely for you." Alla began pulling Osiyar along the narrow path, leaving Dysia to walk behind them. "Osiyar, my dearest, do hurry. Tarik is eager to leave as soon as possible."

"Don't worry about me," Dysia muttered, believing they were far enough ahead so they could not hear her. "I can find my own way." Feeling decidedly left out, she was only partially cheered when Osiyar looked back to smile at her as if in apology for Alla's rudeness.

"That is all of the information conveyed to me by the birds," Osiyar said a few minutes later when he, the still clinging Alla, and Dysia had all rejoined the group in the headquarters building, where preparations for the search were nearly complete. "The Chon have confirmed that the *Space Dragon* did land safely. The man and woman outside the ship appeared to be in good health."

"I thank all the ancient gods of Demaria for that." Kalina closed her eyes for a moment, "Osiyar, did the bird tell you anything more about Halvo? About his physical condition, perhaps?"

"No." Osiyar paused. "There was something strange though. The bird was aware of the woman's attempt to make contact with it."

"A Regulan telepath? Impossible!" Kalina scoffed. "More likely, that scurrilous pirate was planning to harm the bird in some way and the bird sensed it. At least we now know in which direction to search."

"The birds will fly with us," Osiyar said. "This will not be the first time they have guided us to a rescue."

"Then let's move," Tarik said, heading for the door. "We want to reach Halvo before the Regulans take it into their heads to begin a search of their own—if they haven't done so already. Jyrit, I assume you are still coming with us? If so, I will send my men, Reid and Pelidan, along in your shuttlecraft in case we need reinforcements."

There followed a purposeful bustle as the last of the medical supplies, weapons, and food and water were loaded onto the waiting shuttlecraft. Kalina insisted on being as well armed as the other members of the expedition.

"I remember that you do know how to use one of these," Tarik said, handing her a weapon. "Just choose your target with care. Until we find them, we can't be absolutely certain of the identities of those two people the bird discovered.

We only have the word of the Regulans that they are Halvo and his captor. You don't want to make a hasty mistake."

"I won't." Kalina tucked the weapon into her belt. "But I give you fair warning, Tarik. If the second person on the *Space Dragon* proves to be the same dreadful young woman who kidnapped my poor Halvo, I may personally end her miserable life before the Regulans can get their hands on her!"

Chapter Seventeen

Perri knew she was dreaming, but she could not make herself wake up, no matter how hard she tried. In her dream she was back in space, in the badly damaged *Space Dragon*, and she was all alone, not even Rolli was with her. It was taking all of her energy and her newly learned piloting skills to keep the ship steady while she rocketed through the star-strewn blackness. Most of the instruments were malfunctioning and she knew she could not continue much longer. Already the *Space Dragon* was losing speed. Soon it would stop altogether. Then, while she lay helpless and unable to defend herself, her pursuer would overtake her.

She could see his face on the viewscreen, and

she could hear his laughter mocking her efforts to escape him.

"What do you want with me, Elyr?" she shouted at his image. "I am gone from your life. I will never return to Regula. Why don't you leave me alone?"

"You know why not," he said in the maddeningly superior way he habitually used with her. "The answers you want are in your own mind. If you would pause to think, Perri, instead of constantly asking futile questions, you would understand everything."

"I understand that you never loved me," she cried. When he shrugged as though his love or lack of it were of no consequence, she added, "I tried so hard to love you because my parents wanted us to marry. I thought I had succeeded, but I know better now. I tried to love you, Elyr, and I was always completely loyal to you. But in spite of your solemn and unbreakable oath to take me as your wife and cherish me, you were loyal only to yourself."

"Oaths are made to be broken," Elyr said.

"If that is so, what good are they? Who can believe in any promise? Elyr, you disgraced both of us when you put me into a position in which I was forced to become a pirate in order to save your life," Perri said. "You were willing to see me killed without any chance to defend myself. Worse, you would have seen Halvo killed, too, because he would never have kept silent about what he knew of your plot. Why, Elyr? Why did you do it?"

"Halvo should have remained ignorant of the truth," Elyr said. "You were instructed to tell him nothing. You never could obey orders properly, Perri. It is a great fault in you and most unwomanly."

"Your complaints about me cannot hurt me anymore. Answer me, Elyr! Why did you and the Chief Hierarch concoct this plot against me? Why did you include Halvo?" When Elyr's only response was another maddeningly indifferent shrug, Perri screamed at him, "Before you kill me, I have a right to know why I am dying. Why? Why?"

"You think it was all about you, but as usual, you are wrong," Elyr said with a smile that degenerated into a smirk. "It was Halvo. Pirates and Halvo, you stupid girl."

"Pirates?" Perri said. "I don't understand. What are you saying, Elyr? What pirates? Where? Elyr! Elyr, answer me!"

"Perri, wake up!"

A hand was shaking her gently; a supportive arm was around her shoulders. Perri went trembling into Halvo's secure embrace.

"You were having a nightmare," he said. "You were screaming about Elyr and pirates."

"He was going to kill me. Halvo, he still wants me dead. I know it." Clinging to him, shaking from a terror she could not dismiss, Perri recounted her dream. "He will kill you, too, if he can."

"Hush," Halvo said. "It was only a dream."

"On Regula, we believe dreams have meaning," Perri said. "That book I read about space flight spoke of the dreams inflicted on travelers in the Empty Sector, dreams more real than reality, dreams that can drive the most stable personalities into madness. Is that what is happening to me? Was my nightmare the effect of being here in the Empty Sector?"

Perri sat up straight, pushing herself out of Halvo's arms, leaving him to lie upon the narrow bunk while she looked wildly around his cabin, trying to reassure herself that the walls were solid, that there were no other strange effects occurring.

"Or was it the bird?" she whispered. "When that huge bird flew so close to me I saw something, Halvo—a scene clear in my mind. Am I going mad?"

"You are more likely suffering the aftermath of severe, prolonged stress," Halvo said. When he tried to pull her back into his arms Perri stiffened her spine and refused to accept the comfort he was offering.

"Elyr said pirates," she repeated. " 'Pirates and Halvo, you stupid girl.' Those were his exact words."

"You are not stupid," Halvo said. "Just the opposite, in fact. Perri, is it possible that while you

were with Elyr before you left Regula, you overheard something or saw something that he
might fear would put him into jeopardy if you
were to reveal what you had learned?"

"Elyr kept me ignorant of the most important
aspects of his life," she said. "I spent my days
inside his house or in its garden, with his
mother and the servants, and they did not speak
freely to me. I was always aware of their re-
serve. They never told me what Elyr was doing
when he left the house, never explained what I
needed to know about—about intimate matters." She paused, blushing a little.

"So you have said." Sitting up beside her,
Halvo linked his fingers into hers and Perri did
not resist the gesture. "With Elyr a secretive
type and everyone in his household being so
cautious, it is unlikely that you could have
stumbled on anything he did not want you to
know. What about contacts outside his home?"

"I seldom left the house," Perri said, "and then
only with Elyr's mother or her most trusted
maidservant, and also with Rolli in attendance.
I was protected from all unpleasant influences.
That is what they called it. At the time, I believed they meant well and I accepted the restrictions. Now their protection seems to me
like a form of imprisonment."

"It was," Halvo agreed. "All right, then. As
sources of forbidden knowledge we have just
eliminated Elyr, his mother, their servants, and

what they would doubtless consider pernicious outside influences. If Rolli knew anything she would have said so long ago in hope that together she and I could keep you safe from Elyr and the Chief Hierarch. Which leaves your interview with the Chief Hierarch himself. Did he say or do anything that struck you as unusual?"

"The entire interview was unusual, beginning with his consent to see me."

"Think, Perri. Did he mention pirates?"

"Well, of course, he did. I have told you so before, Halvo."

"Tell me again. Exactly what did the Chief Hierarch say?"

"That you had received superficial wounds while commanding the winning side in a battle against pirates on the Styxian border. But now a pirate was going to win against you, because I was to pose as a pirate while abducting you and carrying you off to Regula. But he told me lies. I have learned that your wounds were not superficial. They were terrible. And I know the Chief Hierarch's intentions toward me were dishonest."

"What was your reaction to the idea of pretending to be a pirate?" Halvo asked.

"I thought it was a bad joke," Perri said, "but at the time, I believed he wanted me to have a credible disguise. Later, after I learned it was all a trick and he and Elyr were using me for their own purposes, I thought the Chief Hierarch must be hoping the Jurisdiction government would believe that pirates really were responsible for your abduction and thus would not blame Regula for what happened to you."

"I am sure that line of reasoning was part of it." Halvo considered for a moment before continuing slowly, as if he were thinking out loud. "Pirates. Yes, I did wonder earlier. . . . "

"Wonder what?" Perri asked.

"Let me think about it a little more. I promise I will tell you what my conclusions are, as soon as I reach them."

"I trust your promises," Perri murmured, at last allowing him to draw her down on the bed beside him. "Yours and no one else's."

Some hours later Perri stepped outside the *Space Dragon*, pitcher in hand, heading for the stream. With only a few crumbs left from their supply of bread, water would be their breakfast that morning instead of the cups of hot, steaming qahf, the fried blueflour bread, and the broiled darahfish eggs for which she longed. Halvo was planning to work on the communications system and when it was repaired—assuming it could be repaired—he would move on to the food processor.

"If I need to work on it at all," he called through the hatch after her. "We may be rescued before we have a chance to starve."

"If a rescue is to happen before I starve," Perri

said, putting a bit of teasing into her voice, "it will have to happen within the next hour."

Laughing in response to his sympathetic chuckle, she looked up toward the sky. There was not much to see. The bright weather of the previous day had given way to a bank of thick fog, which had rolled in from the ocean during the night. All Perri could see was the area immediately surrounding the *Space Dragon*. No birds would fly that day, and searchers relying on visual contacts would have a difficult time finding the *Space Dragon*.

As she walked in the direction of the stream Perri could hear the surf, muffled by the fog, and she heard Halvo talking to Rolli as if the reactivated robot were a close personal friend. There were no other sounds, at least not until she was returning from the stream. Then what she heard made her hasten to the *Space Dragon*.

"Halvo, do you hear it?" Her empty stomach forgotten, she set the filled water pitcher down in the galley and hurried into the cockpit, where Halvo and Rolli were taking the communications system apart in preparation for their repairs to it.

"Hear what?" Halvo lifted his head, listening. "That's a shuttlecraft, coming in low."

"Can you tell by the sound whether it is your brother or—"

Perri could not finish the sentence.

"They all sound pretty much alike. We'll have

to wait until we can see it. Stay inside, Perri." Halvo went to the entrance hatch and stared out at the fog. Perri was right behind him. The noise grew louder until, as if stirred by the approaching ship, the fog parted and a brown shuttle-craft not much bigger than the *Space Dragon* emerged. Seeing it, Halvo's mouth tightened.

"I can read those markings." Perri pressed closer to Halvo. "It's a shuttlecraft from one of the Regulan ships."

"If the Regulans were able to find us," Halvo said, "then Jyrit's people cannot be far behind. We have to stall for time until they get here."

"How?" Perri asked.

"I will go out and talk to them. You stay hidden. Perhaps I can convince them that you have left me and fled toward the south, where those thick woods are. If they decide to search for you, their plans will be delayed—whatever their plans might be."

"They will only have to use their sensors to know I am aboard the *Space Dragon*," Perri said.

"Any delay, even a few minutes, could be crucial to us," Halvo said. "Please, Perri, trust me."

"I do trust you." She moved away from the hatch when Halvo went through it. "But I do not trust the Regulans."

"What are you doing?" Rolli turned from the controls to fix blue eyelights on Perri.

"Arming myself." Perri took up the hand

weapon that had been issued to her back on Regula at the start of her adventure. "Rolli, how are the repairs on the communications system coming along? Could you at least get a homing beacon working?" Nothing could help her then, but if Halvo's brother, or a shuttlecraft from the *Krontar*, could locate them before the Regulans took them captive, then Halvo might be saved. It was the most Perri dared hope for at that point.

"The Regulans can block all communications from the *Space Dragon*," Rolli said. "We were hoping to send out a message before they found us."

"Then I am going to fight." Perri glared at Rolli. "Don't you dare tell me it will be a dangerous course. It is the only thing left for us to do."

"As always, I am compelled to warn you of danger," Rolli said. "However, your decision makes sense. To go into Regulan custody would be more dangerous than open defiance."

"I am glad you agree, because you couldn't stop me," Perri said.

By that time, Halvo was standing outside the *Space Dragon* and half-a-dozen men in the plain brown uniforms of the Regulan Space Service had alighted from their shuttlecraft and were approaching him. All of these men had gold or red hair and the usual green Regulan eyes. All were strangers to Perri, a fact which did not surprise her, since she had not been allowed to meet many Regulan men. Being careful to keep out of sight, Perri peered around the edge of the hatch opening.

"I am Admiral of the Jurisdiction Fleet Halvo Gibal." Halvo took a step toward the Regulans, who stopped as he approached. "I assume you are here to offer your assistance."

"We are under orders to return you to Regula," the Regulan leader said.

"Thank you for the hospitable offer, but that won't be necessary." Halvo spoke pleasantly and even smiled. "All I need is a little help with repairing my ship."

"It is a stolen Regulan ship."

"Is it indeed?" Halvo feigned surprise. "Well, then, Captain—"

"Capt. Mirar." The identifying words were snapped out in a brisk manner and Capt. Mirar stood stiff and unbending, his face serious. Perri could tell he was puzzled by Halvo's easy, unafraid attitude.

"A pleasure to meet you." Politely, Halvo inclined his head. "I admire your daring in venturing into the Empty Sector, since you must be aware that it is forbidden territory."

"You are here."

"True, and most inadvertently, I assure you. I was thrown off course by a defect in my navigational system. Otherwise, even the Admiral of the Fleet would not presume to break Jurisdiction law." Halvo's last words took on a distinct warning edge and Capt. Mirar shifted uneasily.

"Where is the woman, Perri?" he demanded.

"Who?" Halvo spread his hands. "As you can see, I am quite alone—and unarmed." Those words were said with a glance at the hand weapons held by Mirar and all of his men.

"You are not alone. Our sensors show two humans aboard the *Space Dragon*."

"Really? Well, Capt. Mirar, you may be right. However, I do feel obliged to point out to you the interesting fact that, here in the Empty Sector, reality is not always what it appears to be."

"What do you mean?" Mirar took a menacing step toward Halvo. Seeing him move, Perri took the safety catch off her weapon.

"Surely, Captain," said Halvo, "you have noticed how undependable your ship's systems have become?"

"I have noticed nothing of the kind," Mirar snapped. "You have delayed me long enough. Step aside and let my men search your vessel."

"By whose authority?" Halvo asked, his voice cool, his demeanor commanding.

"By my authority," Mirar growled, his face beginning to flush.

"Must I remind you, Captain, that I am an admiral?"

"Bah!" Mirar's mouth twisted in disdain. "You have been retired, invalided out of active duty. I take my orders from the Regulan Hierarchy. Get out of my way, Admiral!"

It was then that Rolli spoke. The robot had moved nearer to Perri and like her remained hidden just inside the entrance hatch.

"There is another shuttlecraft coming," Rolli said. "The sound is similar to that made by the first one."

"Has the second Regulan ship also sent out a landing team?" Perri asked. "Or is this one from the *Krontar*? Well, it doesn't matter. Halvo will continue to try to delay this Capt. Mirar, and if Mirar or his men try to hurt Halvo, I know what to do."

"I believe Capt. Mirar is growing impatient," Rolli said. "Perhaps he, too, is aware of the approaching shuttlecraft."

At the moment, Capt. Mirar was standing almost nose to nose with Halvo, attempting to stare him down. Halvo was not moving an inch from his position blocking the entrance hatch.

"Men," Capt. Mirar said, "take him!"

Halvo raised an arm to fend off the hands of the Regulans who were reaching for him. Perri saw him go white and stumble, putting his hand to his head instead of hitting one of his opponents. Perri knew Halvo's dizziness had returned. There was no time to think about how inconvenient his weakness was. She could wait no longer. Halvo's life was in danger. Perri stepped into the hatch opening. Lifting her hand weapon she aimed it at Capt. Mirar and fired. At once she ducked back into the ship.

Her fire was returned. A blast sizzled through the hatch to hit the opposite bulkhead and send white-hot sparks flying around the cockpit.

"More damage," Rolli said. "If this keeps up, we may never complete repairs to this ship."

Perri wasn't paying much attention to the robot. Instead, she was worrying about Halvo. She wanted to go to him, but she decided she might be of greater help to him if she stayed hidden for a while longer. Halvo was picking himself up off the ground while three Regulans held their weapons pointed at him. Nearby, Capt. Mirar was cursing and clutching his left arm where Perri had inflicted what looked like a minor, if painful, wound.

By then everyone near the *Space Dragon* could hear the engines of the arriving shuttlecraft. Capt. Mirar looked up, searching the fog for a sign of it, and several of his men also craned their necks to see what was approaching. By the murmuring among them, Perri decided they were afraid it would prove to be a shuttlecraft sent out from the *Krontar*.

The noise grew louder and a dark shape could be seen, lowering itself slowly to the ground. It came to rest right next to the Regulan shuttlecraft. When the hatch opened, a Jugarian male appeared, followed by a dark-haired human female. Both of them were wearing the dark blue

Jurisdiction Service uniform and both held weapons in their hands. Behind them, two other human shapes waited in the hatchway.

"Jyrit, my friend! Lt. Dysia!" Halvo called. "I knew you would find me."

"Good day to you, Admiral." Jyrit's antennae flared an agreeable orange red, but then turned a darker, warning red as he spoke to Capt. Mirar. "Tell your men to put down their weapons. I am here to take Admiral Halvo back to Capital."

"And I am under orders to take him to Regula," Capt. Mirar said.

"Jurisdiction government orders supersede the routine orders of planetary governments," Jyrit stated firmly.

"Your admiral is traveling with a known criminal!" Capt. Mirar shouted.

"He is not doing so voluntarily," Jyrit said. Pointing his weapon at Mirar's heart, Jyrit added, "Adm. Halvo will now step into my ship."

"He will not!" Mirar's own hand weapon was aimed at Jyrit's abdomen, where the most vital Jugarian organs lay.

"Why don't we all put down our weapons?" Dysia said. "Then we can talk about the problem calmly."

"Be silent, woman!" Capt. Mirar said. "You may not speak unless a man gives you permission."

"Don't talk that way to a Jurisdiction officer." From the *Krontar's* shuttlecraft one of the men in civilian clothes came to stand beside Dysia. The other went to back up Jyrit.

"I knew they were good men when Tarik chose them," Halvo said softly to no one in particular. Perri heard him.

"Those two are from your brother's colony?" she asked, speaking to him through the hatch. "Then he must be searching for you, too."

"I believe Tarik is about to join us." In spite of the threat the Regulans presented, Halvo seemed to be enjoying himself hugely. When the sound of a third shuttlecraft broke loudly through the fog, Halvo's grin nearly split his face.

Two men stepped from this new shuttlecraft, one black of hair, the other blond. Both were strikingly handsome. The two looked around at the tense scene; then the black-haired man walked to where Jyrit and Capt. Mirar were still standing.

"I suggest that you end this contest now," the new arrival said. "Regulan, if you do not put away your weapon and tell your men to do the same, the full force of the *Krontar* will be turned upon your two vessels in orbit. I need not tell you what will happen to those ships or to their crews. And your landing team will be left here, at the mercy of Capt. Jyrit."

"I am honor bound to obey my orders," Mirar said.

"Just exactly what are those orders? And who gave them to you?"

"I am to return Adm. Halvo and the woman, Perri, to Regula. By order of the Chief Hierarch. I dare not fail." Mirar gestured to his men. "Take Halvo under guard to the shuttlecraft and confine him there. Then search for the woman."

"I will not allow that!" Jyrit's fingers tightened on his weapon.

Capt. Mirar was faster. He fired right at Jyrit. The Jugarian crumpled to the ground. A split second after Mirar fired, Dysia fired, too, hitting Mirar in his already wounded left arm. Then the air was filled with the crackle and sizzle of hand weapons. Perri tried to get out of the *Space Dragon* to reach Halvo, but repeated weapons fire pinned her down just inside the open hatch.

The conflict lasted for only a minute or two before the Regulans were standing with their hands on top of their heads while the men from Jyrit's and Tarik's shuttlecraft searched them for concealed weapons. Mirar was the only Regulan who had put up a real fight, and he was one of three who were slightly wounded. The sole serious wound had been sustained by Jyrit. Dysia and Osiyar bent over him.

"Is Halvo safe now?" Jyrit asked in a weak voice.

"Yes," Dysia said, "all of the Regulans have been captured."

"Then my honor is redeemed. I die at peace." Jyrit looked as if he were dead already. His gray skin had faded to a chalky white shade and his antennae were beginning to turn a pale, translucent blue, the color of death.

"Herne!" Osiyar shouted. "We need you here."

"Get out of my way." A large man elbowed Dysia aside and knelt by Jyrit. Dysia recognized him as Herne, the colony physician. "I said clear off so I can work."

"His bedside manner certainly leaves something to be desired," Dysia said to Osiyar, who took her elbow to help her rise.

"His concern for his patients makes him forget his manners," Osiyar said, "but Herne is an excellent physician. If anyone can save your captain, Herne will do it."

"Is there something you could do?" Dysia met Osiyar's blue eyes. "Jyrit thinks he owes his life in forfeit for what happened to Halvo. Someone ought to change his mind, to convince him to fight to stay alive. The Service needs officers like Jyrit."

"Let Herne do his best first," Osiyar said. "Then if Jyrit consents, I will try to help him."

"Thank you," Dysia whispered. "He is a good captain."

"And you are a good and loyal officer—and friend." As if he had just become aware of his hand still on Dysia's elbow, Osiyar released her and stepped aside.

"Tarik," Herne said, "we are going to have to take Jyrit back to Home. I am going to need the operating room there and Alla's help. And, possibly, Osiyar's," he added under his breath.

"We have a fully staffed hospital aboard the *Krontar*," Dysia said.

"We don't have time to take him there," Herne said. "It's Home, or he dies."

"Then do it your way." Dysia made the decision at once. "Osiyar and I will go with you."

"Reid, Pelidan, bring the stretcher on the double," Herne called.

Within a very few minutes the *Krontar's* shuttlecraft took off, bearing Jyrit away.

During all of those preparations, Halvo had stayed where he was leaning against the *Space Dragon*, trying to regain his balance. When Perri made a fresh move to leave the ship and help him, he ordered her to stay inside in a voice that permitted no disobedience. But with the brief battle over, the Regulan prisoners secured, and Jyrit on his way to good medical care, Tarik stalked toward the *Space Dragon*. He stopped a few feet away, planted his fists on his hips, and stared at his brother.

"Will Jyrit live?" Halvo asked, straightening to a fully erect stance.

"Probably. Herne knows what he's doing." Tarik's eyes narrowed. "I thought I was the brother who always got into trouble."

"Well, it was your turn to rescue me, Tarik," Halvo said.

"You aren't armed," Tarik said. Inclining his head in the direction of Capt. Mirar, he asked, "Before we got here, who shot the Regulan captain?"

"I did." Weapon still in hand, Perri at last left the *Space Dragon*, stepping from the hatch to stand beside Halvo. Tarik's eyes went wide and Perri could see he was trying to repress a smile.

"I should have known," Tarik said to his brother, "that, if you were ever kidnapped, it would be by a beauty. For a badly wounded man, you look remarkably healthy."

"Thank you," Halvo said stiffly. "It's good to see you, too."

"You actually came here in this?" Tarik kicked at the hull of the *Space Dragon*. "This laundry tub?"

"She's not a bad little ship." Halvo laid an affectionate hand on the hull. "With a few repairs and a new program in her food processor, I could take her almost anywhere. She comes equipped with an interesting robot and a fine copilot."

"I didn't know Regulan women were allowed to touch the controls of any machine." Tarik gave Perri a searching look.

"They aren't," Halvo said. "I taught her myself."

"You had that much patience with her?" Tarik chuckled.

Perri had been watching and listening to their conversation with growing bewilderment. Like most citizens of the Jurisdiction, where the law limited all but a few couples to one child, she had no experience of sibling behavior. She had expected Tarik to embrace his brother and say how glad he was that Halvo had survived both his battle wounds and the mad voyage across the galaxy. Their cool discussion of the condition of the *Space Dragon* and of Perri's own piloting abilities was beyond her comprehension. Nor could she understand why Tarik turned on Halvo, speaking in a voice suddenly fierce with emotion.

"Now, Admiral, would you care to tell me why you broke security and not only intruded into this space but led three other ships here as well? How dare you endanger my colony? What possible justification could you have for giving the Cetans a chance to abrogate their treaty with the Jurisdiction?"

"What is there to explain?" Halvo looked toward the Regulans. "My reasoning is obvious."

"Not to me, nor to the people on this planet whom you have put into harm's way," Tarik said.

When Halvo only shook his head at this accusation, Tarik clenched his fists. With the speed of a lightning bolt he threw a punch at

Flora Speer

Halvo. Halvo's own hands shot up to block the blow. Wrist pressed against wrist, the brothers stood glaring at each other, breathing hard, looking as if they were ready to kill.

"Stop this at once!" A sturdy, red-clad figure hurried from Tarik's shuttlecraft toward the *Space Dragon*. "Can you two never meet without quarreling? Tarik, leave your brother alone. Can't you see he is unwell?" In fact, Halvo had gone pale. Breaking away from Tarik, he stepped back a pace to lean against the ship once more, as if he were dizzy again.

"Mother," Halvo said with a gasp, "what are you doing here?"

"Looking for you." Kalina, having subjected her older son to a thorough inspection, turned her attention to Perri. "I assume you are the despicable creature who abducted my son. Tarik, take her into custody at once. I am surprised that you have not done so already."

"Actually," Tarik said, "I have been waiting to discover what Halvo wants me to do with her."

"Perri stays with me—and no one touches her." Halvo gave his brother a warning look, to which Tarik responded with raised eyebrows but no protest.

"In that case," Tarik said, "the most immediate question is, what do we do with these Regulan captives? I have no wish to take them to my headquarters. The less they see of Dulan's Planet, the better. But if we turn them loose and

322

send them back to their ships, they may attack us in their determination to get their hands on you, Halvo, so they can follow their orders to return you and Perri to Regula."

"Intern them on the *Krontar*," Kalina said.

"No," Halvo said. "That might only precipitate another battle in space. I have a better idea. We will tell them the truth about their orders."

"Do you know what it is?" Tarik asked. All of his previous antagonism toward Halvo appeared to be gone, a change that mystified Perri.

"I have begun to suspect a complicated plot," Halvo said. "An intrigue typical of the Regulan Hierarchy and one that extends far beyond Regula. If I am right, Perri has been used as a pawn because her life was considered expendable."

Halvo walked across the rough grass to where Tarik's men, Reid and Pelidan, stood guard over the captured Regulans. Halvo spoke loudly enough for all the prisoners to hear him. "Capt. Mirar, I assume that you are aware of my part in uprooting the pirates who once menaced shipping in the Styxian Sector?"

"I have heard your name mentioned," Mirar said. "What about it?"

"Have you in the Regulan Space Service noticed an increase in piratical activities since they were driven from Styxia?"

"There have been some reports." Mirar

frowned. "But very few Regulan ships have been taken."

"I would be surprised if Regulan interplanetary commerce were suffering much," Halvo said. "However, if you were to do a little research, you might discover that other, nearby planetary systems have been having a problem. It would be quite natural for pirates driven out of one sector to move on to another and to draw to themselves fellow outlaws until soon the pirate bands are as large as before. For now they are hunting in a sector they find more welcoming than Styxia ever was."

"What are you suggesting?" Not only did Halvo have Mirar's full attention, but all of his men were listening intently, too.

"I have been out of commission for more than a year," Halvo said, "so I have no proof of my suspicions. You would know better than I, Capt. Mirar. Although, now that I think about it, I do seem to recall Capt. Jyrit mentioning that pirates have recently become a serious problem just outside the Regulan Sector. Pirates require a safe haven where they can shelter between forays. And being barbarian by nature, they do like to avenge themselves rather crudely upon those whom they believe have done them harm. For example, against Jurisdiction Service officers."

"Of course!" Kalina said, when Halvo paused to let his words sink in. "That is why Elyr has married the Chief Hierarch's daughter. And why Cynri was so worried about him. Whatever else she was up to, Cynri was genuinely concerned for Elyr."

"I beg your pardon?" Halvo stared at his mother.

"Elyr has married?" Perri cried. "But he cannot while I am still alive."

"It is perfectly simple," Kalina said, ignoring Perri and speaking to Halvo. "All you have to do is think like a Regulan—a Regulan man, to be precise—and then it all becomes clear. Capt. Mirar sees it. Don't you, Captain?"

"I am afraid I do," Mirar said. "And I am deeply troubled. Adm. Halvo, I owe you an apology. It was wrong of the Chief Hierarch to assign Regulan ships to capture you and even more wrong of me to follow orders blindly. My excuse must be that I honestly believed this woman, Perri, had abducted you for her own evil purpose and that my mission was to return you to Regula, where Perri would be punished under Regulan law. Then with much ceremony the Chief Hierarch would set you free, thus earning great acclaim for Regula from the Jurisdiction government. This is what I believed when I set out to find you, Admiral. Now I think that after you were taken to Regula you would have been turned over to the pirates. I could not allow such a fate to befall any man."

"Thank you, Capt. Mirar." Halvo put out his

325

hand and Mirar clasped it.

"Be assured that Perri will be punished for what she has done," Kalina said to Mirar, "but by a Jurisdiction court. I will personally see to it."

"We will discuss Perri's future later." Halvo brushed aside his mother's threat. "Capt. Mirar, I have something to show you." Reaching into his belt pouch, Halvo pulled out the clear specimen container he had kept in that safe place. He held it up so everyone present could see the tiny red triangle inside it.

"Do you know what this is, Capt. Mirar?"

"I do." Mirar was white to the lips. "Where did you get it?"

"I removed it from the main circuitry of Perri's personal robot. I believe it was meant to destroy the *Space Dragon*, the robot, Perri—and me."

"Tampering with a robot is against Regulan law." Mirar put out a shaking hand. "One of our primary rules is that robots must never be allowed to impinge upon the safety of the humans they serve. Admiral, I promise I will deliver this device to my superior officer."

"I believe you would, but I cannot give it to you." Halvo replaced the container in his belt. "I will require it for evidence when I reach Capitol. But you have seen it with your own eyes, Mirar, and these men of yours are also witnesses that the device does exist. Your combined word ought to be sufficient."

"Admiral, you cannot keep us captive after these revelations. We must return to Regula to tell what we have learned."

"I believe you should do so as soon as possible," Halvo said. "If Lady Kalina and Cmdr. Tarik have no objections, you are free to leave."

"Go," Kalina said. "Only leave this wicked girl in my custody."

"Certainly," Mirar said. "Perri can only cause more trouble if she returns to Regula."

"I place one condition on your immediate release," Tarik said. "Capt. Mirar, you are aware of the violent tendencies of our new allies, the Cetans. In the interest of maintaining peace, I must ask you to order your men not to mention the existence of our outpost here."

"I understand completely. It is in Regula's best interests to keep peace with the Cetans, since we have an important commercial treaty with them. Those men who have remained aboard our two ships will be told that we of the landing team discovered nothing but an uninhabited world. Contradictory sensor readings will be blamed on the well-known effects of the Empty Sector. And no man who stands here today will say a word of anything he has seen or heard. Is that agreed, gentlemen?" Mirar looked his men over, meeting each one's eyes. Every man nodded his head or said yes aloud.

"Thank you, Capt. Mirar." Tarik shook hands

with the Regulan. "You are free to go."

Perri watched Mirar and his men board the shuttlecraft and lift skyward before she spoke.

"You cannot trust the word of a Regulan man," she said to Tarik.

"I know," he said. "But in this case, I think it is safe to make an exception to that wise rule. Those men know that, if word of this colony gets out, the Cetans will refute their peace treaty with the Jurisdiction. And the second place the Cetans will attack on their violent sweep toward Capital will be Regula."

"What will be the first place?" Perri asked.

"Here," Tarik said. "They will begin by destroying Home."

Chapter Eighteen

"We need to take the robot with us." Halvo turned to Tarik's men. "You two, carry it aboard the shuttlecraft."

"Halvo." Tarik's voice was firm. "I am leader here."

"The robot has vital information in its memory banks," Halvo said. "Rolli can verify my reasons for trying to find Dulan's Planet and why, having located it, we were forced to land here. Perri and I do not leave this place without Rolli. I will not argue the point."

"Reid, Pelidan," Tarik said, his eyes still on Halvo's face, "secure the robot in the cargo bay."

"The habit of command dies hard," Halvo

said. "No offense meant, Tarik."

"None taken." In a softer tone Tarik added, "I am glad to see you again."

"You two love each other," Perri cried, beginning to understand, "yet you are in competition."

"We always have been," Tarik said.

"We always will be," Halvo added.

"You would die for each other," Perri insisted.

"Let us hope it will never be necessary." Tarik turned from his brother to Perri. "Is there anything you want from the *Space Dragon*?"

"Nothing but Rolli," Perri said. "I have no personal belongings."

As the three of them walked toward the shuttlecraft, Perri asked, "What will happen to the *Space Dragon*? Will she just be left here to rot?"

"I would like to see her repaired," Halvo said.

"That little ship reminds me of the first one you ever piloted," Tarik said to his brother.

"The one in which you stowed away." Halvo's voice was stern.

"And which you let me fly for a few minutes," Tarik said.

"You nearly killed us. You were only a child and you did not know half as much about spaceships as you tried to convince me you did."

"I knew you would save me, Halvo."

On a wave of masculine laughter they

reached the entrance of Tarik's shuttlecraft. Kalina was already aboard waiting for them, and she was not amused.

"This dreadful girl ought to be secured in the cargo bay along with her robot," Kalina said.

"Perri sits with me," Halvo said.

"Halvo, I was hoping you would lend Perri to me for the duration of this flight." Tarik interrupted smoothly when Kalina began to protest that she wanted Halvo to herself for a while. "Since Osiyar returned with Jyrit and Herne, I lack a copilot." Behind his mother's back, Tarik winked at Perri.

Kalina did not argue about the sudden elevation in Perri's status. Within a few minutes Halvo and his mother were sitting side by side, Reid and Pelidan were strapped into seats behind them, and Tarik and Perri were at the controls in the bow.

"Cmdr. Tarik, you should have been a diplomat," Perri said.

"Never." Tarik laughed. "I cannot tolerate long, boring ceremonies and I despise vague language. I do know what a strain it has been for our mother not to be able to care for Halvo herself. She could not leave Capital when he was wounded and so she was forced to depend on reports from his doctors instead of going to him, as any loving mother would want to do. Let her spend an hour or so with him now."

"You all have very strong personalities," Perri

said. "Do the members of your family quarrel often?"

"Quarrel, no. Disagree frequently and vigorously, yes. Unlike serious quarrels, our disagreements seldom last long. You will get used to us."

"Do you think I will be allowed time to do so?"

"For Halvo's sake I hope so." Tarik glanced at her, then at the control panel. "You look a bit perplexed, but these controls are not very different from the ones on the *Space Dragon*. Just watch me and you will catch on quickly."

Perri thought he was one of the kindest men she had ever met. He had defused an uncomfortable moment with Kalina, and he was treating her as if she were a friend instead of an enemy who had harmed his brother.

"There they are," Tarik said, in a manner suggesting he had just seen someone he expected to meet.

"Who?" Perri asked.

"The Chon. See them there on the viewscreen?"

"Birds!" Perri exclaimed. "There were huge birds flying over the island."

"Yes, I know. They guided us to you, but they stayed well away from the fog bank. Without their help, we might not have found you before you were forced aboard the Regulan ship. Now the birds have rejoined us for the return flight."

"Halvo told me about them." Perri hesitated

for a moment, deciding, then plunged on, instinctively knowing she could trust this man as she trusted his brother. "When the birds flew close to us, I saw a vision, a picture in my mind. There was an island in a lake and a white building with columns."

"Home," said Tarik. "My headquarters. When we approach it, see if you recognize it. If you do, talk to Osiyar, the blond man who was with me earlier. He understands the birds better than any of the rest of us do."

"Thank you. I will." Perri was silent, thinking for a minute. "What will happen to me?"

"That depends on you and Halvo. May I give you some advice?"

"Please do."

"Don't be afraid of my mother. She is fiercely protective of her menfolk because she loves us so much, but she is a reasonable person. She has even been known to change her mind about certain people."

"She hates me," Perri said bleakly. "I cannot blame her for it. I blame myself for what I did to Halvo."

"I don't think he blames you. Halvo looks remarkably happy to me."

The conversation broke off as Tarik set the course and spoke over the communications link with someone at his headquarters. Once during the ensuing flight Perri twisted around in her seat to look at Halvo. He was deep in talk with his mother. Perri feared they were discussing her future.

"Watch the screen, now." Tarik interrupted her troubled musings. "We are approaching Home. Does the scene look familiar to you?"

"It is the same place," Perri said. "I am not mistaken, yet it is different. I saw it differently."

"You saw it through the bird's eyes."

"Does this mean I am a telepath?" Perri sounded as horrified as she felt.

"I don't think so. My wife, Narisa, has had several similar experiences and she is certainly not a telepath, just an unusually open-minded and sensitive person, as I suspect you are."

Home was a beautiful place. Standing on a beach of fine, pale sand, Perri looked around with pleasure, noting the crystal-clear lake edged by a thick forest. In the very center of the island stood a round white building that, with its row of columns and its domed roof, radiated serenity. At least a dozen blue or green Chon flew above, circling the island as if to welcome Tarik and his companions. The orange sun shone a cheerful afternoon light upon the scene.

"Tarik, did all go well?" A slim, brown-haired woman hurried onto the beach, where Tarik's party was disembarking from the shuttlecraft. "Herne is still operating on that poor Jugarian. I hope no one else was hurt."

"Three Regulans took minor wounds, but they have gone back to their ship. The rest of us are unharmed." Tarik embraced the woman, kissing her tenderly.

"Narisa." Halvo came up to the couple. Breaking away from Tarik, Narisa threw her arms around his brother.

"Halvo, it's good to see you looking so well." Narisa turned her gaze upon Perri, whom Halvo drew to his side with one arm about her waist while he introduced the two women.

"You are both welcome here." Narisa's response was a bit cool, and Perri thought she knew why. From the way in which Narisa and Kalina were greeting each other, Perri could tell they were close. No doubt Kalina had used her previous visit to Home to voice her low opinion of Perri to her daughter-in-law.

When Tarik offered to show Halvo around his island headquarters, and Kalina and Narisa moved off together toward the white building, Perri held back. Reid and Pelidan were removing Rolli from the cargo bay. Perri went to them.

"Where are you taking my robot?" she demanded.

"Tarik wants it in the central room." They were not unfriendly. In fact, they were quite pleasant to her. Perri allowed herself to relax a little, even to smile at the man who had spoken. He was Reid, and he was one of the communi-

335

cations officers for the colony, though he did not seem to mind the purely physical duty of transporting Rolli, to which any Regulan male of similar rank would have objected.

"Is there anything special we should know about Rolli?" Reid asked.

"Just be careful of her."

"Her?" Reid nodded. "I take it she's an old friend."

"The dearest one I have." Perri almost said Rolli was the only friend she had, but she thought of Tarik before she spoke. She believed he was a friend, though she did not delude herself that he would defy his formidable mother for her sake.

"Are you coming?" Reid asked. He and Pelidan paused, holding Rolli between them. "Kalina told us not to leave you out here alone."

"She doesn't need to worry that I will steal a shuttlecraft and try to escape," Perri muttered, trudging behind the two men toward the headquarters building. "Where could I go except to one of the Regulan ships? All I can do now is accept whatever fate and Lady Kalina have decreed for me."

"If you want my opinion," said Reid, who was closer to Perri than his companion and who had overheard her, "I don't think Halvo will let anything terrible happen to you."

Perri wasn't so sure. She knew Halvo liked her and enjoyed making love to her. He had even forgiven her for kidnapping him. But he had never said he loved her, nor had he mentioned the possibility of a future with her. And since Halvo had returned to his family, he no longer needed Perri for companionship. She knew little about his real life. Perhaps there was a woman in the Jurisdiction for whom he cared. With the exact punishment for her criminal act still to be decided and Kalina firmly set against her, Perri did not think she had much of a chance to win Halvo's love.

The inside of the headquarters building was a confusing place. It was not a large building and to Perri it appeared crowded. Tarik had told her there were 12 colonists, ten from the Jurisdiction and two who were native to Dulan's Planet, who had joined the original group after the colony was founded. To that number were added Perri, Halvo, Kalina, Lt. Dysia, and Capt. Jyrit, who was still in surgery. The absence of Jyrit, the two people who were operating on him, and two colonists presently on duty aboard the orbiting ship *Kalina* did little to ease the congestion in the central room.

Then there were the children. Off to one side of the circular room two little boys and a tiny girl played, watched over by a woman with long, silver-gold hair who held a silver-haired baby in her arms.

"That's my wife, Janina, with our two children," Reid said. He and Pelidan had just set

Rolli down in the middle of the room and he had noticed Perri staring at the little ones.

"I have never seen so many children at once," Perri said.

"No, I don't suppose you have. Tarik is much more permissive about couples reproducing than Jurisdiction law allows. If our families continue to increase in size, we will soon be forced to build individual houses to hold all of us. Would you like me to introduce you to my wife?"

"Not just now," Perri said, faltering. "I don't mean to be rude. I know you are trying to be helpful."

"I understand. It must be confusing for you to be set down among so many strangers. But we are a friendly lot. If you want to join any group, just walk up to them and tell them your name and you will be accepted." With a smile and a quick pat on her shoulder, Reid left her to go to his wife.

Perri watched Reid and Janina embrace. With a sad little tug at her heart she saw Reid take the baby into his arms and run a gentle hand over the child's head before he kissed it. Perri could not remember ever before observing an expression of such loving concern. How did it feel to hold a small child in one's arms and know it was one's own, the product of a loving union? Perri did not think she would ever know.

"Oh, Rolli." She crouched beside the robot.

"What will become of us?"

"Most assuredly, some form of atonement will be required," Rolli said, and the answer provided no comfort at all to Perri's troubled heart. Slowly the robot turned completely around on its wheels while it took in the bustling activity in the room. "That is a most remarkable computer. It is very old, yet it has recent components added to it." Rolli fell silent when Tarik and Halvo approached.

"It is a six-hundred-year-old computer-communicator," Tarik said. "Narisa and I discovered it still in working order when we first came to Dulan's Planet. Later we made additions to upgrade its capacity so it could serve the entire colony."

"Have you new components that could upgrade me?" Rolli asked.

"I am sorry," Halvo said, "but it can't be done, Rolli. Like all Artificial Life Forms, you are forever limited by your size and your original programming. Though you have a human personality, you are incapable of growing and changing as real humans do."

"That isn't true!" Perri said. "Rolli was programmed to keep me out of any danger, yet earlier today she agreed with me that I ought to fight the Regulans in order to protect you even though doing so would be dangerous to me. Her decision proved she is capable of modifying her own programming when presented with unusual situations."

"That is an interesting theory." Tarik walked around the robot, looking it over before continuing. "I understand your father created this particular ALF. Perri, would you mind if I do a thorough checkup on Rolli? Halvo tells me she has been damaged and repaired recently. She may need additional work, and I would like to see exactly what is inside this unusual robot."

"I would be grateful." Perri took a deep breath, then said, "There is something you ought to know about Rolli." Tarik was the only other person in the galaxy to whom she would entrust the secret of how Melri's memory tapes had been implanted into Rolli's main circuitry. She knew in her heart that Tarik would not use the information against her or Rolli. Quickly, Perri recounted Rolli's history in a voice too low to be overheard by anyone else. Tarik looked disturbed but not shocked. When Perri was finished it was to his brother that Tarik spoke.

"I am delighted to learn," he said to Halvo, "that my conformist brother is at last breaking a few rules."

"I plan to break more than a few in the near future," Halvo said. In a voice quiet but ringing with passion, he added, "My life has been circumscribed by Jurisdiction laws and Service regulations. I never protested because I wanted a career in the Service. Well, I had what I wanted. I was successful. I reached the highest rank possible. And then, after giving everything but life itself, I was discarded because I no longer met the physical specifications."

"Not entirely discarded," Tarik said. "You have an honorable position waiting for you at Capital."

"A desk job," Halvo said, his contempt for such a fate filling every syllable. "Meetings with diplomats of various Races. Once or twice a year someone will ask my advice on a serious matter. Occasionally, the advice I offer may actually be taken. I will never again be sent on a mission into space. Once, I would have accepted such an end to my Service career. Now, I see how empty my personal life has been. I intend to refuse that position at Capital."

"Good for you." Tarik looked pleased. "What will you do then?"

"I haven't decided yet." With a hint of the same teasing tone Tarik had previously used with him, Halvo said, "Perhaps I'll stay on Dulan's Planet."

"I don't think so." Tarik's voice held a note of warning.

"No," Halvo said. "It wouldn't work, would it? Don't worry, Tarik. I will leave when Mother goes."

Halvo decided it was time to change the subject. He wasn't sure whether Perri had understood all the implications of his discussion with

Tarik or not, but that moment was neither the time nor the place to tell her how he felt about her.

"We will appreciate anything you can do with Rolli," Halvo said to Tarik.

"I will be the only person to work on the robot," Tarik said. "Never fear, Perri. I will keep Rolli's secret."

"Thank you." Her voice was so low and she looked so dejected that Halvo seized upon the most obvious way to raise her spirits.

"Tarik, the food processor on the *Space Dragon* wasn't working," Halvo said. "We haven't eaten since last night."

"I'll speak to Narisa. She usually has something simmering in the galley for people who come in from duty at all hours." Tarik went to find his wife, leaving Perri and Halvo standing together.

"Am I a Jurisdiction prisoner?" she asked. "Reid told me that Kalina wanted me inside this building. Am I forbidden to leave it?"

"Of course not. But you must go to Capital," Halvo said, trying to choose words that would not alarm her. "There you and I will explain to my father exactly what happened."

"After which I will be sent to a penal colony. Kalina will see to it."

"Not necessarily. I will have a few suggestions of my own to make about your rehabilitation. I can't discuss them right now. Narisa is beckoning. It looks as if she intends to feed us."

He had to take an openly reluctant Perri by the elbow to make her cross the room to where Narisa was setting out plates and food on a large table. Halvo knew Perri was hungry and also thought he knew why she was hanging back. He loved his mother too much to be afraid of her, but he knew she could have a frightening impression on those who did not know her well.

"We usually eat in shifts," Narisa said to Halvo. "There is always someone going on duty or coming off it. Tonight will be something of a family meal, with only two nonfamily members present."

"That's us," Dysia said to Perri. "Perhaps we ought to sit together."

"A good idea." Appreciating Dysia's diplomatic suggestion, Halvo agreed quickly, before his mother could intervene. He thought Perri would eat more if she were some distance from Kalina. Unfortunately from Halvo's point of view, Janina and Reid had taken all of the children for a walk around the island before bedtime, so there would be no childish distractions during the meal to draw Kalina's attention away from Perri.

The main course was a meaty Demarian stew, the very dish for which Halvo had been yearning for weeks. He ate heartily of it. The wine was excellent, the bread hot and fresh, and to Halvo's great relief, Tarik seemed determined to

keep the conversation focused on noncontro-
versial subjects. Perri sat quietly between Halvo
and Dysia, speaking little, though she did eat
enough to please Halvo. As the meal was ending, Herne appeared from the room he used as
a surgical clinic.

"How is Jyrit?" At once Kalina was on her
feet, and Dysia also left the table to confront the
colony physician.

"He will live." Herne moved his shoulders and
rubbed the back of his neck as if to release the
tense muscles there.

"I thank all the gods of Demaria for this good
news," Kalina said. "I would not want to lose a
friend like Jyrit."

"How soon can he return to the *Krontar*?" Dysia asked Herne.

"He needs twenty-four hours of complete bed
rest. I have never operated on a Jugarian before,
so I want to watch him carefully during the immediate postoperative period," Herne said.
"Then I would like to monitor him for another
day while he is up and moving around. Your
doctors on the *Krontar* can take care of him
after that. I have been in contact with them and
they agree with me about keeping him here for
a while. Lady Kalina, the first officer of the
Krontar asked me to inform you that, unless you
wish to remain longer, the *Krontar* will depart
for Capital forty-eight hours from now. By then,
Jyrit ought to be able to withstand the shuttle-

craft trip back to his ship with no problem."

"May I see him?" Halvo asked. "I owe Jyrit my thanks, and a full explanation."

"He is asleep," Herne said.

"Herne, I want you to do a complete physical examination on Halvo," Kalina said. "I want to be certain he has suffered no lasting harm over the past few weeks."

"That won't be necessary, Mother," Halvo said. "Besides, Herne is too tired after the long operation on Jyrit to do an examination on me tonight."

They had all left the table and were crowding around Herne, talking and asking more questions about Jyrit's condition. No one was paying any attention to Perri. She slipped out of her chair and made for the entrance.

The long, eventful day had ended. Night was falling and the twin moons sent silvery paths across the lake. It did not take long for Perri's eyes to adjust to the semidarkness. She found a path through the trees and began to walk. She had no idea where she was going. She knew only that she wanted to get away from the scene inside the headquarters building.

It was her fault that Capt. Jyrit had nearly died, her fault that the existence of Tarik's colony was known to both Regulans and Jurisdiction Service personnel who should never have learned of it. Worst of all, because of her, Halvo's life had been put in danger. No wonder he

345

had become so distant, so closed to her. He knew how much blame lay on her shoulders.

Perri reached the side of the island nearest to the cliffs that marked the eastern shore of the lake. Across a narrow channel of water they loomed solid and dark. On that end of the island there was no beach, only rough ground that dropped off into the water. Perri had to climb a little hill to reach the south shore. At the top of the rise she paused, looking at the ground beneath her feet, where there were a dozen stones set in two neat rows. One stone was larger than the others and there was a word carved on it. Perri went closer, bending down to try to read the word. It was too dark for her to see well. She touched the stone, tracing the carving with her fingertips.

"That is Dulan's grave," a soft voice said. When Perri gasped and jumped back, the voice continued, "Do not be afraid, Perri. I am Osiyar."

"I'm sorry. I didn't mean to disturb you. I didn't know anyone was here."

"This cemetery is the quietest place on the island. I was with Jyrit for several hours. I needed silence in which to recuperate."

"Herne says he will live."

"That must be a great comfort to you."

"It is a little less guilt for me to carry," she said. Not certain she would have another chance to be alone with him, she went on. "Osiyar, Tarik advised me to speak to you about a peculiar experience I had with the Chon."

"Indeed? I would be interested to hear of it."

"Good evening, Osiyar." Dysia stepped into view. "Hello, Perri."

"Did they send you to look for me?" Perri cried. "Do they think I will flee the island?"

"I am not sure anyone else has noticed your absence yet," Dysia said. "I thought if we were together when you are found no one could accuse you of trying to run away."

"I do not think Perri was runing away," Osiyar said, "but, rather, running to that which she needs."

Before Perri could ask what the telepath meant, they were interrupted by a shrill, angry voice.

"Can't you leave him alone for half an hour? If he wanted to be apart from me, then you shouldn't bother him either."

"Alla, my dear, we were only engaging in idle conversation," Osiyar said in a mild way that made Perri think he was smiling indulgently, though she could not see for certain because they were all standing in shadow.

"Come back to headquarters and I'll fix an herbal tea for you to drink so you can sleep." Alla put her arm through Osiyar's. Perri could just make out the shape of her white hand clutching at his dark sleeve. "Really, Osiyar, you must learn to refuse the importunities of people who constantly ask you for help."

"I am somewhat weary. Perri, we will talk again before you leave."

"Not if Alla can prevent it," Dysia whispered as the woman led Osiyar off toward the beach. "That is the most possessive woman I have ever encountered. She treats him like a child."

"Or a pet," Perri said to Dysia's appreciative chuckle.

"I was not spying on you," Dysia said, "nor trying to prevent you from doing anything you want to do. I just thought you might need a friend."

"I have caused you and your captain a great deal of trouble," Perri said. "Why should you want to be my friend?"

"Anyone who joins the Jurisdiction Service expects to encounter trouble," Dysia said. "What happened with the Regulans was fairly routine. I have been in worse situations. So has Jyrit. Neither of us holds it against you."

"You are Kalina's friend." Even to Perri's own ears the words sounded like an accusation, but Dysia only chuckled again.

"Oh, yes, the Regulan mind-set. You think that I have some ulterior motive, that some complicated intrigue against you is afoot. Sometimes, Perri, an offer of friendship is just what it appears to be. Perhaps," Dysia said, "I need a friend, too."

"You?" Perri cried. "A woman who holds high

rank in the Jurisdiction Service? You must have many friends."

"The Service demands much of its people," Dysia said, "and some of us don't fit very well into our assigned places."

"Do you mean you are unhappy? I find it hard to believe when you have so many opportunities that are denied to other women."

"Uncomfortable would be a better word than unhappy," Dysia said. "Or, perhaps, uneasy. As if half of my clothes were the wrong size. From what I know of you, I think you felt much the same way while you lived on Regula."

"I ask too many questions," Perri said.

"What's wrong with asking questions?"

"Women are supposed to be silent." Perri was stopped by Dysia's renewed laughter.

"You have so much to learn," Dysia said.

"Halvo says the same thing to me."

"Halvo." Dysia broke off her laughter. "It can be a difficult thing to care for a man who has a possessive woman hovering over him, especially if she has a prior claim on him."

"Kalina hates me."

"She is angry with you. There is a difference. Besides, Halvo is too strong a person ever to be swayed by someone else's wishes. Not when he wants something very badly."

"Above all else, Halvo wants to return to his career as Admiral of the Fleet."

"As I said, Perri"—Dysia was chuckling again—"you do have a lot to learn."

Chapter Nineteen

Because the headquarters building was so crowded, no one could be allotted a private room. To ease the problem of where to put so many guests, Halvo volunteered to sleep upon a couch in the central room, while Kalina, Dysia, and Perri were quartered together in a room with two large beds. Lying beside Dysia, Perri found it difficult to sleep. On the other bed Kalina tossed for a while, then quieted. The room was dark save for a faint line of light along the bottom edge of the door.

Perri was deeply aware of Halvo on the opposite side of that door. She longed to go to him, yet she did not know what her reception would be if she did. After hours spent with his disap-

350

proving mother he might reject Perri. If he became angry enough to waken anyone else, Perri would be humiliated beyond bearing. She decided she would just have to stay where she was. She focused on the light beneath the door and tried to will herself into sleep. . . .

"You stupid girl," Elyr said. "Will you never learn that no man of any discrimination could want you? Questions—always you ask enough questions to drive a man mad. Yet you never find answers, do you?"

"I am sure I could if you would just explain to me why you and the Chief Hierarch tricked me," Perri said. "Surely, you knew I would be compelled by loyalty to do anything I could to help you—"

"And you did do what I wanted," Elyr said. "The trick worked."

"You should have told me the truth!" she shouted. "I deserved that much."

"You deserve nothing. The answer you seek is there in your mind, Perri."

Elyr began to laugh at her and as he laughed his figure began to fade, until there was only darkness surrounding Perri . . . and one faint bar of light shining along a stone floor. . . .

"Elyr, wait! I have more questions to ask." But Elyr was gone and Perri, rearing up on her knees upon the bed, thought she saw a movement in front of the light, a figure blocking it for a moment.

"No! Elyr, answer me!" Perri's voice rose to a shriek. "Elyr!"

"What in the name of all the stars is wrong with you? Do you intend to wake everyone in the building?" The shadowy figure moved again and the light came on, revealing a very annoyed-looking Kalina standing by the switch. "Have the decency to remember that there are small children here who could be frightened by your screeching. Not to mention a gravely injured man who needs his rest."

"I'm sorry." Perri looked around the room, half expecting to encounter a smiling, mocking Elyr. But he was not there. Perri blinked away the last remnants of sleep. "I had a bad dream."

"Perhaps your conscience is troubling you," Kalina said.

"Here." Dysia, also awakened by Perri's cries, handed her a cup of water. "Drink this. Then we can talk about your dream if you want."

"Perri!" The bedroom door burst open and Halvo rushed in. He was wearing a loose robe that Tarik had lent him and his hair was tousled by sleep. "You've had another nightmare, haven't you?"

"Does she do this often?" Kalina asked.

Halvo ignored his mother. He sat down next to Perri and tried to pull her into his arms. She did not know whether to accept his embrace, which was what she wanted to do, or push him away because Kalina was watching them. What she did was brace her hands on his shoulders so she could remain sitting upright while she looked directly at him.

"It was a slightly different dream this time," she said. "There was no spaceship, just Elyr and me in some black and empty place. I could see his face and figure, but nothing else."

"What did he say?" Halvo asked.

"Much the same as in my last dream," she replied. "Elyr called me stupid and said the answers I want are in my own mind. But, Halvo, I don't know what the answers are!"

"It's all right," Halvo said, soothing her. "What happened next?"

"Elyr disappeared and I was all alone in blackness. That is when I screamed. Lady Kalina, I did not mean to disturb you or anyone else. I couldn't help screaming."

"No, I suppose you couldn't, if you were in the middle of a nightmare." Kalina sat down on her bed, still watching Perri closely. "Such dreams are almost always the result of an unquiet mind, perhaps caused by a guilty conscience."

"Mother, please!" Halvo said.

"Of course my mind is unquiet." Perri moved out of Halvo's reach to sit facing his mother. The beds were so close that their knees were almost touching. "Do you think I don't know that what I did might have cost Halvo his life? Do you imagine I don't feel guilty about it?

"I was sent out from Regula to capture Halvo by two men who had their own secret reasons for using me as they did. Lady Kalina, have you considered the possibility that Halvo could still be in danger? Until we discover the reason why they wanted him, we can't be sure that Elyr and the Chief Hierarch won't try to capture him again."

"Perhaps you are more astute than I realized," Kalina said. "During my visit to Regula everyone who mentioned your name called you stupid and irritating—a bias that may have colored my own thinking."

"At the Service Academy," Dysia said, "we were taught that a constantly questioning mind is a sign of intelligence. Moreover, such a mind is irritating to those who have something to hide."

"So it is said." Kalina's clear blue eyes regarded Perri soberly. Then her gaze moved on to her son's face. Finally, Kalina shook herself a little, as if she were making up her mind. Or, possibly, she was just rousing herself as her next words suggested. "If you young people have quite finished, I will attempt to go to sleep again. It has been a long day and I am weary."

"Perri," Halvo said, "would you like to come with me into the central room for the rest of the night?"

"I will not allow it," Kalina said at once. "Perri will be perfectly safe here with Dysia and me."

"Yes, I will," Perri said, refusing to admit how badly she wanted to go with Halvo, to be held and comforted by him until she was able to sleep peacefully. Perri thought Kalina's sharp disapproval of her had been somewhat blunted during the last half hour. If she stayed where she was, Kalina might decide that the young woman she disliked had at least a modicum of courage. "I am sure I will fall asleep quickly now, Halvo."

His gaze held hers a moment. Then, right there in front of Kalina and Dysia, Halvo kissed her lightly, just at one corner of her mouth. From where Kalina sat, it probably looked as if he had kissed her on the cheek, but his lips were almost on Perri's. It was enough to give her the strength to get through the remainder of the night.

"Until morning," Halvo said to her, rising. "Good night, Mother. Lt. Dysia."

"Good night, sir." Dysia was already straightening the blankets, smothering a yawn, and climbing back into bed. Perri lay down and a moment later Kalina put out the light.

"In the morning, Perri," Kalina said in the darkness, "you and I are going to have a long talk."

"From what Adm. Halvo has told me, the fault was not entirely yours," Capt. Jyrit said to Perri. "All the same, honor requires that you should

355

make an apology. Even by Jugarian standards you have fulfilled the obligation handsomely. In return, my honor requires a polite acceptance of your honest words. I do accept your apology, Perri."

"Thank you, Captain." Perri found the Jugarian's formality curiously restful. Dysia had suggested that she be completely honest with Jyrit. It seemed Dysia had been right. Perri only hoped Dysia was correct in her further advice that Perri tell Kalina everything she knew or suspected about the plot against Halvo.

"Jyrit, my friend." Halvo, who had come with Perri and Kalina to the meeting, looked around the spare white room that served as the colony hospital. There were no patients other than Jyrit. "If you feel well enough, I would like to confer with you in private, for I trust your intuition as well as your extensive knowledge of the various Races."

As Halvo spoke Perri noticed Jyrit's antennae changing color. While she had offered her apology they had been a washed-out shade of orange that brightened slowly in reaction to her words. Now they were flushing a warm orange red in response to Halvo's open attitude of friendship.

"Because Jugarian physiology requires continual motion, Herne has told me to practice walking about the room in order to speed the return of my usual strength," Jyrit said. "We can talk while I do so. I hope, when he examines me later, Herne will declare me fit to join you and your family for the midday meal."

"You will not require Perri or me for this conference," Kalina said. "Come along, Perri. We, too, will take a walk."

Halvo gave her an encouraging look but said nothing to contradict his mother's plans. After taking a polite leave of Capt. Jyrit, Perri followed the older woman across the central room and out the door, where both of them paused on the first step. Through the trees Perri could see several people who were apparently working on the two shuttlecraft that were sitting on the beach. She was not surprised when Kalina chose a path leading to the opposite side of the island.

"Now, then," Kalina said as she walked briskly along, "let me begin by telling you that my anger against you has abated only a little as a result of Halvo's explanations about your past and your handsome apology to Jyrit. Whatever excuses you may offer, they do not change the fact that you have done something you knew was wrong. Your abduction of my son was deliberately undertaken. However, in the interest of fairness, I am willing to listen to your own version of this sorry tale."

It was a long story, but Perri told all of it with complete honesty, not sparing herself from blame. The only details she did not reveal were the account of the illegal mind draining of her nurse, Melri, and the implantation of Melri's memories into Rolli. Perri was afraid that information would anger Kalina and prejudice her against both Perri and her robot. Perri did not want any harm to come to Rolli. She could foresee a future in which Rolli might again be her only comfort, and she did not want Rolli's familiar personality to be changed in any way. Nor did Perri speak about her unpleasant intimate encounters with Elyr or her far more enjoyable lovemaking with Halvo. Those were private matters, though Perri believed the knowledge that she loved Halvo would probably have set Kalina even more firmly against her. When Perri was finished, Kalina walked on for a while before speaking.

"You have been criminally foolish," Kalina said.

"I do not deny it. When this adventure began, I was an ignorant girl, trying to help a man to whom I was bound. I am much changed now. Dangers and unexpected experiences have made me wiser." Perri met Kalina's eyes squarely.

"Adding what you have just said to the information Capt. Jyrit, Lt. Dysia, and I were able to obtain during our visit to Regula, and to what Halvo has told me," Kalina said, "I believe that you and Halvo are correct in your assumption that there is more to his abduction than a simple exchange of Halvo's life for Elyr's. The question is, what, exactly, is that plot?"

"I have thought about it until I have nightmares," Perri said. "I cannot find a satisfactory answer."

"Your dreams may be no more than the well-known effects of the Empty Sector," Kalina said. "Speaking for myself, I have felt unsettled since shortly before I reached Dulan's Planet. I do not know how Tarik and Narisa and the others tolerate it."

"Perhaps their bodies and minds have adjusted after being here for several years," Perri said.

"Possibly." Kalina dismissed the idea to return to her original subject. "Your dreams, Perri, along with my unsettled state, may well disappear once we are safely returned to Jurisdiction space and on our way to Capital."

Perri sighed. It always came back to that. There was no way for her to avoid going to Capital to face charges for what she had done.

"Your honesty with me speaks well for you," Kalina said, "but I must tell you that I am not pleased by your close association with my son. I am neither blind nor stupid, Perri," she added when Perri gasped at her blunt words.

"Halvo is an adult." Perri did not know what else to say. "He makes his own decisions."

"True." Kalina's severe expression softened only a little. "That does not mean I always approve of his decisions—or that I hesitate to voice my concerns to him. But I will strive to be fair to you, Perri. I will not allow my personal feelings to color the story I recount to Almaric when next I see him."

"Thank you, Lady Kalina." Perri told herself that was more than she could have hoped for, considering the seriousness of her crime.

"Now, you must excuse me. I want to spend the next few hours with Tarik, Narisa, and my grandson. I do not know when I will see them again after we leave here."

Left to herself, Perri wandered farther along the path on which she and Kalina had been walking. She came out of the trees onto the southern shore, where rocks studded the beach and she had a full view of the length of the lake. Someone was there before her.

Wrapped against the wind in a long, bright blue cloak, Osiyar stood looking at the water. Though his back was toward her, Perri knew who it was by his perfect stillness and by his gleaming golden hair.

"I have been waiting for you," he said as she walked up behind him.

"You knew I would come?" Perri shot a glance at him. They stood side by side facing the lake; Osiyar had not taken his eyes off the water.

"It was a reasonable assumption. Kalina will want to devote as much time as possible to the family she has not seen for years. Alla is with Herne, performing a final examination of Capt. Jyrit. This is a secluded place, where I often come to think. Why should you not find it, too?"

"I suppose everyone expects you to use your telepathy even for such minor matters," Perri said.

"Only those who do not know me well. The Power requires energy and is exhausting to use."

"It must be. I never thought about it before. Osiyar, I am beginning to wonder if I have some telepathic tendencies." She went on to tell him about her brief experience with the Chon and about the nightmares. "Tarik said that Narisa has had similar episodes, but that she is not telepathic. Halvo thinks it is all the result of prolonged stress. What do you think, Osiyar?"

"Do you recall other such instances that happened before you came to Dulan's Planet?" he asked.

"No, never." Perri's answer was swift.

"Then, I would not worry about your contact with the bird. If you had spoken to Herne about this, he might have told you of the day when one of the Chon contacted him. The experience left him with a terrible headache. You were more fortunate than he." Osiyar's face lit with a quick smile, then sobered. "The dreams, however, are another matter. Perri, I believe that you know something you do not realize you know. Through the dreams your mind is trying to release that knowledge into your conscious thoughts."

"I fear Halvo may still be in danger," Perri said. "If whatever is buried inside my mind could help to protect him, then I need to release it as soon as possible. Can you help me? If you want to use your telepathic power on me, then do it. I give you permission."

Osiyar's sea-blue eyes locked with hers. Perri could not turn her glance away from his. As she continued to stare into those blue depths, she began to feel slightly dizzy and at the same time she became aware of a faint prickling inside her mind. It was not frightening, but it was strange, foreign. The sensation was withdrawn as soon as she recognized it.

"Child," Osiyar said softly, "you have been sadly used. I am sorry for it."

"Never mind my past. It doesn't matter now." Perri brushed aside his sympathy. "Just tell me how to help Halvo. What did you discover?"

"I do not know enough about Regulan culture to enable me to put the pieces together properly," he said. "It is possible that there is still another part of this puzzle waiting to be uncovered."

"Then how can I keep Halvo safe?" she cried.

"He will be on a Jurisdiction warship under command of the honest Capt. Jyrit," Osiyar said. "So long as you are near, I do not think

362

Halvo will be tempted to leave the *Krontar* a second time."

"He cannot stay on the *Krontar* forever." Perri's growing frustration sounded in her voice. "Sooner or later, I am going to be sent off to some distant prison planet. If I remember something important then that might help him, it will be too late. Halvo is too old to obey his mother's insistence that he stay safely at home, and he hates the very idea of a life spent at Capital. He will leave. He will relinquish the security his parents can offer—and what will happen to him then?"

"Perhaps Halvo feels that a life without risk is no life at all," Osyar said.

"There must be some way for me to dredge up whatever information is lodged in my deepest mind and to recognize what I need to know," Perri said.

"When a dream occurs," Osiyar said, "do not resist it. If you are aware of dreaming, then try to learn as much as you can."

"I do," she said, "but Elyr just laughs at me."

"Elyr may not be the key to the answer you seek."

"Then who? The Chief Hierarch?"

"Do you think it is possible?"

"Of course it is. He is the most powerful person on Regula."

"In my youth," Osiyar said, "I was no stranger to intrigue, myself. It is amazing how the powerful scheme and plot. When next you dream, think of the Chief Hierarch."

"Is that all you can tell me?"

"I know you are disappointed. You were hoping for a simple, definite answer. But sometimes, Perri, the most important answers are the ones we must struggle to find for ourselves."

"You sound just like my father," she cried.

"It was my intention."

"He always told me to work out my problems for myself."

"He taught you well." Osiyar was smiling again. "Better than you think."

The midday meal was over, the afternoon was well advanced, and farewells were being said outside the headquarters building. Jyrit, though still rather weak, had recovered enough to join the party and to walk to the shuttlecraft on his own. Halvo had insisted that he would pilot the craft to the *Krontar* with Dysia as his copilot, a decision that made Perri feel left out. Halvo had paid no attention at all to Perri since accompanying her on her morning visit to Jyrit the previous day.

"Under other circumstances, I might enjoy living here on Dulan's Planet," Perri said to Dysia. She was wishing she did not have to leave at all.

"Perhaps you will return some time in the future." Dysia's eyes were on Osiyar, who was at that moment accepting Jyrit's thanks with dignified grace. "I know I will come back if I possibly can.

"Meanwhile," Dysia said, as if giving herself a lecture, "I have my career to think about. And my first duty is to get my captain back to his ship—after I try to tear Kalina away from her beloved grandson."

Chapter Twenty

From her previous views of the *Krontar* while she was on the *Space Dragon*, Perri knew the ship was huge, but she had not imagined what it would be like to be aboard the giant warship. The corridors seemed to go on for miles, crossing each other in a bewildering maze. There were uniformed Jurisdiction Service personnel everywhere.

Immediately after disembarking from the shuttlecraft on the docking deck Halvo and Jyrit left for the bridge to confer with the first officer, who had been in charge of the ship while Jyrit was absent.

"The robot is to be placed in sealed storage in the same cargo bay with the *Space Dragon*,"

Jyrit said as he went through the hatch.

"No, I want Rolli with me," Perri cried. The hatch slid shut behind Jyrit before he could answer. Perri wasn't even sure he had heard her.

"Your ship and robot are evidence," Kalina said. "They cannot be tampered with until we reach Capital, where Almaric will decide what is to be done with them." Kalina's two aides were waiting for her. She went off with them, leaving Perri with Dysia. Immediately, half-a-dozen security guards moved into position around them.

"Don't mind the guards," Dysia said, leading the way out of the docking deck. "It's just regulations to have them here."

"I must be an important prisoner of state." Perri tried to sound more cheerful than she felt. "I didn't know the *Space Dragon* had been brought aboard. There is certainly enough room on this ship to hold it," she added as they turned yet another corner and started down a long corridor. She was already thoroughly lost and could not help wondering how those serving aboard the *Krontar* ever learned their way around the vessel.

"Captain's orders," Dysia said, "and Halvo concurred. Don't worry, Perri. I have a feeling that both Rolli and the *Space Dragon* will be released into Halvo's care after the technicians at Capital inspect them and make their reports to Leader Almaric."

With the guards marching before, beside, and behind Dysia and her, Perri fully expected to be shown to a holding cell. Instead, Dysia halted during their progress down the latest corridor to push a button. At once a sliding door opened upon a large, well-furnished cabin. At Dysia's gesture Perri walked inside.

"If I weren't a prisoner, I would like this," Perri said, looking around. The carpet was light gray and the walls were blue. On one side a large bed extended into the room. Several built-in cabinets and a door filled the opposite wall. Two easy chairs with a low table between them completed the furnishings. The most striking features of the cabin were the three long windows that allowed a clear view of the black space outside the ship.

"Are they real?" Perri went toward the windows to look at them more closely. "The *Space Dragon* has only viewscreens. I didn't know it was possible to have windows in a spaceship."

"Technology is wonderful." Dysia appeared to find nothing unusual about the windows or the view they revealed. "It's not glass, of course, nor even plastic, but a special compound developed by the Famorat, who, as a result of their inventiveness, are now growing rich making and installing windows in all kinds of space vessels."

"The Famorat," Perri said, recalling what Halvo had told her about the mating customs of those folk. Then she decided it would be well for her to pay close attention to what Dysia was saying.

"This is the lighting control." With her fingertips Dysia stroked a panel near the entrance and the light in the cabin dimmed. There were no lighting fixtures to be seen. Illumination came from the walls and ceiling in a manner Perri did not understand. "You can make the room completely dark or as bright as noon if you prefer." Dysia proceeded to demonstrate.

"I like it the way it was when we first came in," Perri said, and Dysia returned the cabin to a soft, early morning glow that was remarkably like natural daylight on Regula. The overall effect was heightened by the way in which the sky-colored walls and ceiling brightened or darkened at a touch.

"The food processor is over here in these wall components. After your time on the *Space Dragon*, you won't have any difficulty using it," Dysia said, moving to the bank of cabinets. She opened a long door next to the food processor. "This section is for your wardrobe. Push this button and you can speak directly to the ship's computer. Tell it exactly what you want and it will measure you and produce the garments you request, though it does take a few minutes. And finally, through this door is the bathing room." Quickly, Dysia explained the functioning of the sonic shower stall, the sink, and the waste receptacle.

"If you should need something that isn't available in the room," Dysia said, "the guards outside the door can help you."

"What I want is to talk to Halvo," Perri replied.

"I'm sure he will be in touch with you soon." Dysia paused at the sliding door to the corridor. "When I see him, I will tell him you want to speak with him. In the meantime, why don't you relax, Perri? Have a shower and change into fresh clothes. That's what I intend to do as soon as I possibly can. I'll check back on you later, but right now I do have a report to hear from the junior armaments officer who has taken my post while I have been off ship."

Left alone, Perri decided to follow Dysia's advice. Stripping off her clothes, she stepped into the shower, which cleaned by sonic waves. She had used a similar shower while on the *Space Dragon*. It worked well enough, though she did not think she would ever prefer it to real water and scented soap.

At least she did not have to close the curtains over the cabin windows. Still naked, she stopped for a moment to gaze out at blackness and a few stars. In the distance she could just discern the faint, pinkish traces of the luminescent gas that marked the boundary between the Jurisdiction and the Empty Sector. She knew the *Krontar* had departed Dulan's Planet, heading back toward the Jurisdiction before she and

Dysia had left the docking deck, but Perri had no sensation of motion.

"I wonder if I will feel anything when we cross the boundary," she said to herself, "or if the *Krontar* is so large that I won't even notice the difference this time."

Turning from the windows to the clothing processor she tried to decide what she wanted to wear. Except that she knew she wanted a change from the tunic and trousers she had been wearing for weeks, she could not at first make up her mind. Never before had Perri been allowed to choose her own clothing. When she was a child her mother had seen to her wardrobe, and after she went into Elyr's household his mother, Cynri, had made those decisions. While she was still a growing girl her clothing had been limited to two outfits at a time, which were changed when she outgrew them. Her most recent garments had been a dark gray dress for everyday wear and the purple-blue tunic and trousers she had donned for her fateful interview with the Chief Hierarch and had been wearing ever since.

"I want a lighter color," Perri said aloud.

"A more precise description is required," the computer answered her.

"Green." Perri said the first color that came into her mind. "Pale green."

"Specify style," said the computer.

"I don't know. Oh, wait—that long, loose robe

Halvo was wearing last night that his brother lent to him, except it was blue, not green. Something like that."

"Request is incomprehensible," the computer responded. "Restate design preference more exactly."

Perri did so, describing the robe as she recalled it, asking for the pale green shade she wanted and adding gold embroidery at neck and sleeves.

"Is footwear also required?" the computer asked.

"Yes. Mules, low heeled, in a color to match the robe," Perri said at once before the computer could ask more questions. Under happier conditions, she knew she would have enjoyed the session with a machine programmed to give her whatever clothing she could imagine.

"Specify other accessories," the computer said.

Perri thought for a moment. She had never owned any jewelry. Such adornments were considered highly inappropriate for unwed Regulan females, though married women were encouraged to flaunt their husbands' wealth with multiple necklaces, bracelets, and rings. Perri did not want to wear anything even vaguely Regulan in style.

"I want Demarian earrings, gold with green stones. My ears are not pierced. No other accessories are wanted."

"Processing will require three minutes. Please close the wardrobe door and wait for the light to flash before reopening it."

Perri did as ordered, then wandered around the cabin, occasionally glancing at the silent clothing-processing unit, but mostly wondering what would happen to her and to Rolli. She was certain her future would hold no cell as attractive as her present accommodation.

"I may as well enjoy what I have until they take it away from me," she said to herself.

When the light shone forth on the wardrobe door, Perri held her breath in expectation and pulled it open. The robe she had requested hung there, its soft, pale green folds gleaming when she removed it. The gold thread embroidery along the edges of the sleeve hems looked as if it were stitched by hand. A wider band of gold threads in a similar pattern bordered the high neckline and the slit that reached to well below her bosom. Tiny buttons made of gold thread fit into a series of golden loops to hold the front of the robe together. The garment fit her perfectly, as did the shoes.

The earrings were like no jewelry she had ever seen before. When she put them on, thin golden wires swirled over her ears, with tiny, milky green stones dangling from the wires here and there and one larger green stone hanging at each earlobe. Tossing the waves of her dark red hair over her shoulder to better display the earrings, Perri stared at her reflection in the mirror.

"Is this the way Demarian women dress? Do the men enjoy seeing their mates like this?" The computer did not answer her. It had automatically turned itself off as soon as Perri's requests had been fulfilled. But there was an unexpected sound, a quiet chime that came from the direction of the door. Perri hastened across the room to press the panel Dysia had shown her how to use. The chime stopped when the door slid back.

"May I come in?" Halvo asked.

"Please do." Perri stepped aside and Halvo entered. He was followed by a young man in Jurisdiction uniform who was guiding a covered antigrav table.

"By the window, I think," Halvo said to the young man. "Lower it to chair height and take the cover with you."

"Yes, sir."

Perri watched in silence while the table and chairs were positioned as Halvo wanted and the cover removed from the table. At Halvo's signal the young man saluted and left. Halvo followed him to the door, which he sealed so no one could enter unless admitted from within. Then, before he returned to Perri's side, Halvo dimmed the lighting to a shade approximating dusk.

"I thought you might like company for dinner," he said in a casual way.

"How charming. I notice the guards are still at my door. Did Capt. Jyrit order them posted there—or was it your mother?"

"I cannot deny that you are a prisoner. However, we do not plan to torture you," he added in a dry way that she suspected was meant to make her laugh.

"What a relief." Perri did not know why she did not respond to his humor or why she snapped at him when what she really wanted was to go into his arms and be reassured that he cared about her.

"Shall we eat before our meal grows cold?" Giving no indication that he was annoyed by her attitude, Halvo gestured at the table floating between the two easy chairs at a level exactly right for dining.

"What is this?" Perri regarded the pale blue cloth, the crisp white napkins, the temptingly arranged food on delicate ceramic plates, the crystal and silver. Tiny lights burned in low, cut-crystal holders. A bouquet of blue, yellow, and white flowers completed the setting. Perri sniffed at the fragrant odors of a well-cooked meal. "I thought food was provided by the ship's computer."

"It is." Halvo moved to stand behind one of the chairs. "There is also a galley, where traditional food can be prepared by those who prefer it."

"You never made this yourself."

"There is an excellent cook aboard. Jyrit is something of a gourmet, though I do not think you would care for Jugarian specialities. This meal is Demarian, with some of my favorite dishes. Will you sit?"

He was still holding the back of the chair, and Perri realized there was some ceremony involved. She sat, and after making certain she was close enough to the antigrav table, Halvo took his own seat.

"Regulans don't do that?" He shot her a knowing glance. When she did not respond at once, he lifted a decanter of wine and began to pour it into the tall, stemmed glasses.

"A Regulan man would consider it demeaning to hold a chair so a woman could sit more easily. I am beginning to comprehend how badly Regulan women are treated. The more I see of the respect accorded to women of other Races, the more angry I become. This is delicious," Perri ended on a note of surprise, tasting a thin slice of meat. She chewed and swallowed, then took another forkful, adding a bit of grainy vegetable.

"Roasted peloron fowl and wild hairgrass." Halvo attacked the meat on his own plate with enthusiasm. "If you think this is good, just wait until dessert. We are having stewed rockfruit."

"I will try to contain my impatience."

"Don't wrinkle up your nose like that." Halvo

laughed at her. "It is called rockfruit because it grows only in rocky areas and when it is dug out of the ground it is as hard as the rocks. After it is stewed for several hours and sliced open, it has the taste and consistency of a very rich custard—but it contains no fat, just a lot of necessary vitamins. The first human settlers on Demaria lived on it for months, until they could start their farms and bring the crops to harvest. Now, it is our official planetary dish and an important export."

"I didn't know that story," Perri said.

"You may eat it with crushed nuts on top or with a berry sauce," Halvo said. As he spoke he was removing their empty plates to a compartment under the table. From another compartment he produced a pair of green crystal bowls, each sitting on a matching crystal plate. The rockfruit in the bowls looked to Perri like a yellow-fleshed melon. The berry sauce she chose dribbled into the small seed cavity in the center, where it mixed with the fruit when she spooned it up.

"Well?" Halvo watched her as she took her first bite.

"It is every bit as wonderful as you promised."

"I am glad you like it. And I am even happier to see you smile again, if only for a minute." Reaching across the table, Halvo took the hand that was not holding her spoon.

"I don't have much to smile about, do I?"

"Perhaps more than you think." Halvo's hand tightened on Perri's. "I know how you hate being left in ignorance, but there are times when it is best to be discreet until certain delicate matters have been resolved."

"That statement tells me nothing." She tried to pull her hand out of his, but he only exerted a firmer pressure.

"I don't mean to sound like a mealymouthed diplomat," Halvo said. "It is just that I have learned from past experience when to keep silent. You have trusted me before, Perri. Trust me now. It won't be for long."

His voice was low. She could see in his face and his eyes just how serious he was. There was only one answer she could give him.

"I do trust you, Halvo."

"I will not desert you."

Perri knew it was a solemn oath that Halvo had just spoken. What she did not know was the state of his feelings toward her. As an honorable man he might feel no more than a sense of responsibility for the ignorant girl who had been tricked into abducting him. But she did not want his pity. She wanted his love.

Halvo rose from the table, the hand he still held pulling Perri up after him. And then she was in his arms, his mouth was on hers, and though she might question his feelings, she had no doubt about what he wanted.

She thought of refusing him, but only for a

moment. If she sent him away she would be hurting herself, too, perhaps more than she hurt Halvo. She loved him passionately, totally, without knowing how warm or how lasting his desire for her was.

Nor could she guess how long she would remain relatively free and able to make love with him. The worst torture Perri could imagine was being sent to a prison planet far removed from Halvo, never to see him again. Or touch him. Or hear his voice.

I will enjoy what I have until they take it away from me. Silently, as if they were a magical incantation, she repeated to herself the words she had said earlier.

With his arm at her waist Halvo drew her to the bed. Perri's heart beat faster and she sensed a warming deep inside her. Halvo put one knee on the bed. Perri remained standing close to him, within the circle of his arm.

"Your beautiful eyes reveal everything you are feeling." Halvo kissed each lid. "They tell me how much you want me."

"I won't deny it." Perri felt like crying to know she was so transparent to him. She stood perfectly still, letting him kiss the softness of her cheek.

"But this jewelry must go," he murmured, "so I can taste your delicious ears."

"I asked the computer to give me Demarian

earrings. I thought you would like the way they look."

"I do." His mouth curved upward in amusement. "However, I prefer not to have my nose scratched when I am making love." Halvo gently removed the earrings.

"The robe is also most becoming, but it, too, is a hindrance," he whispered, working at the fastenings between her breasts until the buttons were all undone and he could push the fabric aside. It slipped lightly to the floor. Perri was wearing nothing underneath. Halvo stared at her, taking in every detail of her delicate yet womanly figure. Then he grasped a thick lock of her dark red hair and pulled it forward until it fell over her shoulder and down across her breast.

Perri trembled a little, wanting him, wishing she dared to say aloud how much she loved him. She stayed where she was at the foot of the bed until Halvo had undressed and pulled down the covers. When he bent across the bed and put out his hands, Perri laid both of hers into them. Halvo yanked and Perri went tumbling down onto the cool white sheets. Halvo fell on top of her.

The touch of his warm skin on hers inflamed her senses. She loved the way the rough hair on his legs rubbed against her smoother limbs, loved the tingling sensation of his manly chest pressed on her sensitive breasts. Best of all she loved his fingers weaving through her hair, holding her head in just the right position so he could fit his lips over hers. She welcomed the surge of his tongue into the eager heat of her mouth, rejoiced in the hardness that prodded at her thigh.

She wrapped her arms around him, wanting him closer. She shifted her hips, opening to him and Halvo slid into her as easily and naturally as a sunrise—or a fierce, planet-shaking storm. He drenched her with passion and with unceasing kisses. He touched her in places that made her think he must be a contortionist to be able to reach there—and *there*—until she shook and heaved and cried out for more—and deeper—and harder.

"Please. Please." She gasped.

Halvo found just the right place and exactly the rhythm and pressure she needed. She heard him groan with pleasure a moment before she lost all perception of time or place and joined him in a sublime union of bodies and, on her part at least, of heart and mind as well. Only very slowly did Perri's surroundings resolve themselves once more into two people, a bed, a spaceship cabin.

Halvo stayed with her all night, though strictly speaking, in space there was neither night nor day.

"Ship's time," he said. "Humans require day and night to follow each other in the steady cadence demanded by our bodies and our minds. Without that rhythm we suffer, fall ill, and occasionally die. Other species seem to adapt more easily to different schedules, which is why most spaceships maintain a twenty-four-hour day or something as close to it as possible. And at the moment, it is nearly midnight by the *Krontar's* time."

He made love to her again later and it was even more wonderful than the first time, but to Perri the important part of that night was in the long hours when they lay quietly in each other's arms, talking in soft, disjointed phrases. Though they were still in the Empty Sector, she suffered no bad dreams that night but slept peacefully at last, curled up against Halvo's warmth and strength.

Chapter Twenty-one

"Do I have to stay in this cabin until we reach Capital?" Perri asked.

"Where were you planning to go if you should be allowed to leave it?" Halvo lounged back against the pillows, a mug of qahf in one hand, a chunk of brown Demarian bread in the other. The sheet was loosely thrown across his loins as protection, he had told Perri, against the possibility of spilled hot qahf, since she persisted in bouncing about the bed in a dangerous manner.

In response to that grave insult to her dignity Perri had bounced off the bed, and since by ship's time it was now early morning, she had pulled on the pale green robe. However, she neglected to button it and Halvo's eyes frequently strayed to the enticing slit in the neckline. Noticing his interest Perri returned to sit on the edge of the bed with one bare foot tucked up beneath her. Perhaps they would make love again before it was time for him to leave her. She hoped so. There was nothing else quite like the pleasure, or the sense of security, she found in Halvo's arms.

"I would like to see more of the *Krontar*," she said in answer to his question. "Are prisoners ever allowed on the bridge?"

"If you were captain, would you let a prisoner walk onto your bridge?" Halvo took a bite of bread.

"I just thought it would be an interesting place from which to observe our exit from the Empty Sector and our return to Jurisdiction space."

"You can see that from here." Halvo was watching her with a gleam in his eye that suggested he knew what she was trying to do.

"Then I would also like a tour of the galley where our delicious dinner was prepared."

"Um-hmm." He never took his eyes off her, though he swallowed two large gulps of qahf.

"Is there an observation deck on the ship?"

"Of course." Halvo popped the last of the bread into his mouth.

"Dysia mentioned a recreation area for the crew. Did you know she is a swordswoman?"

"She won the Jurisdiction champion[...]
years ago." Halvo paused, then said, "You for[...]
to mention the cargo bays."

"Did I?" To Perri's own ears her voice
sounded too bright, too surprised, too falsely innocent. "I suppose I did. I do want to see all of
the ship."

"You may not visit the cargo bay where Rolli
is stored." Halvo spoke in his admiral's voice
rather than in a lover's tone.

"But I miss her! Rolli has been with me every
day since I was nine years old."

"I would be jealous of that robot if I did not
know there are things I can do for you that Rolli
cannot." Halvo moved swiftly to kneel on the
mattress next to Perri. "You are afraid the technicians at Capital will uncover Melri's memories, aren't you? And you fear that, as a result,
Rolli will be destroyed and a heavier punishment laid on you."

"There are enough reasons for your mother
to hate me, and for your father to punish me,
without them learning about those implanted
memories."

"I can tell you this much," Halvo said. "While
we were on Dulan's Planet Tarik, who knows far
more than you or I about such mechanisms—
and probably more than any technician at Capital—took great care to disguise that portion of
Rolli's circuitry."

"Tarik did?"

385

...ormous pleasure from

...les that he considers un-

...aid. "Tarik has been known

...s on occasion, too. He was all

...ork on Rolli."

... for telling me, but I still want to

... be done. Not on this trip. Rolli and the *Space Dragon* are under heavy guard. However, there may be something I can do to alleviate your loneliness. I believe there is just enough time before I am scheduled to meet with Capt. Jyrit." Halvo lifted Perri, settling her across his thighs. One of his hands slipped inside the open neckline of her robe to stroke and caress her breast. His mouth quickly followed his fingers. With her own emotional temperature rising, Perri could feel Halvo hardening against her. She pulled at her robe, lifting it up until it was bunched at her waist and she and Halvo were flesh to flesh. Her arms stole around his neck just as Halvo pulled her nearer still.

"You really are the most inventive man," she whispered.

"Do you still want to get out of this guest cabin that you regard as a jail?" It was almost noon by ship's time and Halvo had been with Capt. Jyrit for several hours. He had just returned and now stood lounging in the doorway of Perri's cabin, looking incredibly handsome in his fresh Jurisdiction uniform.

Perri had used her time alone to invent new clothing for herself. She could tell from the way Halvo was regarding her that he approved of the costume she and the helpful computer had created. Her hair was pulled behind her ears, securely fastened there with a pair of mock tortoiseshell combs, which, nonetheless, allowed the dark red waves to flow loosely down her back. Her dress was a soft, pale beige, the neckline wide and just low enough to reveal her collarbones. The sleeves were long and tight and the body of the dress was designed to cling, but the skirt flared out from hip to midcalf. Her tights matched the dress exactly, as did her plain, low-heeled shoes. It was a simple outfit, yet the mirror had revealed to Perri how well the color and the cut of the dress showed off her lithe figure and the startling combination of her hair and eyes.

She had dumped her Regulan clothes into the recycling slot. Ridding herself of them and putting on the new garments of her own choice marked for Perri the beginning of her life as a real adult. No longer a girl in any sense, she was determined to accept whatever fate—and Jurisdiction justice—might deal to her. As an adult she would take full responsibility for what she had done. And she would never stop loving Halvo.

"I have learned so much from you," she said

to him. "I never laughed before I met you. I never made up my own mind on any subject."

"It hasn't been one-sided, you know." He came to her to lift her chin and kiss her lightly. "I had become remarkably stuffy. I had forgotten how to have fun."

"While I had never learned how." Perri touched his cheek. "If it is permitted, I would like to see as much of the ship as possible. I have a lot to learn, and it seems that most of my schooling must be completed before we reach Capital." She did not finish the thought, which was that once she was in a Capital jail cell or, later, on a prison planet, she would not have the opportunity to study the cultures of the many Races of the Jurisdiction or their history and various sciences. Her education would be brief, limited to the days she spent on the *Krontar* and the facilities the ship had to offer.

"I have Jyrit's permission to show you around," Halvo said.

"Then let us not waste time." Perri was out of her cabin and into the corridor before she finished speaking. She indicated the guards standing on either side of her door. "Do they have to come with us?"

"Gentlemen, I believe I can handle the prisoner on my own," Halvo said to the guards. "On my authority, you are dismissed. Check with security and your chief will tell you when to begin your next watch at this post."

"Aye, sir." Outwardly the guards appeared to be serious, but Perri thought they were secretly amused.

With Halvo as a guide to explain why the ship was arranged as it was, the layout of the *Krontar* soon became clear to Perri. It was not only a warship. Arrangements were necessary to house, feed, clothe, and at least occasionally, to entertain the several hundred souls who served on her. Nor could the care of personnel who were ill or injured by accident or in battle be neglected. Perri met the chief cook, the ship's three doctors, the head nurse, and the recreation director. She even met the Chief of Security, who, as she expected, regarded her with cold disdain.

"You already know Lt. Dysia, the Chief Armaments Officer," Halvo said as they walked along a corridor on one of the upper decks.

"It is amazing to me that a woman could be given so great a responsibility," Perri said.

Then she stopped in her tracks, because a cabin door had just opened and Kalina had stepped into the corridor. She looked as surprised to see Perri as Perri was to see her. One swift glance took in Perri's new clothing and the fact that she was with Halvo. A longer look assessed the quick upward tilt of Perri's chin and the way she met Kalina's eyes without faltering.

"Where are you going?" Kalina asked.

"With Capt. Jyrit's permission," Perri answered, "Halvo has been showing me over the ship."

"I see." Again Kalina looked from Perri to her son and then back to Perri. "Your appearance is much improved."

"I hope so," Perri said. "It is my intention to improve all of my life."

"Indeed?" Kalina almost smiled. "Why are there no guards with you?"

"Perri will not misbehave while she is in my custody," her son said.

"Let us hope you are not mistaken. Halvo, would you care to join me? My aides and I have been invited to the bridge to observe our reentry into Jurisdiction space."

"Thank you, Mother. Perri and I would be delighted."

Perri could tell that Kalina was taken aback. She had meant her invitation only for her son. But Halvo laid a hand on Perri's arm, keeping her close to him when he took his place at his mother's side and began to walk down the corridor with her. Kalina's two aides fell in behind them. Kalina said nothing, either to protest or to agree with Perri's inclusion in the party.

When they reached the bridge they all paused at the entrance. Deferring to his mother, Halvo stepped aside to let her go first. The double door slid open and Kalina moved to the exact middle of the threshold.

"Permission to enter the bridge, Capt. Jyrit?"

Kalina spoke the formal request.

Jyrit was standing in front of his captain's chair, his gaze intent upon a giant viewscreen across which swirled the image of the pink, gaseous outer boundary of the Empty Sector.

"Permission granted, Lady Kalina." Jyrit did not turn to look at his guests until all five members of Kalina's party had entered and the doors had closed. Then with perfect Jugarian formality he bowed to Kalina and to Halvo. He paused for only an instant before bowing to Perri, too. Halvo had told her that good manners and a sense of formality were important to Jugarians. Still, Perri marveled at Jyrit's unshakable poise at finding a prisoner on his bridge. Halvo had made no explanation of her presence, so Perri decided she was not obliged to make one either. She simply bowed to Jyrit as the others were doing.

"Where would you like us to stand, Captain?" Kalina asked. "We do not want to be in your way."

"Only the raised area immediately around my chair is off-limits," Jyrit said.

"Then we will remain behind that area and disturb you no further."

Again there were polite bows all around, after which Jyrit resumed his survey of the viewscreen. Dysia, who was sitting at a console off to one side of the bridge, looked over at Perri, took in her new clothes with a nod of approval, and sent a friendly smile her way.

As the *Krontar* drew nearer to the boundary the streaky, illuminated gas clouds through which they were passing became more dense and more frequent until they filled the viewscreen. The light from the clouds was reflected onto the bridge, turning the dull gray metal bulkheads and the businesslike consoles to glowing rose. The very air of the bridge seemed pink.

"It wasn't like this when we came into the Empty Sector," Perri whispered to Halvo.

"This is a better viewscreen than we had on the *Space Dragon*," Halvo replied. "It registers every particle of light to produce a more detailed picture. Nor are we traveling at Starthruster speed. This exit should be far smoother than our entrance."

It was. Instead of the rocking jolt and the heart-stopping sliding sensation that had nearly shaken the *Space Dragon* apart, Perri felt only a few mild bumps. With the Empty Sector behind them, the gas clouds cleared, the glow disappeared from the bridge, and the view of space shown on the large screen once more became a velvet black interrupted only by the light of distant stars.

"Lovely," Kalina murmured. "Thank you for allowing us to be here, Capt. Jyrit. This was a memorable experience."

"As always, Lady Kalina, your presence is a

great pleasure to me." Jyrit bowed to Kalina as she and her company moved toward the doors, preparing to leave the bridge.

"Captain," said the communications officer, "a ship is approaching."

"What markings?" Jyrit demanded. "Did one of those Regulan ships that followed us into the Empty Sector wait to be sure we would come out again?"

"No, sir, it's not one of those two ships," the communications officer replied.

"Sir, it is a warship, and heavily armed," Dysia said. "It bears no identifying markings at all, not even a number."

"That is against Jurisdiction law."

"Perhaps it isn't a Jurisdiction ship," Dysia said. "It might be a pirate vessel."

By then the approaching ship was visible on the viewscreen as a shadow only slightly less black than the space around it.

"Magnify that image." Jyrit's order was obeyed at once. The strange ship grew larger and more menacing looking.

"It displays no running lights," Jyrit said. "I take that as a sure sign of aggressive intentions."

"Mother," Halvo said to Kalina, "you and your aides ought to leave. A warship bridge is no place for you if there is trouble."

"Go back to my cabin and wait for me there," Kalina said to her aides. "I shall remain here until we discover what the appearance of this ship portends. There may be something I can do to help avert a problem."

"Mother, I wish you would go. If they prove to be pirates," Halvo said with a nod toward the viewscreen, "then it's better if they don't know you are aboard. You would be a great prize to a pirate captain."

"No more than you are," Kalina said. "I will not leave unless Capt. Jyrit specifically orders me to do so."

Jyrit wasn't paying any attention to the discussion between Halvo and his mother. The *Krontar's* captain was fully occupied with issuing a series of commands to his bridge crew. The *Krontar* slowed as the unknown ship continued on an interception course. At Jyrit's order, Dysia released the safety monitors and readied the ship's weapons for firing.

"I am beginning to think they would prefer not to talk to us," said the communications officer, who was trying to establish contact with the unidentified ship. "Ah, there they are. Sir, they have finally accepted a video link with us. The picture is coming on the viewscreen now."

The image of the oncoming vessel faded to a picture of one section of its bridge. A man so young he could only be a junior officer had the helm, but he wore no uniform. At once Jyrit identified himself and his ship, stating that it was returning to Capital.

"Identify yourself." Jyrit paused, awaiting that act of courtesy common to all space travelers who were on respectable business.

"We prefer to remain anonymous." The young man spoke with no trace of politeness. Perri watched in fascination as Jyrit's antennae began to turn red with anger at the deliberate rudeness.

"Are you the captain?" Jyrit demanded.

"You have passengers whom we wish to welcome aboard our ship," the young man said without answering Jyrit's question. "You will send a shuttlecraft to us with the Lady Kalina and Adm. Halvo Gibal aboard."

"If we do not?" Jyrit said through gritted teeth.

"We will reduce you to atoms."

"They are pirates," Halvo said. "They want prisoners for ransom."

"Before I allow any of my passengers to visit an unknown ship," Jyrit said to the face on the viewscreen, "I must speak to your captain."

"Why?"

The response was so insolent that Jyrit's antennae fairly glowed with outrage. But he kept his voice firmly reasonable. "I want your captain's word of honor that these two passengers will not be harmed."

There followed a whispered conversation between the young man and someone who was positioned offscreen. While it went on, everyone on the bridge of the *Krontar* stared at the viewscreen, straining to discover any sign that might reveal the origin of the ship they were confronting. Perri gazed as fixedly as anyone else, but all she could see was a communications station bare of everything except the necessary console equipment. The area behind the young man was also blank, just a pale, painted background—until he leaned closer to whoever was speaking to him.

"Halvo," Perri said, keeping her voice soft, "when he moved just then, his shadow moved over a raised marking on the wall."

"Bulkhead," Halvo said. "I saw it, too. Something has been deliberately covered over."

"An identity mark?" said Kalina, who was close enough to hear them talking.

"Possibly," Halvo said, "but I can't tell what it is. Not unless he changes position again so his shadow slides along that bulkhead."

"It looked to me like a circle," Kalina said. "Which isn't much help to us. There are hundreds of governments that use some kind of circular device as their emblem."

Or a spiral. Perri could not make herself say the words out loud. Not yet, not until she was sure of what she was beginning to suspect.

"If these are pirates, that could be a stolen ship, and any emblem on it would be meaningless," Halvo said.

"Our captain will speak to you," the young man said to Jyrit.

Jyrit moved forward a pace or two to stand directly in front of the screen. The young man who had been speaking to Jyrit stepped aside and an older person in plain dark tunic and trousers came into view. This man had light brown hair streaked with gray, and though she could not see his eyes on the viewscreen, Perri knew they were green.

"Halvo," Perri hissed. "I know him."

"What?" Kalina stared at her. "Who is he?"

"It is Vedyr. It is Elyr's servant. He carried to me the news that Elyr had been condemned to death. False news!" Raising her voice, Perri said, "Capt. Jyrit, that mysterious ship must come from Regula. Now that I have recognized the captain, I can identify that covered-up symbol on the bulkhead behind him as the Regulan spiral." As she spoke, Perri moved out of the shelter of Jyrit's back and into full view of the man on the screen.

"Perri?" Vedyr looked stunned.

"He probably expected you to be confined to a cell," Halvo said, "and never guessed you would be on the bridge to see and recognize him."

"It is a good thing for us that she is here," Kalina said. "Thank you for the information, Perri."

"If you do not deliver Lady Kalina and Adm.

Halvo to us promptly," Vedyr said to Jyrit, "you will be destroyed."

"I would say he has recovered from his surprise," Halvo said.

"Capt. Jyrit, may I speak to him?" Perri asked. "I have an idea."

"Go ahead. Take as much time as you like." Jyrit motioned to Perri to take his place while he stepped closer to Dysia, with whom he began to speak in a low voice. Perri understood that Jyrit was planning his next move and would appreciate having Vedyr's attention fixed on her for a while.

"Vedyr." Perri faced him, unafraid.

"Woman, you may not speak without my permission," Vedyr said.

"You just heard Capt. Jyrit. I have his permission to speak. Vedyr, you do not want Lady Kalina or Adm. Halvo. I am the one you want to take back to Regula. As you can see by my lovely new clothing and by the freedom with which I move about this bridge, I am not a prisoner here. These people think well of me. I offer myself as hostage in place of Lady Kalina and Adm. Halvo. I will willingly join you aboard your ship. I will return to Regula without protest, and once there, I will offer myself to the Hierarchy for punishment."

"You?" Vedyr looked as if he might burst into scornful laughter.

"I am sure Capt. Jyrit will agree to let me have

398

a one-person shuttlecraft. I can be with you within the hour."

"Women cannot handle machinery," Vedyr said.

"During my absence from Regula, I have learned to pilot the *Space Dragon*."

"Outrageous! Scandalous!" Vedyr did not trouble to hide his shock. But he pulled himself together quickly. "You are of no use to us, Perri. Enough delay! I want an immediate answer from Capt. Jyrit."

"Sir," the communications officer said to Jyrit, "our sensors indicate only a skeleton crew aboard that ship."

"No more than half their weapons are operational," Dysia said, adding the data provided by her instruments. "This confrontation is only a bluff. They don't know us very well if they thought we would be fooled by it."

"Just as I thought." Jyrit paused for a second. "Vedyr may be able to answer some of our questions. I want that ship disabled, not destroyed. And I want the crew captured alive. Fire when ready, Lt. Dysia."

"Aye, sir." Dysia pressed the buttons on the weapons console. At first nothing happened, but then everyone on the bridge witnessed the results of their attack on the viewscreen. Sparks flew from the communications console next to Vedyr. With a shout he jumped away from it.

"Can you still hear me, Vedyr?" Jyrit was back

in the captain's position, standing next to Perri. "It is you who will be destroyed if you do not surrender."

"Fire!" Vedyr screamed. The image of his ship's bridge vanished, changing to an exterior view of the entire ship. The weapons tubes flared bright yellow. The aim was true and a moment later the *Krontar* rocked as the blasts hit her hull.

Perri was thrown off her feet and onto the deck. Halvo caught her, setting her upright again.

"Lt. Dysia." Jyrit was as cool as if he were attending a party. "Blast those Regulans to a standstill now. I want no injuries or deaths on my ship."

"Aye, sir."

"Why is Vedyr doing this?" Perri cried. "He has never been a violent person."

"You heard him," Kalina said. "He wants me and Halvo for hostages. Some people will turn violent for large sums of money."

"No, there is more to what Vedyr is doing. There must be," Perri insisted.

"Are you hurt?" Kalina asked, seeing Perri rub her wrist.

"I just landed hard on my hand and twisted my wrist. There's no serious harm done."

"Would you actually have gone to that ship in place of Halvo and me?"

"Of course." Perri's green eyes met Kalina's

blue ones with open honesty. "I have much to answer for, Lady Kalina. I am sure it is at least partly because of me that we are in this dangerous situation. If I can help Halvo or you or, indeed, prevent the taking of a single life aboard this ship, then I will do whatever is required of me."

"Capt. Jyrit." Dysia's voice rang through the bridge. "All weapons on the Regulan ship have been disabled. Their air-circulation system is no longer functioning. They have only two shuttlecraft and both are out of commission."

"Good work, Lieutenant. Comm officer, get the bridge view back on screen. I want to see Vedyr face-to-face." It took a minute or so, but Jyrit's order was carried out and a wavering, smoke-obscured image appeared. "Now, Vedyr, you cannot live much longer in a deteriorating atmosphere. As I understand your culture, suicide is not acceptable to Regulans under any circumstances. We will send shuttlecraft to pick up your crew. How many survivors have you?"

"There are twelve of us." Vedyr appeared to be utterly defeated.

"My communications officer will make the arrangements with you. We will take your damaged ship in tow. Jyrit out." With a slash of his hand Jyrit indicated that the video link with Vedyr should be severed.

"Thank you for your help, Perri." Jyrit's nod in her direction was almost a bow.

401

"Captain, something is wrong here," Perri said. "Vedyr is not a space pilot, he's a servant. Why was he put in charge of a ship with a minimal crew and only half the weapons in working order? It doesn't make sense."

"I agree." Jyrit gave her a quick look of approval.

"Their apparent surrender may be a trap," Halvo said.

"Are there any other ships in this area?" Jyrit asked his communications officer.

"No, sir," came the immediate response. "All clear between here and the Cetan border."

"Then our best hope of solving this intriguing mystery would seem to lie in intensive questioning of Vedyr and his crew," Jyrit said. "And you, Perri, will have the chance to prove you meant that rash claim you made to the effect that you are willing to do all you can to help us."

Perri stared into the holding cell, grateful that she was not being kept in one. It was a gray metal cube containing only a padded shelf for sitting and sleeping and a pull-down lavatory for the prisoner's personal needs. A strained-looking Vedyr was standing well back from the charged mesh that stretched across the open side of the cell. If he touched the mesh, the shock it generated would leave him unconscious.

Jyrit had decided not to attend this initial interview, saying he would interrogate the prisoners later, after giving them time to think over their misdeeds and contemplate what kind of justice might await them. Thus, it was Halvo and Perri who stood facing Vedyr, along with Dysia and a security officer, who were there to serve as corroborating witnesses. In one hand Halvo held a recorder. He pressed the button to start it.

"Perri of Regula, your official identification of this man is required," Halvo said to her.

"It is Vedyr of Regula, the servant of my former betrothed, Elyr," Perri said. "I know him for a liar, but he is completely loyal to Elyr. I do not believe he would stop a Jurisdiction ship on his own. Elyr must have sent him—or perhaps the Chief Hierarch did."

"The identification and your comments are formally noted." Halvo looked toward Vedyr. "Have you anything to say for yourself? I warn you, interrogation by Capt. Jyrit's security people will not be a pleasant experience. You would do well to speak now to me."

"You do not frighten me." Vedyr sneered. "Capt. Jyrit will not break the laws, not on a Jurisdiction ship with Lady Kalina aboard it. Torture is forbidden by Jurisdiction law. So are truth drugs and mind draining. I have nothing to say, not to you, Admiral, or to your Capt. Jyrit."

"But I have," Perri said. "In fact, I have already told my story several times. You were involved in the plot to abduct Halvo from this very ship. Surely you know about Jugarian honor, Vedyr. Capt. Jyrit will not rest until you—and Elyr—are punished for your parts in that crime. If you are still as loyal to Elyr as you have always been, then you will tell everything you know about the plot against Halvo. You see, I believe and I have so informed Capt. Jyrit and Lady Kalina that the true instigator of the abduction scheme was the Chief Hierarch. If I am right, then you and Elyr may be able to lessen your punishment by revealing the truth."

Those statements were what Perri and Jyrit had agreed that she would say to Vedyr. Still, the words were hard for Perri, because she believed Elyr was as much to blame as the Chief Hierarch. But she was eager to prove that she had been a pawn and not one of the conspirators. While on the bridge of the *Krontar* Perri had found the qualified approval of Lady Kalina and Capt. Jyrit to be extremely gratifying. She was determined not to disappoint them.

"Tell us what you know, Vedyr," she said.

"Woman." Vedyr spoke in the scornful tone that Regulan men ordinarily used with females. "You are every bit as stupid as Elyr always said you were. Not Capt. Jyrit, nor Lady Kalina, nor even Leader Almaric can touch Elyr now. You haven't heard the latest news from Regula, have you?"

"What news?" Perri demanded. She was aware of Halvo's rising annoyance with Vedyr's manner toward her. She just hoped she could make Vedyr say something important before Halvo cautioned him to be more polite, an order that would effectively silence Vedyr out of sheer outrage at the idea that a woman's feelings ought to be considered.

"Your former betrothed," Vedyr said to Perri with malicious relish, "cannot be punished by the Jurisdiction."

"Why not?" Perri expected Vedyr to say that Elyr was dead. It was the only reason she could think of for such a declaration. Vedyr's actual response was the last thing she expected to hear.

"Because Elyr is the Chief Hierarch."

"What?" Perri stared at him in disbelief. "It cannot be. Where is the real Chief Hierarch?"

"That old man?" Vedyr's voice dripped contempt. "We have removed him."

"But he is Elyr's father-in-law," Perri said.

"What does that signify? Women never understand these governmental matters," Vedyr said to Halvo, "certainly not one as stupid as Perri."

"This interview is over." His mouth hard with anger, Halvo turned off the recorder. Without another word he stalked out of the ship's brig, his companions following him.

In Jyrit's conference room Perri, Halvo, Kalina, Dysia, and Jyrit were gathered. While the others listened to the recording of the interview with Vedyr, Perri glanced about the room, which was decorated in Jugarian style. The walls were stark white, there was a grass mat of some kind on the floor, and the dark wood chairs were cushioned in bright red and gold. A tall gold vase containing two red flowers and a swirl of bare branches stood in one corner. Four tall windows showed the wide vista of space. Perri found the very spareness of the room relaxing and peculiarly elegant, perhaps because it was so different from Regulan decor. At the moment, she was not feeling charitable toward anything—or anyone—with the slightest claim to being Regulan.

"So Elyr has made himself Chief Hierarch," Jyrit said. "I wonder how he did it."

"Marriage to the old Chief Hierarch's daughter would give him a claim to become a member of the Hierarchy." Perri tore her eyes from contemplation of the red flowers to respond to Jyrit's remarks. "Ascension to the Hierarchy by right of marriage has occurred in the past. But the men who reach the Hierarchy by such means do not usually aspire to the foremost position of power."

"I wonder what Vedyr meant by saying that the former Chief Hierarch has been removed," Kalina said. "Is the old man still alive or have they killed him?"

"In a legal sense, it hardly matters," Halvo said, "since Jurisdiction law forbids interference in the internal affairs of any Member Planet. So Vedyr is right when he claims that Elyr cannot be touched."

"Except by other Regulans," Perri said. "Elyr must have made enemies among the six men who have been members of the Hierarchy for years, each of whom will no doubt think he had a greater right than Elyr to become Chief Hierarch."

Perri fell silent under Kalina's intense gaze. "Whatever your complicity in this matter may be, it is clear to me that you are not the witless creature those men believe you to be. However, Elyr is a fool."

"At the moment, he appears to be a successful one," Dysia said.

"Not for long." Kalina's lips curled into a smile that Perri was sure must have made many a miscreant tremble. She was glad Kalina had not turned that smile on her. "As Halvo has rightly noted, so long as Regulan intrigues were confined to Regula, the Jurisdiction government could not legally take action against the Hierarchy. But no planetary government, whether it is a Member of the Jurisdiction or not, can order the kidnapping of the Admiral of the Jurisdiction Fleet without expecting retribution."

"Never mind how useless to the Jurisdiction that admiral may have become," Halvo muttered.

"You are not useless, Halvo. Not at all." Kalina gave her son a long look before she turned to Jyrit. "Before he left his ship, did Vedyr send a message to Regula?"

"No," Jyrit said. "My communications officer was monitoring all messages from that ship. The only ones sent were to the *Krontar*."

"Still," Kalina said, "when Elyr does not hear from his friend, Vedyr, he may send another vessel to intercept us. Jyrit, I suggest you have your communications officer send a full report of this incident to Capital and also request an escort to see us safely there. This is no slur on your honor or on your determination to protect us to your last breath, my friend. It is merely a realization of the great distance that lies between us and Capital—and of the ceaseless treachery of the Regulans."

"I agree with you," Jyrit said. "I shall give the orders you wish."

"Before we proceed to Capital," Halvo said, "we ought to make a stop at Regula."

"No!" Perri cried in dismay. "I never want to see Regula again."

"In the name of all the stars, why should we

go there?" Kalina asked.

"For two reasons," Halvo said. "First, to confront Elyr and try to unravel the mystery of why I was kidnapped and why Perri was used as the Chief Hierarch's agent. And second, to discover what has happened to the former Chief Hierarch. We will need to know whether he is dead or still alive before the Jurisdiction can bring charges against the Hierarchy. If the old man is dead and Elyr claims that he was in some way a victim of the old Chief Hierarch, then the Jurisdiction may not have a case against him."

"I see your point," Jyrit said. "I also have personal reasons for wanting this mystery solved. My honor was blemished by the scheme that old Chief Hierarch set in motion."

"Jyrit," Kalina said, "any stain you imagine upon your honor has been wiped out by your bravery in rescuing Halvo. My dear friend, you were nearly killed for your efforts in Halvo's behalf. Not even your sacred honor could require more of you."

"But Halvo is right," Jyrit said. "Before we travel to Capital, we stop at Regula."

Chapter Twenty-two

"Ah, Perri, you are wonderful." Drawing her nearer on the bed they shared, Halvo buried his face in her hair. "You are everything a man could want. Beautiful, intelligent—"

"You are the only man who thinks so," she said. "You heard Vedyr call me stupid, just as Elyr always did."

"They are blinded by their distorted Regulan attitudes toward women," Halvo said.

His hands caressed Perri's body, his mouth was on her throat, her shoulders, her breasts. Perri felt herself warming to him as she always did when they lay together, but this time a portion of her mind was separate from what they were doing. A small corner of her brain was mulling over a problem, considering something she had seen . . . or heard . . . something she ought to be able to put together. . . .

Halvo moved over her, his mouth on hers again, making her dizzy with sensual pleasure. His thigh slid between hers. She was aware of his masculine weight pushing against her, seeking entrance. She slipped a notch closer to ecstasy, toward acceptance of his desire and the sweet oblivion of throbbing passion. Then that odd, busy, little corner of her mind opened wide with comprehension.

"Pirates!" she said, trying to push Halvo away. "Halvo, wait."

"I can't." He pressed more firmly against her. "Not even for another pirate attack."

"No, please listen to me. I have just put the pieces together."

"It is what I am trying to do, too. Now, if you will only—"

"No, Halvo, you must stop. This is so important." She tried to wriggle away from under him, and she pushed at his shoulders as hard as she could. She saw his face go dark with frustration before he controlled himself and pulled back to kneel between her thighs.

"What is it?" he asked. "I know you would not stop me at such a moment for some trifle."

"You asked me once if I could remember seeing or hearing anything during my interview with the Chief Hierarch that might cast some light on why I was sent to abduct you or why the Chief Hierarch wanted you kidnapped."

"And?" He was watching her intently and she could tell he was intrigued rather than angered by the way in which she had stopped him at the height of his passion.

Blessed Halvo. She did not think any other man would take her insistence on waiting quite as well as he was. She wanted to touch him and whisper a promise that she would make the delay up to him because his consideration of her wishes warmed her heart as few other gestures could have. However, she decided it would be best not to stir that particular fire at the moment. Passion would have to be postponed, at least for a little while.

"Perri, you are going to explain, aren't you?" Halvo cocked an inquiring eyebrow at her.

"The Regulan spiral was the key," she said.

"The one we noticed on the bulkhead of Vedyr's ship, the sign that was covered up?" he asked when she paused.

"Yes. That disguised sign reminded me of the two Regulan spirals in the Chief Hierarch's private office. I mean, in the office of the former Chief Hierarch. Who knows what changes Elyr has made to that chamber?"

"Since the spiral is the Sign of Regula, it would not be unusual for the design to be in the Chief Hierarch's office," Halvo said.

"It was the combination of elements in the

office that I found so unusual," Perri said. "The silver spiral on the wall and a second spiral inlaid on the Chief Hierarch's desk. A Cetan sword on another wall. And a gold Styxian lizard sitting on the desk. I understood why the sword was there, because Regula has a commercial treaty with the Cetans. I could recall watching on the telscan the grand diplomatic ceremony when the treaty was signed and the sword was presented. I remember that I wanted to ask the Chief Hierarch why he also had a Styxian lizard, but I was too much in awe of him when I first saw him. By the time I had recovered enough to ask questions, I was so stunned by what he was telling me that I forgot all about the lizard."

"Regula has always been on cool terms with Styxia," Halvo said. "The two planetary systems are on opposite sides of the Jurisdiction, a distance that does not make for neighborly familiarity. And then, like many warm-blooded people, Regulans find the Styxians difficult to deal with since Styxians are descended from reptilian life-forms. Many of the humanoid Races of the Jurisdiction consider the Styxians untrustworthy, though I have never found them so. They were certainly honest and cooperative in the matter of the pirates whom we chased away from their border."

"Chased where?" Perri asked.

Halvo stared at her for a moment and she saw

413

Flora Speer

understanding come into his eyes.

"Are you suggesting that the Hierarchy gave the surviving pirates shelter after they fled the Styxian border?" he asked. "Perri, this is what I suspect, too, but so far I have not been able to put the whole story together."

"The entire Hierarchy may not be involved in the scheme," Perri said. "You will remember that Capt. Mirar had also been told a false tale to explain his mission. Perhaps it was only the Chief Hierarch who was directing the plot. He alone holds the power to grant dispensation from punishment in criminal cases. That is why I went to plead with him about Elyr's supposed death sentence. If the Chief Hierarch was in league with pirates, it would explain why he wanted me to abduct you."

"Because I led the force that defeated the pirates at Styxia," Halvo said. "The pirates must want revenge against me for that battle. Personal vengeance is a well-established custom with them."

"I can imagine an exchange of a different kind from the one the Chief Hierarch suggested to me during my interview with him," Perri said. "An exchange of a priceless piece of loot, the golden Styxian lizard I saw sitting on the Chief Hierarch's desk, plus a share of the profits from the pirates' raids, paid to the Chief Hierarch by the pirates in return for sheltering them in the Regulan sector—and for turning you over to them to do with as they liked. Any pirate would consider that a fair bargain. And so would the old Chief Hierarch from what I know of him. He liked money and power, but he loved intrigue even more. It would be a constant source of pleasure to him to know he was keeping the double secret of your disappearance and the location of the pirates' hideaway."

"Two dangerous secrets, and not entirely secure ones either," Halvo said, smiling as they worked their way through the maze of intrigue. "Just suppose that Elyr found out what the Chief Hierarch was up to and tried to blackmail him. And was paid off with a promise of marriage to the Chief Hierarch's daughter, which would guarantee Elyr a claim to a seat on the Hierarchy the next time one fell vacant."

"But Elyr was already betrothed to me," Perri said, taking up the story. "By Regulan law a betrothal can only be broken by death, which was why Rolli was programmed to blow up the *Space Dragon*—but only after you had left it, because they wanted you alive to hand over to the pirates. How furious those two conspirators must have been when you would not accept their false story that I was acting alone. And then you refused to leave the *Space Dragon*."

"They wanted you dead," Halvo said, "and me in the hands of the pirates so neither of us could tell our side of the story and so Elyr could be free to marry Thori. My dear, I do believe you

415

have solved this mystery."

"But why is Elyr now the Chief Hierarch?" Perri asked.

"Isn't it obvious? It's yet another Regulan intrigue, and from Elyr's point of view, it must be simple common sense. He knew too much. Elyr must have believed he would never be safe so long as the old Chief Hierarch held power. Nor could the Chief Hierarch feel secure with Elyr knowing about his illegal agreement with the pirates. One of the two was bound to destroy the other. Elyr got his blow in first. In the Service, we call it a preemptive strike."

"Then Elyr must have had the old Chief Hierarch killed," Perri said.

"No doubt." Halvo did not look at all upset by the conclusion. "I would guess that along with his title, Elyr has inherited the old Chief Hierarch's profitable connection with the pirates. That is probably why he sent Vedyr out to abduct me again, a role for which Vedyr was sadly miscast. The man doesn't have the nerve to play a pirate and be convincing about it. I am amazed by what poor judges of character Elyr and the Chief Hierarch have been. They used Vedyr beyond his capabilities and they misjudged you, Perri. They thought they could manipulate you as they pleased and, since you are a woman, you would do as they told you."

"Elyr is using Thori now." Perri's mind had moved on to another area of speculation. "Poor

Thori. I know her, Halvo. She loves her father, and she places a high premium on the importance of her family. Thori will not take kindly to what Elyr has done. I do not think their marriage can be a happy one." Perri paused, thinking. "Shouldn't we tell Capt. Jyrit about this right away? And your mother?"

"There will be time enough before we reach Regula." Halvo's eyes were glowing with a silver heat as he regarded Perri. "Do you have any idea just how stimulating I find intelligence in a woman? When combined with a kind heart and a passionate nature, brain power can be sexually devastating."

He was grinning at her, and Perri immediately saw why. Halvo was, as he had said, highly stimulated by her display of intuition and reasoning power.

"I am sorry I made you wait," she murmured.

"Don't apologize. The delay was well worthwhile." Catching Perri in his arms, he bore her down onto the mattress again. "May I assume that you are equally excited by what we have deduced? Or perhaps, since it is my understanding that women are sensitive about interruptions to passionate interludes, a bit more stimulation would be in order?"

"You may stimulate me as much as you like," she replied, "but be warned, Halvo. I intend to give as much stimulation as I get."

"That's what I was hoping," he said.

*   *   *

"You have a Regulan ship in tow?" On the viewscreen Elyr's deliberately bland expression lapsed into fear, which was quickly superseded by a display of controlled anger. "Capt. Jyrit, this is outrageous. By what law does a Jurisdiction Service vessel apprehend a friendly ship?"

"By the law of self-preservation," Jyrit said. "Your so-called friendly ship threatened us and ordered us to hand over hostages. Not that there was a chance they could do us much harm if we did not comply with their demands. The ship was insufficiently manned and armed, and its captain was completely untrained for warfare. By the way, Elyr, he claims to be a particular companion of yours."

Perri, who with Halvo and Kalina was standing off to one side of the bridge where Elyr could not see them, knew Jyrit was enjoying their meeting. She could tell that Elyr was not.

"You will address me as Chief Hierarch." Elyr attempted to regain the dignity he had lost over the last few minutes. "As head of the Regulan government, I order you to turn over to me any prisoners who may be Regulans. I also expect you to return the ship."

"You may have them, ship and men alike," Jyrit said. "We have examined every inch of that vessel and know it to be Regulan made. As for the men, they have been thoroughly interrogated. What they know, I know."

At those words, Elyr went white.

"Would you care to provide me with your personal explanation of recent events on Regula?" Jyrit asked. "I will be happy to carry your words to Leader Almaric. He will be curious to know how you have become Chief Hierarch at so young an age."

"When I discovered proof of the former Chief Hierarch's complicity in the abduction of Adm. Halvo Gibal," Elyr said, "I had no choice but to remove him from office."

"Where is he now?" Jyrit asked.

"That need not concern you. Merely convey my greetings to Leader Almaric and assure him the Regulan Hierarchy is conducting planetary business as usual."

"Jyrit," Kalina said, "may I have a few words with Elyr?" At Jyrit's assent, she moved forward to face the viewscreen.

"Lady Kalina." Seeing her, Elyr began to look nervous again.

"How is your mother faring after this unexpected change in your fortunes?" Kalina asked. "When last I spoke with Cynri, she was greatly worried about you."

"She is well," Elyr replied, "and no longer worried."

"Perhaps she ought to be more worried," Kalina said in a silky-smooth voice. "And Thori, your dear wife—how is she?"

"Thori is also well." Elyr frowned as if he

could not understand the purpose of Kalina's questions.

"After my delightful and remarkably enlightening visit to Regula not long ago, I regard both of those ladies as dear personal friends," Kalina said. "I would be deeply distressed were any harm to come to either of them. Leader Almaric would, of course, share in my distress."

"I thank you for your kind thoughts," Elyr said. "I will inform Thori and my mother that you were asking about them."

"The welfare of Regula and of the Regulan people is always a matter of concern to the Leader of the Jurisdiction," Kalina said. Deepening her voice she added, "Any misfortune to befall the Regulan Hierarchy, and any accident or ill health occurring to any Regulan, male or female, would call forth immediate help from the Jurisdiction Service. You may depend upon us, Elyr. Ah, forgive that slip of my tongue, *Chief Hierarch*. Your title is still so new to me. I beg you not to forget what I have said." Kalina stepped aside, leaving the viewscreen to Jyrit.

"If you have no other messages for anyone at Capital," Jyrit said to Elyr, "then we will return your ship and its crew to you, with the suggestion that you train those men better before sending them out into space again. We intend to leave the Regulan Sector in two hours." Jyrit paused, but Elyr said nothing more. At a nod from Jyrit, the communications officer closed the video link with Regula.

"Mother, you were wonderful," Halvo said, laughing. "What a marvelous example of diplomatic double-talk. Elyr won't dare to harm Thori now."

"Let us hope not." Kalina looked at Perri. "Thank you for suggesting that Thori will need protection from her scheming husband, since he has achieved his goal and does not need her anymore."

"It was your idea to include Cynri in the warning," Perri said, adding, "though I do not seriously think Elyr would harm his own mother."

"You never can tell with Regulan men," Kalina said. "They cannot be trusted."

"How well I know that. Lady Kalina, I hope you believe my story now."

"What I believe or do not believe does not matter," Kalina said. "The fact remains that you did, by your own admission, deliberately and willfully abduct my son, and for that crime you must face trial on Capital. What happens to you then will be up to Leader Almaric."

Chapter Twenty-three

Perri had never seen a city as magnificent as Capital, nor a house quite like the one where Kalina and Leader Almaric lived. With the *Krontar* docked at the orbiting spaceport high above the planet, Kalina, Halvo, Perri, Capt. Jyrit, Lt. Dysia, and a still deactivated Rolli had all boarded a shuttlecraft, which Halvo then piloted to a landing spot in a park that faced the Leader's house.

"As soon as he became Leader of the Jurisdiction, Almaric insisted on having a more convenient place to land than the main city strip," Kalina said. "This does save time, and since we had these trees and bushes planted, the view remains an agreeable one. As you see, we can walk to the house."

The instant they stepped off the shuttlecraft they were surrounded by Service guards. Two of them carried Rolli, while two more walked on either side of Perri.

The house to which they went presented a pale stone face, with stone steps leading up to the wide entrance. Once inside they paused only briefly in the stone floored entry hall before their group was ushered down a corridor to closed double doors of black wood that had a swirling design carved into them. In the design Perri recognized many of the symbols of the various Member worlds of the Jurisdiction, including the Sign of Regula, the familiar spiral. Two of the guards flung open the doors, and Kalina led everyone into the room beyond.

It was an office, with dark, paneled walls and shelves that held audio and video records. Even a few antique books had their places on those shelves. There was a green-and-red carpet on the red stone floor, a couch and several chairs grouped for easy conversation, and a wall of floor-to-ceiling windows that opened onto a stone terrace and the garden at the back of the house. A bowl of fruit, a thermal qahf jug, and a plate containing pastries sat together on a table.

Perri glanced around quickly, taking in those simple domestic objects before her eyes were drawn to the wide desk at one end of the room. A man sat at the desk, his head bowed over his work. Perri needed no introduction to recognize him. The Leader of the Jurisdiction looked up as Kalina entered.

"My dearest! Welcome home. I am happy to see that you are here at least an hour earlier than I expected." The man rose and came around the desk to Kalina. They went into each other's arms for a long, tender kiss.

"You are too thin, Almaric," Kalina said. "Every time I go away, you lose weight."

"Now that you are with me once more I expect to regain all of it." Almaric's attention moved from his wife to his son. He opened his arms. "Halvo, my boy, I feared I would never see you again."

As the two men embraced, Perri noticed Kalina brushing at her eyes.

"Capt. Jyrit, welcome and thank you for all of your help," Almaric said, gripping Jyrit's hand. "And you, too, Lt. Dysia. It's good to see you again."

Then all the pleasant warmth left Almaric's face. The look he gave Perri was icy enough to freeze the blood in her every vein. "I need not ask who you are."

Perri regretted that look. Almaric so closely resembled his younger son, Tarik, that Perri had at once experienced a rush of friendly emotion toward him. Like Tarik, Almaric was tall and slim, though the father's once dark hair was almost completely silver, and his sharp-featured face was lined. His eyes were a lighter shade of blue than Tarik's and cold when they looked at Perri. So very cold. With a chill in her heart, Perri saw that Almaric might never forgive her for abducting the beloved son of whom he was so proud.

It was Halvo who saved Perri from collapse in the face of his father's coldness. Halvo put an arm around her and drew her against his side. With a question forming in his icy-blue eyes, Almaric regarded his older son.

"This is Perri." Halvo's tone of voice made it clear that she was important to him. "She and I have an amazing story to tell you."

"Indeed?" Almaric's lips barely moved when he spoke.

"Capt. Jyrit, Lt. Dysia, and my own mother are witnesses to much of the tale," Halvo said. "We also bring news from Regula."

"Unless you have been in direct contact with Regula during the last day or two, I expect the news I have of that benighted planet is more recent than yours. I shall wait to reveal what I know of Regula until after I have heard all you can tell me of your adventures. After listening to your story, I am sure what has happened on Regula will hold greater meaning for me, allowing me to interpret events more accurately." Almaric gestured toward the grouping of couch and chairs. "Please be seated."

All of them did as he ordered, except Perri, who hung back. Going to where the guards had set Rolli down before departing, she laid a hand on the robot's shoulder.

"I want Rolli reactivated," she said to Halvo. "Rolli is a witness, too."

"I will decide when that thing should speak," Almaric said.

"Father," Halvo said in a voice that suggested to Perri the beginning of a dispute.

"Actually, Almaric, my dear," Kalina said, breaking into the tension between father and son, "Perri is correct in this instance. I also suggest that the robot be included in our discussion."

"I see." Almaric let them wait for a minute or two while he pondered his decision. "Very well, Kalina, I will accede to your request. Let the robot be activated. No, Perri. Take your hands away from it. Halvo will do it."

"As you wish, Leader Almaric." Perri sat down in the chair Kalina indicated to her.

"Admiral," Rolli said, blue eyelights scanning the room, "where are we now?"

Halvo explained, introducing those members of their company whom Rolli did not know.

"I ought to be the one to begin this story," Halvo said, taking the chair next to Perri. "As you know, Father, I was returning to Capital from the hospital planet where I had been recovering for a year. It is difficult for me to remember now just how bored, how listless and weary of life I was after months of a strict schedule of intensive therapy."

"You had the best of care," Almaric said with some irritation.

"I know I did, and I thank you for arranging it," Halvo said. "It is not your fault that I could not deal with what my life had become or with the future I knew I would face once I reached Capital. When the *Krontar* was hailed by a tiny pirate ship and a robot's voice declared that a meeting with me was desired, my curiosity was aroused. It was the first time since I was wounded that I had felt any spark of interest in what was happening around me.

"I want to make it very plain," Halvo said, "that nothing that followed was in any way the fault of Capt. Jyrit or of any member of his crew. I was repeatedly warned against meeting with anyone from the pirate ship and warned again about the possible danger in boarding it."

With Halvo suggesting when each of them should speak, the others told their respective versions of the story roughly in chronological order. When Halvo produced the specimen capsule containing the device that had been intended to make Rolli destroy the *Space Dragon*, Almaric took it with an angry exclamation.

"This is damning evidence," Almaric said, "though it may prove to be irrelevant."

"I don't see how that can be," Kalina said.

427

"When the tale is done, I do not doubt that you will all understand." Almaric looked at his wife. "Tell us now about your first visit to Regula."

Not having heard that part of the story, Perri listened to Kalina with great interest. She was aware that Leader Almaric's eyes were often fixed on her face, and she feared he was agreeing with every unkind thing the Regulans had said about her.

Though when it was his turn to speak again Halvo repeatedly pointed out that Perri had been little more than an unknowing pawn in the schemes of Elyr and the Chief Hierarch. Perri did not think Almaric was impressed by that argument, not even when Rolli also attested to Perri's ignorance of any intrigue and spoke of Perri's simple and perfectly natural desire to help her betrothed. Rolli spoke eloquently of Perri's hurt and her rage at Elyr's betrayal.

Rolli then went on to mention the subservient position of women in Regulan society. At that point Almaric appeared to be having some difficulty in controlling an impulse to laugh. Perri thought his reaction was probably caused by the fact that she was no longer a typical Regulan woman, which the shrewd Almaric must have noticed. During the course of her adventures with Halvo she had changed until she was anything but subservient. And she was certainly not passive either. Recalling her last night with Halvo aboard the *Krontar*, Perri was forced to admit that on Regula she would no longer be considered a woman of acceptable temperament.

When at last they all fell silent, their story told, Almaric looked from one to the other. The gleam in his eyes reminded Perri once again of Tarik. In her brief acquaintance with Tarik, he had often had the appearance of a man who was hiding a delicious joke that he could scarcely wait to reveal.

"Will you accuse Elyr of abetting pirates?" Jyrit asked Almaric.

"I do not believe it will be necessary to do so," Almaric said.

Perri could tell he was teasing them. His humorous gaze even included her.

"But, sir," Jyrit protested, "those cursed Regulans dared to have an Admiral of the Fleet kidnapped! An example must be set or the crime could be repeated, if not by the Regulans, then by some other Race. Not all the Members of the Jurisdiction are entirely law-abiding Races."

"Capt. Jyrit makes an excellent point," Kalina said with a smile for her Jugarian friend.

"I do not want a war, Kalina. This present peace was too hard won," Almaric said. "If we accuse the Regulans or attack them, their trading partners, the Cetans, are sure to join the dispute, and where will our peace treaty with Ceta be then?"

"I was thinking more of strict economic sanctions," Kalina said.

"Such restrictions would greatly anger the Regulan merchants," Almaric said. "Every one of them would be furious with the Hierarchy for bringing Jurisdiction sanctions down on them. You know how the Regulans are. There would be intrigue upon intrigue upon intrigue. I have no desire to cause any difficulty for the present Hierarchy." Almaric paused, his face a remarkable study in laughter and the attempt to prevent it.

"I think," Kalina said, looking into his eyes, "that you ought to reveal to us exactly what the latest news from Regula is."

"How perceptive you are, my dearest," Almaric murmured. "How could I possibly lead the Jurisdiction without you by my side?"

"Almaric." Kalina tried to look stern, though love for her husband was written clearly on her face for everyone in the room to see. "Speak before I strangle you."

"When Elyr made himself Chief Hierarch," Almaric said, "the other six Hierarchs were greatly displeased by his presumption. They immediately fell to squabbling among themselves about how best to remove him."

"I am not surprised to hear it," Kalina said. "Are you telling us that Elyr has been deposed?"

"He has," Almaric said, "but not by the other Hierarchs. They were too busy devising intrigues against each other to form a coalition strong enough to remove Elyr."

"Then who did remove him?" Kalina asked.

"His mother and his wife," Almaric said. Laughter threatened to overwhelm him, but he swallowed hard and kept his composure.

"What?" Kalina's jaw actually dropped open at that piece of news.

"Thori and Cynri?" Perri said. "Those quiet, peaceable women who would never dare raise their voices to any man?"

"They claimed to me that they were inspired by Kalina's example," Almaric said.

"I knew it!" Halvo burst into laughter. "Perri, didn't I tell you once that, if ever my mother went to Regula, she would turn the planet upside down?"

"I did nothing of the kind." Kalina sent a quelling look toward her laughing son before turning to Almaric again. "I assure you I was the very model of diplomatic propriety during my visit to Regula."

"Sir," Jyrit said before anyone could dispute Kalina's somewhat exaggerated claim, "may we assume from what you have said that Elyr was dispatched once he was removed from office?"

"Not at all," Almaric said. "Elyr is currently under house arrest, held there by Thori's authority. Thori says she will decide later what to do with him, but she suggested that she may keep him alive, since she wants to have a daughter and Cynri has expressed a wish to be a grandmother."

"How can Thori bear to lie down with Elyr after he killed her father?" Perri cried.

"It seems that Elyr lost his nerve and neglected to kill the former Chief Hierarch," Almaric said. "Elyr only imprisoned his father-in-law, and in prison the man will stay since, like Elyr, he is now accused of dealing with pirates."

While they all digested the unexpected news, Dysia spoke. "If the women are determined to pay the men back for past injustices, then I cannot think the Regulans will be any better off under female rule. They will simply reverse the situation instead of improving it."

"Apparently, Cynri takes the same point of view," Almaric said. "According to the report she made directly to me, she intends to keep a hierarchal system of government in place. Cynri herself has been installed as the new Chief Hierarch. In her capacity as head of the Regulan government, Cynri has made a profound apology for the previous government's involvement in the kidnapping of Halvo.

"She has also offered an explanation of the motive behind your kidnapping that accords with what you have deduced," Almaric said to Halvo. "According to Cynri, the old Chief Hierarch and his pirate friends were making so much profit from their illegal activities that they could not risk having the flow of money cut off if Halvo should decide to continue his crusade against the pirates. Whether you were healthy and commanding a warship, Halvo, or here at Capital where you could influence me to act against them, you represented a threat to pirates and Chief Hierarch alike."

"So," Halvo said, "greed was the ultimate reason for this intrigue. What reprisals will be made against Regula?"

"I consider myself a civilized man," Almaric said, "and I try to run a civilized government. Therefore, I will not call for vengeance. I assured Cynri that I believe her assertions about the great changes currently taking place on Regula. Of the six Lesser Hierarchs recently installed, three are women and three men. At Cynri's insistence, Thori is one of the female Hierarchs. Furthermore, Regulan women have at last been given equal citizenship with men, though I personally believe it will take many years for them to learn how to cope with their new freedoms—and their new responsibilities."

"The Jurisdiction could help them learn to be fair to both men and women," Kalina said.

"I have already offered our help, and Cynri has accepted." Almaric smiled at his wife. "I am so proud of you, my dear. These changes on Regula represent yet another diplomatic triumph to your credit."

Almaric looked around at his audience before

continuing. "Capt. Jyrit, I have a new assignment for you. The Regulans have requested our assistance in dealing with the problem of those pirates who are lurking in their sector. A certain Capt. Mirar particularly asked that you be sent to help. I gather that he holds you in high respect. I know you are overdue for leave, but would you have any objection to postponing your time off so you can return to Regula for a while?"

"No, sir." Jyrit's antennae were a bright and startling shade of orange. "I would be delighted."

"Despite the fact that he wounded you, Jyrit," Halvo said, "Capt. Mirar impressed me as an honest man. Perhaps not all Regulan males are addicted to intrigue."

"An interesting possibility," Jyrit said. "It would mean there is hope for the future of Regula."

"As for you, Lt. Dysia"—Almaric's eyes were dancing with amusement—"several days ago, I received a recommendation from your commanding officer, citing your exemplary service during a time of peril. I am happy to approve Capt. Jyrit's commendation of you and to promote you to the rank of lieutenant commander."

"Thank you, sir." Dysia looked from Almaric to Jyrit.

"No thanks are needed," Jyrit said. "You have

earned your promotion."

"Well, Halvo," Almaric said, turning to his son, "the next question is, what to do with you? For administrative reasons it was necessary to place someone else in the position being held for you. However, posts here at Capital do open up with some frequency."

"Of course they do." Halvo interrupted his father with sudden, barely controlled anger. "Since most of those administrative positions are held by Service personnel who are too old, or who have been too badly injured to remain on active duty, we can't expect them to live very long, can we?"

"We do our best for those who have retired from active duty," Almaric said. "The Jurisdiction owes to loyal Service personnel the dignity of continued employment for as long as they wish, or for at least as long as they are able to sit at a desk. Nor is such a job a matter of pure charity. The experience of such personnel is frequently useful."

"I am not so old, or any longer so disabled, that I can only perform a desk job," Halvo said.

"Yes, I am happy to see that you do appear to be restored to your usual excellent health," Almaric said. "My own eyes confirm the medical reports I received of you from the *Krontar*."

"Then give me an active man's job to do," Halvo demanded.

"Halvo, my boy, surely you understand that

Flora Speer

any officer in the Jurisdiction Service would be embarassed to have the former Admiral of the Fleet serving under him, to be forced to give orders to the man who was once his commander-in-chief. Nor am I willing to disrupt the Service order of promotions by removing the present Admiral of the Fleet and reinstating you. Such a move would be too destructive to morale."

"I have no desire to be Admiral of the Fleet again," Halvo said. "But I absolutely refuse to remain here at Capital in a desk job. I belong in space."

"Almaric," said Kalina, who had been listening to the altercation with growing concern, "I have a suggestion."

"I would be grateful to hear it, my dear," Almaric said.

"Since you became Leader of the Jurisdiction, I have been your only personal ambassador, the one person you trust to travel throughout the Jurisdiction, and sometimes beyond it, to help in settling disputes in an unofficial way. We have both complained that, while my work is vital to the smooth functioning of this extremely disparate organization of planetary governments, there is too much work for one person, and I am far too often away from you."

"I believe I understand what you are getting at, Kalina. With his vast experience of the many

Races of the Jurisdiction, Halvo could serve as my second unofficial ambassador. I say my second ambassador, for I do not delude myself that you will ever be willing to give up interplanetary travel, my dear. Like our sons, you love space too much to remain on any world for very long without becoming restless.

"Halvo, what do you think of your mother's idea?" Almaric turned back to his son. "I assure you, this would not be a made-up position designed to keep you happy. It will require hard work and a lot of travel, and it will sometimes be dangerous. But it would be a way for you to continue to serve the Jurisdiction without tying you to the desk job you appear to dread. If you say yes, I will begin by sending you to the Famorat, who are presently embroiled in a bloody dispute with their nearest neighboring star system over who first invented that new material for spaceship windows."

"The Famorat?" Perri said, unable to restrain herself at the mention of the intriguing name.

"Yes," Almaric said. "Do you know anything of that Race?"

"Only what Halvo has told me. The Famorat live too far from Regula for the Race to be familiar to me." Perri hoped she was not blushing. She knew Halvo was looking at her in a peculiar way, as if he were considering a fascinating possibility he dared not discuss with her in front of other people.

"I will consider your proposition," Halvo said to his father, "only after you agree to several conditions. First, when I travel as your personal ambassador, I want to use the *Space Dragon*."

"That wretched little ship?" Kalina cried. "Halvo, we can provide a larger, better-equipped vessel for you."

"I like the *Space Dragon*, Mother. She holds special memories for me."

"Can she be made space worthy again?" Almaric looked from Halvo to Jyrit for confirmation.

"Easily," Jyrit said at once. "For all their governmental faults, the Regulans are master shipbuilders. It won't take much to repair the *Space Dragon* and make her comfortable for long-distance space travel. She already has a Starthruster device."

"Very well, Halvo," Almaric said. "You shall have the *Space Dragon*. In fact, now that I think about it, a smaller vessel will be more appropriate for your work. Wherever you go, you won't upset the official Jurisdiction ambassadors by upstaging them."

"I also want Rolli to go with me," Halvo said.

When Perri would have protested that condition, Halvo, who had risen to stand behind her, put a hand on her shoulder and squeezed tight, signaling her to remain quiet. She sat in her chair, but not without sending a questioning look in Halvo's direction.

"I have found Rolli useful and easy to work with," Halvo said.

"Thank you for the compliment, Admiral, but I prefer to remain with Perri," Rolli said.

"Once Perri's trial is finished, I see no reason why the robot should not be handed over to you." Almaric spoke right across Rolli's words, as people frequently did when robots offered unsolicited remarks.

Perri was further annoyed by Almaric's attitude toward her old friend. She was about to make a complaint on Rolli's behalf when Halvo's hand on her shoulder squeezed again so hard that she almost cried out in pain.

"There will be no trial for Perri," Halvo said.

"The woman has admitted kidnapping you," Almaric said. "Her conviction and sentence are inevitable."

"Not only do I refuse to press charges against Perri on my own behalf," Halvo said, "but I will not act as witness against her if the Jurisdiction presses charges."

"You cannot prevent her trial," Almaric said.

"I can and I will. I intend to marry Perri. I call everyone here in this room to witness that I do so freely. What surer sign could there be that I forgive whatever minor mischief she has committed?"

"Minor?" Kalina gasped. "You could have been killed! If it had been left up to Elyr and the Chief Hierarch, you would have been killed."

"Not only do I remain alive," Halvo said, "but my life has been revitalized and I am happier than I have been since I was a boy."

"I do not know why you have chosen to do this," Almaric said, "but I remind you, Halvo, that once you marry this woman she can no longer be prosecuted for kidnapping you. Are you absolutely certain you want to take this path?"

"I have no doubts at all, Father."

"This is beyond my comprehension." Almaric shook his head in perplexity.

"He loves her," Kalina said to her husband.

"With everything that's in me," Halvo said. "I knew you would understand eventually, Mother."

Throughout the discussion Perri sat, still with Halvo's hand on her shoulder, unable to move for sheer amazement at his declaration. She was not certain she could believe what he had said. She knew he desired her. She thought he took pleasure in her company. But love? Or was this a ruse, Halvo's way of saving her from prosecution? Would he see to it that she was set free, then desert her?

"I cannot say I fully approve," Kalina said to Halvo, "but I will accept your choice."

"I do not approve," Almaric said.

"You will," his wife said, "once you understand how happy she makes Halvo. I was greatly prejudiced against her, Almaric, but the weeks I have spent observing the two of them have begun to change my mind about Perri's character."

"But to have my son, the former Admiral of the Fleet, marrying an accused felon—"

"You could say that she didn't kidnap him, that the abduction was in fact a cleverly planned elopement," Dysia said. "People might laugh at them for a short time, but the explanation would help to defuse a serious interplanetary incident if any Jurisdiction Member planet should decide that Regula ought to pay for its part in Halvo's abduction."

"No! Dysia, I thought you were my friend." Perri was on her feet, throwing off Halvo's restraining hand. "How dare any of you arrange my life for me without even asking me what I want? Tell me, Halvo, did you imagine I would be so grateful to escape a future on a prison planet that I would be willing to marry you instead of facing trial?"

"Actually," Halvo murmured, "I was hoping you might agree to marry me because you are eager to see more of the Jurisdiction. Or did I misunderstand your interest in space travel and in learning about new worlds?"

"You didn't ask me. You just told everyone else first!"

"I am asking you now. Will you marry me?"

"No."

"Why not? Is it because of my age? Do you think I am too old for you?"

"Age is only an excuse for something you don't want to do," she cried. "If you don't know my reasons for refusing, then I am right not to marry you."

He caught her hands and drew them up to rest on his chest. When she tried to pull away he kept his larger, stronger hands around hers, holding her fingers flat over his heart so she could feel it beating. He looked down into her eyes, and his own eyes flamed with the silver light of desire.

"Are you refusing me because I have never said aloud that I love you?" he asked.

"Your mother had to tell me, at the same time she told everyone else in this room!"

"I thought you knew. I thought I had been saying it with every act and every kiss since we first escaped Regula. I do love you, Perri. Without you, my life would be empty and unbearable. You have made me young again. You have given me laughter and warmth and hope. Now I have a universe of love to give to you in return. Please, please marry me. I don't think I can go on living without you."

She stared into his eyes, seeing there a future of honesty, love, and hope. And freedom, too. Halvo would never restrict her as Elyr once had. To Halvo, her love was valuable only if she gave it without coercion.

"Well," she said, "if you put it that way, I can scarcely refuse, can I? You are right. I do want

442

to see as much of the universe as I can, and marrying you seems to be the best way of achieving that particular dream."

"Now I begin to understand," Almaric said. "Kalina, she is very like you when you were young. I suppose I could remand her to Halvo's custody for long-term rehabilitation."

Perri and Halvo were not listening to him or to the laughter of the others in Almaric's office. Perri and Halvo were locked in each other's arms, mouth to mouth, heart to heart.

"Excellent." Rolli's blue eyelights were blinking merrily. "Precisely the outcome for which I hoped. I would remind you, Perri, that despite all the changes recently made to my programing I am still capable of caring for children as I once cared for you."

"If they intend to have children, they will need official permission," Almaric said.

"They already have permission from a far higher power than you," Rolli told the Leader of the Jurisdiction. "They have love's permission."

FLORA SPEER

Bestselling Author Of *Love Just In Time*

Falsely accused of murder, Sir Alain vows to move heaven and earth to clear his name and claim the sweet rose named Joanna. But in a world of deception and intrigue, the virile knight faces enemies who will do anything to thwart his quest of the heart.

From the sceptered isle of England to the sun-drenched shores of Sicily, the star-crossed lovers will weather a winter of discontent. And before they can share a glorious summer of passion, they will have to risk their reputations, their happiness, and their lives for love and honor.

_3816-1 $4.99 US/$5.99 CAN

THE 2022 ROMANCE CHRISTMAS COLLECTION

6 FREE TRADE-SIZE BOOKS IN ALL!

In this loveliest of seasons may you find many reasons for happiness, magic and love, and what better way to fill your heart with the magic of Christmas than with an unforgettable romance from our specially curated holiday collection.

YES! Please send me the first shipment of **The 2022 Romance Christmas Collection**. This collection begins with 1 FREE TRADE SIZE BOOK and 2 FREE gifts in the first shipment. Along with my free book, I'll also get 2 additional mass-market paperback books. If I do not cancel, I will continue to receive three books a month for five additional months. My first four shipments will be billed at the discount price of $19.98 U.S./$25.98 CAN., plus $1.99 U.S./$3.99 CAN. for shipping and handling*. My last two shipments will be billed at the discount price of $17.98 U.S./$23.98 CAN., plus $1.99 U.S./$3.99 CAN. for shipping and handling*. I understand that accepting the free books and gifts places me under no obligation to buy anything. I can always return a shipment and cancel at any time. My free books and gifts are mine to keep no matter what I decide.

☐ 269 HCK 1875   ☐ 469 HCK 1875

Name (please print)

Address   Apt. #

City   State/Province   Zip/Postal Code

Mail to the **Harlequin Reader Service:**
IN U.S.A.: P.O. Box 1341, Buffalo, NY 14240-8531
IN CANADA: P.O. Box 603, Fort Erie, ON L2A 5X3

*Terms and prices subject to change without notice. Prices do not include sales taxes, which will be charged (if applicable) based on your state or country of residence. Canadian residents will be charged applicable taxes. Offer not valid in Quebec. All orders subject to approval. Credit or debit balances in a customer's account(s) may be offset by any other outstanding balance owed by or to the customer. Please allow 3 to 4 weeks for delivery. Offer available while quantities last. © 2022 Harlequin Enterprises ULC. ® and ™ are trademarks owned by Harlequin Enterprises ULC.

Your Privacy—Your information is being collected by Harlequin Enterprises ULC, operating as Harlequin Reader Service. To see how we collect and use this information visit https://corporate.harlequin.com/privacy-notice. From time to time we may also exchange your personal information with reputable third parties. If you wish to opt out of this sharing of your personal information, please visit www.readerservice.com/consumerschoice or call 1-800-873-8635. Notice to California Residents—Under California law, you have specific rights to control and access your data. For more information visit https://corporate.harlequin.com/california-privacy.

XMASR2022

Get 4 FREE REWARDS!

We'll send you 2 FREE Books plus 2 FREE Mystery Gifts.

FREE Value Over $20

Both the **Romance** and **Suspense** collections feature compelling novels written by many of today's bestselling authors.

YES! Please send me 2 FREE novels from the Essential Romance or Essential Suspense Collection and my 2 FREE gifts (gifts are worth about $10 retail). After receiving them, if I don't wish to receive any more books, I can return the shipping statement marked "cancel." If I don't cancel, I will receive 4 brand-new novels every month and be billed just $7.49 each in the U.S. or $7.74 each in Canada. That's a savings of at least 17% off the cover price. It's quite a bargain! Shipping and handling is just 50¢ per book in the U.S. and $1.25 per book in Canada.* I understand that accepting the 2 free books and gifts places me under no obligation to buy anything. I can always return a shipment and cancel at any time by calling the number below. The free books and gifts are mine to keep no matter what I decide.

Choose one: ☐ **Essential Romance**
(194/394 MDN GRHV)

☐ **Essential Suspense**
(191/391 MDN GRHV)

Name (please print)

Address   Apt. #

City   State/Province   Zip/Postal Code

Email: Please check this box ☐ if you would like to receive newsletters and promotional emails from Harlequin Enterprises ULC and its affiliates. You can unsubscribe anytime.

Mail to the Harlequin Reader Service:
IN U.S.A.: P.O. Box 1341, Buffalo, NY 14240-8531
IN CANADA: P.O. Box 603, Fort Erie, Ontario L2A 5X3

Want to try 2 free books from another series! Call 1-800-873-8635 or visit www.ReaderService.com.

*Terms and prices subject to change without notice. Prices do not include sales taxes, which will be charged (if applicable) based on your state or country of residence. Canadian residents will be charged applicable taxes. Offer not valid in Quebec. This offer is limited to one order per household. Books received may not be as shown. Not valid for current subscribers to the Essential Romance or Essential Suspense Collection. All orders subject to approval. Credit or debit balances in a customer's account(s) may be offset by any other outstanding balance owed by or to the customer. Please allow 4 to 6 weeks for delivery. Offer available while quantities last.

Your Privacy—Your information is being collected by Harlequin Enterprises ULC, operating as Harlequin Reader Service. For a complete summary of the information we collect, how we use this information and to whom it is disclosed, please visit our privacy notice located at corporate.harlequin.com/privacy-notice. From time to time we may also exchange your personal information with reputable third parties. If you wish to opt out of this sharing of your personal information, please visit readerservice.com/consumerschoice or call 1-800-873-8635. **Notice to California Residents**—Under California law, you have specific rights to control and access your data. For more information on these rights and how to exercise them, visit corporate.harlequin.com/california-privacy.

STRS22R3

#455 HOME WITH THE RODEO DAD
The Cowgirls of Larkspur Valley • by Jeannie Watt

Former rodeo rider Troy Mackay has given up risk-taking and wants to settle down with his baby. He only teams up with local farmer Kat Farley out of necessity—but now he's ready to take the greatest risk of all.

#456 HER VALENTINE COWBOY
Truly Texas • by Kit Hawthorne

With her horse-boarding business barely staying afloat, Susana Vrba offers newcomer Roque Fidalgo a deal—twenty hours of work a week *and* she'll even board his horse for free. But falling for the cowboy was never part of that deal!

#457 A MERRY LITTLE CHRISTMAS
Return to Christmas Island • by Amie Denman

When Hadley Pierce tells her good friend Mike Martin that she's pregnant—and he's the father—Mike can't propose quickly enough. But Hadley won't accept *any* proposal that isn't based on true love...no matter how much she wants to!

#458 A FAMILY FOR THE RANCHER
A Ranch to Call Home • by M. K. Stelmack

Mateo Pavlic intends to buy back his family's ranch land from onetime friend and neighbor Haley Jansson. But the cowboy hurt her once before. How can Haley trust him now with her land, her newborn son...and her heart?